BRITTANICA

THOMAS EMSON

snowbooks

Proudly Published by Snowbooks in 2010

Snowbooks Ltd
Kirtlington Business Centre
Oxfordshire
OX5 3JA
Tel: 0207 837 6482
email: info@snowbooks.com
www.snowbooks.com

British Library Cataloguing in Publication Data
A catalogue record for this book is available from the British
Library.

Paperback 978-1-906727-37-6
Library Hardcover 978-1-906727-29-1

ZOMBIE

BRITTANICA

THOMAS EMSON

THIS IS REAL …

AN outbreak of zombies will result
in the collapse of civilisation, with
every human infected, or dead …

From *Infectious Diseases Modelling Research Progress*, Chapter
4: "When Zombies Attack!" by Philip Munz, Ioan Hudea, Joe Imad,
Robert J. Smith? (Carleton University, Ottawa; The University of
Ottawa), featured on bbc.co.uk, August 18, 2009

PART ONE.

HEATWAVE.

CHAPTER 1.
SACRED PLACES.

THE dead burst in while Carrie Asher spoke on the phone with Boyd, begging him not to go to the pub today of all days.

"Not today, Boyd, not after this," she'd said, and he'd said, "Oh Christ! Are you sure?"

The zombies stormed in through the main entrance of the Abbey. They stumbled into the nave and pounced on a red-cloaked marshal.

Carrie gawped, Boyd in her ear going, "Are you sure, are you absolutely sure?"

The zombies tore at the marshal's throat. Blood sprayed, and his screams echoed around the building.

More zombies flooded the Abbey. Their faces twisted with hate, lips curled back to show rotting teeth or toothless gums. Their jaws snapped, biting the air. Saliva oozed from their mouths. Some of the creatures were little more than skeletons, their flesh nearly transparent or rotted away to show the bones beneath. Rags of cloth flapped on their scrawny frames. A smell of decay tainted the air.

The zombies swooped on the terrified humans. Screams echoed around the Abbey.

Boyd, on the phone, said, "What's that? All that screaming."

Carrie didn't answer. She could only stare at the invaders as they assaulted worshippers, tourists, and staff. And ate them.

Eating them, she thought, *they're –*

Eating us.

And a zombie reared up, lifting its bloody face from a man's stomach, intestines trailing from the creature's mouth.

Carrie retched.

She'd been loitering in the quire, packing away her cleaning products and dusters, when she'd called Boyd.

Now he said, "Carrie, is everything all right? Are you taking the – "

And he became quiet.

Carrie backed up along the benches where the choristers usually stood.

Three zombies pinned an elderly woman to the floor. They tore at her with teeth and hands. Blood soaked the woman's yellow cardigan and splashed across the quire's chequered floor. The pensioner screeched, and her husband cried out, reaching for his wife as four creatures tugged at his arms and his legs. They held him by each limb and pulled. Carrie felt bile rise up into her throat. His bones cracked. An arm came away. Blood spouted from the stump of the old man's shoulder. His screech broke Carrie's stare.

She raced along the benches, towards the nave. Her heart pounded. Fear coursed through her. The phone was pinned to her ear. Visitors and staff members scattered, screaming. Zombies trampled through the nave, spreading right into the north transept, left into the south transept. Sweeping forward towards the sacrarium, where kings and queens had kneeled to be crowned.

Carrie said into the phone, "I don't know what's happening."

Boyd said, "There's a commotion in the street."

"Don't go out, Boyd, please, please. Stay with Mya today. Please."

"No, but … Carrie, there's something kicking off out there – "

"Boyd! No, stay on the phone. Stay in the house."

She ran down the nave. Blood splattered the floor. Zombies fed on flesh. Their eyes white – no life in them, no colour. Mouths tearing and chewing. Meat wedged between molars and incisors.

Their victims lay strewn across the Abbey. Disembowelled. Dismembered. Decapitated. Amputated. Some were still alive. Howling in agony. A priest in purple tried to gather up his own guts. A legless man crawled along the nave, leaving a trail of blood behind him.

Carrie sobbed, tears streaming down her face. She thought of Mya and wanted to be sick. She grew nauseous, her head swimming.

Someone told her to hurry. Grabbed her sleeve. Dragged her along towards an exit. She didn't know where she was going. Bundled along with other screaming people. Blinded by tears. Dizzy with panic. She yelled her daughter's name into the phone:

"Mya! Mya!"

She felt herself being swept along in a crowd. The noise was incredible. Screams and shouts echoed inside the Abbey, sirens and horns blared outside.

Carrie knew she was shouting Mya's name, but she couldn't hear herself, and then light blinded her, and she was outside the Abbey, in the heat and the light and the chaos. Someone knocked into her, and she whirled, screaming Mya's name again but not hearing it, the noise of the world falling apart overwhelming and deafening.

Someone pulled her, and she sprawled and fell through a door, wheeling, head spinning. She barged into a shelf, spilling books, the shelf toppling.

Carrie came to. Blinked and panted for breath, eyes flitting around her surroundings.

She was in the Abbey's shop, situated outside the exit.

How had she –

"We'll be all right here," said a voice.

Carrie turned.

A marshal, in his red gown, gazed through the door at the chaos outside. He was young, late twenties with trendy, black-framed glasses. Sweat poured from his black hair.

"I'm sorry," he said, "I just grabbed whoever was closest… I'm really sorry, if I… if I scared you."

She ignored the marshal.

"Boyd," she said into the phone, frantic now, "Boyd." But Boyd had gone. Silence on the line. Carrie's legs gave way, and she staggered over towards an alcove of shelves near the counter and leaned against a ledge of souvenirs. From here, she couldn't see through the glass doors at what was happening outside. She didn't want to. But the muffled sound of carnage still filtered into the shop, despite Carrie's efforts to ignore it.

The marshal came over and said, "What's going on, do you know?"

His eyes were wide with fear.

Carrie said, "You're the one with access to God. I'm only a cleaner, mate." And then she calmed down and said, "I don't know. I'm sorry. My daughter, she's with her dad, and he's – "

Something thumped against the door.

The marshal glanced and said, "Oh dear Lord, they're… they're trying to… "

Carrie jerked. "Will it hold?"

He looked at her, his face ashen. He said nothing, so Carrie asked, "Well?"

Something raked at the door, trying to get in, so she stayed behind the shelf, not wanting to see.

The marshal gave a nervous laugh and said, "They… they want to eat us."

Carrie blocked out the devastation occurring outside and focused on her child.

How will I get to Mya?

She raised the phone to her ear and called out to Boyd, but she couldn't hear anything. She whimpered and thought of Mya alone in the house. Alone with her useless, drunk dad, who'd promised to sort himself out. Promised to stop drinking and never, ever get off with anyone again.

"If I sleep with someone ever again, you can cut my balls off, Carrie, honest," he'd said.

She'd looked him in the eye and said, "I will."

Carrie had wanted to believe him. Believe he'd stop drinking and shagging around. Wanted to believe him for Mya's sake, because Mya needed her dad, and loved her dad – despite his faults. Carrie had the ideal family photo in her head. A picture she'd never had as a child. A photo of the three of them on a beach in Morocco the previous summer, before things went pear-shaped again. She decided to fight for that image, now.

"We've got to get out of here," she said to the marshal.

He said no, they couldn't. "It's not safe."

"No, we've got to get out."

She moved behind the counter, from where she could see both doors.

The marshal said, "We should wait. I think they... they might be all over the place. London, I mean."

Carrie looked from one door to the other. Figures flashed past. Screams could be heard from the square outside.

"Why don't you pray?" she said.

"What?"

"Pray to your God."

"Praying's... praying's not really what I do... I... I'm just a guide, a – "

She shoved past him and strode towards the door.

He stumbled after her, saying, "No, please… " and he threw himself in front of her, blocking the way.

A zombie with meat in its jaws and its brain showing through a gouge in its forehead slammed itself against the door behind the marshal.

Carrie flinched. "I have to get to my daughter," she said.

"I… I know; I can see in your eyes that you are very determined, very… angry. But… but I think, for a while, we should stay here. Just for a while. I… I'm sure the authorities will… they'll get things under control again. And then… then we'll… "

"I'll beat you up if you don't move."

The marshal swallowed, and Carrie saw he believed her.

He slid away from the door, whimpering.

Carrie stared at the creature outside. It gnashed its teeth, biting at the glass, smearing it with blood from its mouth. She quaked, not knowing what to do, thinking, *I have to do this – for Mya*.

She reached for the lock, her hand shaking. A small voice made the hairs on the back of her neck stand on end. She pressed the phone to her ear, and the voice was there. And the word it said split Carrie's heart:

"Mum?"

Carrie sobbed and tried to speak, but only blubbed.

"Mum?"

"Mya, baby, are you okay?"

"Mum… "

"Mya, where's Dad?"

"Mum, he's gone out."

"Oh God." Her daughter was alone.

"Mum," said Mya again.

"Yes, baby?"

"Mum, there are zombies outside the house."

CHAPTER 2.
THE SMELL OF A STORM.

"YOU forgot to leave the light on for her," said Carrie.

Boyd rubbed sleep from his eyes. He yawned and ran a hand through his blonde hair. "She's six; she needn't be afraid of the dark."

"Well, she is – and so am I. I'm twenty-seven."

"It's irrational."

"What is irrational, Boyd, is for Mya to have a dad who thinks he's Jeffrey Bernard without the amusing stories, just a boozy layabout – that's irrational."

He furrowed his brow. "Hey, I'm dealing with it, okay?"

Carrie grabbed a piece of toast from the rack on the kitchen table and clenched it between her teeth while she piled her clothes into the rucksack. She glanced at Boyd. He wasn't watching. She tucked the pregnancy test into the rucksack. She'd check it again when she got to work. Check it in case she'd made a mistake.

She hoisted the rucksack onto the chair and looked at Mya, who was eating Coco Pops at the table.

"I'm sorry, darling," said Carrie and kissed her daughter's hair.

"Why sorry?" said Mya.

"Don't talk with your mouthful, angel."

"Her mum does," said Boyd.

Carrie glowered at him. "Don't go to the pub today," she said.

He shrugged. "I don't anymore."

"Don't lie to me. Are you going to ring that man about the job?"

He flapped a hand at her and said he would, and not to hassle him.

"I'm not hassling you, I'm mothering you – and that's not what I want to do to you." She touched her stomach without thinking. Snapped her hand away when he smirked at her.

He said, "What do you *want* to do to me?"

Carrie gave him a look, and his face darkened. He swiped the copy of *The Mirror* from the counter and plonked himself in a chair. He opened the paper and held it up in front of his face.

She looked at him sitting there in his Superman pyjama pants and shook her head. "I'm late. I'll phone you later."

He drew the paper down and showed his creased brow. "You'll phone me?"

Carrie felt herself blush. "Yes, Boyd. It's what couples do. They ring each other."

"You checking up on me?"

Carrie embraced her daughter. Kissed her and told her to be a good girl for Dad. Then she looked at Boyd and said, "Do I need to be checking up on you?"

She kissed Mya again and told her she loved her and said goodbye to Boyd before walking out of the door.

Outside, it was searing. The radio had said something about high temperatures. "Unprecedented" was the word they'd used. Carrie had heard the word while arguing with Boyd. It was going to be hot. She'd be drenched in sweat by the time she got to work.

The cycle ride from Wood Green to Westminster Abbey was

an hour. She'd get to the gym near work and shower there. Then she'd dress in the short denim skirt and T-shirt she'd packed into the rucksack.

She looked up at the sky and grimaced. No clouds. Perfect blue, that was all. But the odour of static clung to the air.

The smell of a storm.

Carrie cycled down Mayes Road and thought about Boyd. Thought what an arse he was but how much she loved him. But did she? She didn't know. What was she supposed to feel? He excited her, and he saddened and angered her, too.

She'd wanted to tell him that morning, but she couldn't. Maybe it was his attitude, his childish behaviour. But then, that was how he always behaved. Maybe she could never tell him. Maybe she shouldn't. Maybe she and Mya should go.

She cycled down Hornsey Park Road, past the two gasometers shimmering in the heat.

Perspiration poured down Carrie's face. She puffed, and her heart raced. They'd mentioned record temperatures, she remembered now. Over forty degrees centigrade and possibly approaching fifty, they said. The temperature reminded her of that Moroccan holiday – the last getaway they'd had before Boyd lost it again.

Before he got back to his drinking and walked out on her.

And he'd been gone until three months previously. They'd kept in touch, though. Carrie was desperate to heal him. Thought she could make him better. But he refused to accept he had a problem.

"I like a drink," he'd say.

The typical *I'm a drinker, not a drunk* nonsense spouted by alcoholics, according to Carrie's counsellor friend.

A week before he came home, he had called Carrie to say he was clean. He'd cut down the drinking. Could he come back, please?

16

She'd greeted him at the door, arms folded and brow knitted like some Nora Batty figure, and he had trudged in with his Adidas bag and his blue eyes, and she'd melted again.

But it didn't take long for Boyd to rediscover the pub.

"You're a dad," she'd told him. "Mya needs you. We both do."

"I'm there for Mya."

"Not when you're pissed."

"I'm never pissed around her."

"You're a liar, too."

"Sod it," he'd say and stomp out. Carrie would ask him where he was going. He'd say "out", and she'd know what "out" meant.

He'd come back reeking of booze a couple of hours later.

For him, that was good. Before, he'd've been out all night. All night and the following day. He'd come back pissed and bloodied. Been in a fight or fallen over or something.

But at least now he was coming back after two hours. Or three, once or twice. So she ignored the problem, thinking, *That's better than nothing*, and let him get on with his boozing.

But not today.

Please not today, she thought as she swept past Finsbury Park.

Not today, when you're going to be a father again.

* * * *

Carrie flicked two fingers as she cycled past Arsenal's Emirates Stadium and smiled, thinking about her dad doing that with her when she was young.

They were Spurs fans, she and Dad.

Arsenal were the enemy.

"Give them the salute," Dad would say when they drove past.

Carrie would imitate him, jutting two fingers at Highbury stadium, where Arsenal played back then. And they'd laugh, she and Dad. Laugh till her tummy hurt.

17

She cycled on. The traffic was heavy. She weaved through cars and buses and cabs. The heat seemed to melt the road, making the asphalt sticky. She couldn't remember it being this hot, ever. Beneath her cycling gear, Carrie sweltered. Perspiration plastered the material to her body. It would be a task to peel away the layers.

She passed Smithfield Central Market. The odour of food carried from the stalls. Carrie furrowed her brow. The reek of decay hung in the air. She tilted her head and sniffed the air. Six black helicopters sliced the blue sky, flying in formation: one in front, then two, two, and one at the rear. Carrie thought they looked like birds of ill omen or something, and a chill raced down her spine.

Because she was looking up, she didn't see the people crossing the road.

Someone shouted "Hey!" and it drew Carrie's attention away from the helicopters. The lights were red. The pedestrians marched over the crossing. Carrie squeezed the breaks and held her breath. The tyres squealed. The bike slid forward. A man glowered at her as he strode across the road. He shouted at her to be careful.

Carrie came to a halt. Her heart thumped, and her lips felt blistered. She looked at the man and couldn't speak, couldn't apologize. She sat at the lights. A horn honked, and she recoiled. She glanced over her shoulder. A bus driver gestured for her to get moving.

Carrie shivered.

Things weren't right this morning.

They weren't right, because she was pregnant, and she was waiting to tell Boyd. Waiting to hear what he'd say.

The shower felt good when she got to the gym. The cold water helped wake her up, and washed away the sweat and the grime that filmed her body.

She packed her cycling gear into the rucksack. Dressed in the denim mini and a t-shirt. She bunched her hair up and pinned it messily into place. She perfumed with a spray of Elizabeth Arden, then popped the bottle into the pocket of her skirt.

She caught her reflection in the mirror and stared.

What are you doing, Carrie? she thought. *Why do you stay with him?*

She broke the stare and shook her head, refusing to confront the questions.

Outside, the heat stifled her. She puffed, the sweat pouring off her again. The stormy smell continued to hang in the air.

Carrie chained the bike to the railings outside the Abbey. She checked her watch. A few minutes late, but she might get away with it. Blame it on the heat.

"Boiling, isn't it," she told one of the other cleaners when she got to the storerooms to pick up her equipment.

The cleaner said he'd never known it so hot: "Global warming for you."

Carrie smiled. She made her way through to the Abbey. She started at 8.00 a.m., usually. It was ten-past now. No one had said anything. A shift of cleaners had already been in since 6.00 a.m. Carrie's shift would make its way through the public areas first, making sure they were done by 9.30 a.m., when the doors opened to sightseers. The cleaners would then sweep through the rest of the grounds, the areas that weren't open to visitors. Carrie would be done by 4.00 p.m. Home, then, by five-ish. Home to face Boyd – if he'd bother staying after what she was going to tell him.

Maybe it was too much to hope that the news would persuade him to deal with his problems and trigger a yearning in him to commit to her, Mya, and the –

She laid a hand on her tummy.

It was 9.25 a.m., and she was done in the quire. She got her phone out and dialled Boyd.

He answered, groggy.

She warned him not to go out and leave Mya or foist her on Louise next door again.

Then she told him.

"I'm pregnant."

Silence filled the line for a few moments.

Then he said, "Who's is it?"

"You bastard, it's yours."

She said it quietly, but it sounded as if her words were echoing around the Abbey.

Then the dead came in.

And Boyd said, "Oh Christ! Are you sure?"

CHAPTER 3.
SAWYER.

"NOT your real names, dickheads." That's what the blind man had said. "Make something up; I don't give a shit. Do I look like I do? I can't *see* if I do, but do I?"

The driver didn't think the blind man *did* give a shit, so he chose Sawyer.

He chose Sawyer from "Tom Sawyer". The only book he'd enjoyed as a kid. The only one he'd *read*. Not much reading went on when he was growing up. Fighting and nicking and cheating, maybe. And killing, too. But not much reading.

He tightened his grip on the steering wheel and told himself, *This is the last job, the last one. You're out after this. You do good work after today. Salvation and redemption. You make peace with your past, and you leave it behind.*

It wasn't the first time he'd lectured himself like that.

He blew air out of his cheeks.

"So that's not your real name, eh?" said the one who called himself Daddy.

21

Sawyer glanced in the rear-view mirror. Daddy was heavy. He wore his silver hair in a buzzcut. The skin on his face looked like leather, and Sawyer wondered if he'd spent time hiding from the law in Spain, sunning himself while waiting for the next job.

Sawyer said, "Is Daddy yours?"

Daddy laughed and looked at the one called Sonny, a teenager with sparkling green eyes. Eyes that glinted like a razor, in Sawyer's opinion. Eyes that said, *I'll do anything – I've got no limits.*

Sawyer said, "You don't look alike."

"Oh, we are," said Daddy. "You done a lot of driving?"

"Enough," said Sawyer.

"Where d'you get the wheels? Nice wheels. What is it?"

"Vauxhall Vivaro."

Daddy nodded, lower lip curled out. Sonny gazed around the rear of the van, admiring. The pair sat in the back, on the bench that lined the sides of the van. The men were dressed, like Sawyer, in blue cotton boiler suits. Sawyer sweated under his. Perspiration had saturated the material already, making it heavy. They said on the radio that it was going to be a hot one.

Gold star for Michael Fish for that forecast, thought Sawyer.

He looked at the clock on the dashboard.

"Nine o'clock," he said.

"Another ten minutes," said Daddy.

They were parked on the pavement next to a pub. The bank stood across the street. A queue waited outside for the doors to open. Sawyer noted an elderly man wearing a trilby and a brown overcoat. The pensioner was bent, and he wavered in the heat, leaning on his walking stick. Sawyer felt sorry for him. The old fellow must've been drenched in sweat. Must've been wishing that death would come to cool him.

Sawyer heard the break action of a shotgun being unlatched and then latched again. He glanced in the rear-view mirror. Daddy checked his sawn-off shotgun. Sonny weighed a 12-bore in his hands, like he was guessing the weight of a baby.

Sawyer glanced up and down the street. Commuters packed the pavements, sweating and struggling in the heat. The men had flung their suit jackets over their shoulders, the women scorched themselves in summer dresses.

Traffic choked the street. Horns blared as the vehicles crawled along. He shuddered. Something wasn't right. It shouldn't be this slow on the roads. Yes, it was Central London. But not this slow. He furrowed his brow. He was thirsty and reached for the water bottle and took a few gulps. He turned on the radio, thinking the broadcasters would tell him something.

Because there *was* something.

He knew it.

"...and the advice is, stay in your homes or, if you're already out, make your way to the nearest large venue and... if you'll just bear with me... I have a list here of places where you should go... "

Daddy said, "What the fuck's going on?"

Sawyer said, "I don't know. Listen."

And they listened. The newscaster gave a list of places. Football stadiums. The O2, he mentioned. Smithfield market. Euston station and St Pancras station, as well.

"Why are they doing that?" said Daddy.

"I don't fucking know," said Sawyer. "I'm trying to fucking – "

He knew it was a gun barrel pressed against the back of his skull. Knew because he'd felt one there before – a few times.

Daddy, his voice low, said, "You don't speak to me like that, kid-o, or I blow your head off. I'll drive this fucker myself if I have to."

Sawyer said nothing. The barrel moved from his head.

The newscaster said, "We've no reports of anything in Central London as yet, but they – "

They? thought Sawyer. *Who's "they"?*

"...seem to be sweeping south – "

"Who's fucking sweeping south?" said Sonny, the first time he'd spoken. His voice shaking. His eyes glittering in the van's dimly lit rear.

The screams made Sawyer jerk. A Seat ploughed into the back of a bus. The car's driver shot through the windscreen. *No seatbelt*, was the first thing that came to Sawyer's head. The second thing was: *Why are those people stampeding down Victoria Street?*

He switched on the ignition.

"What are you doing?" said Daddy.

"Getting out of here."

"You can't do that, we're – "

Daddy faltered. Sawyer knew why. They were looking at the same thing. People pouring out of House of Fraser on the corner. Their faces stretched in terror. Screams filling the air. Drivers leaping out of their cars and stumbling away. Passengers spilling from buses.

Panic had gripped London.

The screams grew louder. The radio spat out static. Sawyer gawped.

What the hell's going on? he thought.

It was Sonny who solved the riddle.

He screamed the word:

"Zombies!"

Sawyer flinched.

"Zombies! Eating people!" said Sonny.

Sawyer saw the dead barrelling out of House of Fraser after the living. Saw them swarming down Victoria Street. Hundreds of them. He knew they were dead because they –

"They're skeletons. They're rotting corpses," said Daddy, a tremor of fear in his voice. "Look at 'em, for Christ's sake. Skin hanging off 'em. They – they've been dead years."

"Yeah," said Sonny, "and they're hungry."

Half a dozen zombies, faces twisted in fury, jaws snapping and drooling spit, ploughed towards the van. Sawyer gawked at them through the windscreen. Their hands clawed towards him. Their eyes were white and empty but still managed to express rage and hatred.

"Get us out of here," said Daddy.

The zombies slammed into the van. Sawyer shot a glance along the road. The dead crawled over cars, prying open doors to get at the drivers and passengers inside. They hauled down fleeing pedestrians and tore at them with their teeth. A zombie, its face a bloody mask, loped along the street with a rope of intestines in its hands. Every now and then it buried its face in the viscera, biting chunks from it.

Sawyer felt sick.

He slammed the accelerator. Drove over the zombies that scoured at the windscreen. The van bumped over their bodies. He wheeled round. Traffic gridlocked Victoria Street.

Daddy and Sonny shouted in the back of the van. They were telling him to drive, to get them out of there. But Sawyer couldn't. He revved, but that did no good. No traffic moved.

Sawyer thought about the bank, the money he'd make out of the raid – the money he needed. He glanced at the building. Zombies were eating a customer. It was the old man. His trilby lay on the pavement. The top of his head was still inside the hat. A zombie had its face buried in the pensioner's skull, eating his brain.

The old man blinked. And for a second his watery eyes fixed on Sawyer, and his mouth made a shape.

The shape of "help".

Sawyer made to open the driver's side door, leap out. But then the zombies swarmed over the pensioner, and he was gone. In seconds, he'd be nothing.

Sawyer stared in horror at the sight.

"Sawyer, get us the fuck out of here," said Daddy.

Sawyer rammed the van into reverse. It mounted the pavement. Hit something, Sawyer didn't know what, and he didn't care. He spun the wheel.

Zombies feasted on humans.

The brakes shrieked. Sawyer turned the van round. Faced west and saw, down the street, the towers of Westminster Abbey.

He sped up the road, driving on the pavement, crushing zombies under the wheels, looking towards the Abbey and thinking maybe he'd find salvation there – salvation and redemption.

CHAPTER 4.
MY KNIGHT.

BEAUMARIS, ANGLESEY, WALES – 9.01A.M., JULY 3

VINCENT Maskell watched the boats glide along the Menai Strait, the channel separating the island of Anglesey from mainland Wales. The sun splintered off the water's surface, and Holly Jones, sitting next to Vincent on the sea wall, said, "It's really beautiful, isn't it?"

"I suppose it is," said Vincent.

He drank from his bottle of water and then offered it to her.

She shook her head and then said, "You *suppose* it is?"

"Yes, I suppose."

"How long have you lived here?"

He looked down at his feet, dangling a yard above the water. "Seven years, now. After Mum and Dad split. Mum's from here – she came back – I came with her."

"So don't you find it beautiful?"

He looked across the channel towards the mainland. The hills, thick with trees, stretched towards the cloudless blue sky. The sun beat down. Hottest day on record, they'd said on GMTV.

"I was thirteen, you know. Thirteen, you don't think places are beautiful. You think girls are." He smiled at her. "But not places."

"You're not thirteen now."

In his head he was. In his head, he was also going out with Holly. But outside his head, in the real world, she wasn't having any of it.

"Well, I find it beautiful," she said.

So are you, he thought and felt embarrassed, as if she'd heard him.

Holly and her mum had moved in next door to Vincent two weeks ago. He lived alone now and worked at the Victoria Hotel in the evenings. He'd woken up one morning the other week to someone knocking on the front door. He'd opened it to find this seventeen year old with long brown hair and green eyes smiling at him, asking to borrow two teabags.

"Only if I can have them back," he'd said.

"Okay," she'd agreed, and an hour later returned them, used.

Holly was an Anglesey girl who'd moved south-east across the island from Holyhead. And she'd moved for the same reason as Vincent – her parents divorced.

He'd phoned his brother for advice. But his brother, his voice slurring, had said, "You're twenty – you don't need advice."

"You drinking again?" Vincent had said.

"That's none of your business, is it."

"Mum keeps asking me if you are."

"Yes, well, she abandoned me."

"You were twenty-three, Boyd. We never saw you."

"Twenty-three, you still need parents, you know."

"Yeah, okay. What should I do about this girl?"

"I don't know, take her down to the river. You got a river there, haven't you? Take her to that fucking castle. I don't know, do I. I've got my own problems. How am I supposed to sort yours out? Fucking hell – "

28

And Boyd had slammed the phone down.

Vincent thought about Boyd now. A week had passed since that conversation. He'd brought Holly down to the river. And now he looked back across The Green towards the castle. He wondered how they did this romance stuff in the old days. They were straightforward about it, he guessed.

"Holly, listen."

She smiled at him, and her eyes glittered. "All ears," she said.

"I fancy you, okay."

"Okay."

"And basically, I want to go out with you."

"Okay. That's nice."

But the way she said it made him think it wasn't that nice.

"I don't get it," he said. "You hang out with me. You give me all that – "

"All what?"

"Smiles and flirting and all that. And then you don't want to go out with me."

She looked at him, and her smile had gone. The fire had gone left her eyes.

She said, "Am I supposed to give it away? Is that what you think? I want a romantic, Vincent. I want a hero. Like the heroes who lived in that castle."

"I don't think they were heroes. They were pretty cruel. And not so romantic. Wouldn't chat too long with a woman, you know. They'd just take you if they wanted to."

"They were chivalrous."

"They were bastards."

"I bet some of them were chivalrous. They could be if they wanted to. All it takes is to want to be."

"I think that's against nature."

He regretted the words as they came out of his mouth, and he cringed.

"Against nature?" she said.

He shrugged, blushing. "You want to go see the castle, then?"

She folded her arms and looked at the water.

"Do you want to take me?" she said.

"I do, actually. Get out of this heat."

"You don't like the scenery. You don't like the heat, *either*. What do you like?"

"I like you."

She looked into his eyes and blushed. "You've got a funny way of showing it."

"I'm a funny bloke."

"Bet you don't like sailing either, do you."

"That lot?" he said, gesturing towards the yachts slicing along the water. "They're just a bunch of snobs. Marina's full of them."

"Okay, take me to the castle then – we might make a knight of you yet."

"I doubt it," he said.

CHAPTER 5.
THE SIEGE BEGINS.

HOLLY said, "I bet you've never been here, have you. Famous castle on your doorstep, and you've ignored it."

He said nothing.

They stood in the inner ward of Beaumaris castle. Vincent scanned the expanse of lush, green grass and imagined what it would've been like when work began on the stronghold in the 13th century.

He stared at the eastern curtain wall. He thought about the people who'd built it. Pictured them slaving over the stone – but not in heat like this, surely. He wiped his brow and thought about how the walls still stood, a thousand years after they had been laid.

"Let's go sit over there," he said and led her to a bench beneath the remains of a fireplace, the centrepiece of a grand room that was never built.

They sat down. She folded her arms but was close enough that her elbow touched his bicep.

"This is the inner ward," he said.

His gaze wandered over the three-quarter acres of grounds.

A big, fat American and his small, thin wife sat on the next bench along. The big, fat American fanned himself with his LA Lakers cap. The small, thin wife wore sunglasses so large they made her look like an owl. A baseball cap sporting a Welsh dragon perched on her head.

A man with a mullet played football with two boys. The man wore an England football shirt, his belly straining at the material. The boys – his sons, Vincent guessed – looked alike. Twins. And clones of their dad, too, with their mullets and their England football shirts – and their bellies.

A woman with platinum-blonde hair and orange skin sat on the grass nearby. She photographed the boys and the man with a Kodak disposable camera. She said, "Shame about that knee of yours, Roger, or we could've had father and sons play for Doncaster Reserves together," and she cackled.

Roger scowled at her and puffed: "Shut up, you cow. Could've played for England, me, if it weren't for me knee. And you know it."

"Bollocks," said the woman.

A middle-aged man in shorts and socks and brown leather shoes pondered the walls. He had a notebook, and he'd scribble in it for a few seconds, then gaze up at the walls again. Behind him stood a tall, thin woman with crow-black hair. She fanned her face and looked bored, glancing at her watch. She nudged the man in shorts, and he turned and seemed to be appeasing her.

Vincent wanted to take his T-shirt off and get a suntan. But he thought it was too obvious, showing off his body to Holly. He was a bit scrawny, but at least he wasn't fat.

He said, "But in 1296 or whatever, there were huts filling this place and 2,000 people living here. Working on the castle."

She gawped at him. "How do you know that? I thought you weren't interested."

He blushed and shrugged his shoulders.

"Why are you embarrassed?" she said.

"I dunno."

She laughed.

He said, "I started coming here when I was at school, you know. Got interested, that's all. I didn't tell my mates, though. They took the piss. But anyway… "

He turned away from her, not wanting her to see his reddened cheeks. He set his gaze on the north gatehouse. Five windows peered down. An archway led through into a passage.

Holly said, "I think it's cool."

He faced her. "You do?"

"Yeah, really. Why didn't you think I'd find it cool? Or what did you *think* I'd find cool?"

"No idea. Girls are complicated."

"Not really, we're not."

She looked at him, and her pupils flared. He leaned towards her, and she tilted forward.

Screams came from outside the castle.

Vincent ignored them and touched her arm, but Holly had turned away.

"What was that?" she said.

The screams grew louder.

"Fuck's sake," said Vincent.

"No, wait – listen."

Through the noise, Vincent picked up a panicked voice saying, "They're everywhere! Oh my God, they're everywhere!"

"Come on," he said to her.

They ran across the lawn towards the south gate. He led her through a doorway and then up a set of narrow stone steps. The sun blinded him as he came out on the top of the wall. He raced along the walkway, Holly close behind, and he stared out over the town.

His blood froze.

Beside him, Holly said, "Oh my God."

The sun glinted on the Menai Strait. The yachts glided across its surface. The figures came out of the water. Hundreds of them, hauling themselves from the depths. Dark and damp, covered in seaweed, the army of marine monsters waded out of the river. They swarmed up the sea wall and swept across The Green.

Holly gasped and tugged his sleeve. She pointed down.

"Those things, they're… they're attacking people… Vincent… Vincent… they're – "

She shrieked.

Eating them, he thought, finishing what he guessed she was going to say.

The first word, then, that came to his mind was *zombies*.

And he voiced it: "Zombies."

Down in the street, six of the creatures pinned a man to the ground. They were eating him. He screeched and writhed.

Four zombies dragged down a woman. They fell on her, and she thrashed and screamed as they went at her with their mouths, ripping away her flesh.

Zombies packed The Green and filled the road running past the castle.

Cars skidded to a halt. Drivers and passengers were locked inside their vehicles, and Vincent could see the panic in their faces – especially the children.

Some people had leapt out of their cars, hoping to flee.

But zombies poured from everywhere. They clambered out of the water and funnelled down the streets. They attacked anyone who was out in the open. You had four, five, or even more zombies hauling down one human – and then eating them.

Terror coursed through Vincent, making him quake.

The entrance, he thought.

He looked down into the outer ward, the narrow strip of grass that lay between the castle's inner wall and outer wall. The zombies had not penetrated the castle yet.

He looked over the outer wall, where the moat encircled the castle. Beyond the moat, a path ran from where you paid to get into the castle, along the railings, to the bridge. You had to cross the bridge, a narrow, wooden structure that would probably snap if it were crammed with zombies. You then came to the Gate Next the Sea, where you entered the castle. It had double doors. Vincent knew they had to be closed, or the zombies would swarm into the castle.

Zombies were already reaching through the railings, squeezing their rotted bodies through on to the path.

A youth in a vest tried to clamber up the railings. The zombies grabbed at his legs and dragged down his trackie-bottoms, baring his backside. He scrabbled, trying to pull himself up. The zombies began eating his legs, ripping chunks out of his thighs and his calves. Vincent looked away, but the youth's screams made his belly churn.

Two women who manned the booth where Vincent had paid £7 to get in raced along the wooden bridge and into the castle just as two zombies slithered through the railings.

The creatures stumbled into the moat and splashed about. A swan flapped its wings, attacking one the zombies. The creature grabbed the bird's neck and wrenched it, and bit into the feathers. Blood sprayed as the zombie tore through the swan's throat. Feathers filled the dead thing's mouth.

More zombies pressed through the railings now.

The creatures were skin and bone.

Dead for centuries, thought Vincent.

Rags flapped from their bony figures, and their wispy hair wafted as they staggered around.

The zombies poured across the bridge, and Vincent shouted, "Shut the gate, shut the gate!" The creatures piled up, clambering over each other. The bridge creaked but held. Some zombies toppled over into the moat and splashed about in the water.

"Vincent, what's happening?"

He turned to Holly. She looked terrified. He said nothing. He didn't know what to say. He got out his phone and tried to ring his mum. While he was waiting for her to answer, he told Holly to ring her mum, too. She got out her iPhone, her hands shaking, tears streaming down her face.

He watched the zombies flood the town. He swivelled and fixed on the playground that lay to his left, just outside the walls of the castle.

Children had played there earlier.

Now zombies fed there.

Something cold crawled up from Vincent's belly and seeped through his chest. He turned his back on the swings and the slides and the gore, and a voice on the phone blanked what he'd seen in the playground from his mind.

"Mum?" he said.

"Vincent? What's the matter? Where are you? Have you seen the news?"

Static drowned her voice. Vincent furrowed his brow, trying to hear.

"Mum, listen… Mum, get in the car – get out of here."

"But – but the news – oh my God. There's pictures of London. There's – oh God, Vincent what *are* they? All over the streets. Westminster Abbey's under attack. Vincent, where are you?"

"At the castle, Mum." A clatter on the other end of the line made him flinch. "Mum, what was that?"

"Someone – oh God – I left the back door –"

And his mother screamed, and he heard snarls and her muffled shrieks.

And he screamed for her, his voice lost in the noise of panic and murder.

He fell to his knees, listening to his mum being butchered.

He couldn't speak and could hardly breathe, the phone pinned to his ear, her death loud and violent.

Someone spoke his name.

A gentle voice coming through the screams.

The phone slipped from his grasp.

He looked up through his tears, and a figure loomed over him, blocking out the sun.

His name came again:

"Vincent."

"H-Holly?"

He blinked and focused on her. Tears streamed down her cheeks. But she looked calm.

She said, "My mum's not there. No one's there."

CHAPTER 6.
DON'T GO OUT THERE.

CARRIE told Mya, "Stay where you are," but she didn't know if that was the right thing to do. She didn't know anything. She grabbed a handful of her own hair and tugged at it, making her scalp burn. Tears rolled down her cheeks. A frenzied feeling raced though her, as if she were going mad.

She asked if Boyd was there. Mya said he'd gone outside, and there were people in the street who were making horrible noises.

"Listen to them, Mum," said Mya, and she must've held the phone out because Carrie heard shrieks and moans. Her skin crawled with fear.

The sounds of sirens came from outside the Abbey's shop, tangling with the constant screaming Carrie could hear through the solid, glass doors.

Mya said, "Mummy, I'm scared."

The words went through Carrie like acid, searing her insides, withering her.

"Everything… everything will be okay, darling," she said.

"Mum, Dad's gone."

Carrie whimpered and bit her knuckle. She imagined her daughter being assaulted by these creatures.

Eaten by them.

Carrie gave a shout of desperation. She turned back to the door. The zombie that had been gnashing there was gone. But more of them swept past the door, pouring in and out of the Abbey, bringing down anyone who hadn't found shelter.

The marshal, a Bible in his hands, said, "You mustn't – we have to wait."

"Wait for what?" She pulled the phone away from her ear. "My daughter's out there."

The marshal whined.

Carrie said, "I'm going to get her."

"I… no… don't open the… "

"I'm going – "

"She'll be all right, your daughter," he said. "Yes. Yes, this is a Central London issue, I'm sure. You stay, wait for the authorities. They'll come to get us, you'll see. Then you can go home, see your… your daughter."

Carrie stared at him. Sweat glazed his face and slicked his hair.

She said, "They're everywhere, those things. Not just in Central London. Everywhere. They're outside my house where my six-year-old daughter is right now."

"Ring the police on your phone. Tell them the address. I'm sure they can go and see if she's all right."

"Don't you think that the rest of London is doing that? The police might be slightly busy at the moment. Or slightly eaten, like everyone else."

"You're panicking."

"Too right."

She reached for the door. He struck her from behind, and she spun round, seeing him brandishing the Bible in both hands. Her head throbbed and the room blurred.

He came at her again, raging.

She flailed, trying to get him off her as he swiped with the book, thumping her arms and shoulders.

Carrie and the marshal reeled, overturning shelves, knocking over displays. She saw stars but gritted her teeth, whirled away from him.

He screamed and came at her again saying, "I can't let you go – I can't let you open the door and kill me."

Carrie grabbed a china tea cup decorated with an image of the Abbey and flung it at the marshal. He batted it away with his Bible, but she launched another one that clipped him just above the eye.

He blinked and staggered, giving Carrie time to scoop up a paperweight. She hurled it, and it cracked the marshal in the forehead. His eyes rolled back in his head, and he toppled over, smashing into a cabinet. Glass showered the floor.

Carrie grabbed a shard of glass the length of a bread knife and then raced for the door, throwing it open without thinking.

The noise struck her like a wave, and she flinched.

Screams came from all over. Sirens wailed and horns blasted. Helicopters roared overhead. Blue lights flashed in the street outside the Abbey.

Hundreds of sightseers, locals, and commuters stampeded.

And zombies… zombies chased them.

The dead, all bone and flesh, stormed through Central London.

She stood there in the doorway for a second, feeling as if she were watching a film.

Then a zombie exiting the Abbey veered towards her. She gawped at the creature. The flesh on the lower part of its face was missing. Ribbons of skin flapped around its throat.

Carrie shrieked.

She sprinted out of the door.

The zombie raced after her. Its arms windmilled, and its mouth snapped open and closed. The creature ran on bony legs, the flesh rotted away.

How long have these things been dead? she thought.

She ran out of the Abbey grounds, towards the railing where she'd fixed her bike. She halted, holding her breath. A double-decker bus lay on its side where the railing should've been, where her bike should've been.

Zombies crawled over the bus. Passengers heaved themselves out, only to be attacked by the dead.

Carrie's legs buckled. The heat was intense. But the terror flushing her veins felt like ice, freezing her to the spot. She spun round. The zombie charged for her. She retreated, stumbling. She was going to fall, hit the pavement. The zombie seemed to sense this and appeared ready to pounce.

Carrie bumped into someone. It helped her regain her balance. The zombie hadn't reckoned to that and ploughed forward, head exposed.

Carrie sliced downwards with her glass dagger. Drove the shard deeply into the zombie's skull. A tar-like fluid spurted from the wound. Carrie shrieked and wheeled away. The zombie staggered about. The fluid ran into its eyes, blinding it.

The creature whined. Its white eyes stood out from the black goo masking its face. And it came stuttering towards her, arms flapping.

Carrie stiffened, looking about for a weapon, eyes fixing on the chaos around her: the human versus zombie war escalating, zombies winning.

She faced the creature. Its head lolled, and as it neared, its legs gave way. It shook its head and clawed at the glass buried in its skull as it fell to its knees.

Carrie took her chance and kicked out. Cracked the zombie under the chin. Its head snapped back. A black grin appeared across its throat. She'd given it such a kick, its throat had been sliced open. The tar-like substance poured out of the gape in its neck. The head lolled back. The arms waved about. The creature squealed like a distressed animal.

The zombie toppled forward, hitting the pavement chest-first. The black fluid splashed. The head nearly snapped off.

The thing's face, resting on the back of its shoulders, stared up at the brilliant, blue sky.

Carrie backed away and scanned the street. Everywhere she turned, zombies hunted humans. She cowered, trying to make herself invisible. She put the phone to her ear. She was still connected.

"Mya? Mya, are you there?"

Silence came back at her and something uncoiled in her stomach. She laid a hand on her belly, thinking about the baby in there.

"Mya?"

"Mummy?" came the tiny voice.

Carrie nearly fainted.

"Mummy, I'm scared."

"Baby, baby, you've got to hide. Hide in the cupboard, baby. Or the cellar, can you get in the cellar?"

"It's dark there, Mum, I – I don't – I don't have my blanket, I…"

"It's okay, Mya. Please. Get… get your blanket and… hurry… but, please, baby, please be… be brave and hide in the dark. Mummy's coming, okay? I'm coming to get you."

CHAPTER 7.
ROAD KILL.

M8, Glasgow, Scotland – 9.21am, July 3

CRAIG Murray, fifteen and fucked off with his life, blew air out of his cheeks and wondered when the fuck this traffic jam would get moving, or they'd be late for their fucking flight.

He rested his head against the Ford Sierra's window. Sweat coated his scalp and poured from his hair and down his back. Samantha, twelve and a pain in the arse, moaned next to him that she was hot and why didn't they have air-con like Carly's dad's car had.

"And why don't they start moving, Mum, I'm dying," she said.

"It'll move in the while, darling." Mum's English accent was soft compared to Sam's Glaswegian drawl. And her voice was silky, too. It was the only thing that calmed Craig down. When he heard it, he didn't want to smack people or smash their windows or nick their cars. He didn't want to drink himself into a frenzy, sniff glue, smoke dope. When he heard his mum's voice, he wanted to lie down and go to sleep.

"You been saying that for twenty minutes, Mum," said Sam.

"We're going to miss the bloody flight," said Dad, knuckles going white as he gripped the steering wheel.

"Don't swear in front of the children."

Craig squirmed. He hated being called "children." And "bloody" was hardly a swear word. Parents were ridiculous sometimes. Even parents like Mum, with her silky voice.

"Have some ginger," said Mum, and passed the two-litre bottle of soda into the back.

Sam folded her arms and curled out her bottom lip. Craig took the bottle. Mum said, "What do you say, Craig?"

"Christ, Mum, I'm not" – he glanced at Sam – "a kid, you know."

"You behave like one, sometimes."

"Oh, Jesus – "

Mum ignored his curse and went on:

"Which is why we're all here, isn't it. Now, what do you say?"

"Thank you," he said. He drank from the bottle. The soda was tepid. He grimaced at the sugary warmth in his mouth. His stomach churned.

He thought about what his mum had said. About why they were here.

Fifteen, he thought, *and I'm off on a family holiday.*

How embarrassing was that?

You nugget, Craig, he said to himself.

The judge had said, "I've got a good mind to incarcerate you, Murray. I've seen enough of you over the years."

But then Mum and her silky voice begged for another chance:

"I promise you, Your Honour, this time he'll learn."

The judge curfewed him. Banned him from seeing his mates, Nacker and KP. Imprisoned him in the house between 6.00pm and 6.00am. Threatened him with a young offenders' unit "if I ever, ever see your face in this court again, Murray".

The order lasted for three months. Till October, for Jesus's sake. And by then it would be winter, nearly.

He ground his teeth. The rage flared in him. He hated them all. Every one of them – police, judges, social workers, probation… family.

Because of the curfew and what the nugget judge had said, he wasn't allowed to be on his own. So he had to go on the family holiday. The first time in two years he'd gone on the traditional break with Mum, Dad, and Samantha.

Majorca would be good, though. But he wasn't going to say that to Mum and Dad. He'd make it clear this was "an inconvenience of the highest fucking order", as KP would say when police arrested him.

Sod them, he thought. *I'll get a tan, get pissed.*

The curfew didn't cover Spain. He'd already checked.

Not as much of a fucking nugget as they think I am.

He'd ogle girls and have some Nat King Cole "get yer hole" with a few of them, and he'd go clubbing and smack some students, and he'd get bladdered on sangria and beer, and get stoned, and puke and piss in some cunt's garden.

He'd do what he liked.

And Mum and Dad and police and judges and all of them could do fuck all about it.

But he wouldn't be able to do any of that unless this traffic got moving.

Dad was right: they'd miss their flight.

But they weren't budging. Traffic clogged the M8, north and south. Every lane snarled with cars and lorries. Motorbikes weaved through the congestion. Drivers, angry at the bikers' freedom to move, waved fists and swore at them as they threaded through the jam.

They'd been on this stretch of the motorway between Junction 14 and 15 for twenty minutes. Craig looked at the scenery for the millionth time. To their left stood Glasgow Infirmary. Looming over the opposite lanes, rows of flats peeked through the trees. A haze had settled over the landscape, and the intense heat made everything look as if it were flickering. It gave Craig a headache.

The car's windows were rolled down, but no breeze wafted in – it was stifling.

The radio said temperatures had soared to over forty degrees centigrade. The word they used was "unprecedented", which Craig guessed meant "never before".

Temperatures in London, where Mum was from, edged towards fifty degrees centigrade, they said.

That was hot.

Hotter than Majorca.

He drank from the soda bottle again.

"Give us a drink, you big shite," said Sam.

He looked at her and scowled. "Shut it. Little cow."

"Give us a drink, Craig."

He said nothing, kept hold of the bottle.

"Mum – " said Sam.

"Craig, give your sister the bottle – please."

He handed the bottle to Sam and mouthed, *Little cow.*

She took a drink and made a face. "It's warm, Mum – it's horrible."

"It will be in this weather, Samantha. I'm sorry about that."

"Right, that's it," said Dad, and he got out of the car.

He wasn't the first one, though. Drivers milled around on both sides of the highway.

The Murrays had left home an hour ago, driving through the grey streets of the estate, leaving it behind for a week. Craig felt sad and empty, as if someone had ripped out his guts. These streets were home – his patch. It was where he felt safe and strong, where he could do what he liked, when he liked.

It would be a test to be tough in Spain, especially without Nacker and KP.

He cursed the pair of them, now. They'd been at fault for the car.

The three of them had been guzzling Red Stripe nicked from an off-license. KP has grabbed the booze. Nacker and Craig had shoved over a stack of bottles and cans to trip up the owner as he chased them out of the store.

They'd sprinted down the road and into the estate and then slowed and panted and laughed and swaggered down to the underpass.

They drank and smoked KP's dad's fags till midnight. They'd shoved a man off his bike and gave him a kicking. Three girls had walked by, and they'd flirted with them, pressing them against the wall of the underpass, rubbing up against them. Craig's girl had liked it, though she cried, but Nacker's bitch clawed his face, and they'd all scarpered, screaming.

"Fuck this," Nacker had said as the girls' screams dwindled, "I'm going home."

Walking back towards the estate, KP had said, "Look at that – you don't see a lot of that round here."

You didn't, either. It was an old Rolls Royce. None of them knew much about cars. Couldn't tell you its value. Nothing like that. But what they *did* know was how to break into them, hotwire them, race them around the streets, and torch them – which was more than enough.

"Go on, you queer," said KP.

"No way," said Craig.

"Go ahead. We agreed – next car we see, you're driving," said KP.

Craig had gazed at the Rolls.

"Hurry your arse, Murray," said KP.

"Aye, you're like a fucking girl," said Nacker. "Do it or not do it."

"Fuck it," said Craig. He picked up a brick. Tossed it at the driver's side window. The glass shattered and showered the street. The alarm wailed. He cracked open the door. Easy. These old cars had barely any locking system.

The lads dived in the back. Craig ripped away the ignition casing. Tore at the wires, hands shaking, mates in the back hurrying him along.

Bastards, he thought at the time.

The engine started.

The lads whooped, and then a voice saying, "Hey! Hey, you bastard!" made him and Nacker and KP laugh because they knew it was the owner.

Craig slammed the car into gear and hammered the accelerator. They sped away. But two hundred yards down the road, he lost control and smashed the Rolls into a wall. The impact threw him against the steering wheel, and everything went fuzzy.

Nacker and KP had legged it.

Dizzy, Craig had stumbled out of the car. Someone grabbed him by the collar and spun him round. Craig's vision swam. A big bastard with tattoos on his tree-trunk neck glowered at him. The big bastard called him something and then punched him in the face three or four times before the cops arrived, the flashing lights making Craig sick.

Craig had been out of it. Didn't know where he was. But his instincts kicked in, and he started to cry and pretend he was sick, hoping the cops would let him off.

They didn't. They phoned his mum and dad.

"Better make sure you've got your hat on when you get home, sonny," said the sergeant, "because the shit is going to bloody well hit the fan and pour all over your lovely, highlighted, girlie locks."

"Yeah, what's fucking new?" Craig had told him.

Now, on the gridlocked M8, Dad asked the other drivers, "Anyone know what the fuck is going on?" He lit a cigarette and coughed, grimacing as he did so.

Mum cringed in the front seat.

Craig got out.

Mum said, "Craig, stay in the car."

Anger sparked in his breast again. *I'm fifteen*, he thought. But he said nothing. He ignored her and joined the men, six or seven of them loitering in the middle of the road, smoking.

"Traffic's stretching for miles," said one of them.

Craig looked. The jam snaked south. Vehicles shimmered in the heat. Drivers and passengers milled about all the way down the M8, all the way back north behind them, as well.

And then, in the distance, he made out a wave of dark figures sweeping towards them, and something gnawed at his guts.

He squinted, put a hand to his brow. The figures looked miles away. They shimmered in the haze, a blur of darkness against the glare. It looked like a mirage – or how Craig imagined a mirage would look.

He glanced back at the car and wished he'd brought the soda.

He licked his lips.

"Drink?"

He turned towards the voice. A bald-headed biker-type smiled at him, showing gaps in his teeth. He was offering a jerry can. The kind you carry petrol in. Craig furrowed his brow and looked at the can.

"Cool water straight from the ice box." The man gestured to a lorry, a Scania that gleamed red and gold in the sun. The truck tugged a trailer marked Porter's.

Craig nodded, unable to say thank you. He'd never been conditioned to. He took the jerry can and drank from it, and the coldness of the water made him shudder. It was the best he'd ever tasted. Icy and refreshing. He groaned with pleasure. He handed the can back to the man, who chuckled.

49

"Craig," said Dad, "me and these fellas, we're heading down the road to see what's up. You stick with your mum and Sam."

They strolled off, leaving Craig with the jerry can's owner.

"You staying with the women and the children, eh?"

Craig flushed. "You can fuck off, son."

The man laughed. He had earrings looping through both lobes. Tattoos peeped from beneath the sleeves of his T-shirt. He was thin but looked hard, as if he were made of wire. Looked like he could slice you open if you touched him.

"I'm Art," said the wire, offering a hand.

"Craig." He shook the man's hand.

"Where were you headed, Craig?"

"Airport. Off to Majorca."

"That your car?"

"Uh? Yeah."

"That your mum in the front?"

"Aye."

"Who's that in the back?"

"My wee sister."

"Oh, how old is she?"

"Twelve."

"Take her a drink, laddie." Art offered him the jerry can. "Go on."

Craig looked at the can and thought about it. Then he took it and went back to the car. He stared north and saw the motorway crammed with vehicles. Drivers and passengers wandered about. It was like a car park. Some folks had set up picnic tables. They drank tea from flasks and booze from cans. They munched on sandwiches and pies.

"You want cold water?" Craig said to Sam.

Mum said, "What have you got there?"

"Water, that man – "

Art was at his shoulder, and it made him jump.

50

"Hello, there. Art's the name. Thought the wee lassie there might need water – cold and fresh from the ice box."

Art bent down and looked at Sam.

She took the jerry can off Craig.

"No," said Mum.

Art said, "It's all right, missus. It's only water."

"How do I know that?"

Craig said, "Cause I drank it, and it tastes like water."

"Craig – Craig, you took a drink off a stranger."

Art laughed.

Craig said, "Mum, for Christ's sake… "

"Can I drink it?" said Sam.

"Yes," said Craig.

"No," said Mum.

Art said, "It's perfectly all right. I've been drinking it since Perth, and I've not turned blue yet." He smiled into the car at Sam and winked at her. She drank from the can, and Craig watched her eyes close and the water drizzle down her chin – and he saw something light up in Art's eyes and his tongue flicker over his lips.

Seeing that made Craig's belly squirm, and he was about to say something when screams filled the air.

Mum said, "What's that? Where did your dad go?"

Craig moved away from the car, towards the shouting. It rifled up the motorway from the south – where Dad had gone

"There's – there's people coming," said someone.

Craig shielded his eyes from the sun. The heat was savage. He screwed up his eyes. Through the undulating world, a mass of bodies came racing up the motorway, sweeping over the cars.

Four men ran in front of the horde.

About fifty yards in front.

And one of those men was Dad.

Craig froze.

Dad, flagging, waved his arms above his head as he ran, and his mouth moved, but Craig couldn't hear his words

And then the screams grew louder, and more folk were running – running for their cars and lorries and trucks, or whatever cars and lorries and trucks were nearby.

And he heard Dad's voice come through the noise saying, "Run, Craig, run... back in the car, back in the car," but Craig failed to move, and Dad shot past him and grabbed him by the collar and dragged him towards the car and threw him in the back and slammed the door.

"Roll up your windows," said Dad, panting and sweating, his eyes wide with terror.

Sam shrieked.

Craig's mouth opened and closed. His skin crawled. Fear turned his bowels to liquid.

The first batch of attackers hurtled down the M8 and swarmed over the vehicles up ahead, swamping whoever was stupid enough to be out on the road.

Sam continued to shriek, and now Mum shrieked too.

And Dad said, "What the hell are they?"

Craig knew. He'd known straight away. He'd known in his guts.

"Zombies," he said. "They're zombies."

CHAPTER 8.
THE CASTLE BREACHED.

THE man stepped forward and raised his hands. "Please… please, ladies and gentlemen," he said through the babble.

Vincent gawped at him.

The man said again, "Please… please be quiet, let me have a word… please… " and the jabbering dwindled, everyone looking round at him.

He introduced himself as Oswyn and said he worked at the castle, some kind of supervisor. Perspiration plastered his thinning red hair to his scalp, and his shirt was soaked through. His cheeks purpled, and his blue eyes skipped over his audience. Clearing his throat, he said, "I want to tell you, to reassure you, that we are perfectly safe here in the castle – remember, it was built for this purpose."

"To keep zombies at bay?" said Vincent.

"Please… please, young man… don't be… look, the authorities have been contacted, and they will be here forthwith."

The American man in the LA Lakers cap frowned. "Does this kind of thing happen often in England?"

"We're not in England," said a blonde-haired man with round glasses, trying his best to comfort two girls, both aged under ten.

The American said, "What? What do you – " before his wife nudged him and said, "Wales, Bert. It's Wales, remember?"

Bert said, "Pah! Like it's important."

They were gathered in the inner ward, about twenty of them. The sun beat down, making things uncomfortable for everyone.

The twins Vincent had seen earlier playing football with their dad headed the ball back and forth between them. Their mother, the platinum blonde, nudged her mullet-haired husband and said, "Tell them lads to put a sock in it, Roger, man, or I'll smack 'em round the ears." Roger obeyed, and the boys tutted and put their ball away.

Oswyn said, "If we can all keep calm, I'm sure this will be sorted in no time. And let's have no more talk of zombies, shall we. That only scares the children."

Vincent bristled. "Don't look at me like that, mate," he told Oswyn, "I'm only telling the truth, that's all."

Holly said, "It's okay, Vincent," and she touched his arm, cooling the rage in his breast.

"That's right," said Bert, the American, "you listen to your girlfriend, sonny – "

Vincent glared at him. Bert's wife nudged her husband again. "Bert, don't you go causing any bad energy here."

Bert flapped his hand and blustered.

Vincent said, "Do you hear what's going on out there?"

They listened, canting their heads. Screams came from beyond the castle walls, and they were mixed with wailing sirens. Somewhere in the distance, the rotors of a helicopter growled.

Vincent scanned the faces of his companions. They showed fear, concern, and confusion.

He said, "You hear that? That's the end of the world, that is."

Oswyn said, "Please, ladies and gentlemen, I hear what… "

"Vincent," said Vincent.

"…what Vincent is saying, but we *have* contacted the authorities, and they are on their way – look, I believe that helicopter must be – "

And everyone craned their necks as the helicopter hovered overhead. Vincent shielded his eyes from the sun. The chopper hung there for a few moments. The bleached blonde and her husband, Roger the footballer, waved up. A couple of other women did the same, shouting, "We've got children here! Help us!"

But the helicopter swept away.

"No," said someone and raced across the grass in the helicopter's direction.

Vincent looked at Oswyn and said, "There's no one coming, mate. It's everyone for themselves."

Screams came from the south gate. The two women Vincent had paid to get in now trundled into the inner ward, shrieking. They wore white shirts, nametags clipped to the breast pockets. They wailed and flapped their arms.

The older women, heavy and not made for running, said, "They've got in, Oswyn. I'm sorry, we couldn't stop them."

Three zombies burst through the archway, into the inner ward.

Everyone started screaming and shouting, scattering around, trying to get to safety. But Vincent just stared at the creatures, amazed that such things were real.

Their flesh had rotted away. They were skeletal, dressed in the rags in which they'd been buried. They ploughed forward, growling.

"Vincent… oh my God… " said Holly.

Vincent backed away now.

A woman screeched, saying, "Andrew, no! Andrew!" and Andrew, the blonde-haired man with round glasses, said, "Make sure the kids are safe, Penny."

But before he could defend himself, the zombies crashed into him.

They floored him and fell on him and were like pigs at a trough, their faces buried in his neck, his belly, tearing at him with their teeth, clawing at him with their bony hands.

He thrashed about and screamed. His wife, the woman he'd called Penny, screeched.

Two men raced forward.

Vincent stood frozen, his insides writhing.

The men kicked at the zombies. Andrew moaned and rolled over. Blood poured from his throat. He crawled away, one zombie still tearing at his legs.

The men stamped on two of zombies' heads. The creatures twitched and flapped their arms about.

Then the men grabbed the other zombie, the one still on Andrew's leg, and dragged it away. The creature snapped at them and bit one man on the arm, its teeth tearing away a chunk of flesh. The man howled.

Penny stumbled forward to comfort her husband. She screamed and tried to pull him away. Their children bawled, another woman trying to comfort them.

Vincent felt the panic rise in him. The heat made him sick, and his head ached.

The two men carried the struggling zombie towards the north wall. They rammed its head into the stone. Used it like a battering ram till its skull burst and a black stain blotched the wall.

* * * *

"Thanks a lot, the rest of you, for your help," said Gavin, one of the guys who'd saved Andrew. He stood with his hands on his hips. He wore a sleeveless Wizard Of Oz T-shirt, and two hearts were tattooed on his right forearm. He glowered at them, letting his eyes drill into each one in turn. "You're all very brave, aren't you?"

He crouched over his friend, who was called Neil. Neil had been bitten in the arm and grimaced and rocked, Gavin stroking his hair.

Holly crossed to the men.

Vincent glanced around. Andrew lay on the ground, his wife cradling his head, her legs covered in his blood.

The man was dying. His throat had been shredded. He'd been bitten on his chest and belly, and his legs were also rutted with bitemarks. Another woman, aged early thirties, tried to stem the blood bubbling from his throat.

Vincent thought, *They're going to change.*

Oswyn berated the two women with nametags. "I told you to watch the gate. It was your responsibility. I'm going to have to issue you with a verbal warning – "

Vincent ran over to the south gate.

Oswyn said, "Where are you going?"

Vincent looked over his shoulder. "I'm checking the gate. Making sure nothing else comes through."

He went under the archway and waited there for several seconds in the shadows, letting the gloom cool him down.

He took a deep breath and stepped out into the barbican. He peeked around the corner at the outer ward, the band of grass between the inner and outer walls. This place used to be known as the killing ground, where attackers were assaulted with arrows and fire and whatever else the castle's residents could throw at them.

Vincent thought they might need some arrows and fires over the next few hours. Arrows, fire, and an RAF Sea King helicopter to airlift them to safety.

He crouched. Groans and screams came from beyond the wall. Something scratched at the wooden doors in the Gate Next the

Sea. The doors looked secure, but his heart knocked, and a sweat broke out on his back, cold and clammy. He'd have to check.

He ventured into the passageway, swallowing, trying to wet his throat. He had no spit and kept licking his chapped lips. He took the water bottle and drank. Not much left, now. He decided to ration it and tucked the bottle back into the deep pocket of his combat pants.

The scratching became louder, and now he heard snarls as well – the zombies behind the gate trying to get in, trying to get at the humans inside.

He dashed up to the door. Yanked the handle. Saw it was secure. Whirled round and took a step.

But the dark figure standing in the passageway's shadows made him stop dead.

CHAPTER 9.
MYA'S LAST WORDS.

CARRIE stood on Victoria Street and looked down towards Parliament Square.

"Oh my God," she said.

A photographer raced by and stopped when he saw her standing there amid the chaos.

"It's like a war zone," he said and took Carrie's picture. "This is the end of the world, and I'm going to take pictures of it."

He belted out a laugh. Carrie looked him in the eye. He stared wildly at her and grinned. He darted away, snapping photos as he went. Fixing his camera on a stream of people hurtling down the street. Zombies ran among them. They dragged down a human now and again. Floored their prey and fed on them.

Cars lay overturned. Buses had ploughed into buildings. Ambulances sped through the streets. Armed police swept towards the scene. They shot at the creatures.

Carrie put her hands over her ears, the gunfire deafening.

Blood sprayed as the undead danced. But even when they were riddled with bullets, they still crawled towards the nearest human. They staggered around with limbs missing. Lurched for the closest meal even with their bellies blasted open and their entrails pouring out.

Smoke rose from the Houses of Parliament. On the green outside, where TV crews filmed interviews with MPs, zombies pinned down journalists and cameramen – and politicians too, maybe.

People stampeded up and down Victoria Street.

Carrie knew she had to go through Parliament Square and head for Westminster Bridge.

She tried the phone again. Dialled her home number. The lines had died. She tried to think what Mya's last words had been and what she'd said in return.

What did she say? What did I say?

Her head hurt thinking about it, and the panic intensified.

She tried the phone again, but all she got was a dead tone. The network must've been overloaded. Everyone phoning home, phoning loved ones. The lines jammed across London – across Britain.

She looked back at Westminster Abbey and considered going inside again. She'd be safe there. They could wait until the police and the Army sorted this out.

She backed up towards the entrance.

Scotland Yard was up the road, to her left. She wondered if the Met was hatching a plan to combat this invasion. She watched as half-a-dozen policemen with guns were attacked and quickly turned into rags of blue and scarlet by the zombies.

Carrie whimpered.

She wheeled and made for the Abbey.

Two zombies darted towards her.

She shrieked. Spun to race away and faced another trio of creatures. They came at her not as a pack but as individuals. Five of them, all with one aim.

They're going to eat me, she thought.

She dashed left. The zombies pursued her. She glanced over her shoulder. They were fast but clumsy. They bumped into each other, but kept coming. Carrie cried out, thinking she would be dead in seconds, thinking of Mya alone in the house.

She cursed Boyd for leaving their daughter, and if she got out of this, she'd kill him herself.

A cab swerved down the road, the horn honking. Carrie waved her arms, trying to alert the driver. But he didn't stop. He headed straight for her. And when she didn't move, he swerved and ploughed into a rabble of zombies crouched over a carcass. The wheels churned through flesh, spraying blood and gore.

Carrie ran to the taxi, her pursuers still chasing her. She jerked the door handle.

"I'm not on call, girl," said the driver, his chubby face damp with sweat.

"Let me in," said Carrie.

Screams nearby drew her attention away from the cab. Three women, their business suits torn, hurtled towards Carrie. They rammed into her, shoving her aside. They clawed at the cab's door and screeched to be let in.

The zombies rushed forward. The cabbie pulled away. The women shouted after him, telling him to stop. He sped off down Victoria Street, weaving through the chaos.

Carrie leapt to her feet.

She said, "Look out," to the women, but it was too late.

Three of the creatures that had been chasing Carrie smashed into the women. Their screams made Carrie shake. Two of the women got up, raced away. The zombies pounced on the other one. She hollered as they bit into her face, ripped away her cheeks.

Carrie glared at the horror of it, the woman eaten alive right in front of her.

She backed off and looked way. The woman's screams blended into the cacophony. Carrie let the images of the attack slip from her mind. Now she looked around, thinking how she'd get out of here. How she'd get to Mya.

Zombies attacked the traffic. They clung to speeding vehicles. They were crushed under the wheels of buses. They assaulted pedestrians and commuters.

Carrie stood on the pavement, looking around and seeing the chaos and thinking, *I'm never going to see Mya again.*

Zombies came at her, a pack of them. Their flesh and clothes were rags. Their eyes bulged white in their skulls. Their jaws opened and closed, and they slavered.

She glanced towards the woman who'd been attacked. Zombies were bent over her, gorging. Gore spilled over the pavement from her mutilated body.

That'll be me, she thought, *that'll be me if I don't do something.*

The zombies pelted towards her.

CHAPTER 10.
HELL'S HIGHWAY.

CRAIG'S gaze followed the man in the Rangers shirt as he ran between the cars. His belly wobbled under the shirt. His mouth gaped, and his eyes goggled.

He wasn't going to make it.

The zombies swept over the cars. Roofs buckled and windscreens cracked. They chased the man. He screamed when he realized there was no escape.

Two zombies got to him, diving on him, and the three of them – predators and prey – fell between the vehicles.

More zombies headed towards the point where the man had fallen, and they bundled into the pile-up, while others swept past the feast and chased down other stragglers.

"Terry, we've got to get out of here," said Mum.

"Jesus, what are they?"

"They're zombies, Dad," said Craig.

"Shut your face, you rockit. If you don't have a Scooby, don't say shite."

"Don't speak to him like that, Terry," said Mum.

"He's talking bollocks, Helen."

Sam shrieked. Zombies flooded past the car. Some of them glanced in. Craig stared at them, feeling himself becoming sick.

Their eyes were milky and blank. Pale, chalky skin sagged. Eyeballs hung on tendrils of arteries. Bones showed through craters in the flesh. Thin, colourless hair straggled down to bony shoulders. Their rotting bodies were either naked or draped in scraps of clothing. A female zombie wearing a long-white gown stained with soil and grass raced past Craig's window. A male zombie followed, dressed in a dusty, black suit with spiders crawling all over the jacket.

The dead, he thought, *the dead have risen.*

A zombie rammed its face against the window.

Sam leapt in her seat and screeched.

The creature's jaws opened and closed, as if it were trying to bite the glass. Saliva splashed from its mouth and smeared the window.

More zombies piled into it as they flocked past, crushing it against the car. The creature fell and the others trampled it, and when they'd passed, it struggled to its feet and hurtled after them.

And they kept coming.

Sweeping in from the south.

The numbers thinning out now, but still coming.

"Dad, go down the hard shoulder," said Craig.

They were in the first lane, so it would be easy to slip out of the traffic.

Dad turned, and his face reddened. "That's what you do when you nick cars, eh?"

"Dad, we've got to move."

"Terry, he's right," said Mum.

Sam shrieked

Craig looked at her and said, "Shut up, will you? Little cow."

"You've been asked not to call her that, Craig."

"But Mum, she's doing my head in."

Dad started the engine, but they weren't the only ones trying to escape. Craig smelled fumes. The air filled with smoke. Engines whined and horns wailed.

Craig's heart hammered. *Christ*, he thought, *Christ, we've got to get out of here.*

Cars ground against each other. They bumped and shoved. A LandRover drove over the bonnet of an MG. The MG buckled, the driver's side door snapping off. The man and the woman inside screamed.

Zombies stormed the crippled MG.

The creatures dragged out the couple.

The man disappeared under a press of hungry dead.

The woman got away, tearing down the M8 – directly into another wave of monsters.

They mobbed her, tearing at her clothes, biting into her flesh. Her blood sprayed over a nearby car and splashed on the tarmac.

Craig's balls shrivelled, and he began to pant. Mum and Sam screamed. Dad shouted at them to shut up. They were doing his head in, he said.

The LandRover now trundled forward. Bumped into other vehicles. Ground through the snarl of traffic. The smell of petrol seeped into the Murrays' car, and Craig screwed up his face, feeling he was being choked.

"It's a fucking free-for-all," said Dad.

"Stop swearing when the kids are around," said Mum.

Like that's fucking important, thought Craig, his mind reeling.

Dad forced the car on the hard shoulder. But the drivers up ahead, and those behind, had the same idea. And now the traffic seemed to be crawling along.

Craig glanced through the back window. Zombies ripped open a sports car's canvas roof. They spilled into the car through the slash in the material. The guy inside flailed, but he was soon buried under a pile of zombies, and the car rocked from side to side as they ate him.

A biker roared by on a big red Kawasaki. A zombie clung on to him, riding pillion, trying to bite into the helmet. The bike laced through the traffic. The rider batted at the zombie. He lost control of the Kawasaki. Slammed into the side of the LandRover.

Craig flinched with the impact.

The zombie flew off the bike, somersaulting over the LandRover. The rider smashed into the door of the truck and the door bowed inwards and the rider's body bent and twisted.

Zombies dashed towards the wreckage.

The LandRover's side window had cracked in the collision. Zombies smashed their way through it, into the vehicle. They grabbed the woman driver and hauled her out, her body tearing on the jagged glass. They pulled the woman to the ground, and she kicked and screamed as they sank their teeth into her body, eating her.

Eating her alive, thought Craig, and he wanted to piss, the fear rinsing through him and down into his bladder.

He'd been scared before, but not like this. He clapped his hands over his ears to block out the noise – the screaming, blaring, revving, arguing…

He screwed up his face and was going to cry.

He promised he'd be good, thinking that maybe God were in charge here, and if he started to believe in God, and pray, then things would sort themselves out, and he and his family could soon be at the airport and off to Majorca and the girls in bikinis and the sangria and…

The car jerked.

Craig looked up, his chest tight.

Mum said, "What was that?"

"Something on the roof," said Dad.

That set Sam off again. She curled up on the backseat and screamed, the noise like a drill in Craig's ears.

The roof buckled.

Craig stiffened. They were trying to get in. He looked behind him. Zombies flocked over the cars. Up the bonnets, over the roofs, down again, and then up the next car's bonnet...

They kept coming, streams of them.

And if they kept coming, the roof would give.

It buckled again, and Craig flinched.

Dad banged on the horn, and then every other driver seemed to do the same. But it didn't scare off the zombies. They carried on swarming over the cars, attacking anyone stupid enough to have their windows open or who'd made a run for it.

"Terry, what the hell's going on?" said Mum.

"If I knew that, I'd be a fucking prophet and wouldn't have to drive along the M8 to some airport to catch a cheap flight to Majorca."

"What?"

"If I was a prophet I'd be rich and – "

"What are you talking about? What are these things? Are they human?"

Craig said, "No, Mum, they're zombies – I told you."

His parents ignored him. Mum said, "They must be on drugs or something. Has there been some kind of music festival?"

"Mum, hippies who go to rock festivals don't eat people alive."

She turned and looked at him. She was pale, and her eyes were ablaze. He saw fear in them.

"No one's being eaten, Craig, don't be silly."

"Mum, there are people being eat – "

"Be quiet," she said and turned to Dad: "Terry, what are we going to do?"

The car crawled along the hard shoulder. The rest of the traffic crawled too. Some drivers had turned back and we're headed the wrong way up the motorway. In the northbound lanes, it was the same – traffic creeping along the hard shoulder, drivers trying to wheel their vehicles round, the road looking like a pile-up.

And the zombies kept coming.

Craig watched them. They ignored you if the windows and doors were shut. Maybe they hunted by sense of smell. Or hearing. Or movement, like T-Rex in *Jurassic Park*.

They appeared to be drawn when a car crashed, when someone screamed, or if a window got smashed.

Mum grabbed Dad's arm and said, "Get us out of here, Terry." She was trying to be calm. Craig knew that. But panic shook her voice. And he'd seen the dread in her eyes.

Dad growled. He hammered the horn.

"It's pointless doing that, Terry."

"Jesus, can't these fuckers get a move on?"

"Don't swear in front of the children."

Craig squirmed again at being described as a child. It got to him even when zombies had invaded the world.

"We should go home, Mum," he said.

"Why do you always speak to your mum, eh?" said his dad.

"Cause you never listen."

"Why home?" said his mum.

"I don't know," said Craig.

"There," his dad said, "that's why I don't listen – you talk shite, you bawbag."

"Terry, leave him – for God's sake get us away from this." Mum turned round to check on Sam. "Darling, darling are you okay? It'll be all right. Dad'll get us home, now."

"Home? We're not going home," said Dad.

"Then where are we going?"

"To the airport, woman."

He accelerated and bumped the car in front. Craig jerked.

Mum bawled. "You idiot, what are you doing?" she said.

"Getting a move on, that's what I'm doing."

Craig looked through the back window. Zombies raced around, clambering over cars, scuttling between the vehicles, clawing at partly open windows.

"Dad, turn the radio on."

His dad listened to him this time but didn't say anything. The radio crackled. Dad swivelled the dial. Voices came out of the static, but never anything clear.

Then something came through:

"… advising people to stay in their homes… "

"Stay at home," said Mum, "that's what they're saying."

"… no indication of what has caused this… "

Dad said, "They've not got a clue, the fuckers."

"Terry – Jesus – stop your language with the children here."

Craig ignored the word this time. He was trying to listen to the radio. He heard the presenter say, "… but it seems the dead have risen and are eating the living… thousands dead… "

Craig shuddered. Mum switched off the radio.

"Mum, what are you doing?"

"We don't want to listen – we've got – we've got a child in the car, you understand?"

Dad said, "She knows what's going on. She's not stupid," and he turned to look at Sam. Sweat glazed Dad's face. It poured from his black hair and down his nose. It gave the black eye he'd got last night in the pub a sheen. His split lip looked sore, as well. His fault, though. Shouldn't have let the guy give him a bleachin' with that pool cue. If Craig had been there, he would've glassed the fellow – but he wasn't allowed out.

"You all right, little doll?" said Dad.

Sam said nothing. She was chalk-white. Her eyes were screwed shut, and she was curled up in the seat.

"I'll get you out of here," said Dad.

He accelerated along the hard shoulder again, revving, grunting a curse word at the car in front or a driver trying to force his or her way into the lane.

Traffic was moving now. Only twenty miles an hour, but it was moving.

Engines growled as drivers hurried to flee the carnage, but in their haste they were careless, and Craig saw pile-ups.

And where there were pile-ups, there were zombies.

They headed towards the wreckage, reaching in through broken windows and loosened doors for the passengers inside.

Craig watched with horror as the dead dragged a boy, aged about five, out of a Volvo. The kid kicked and writhed. The creatures threw him to the ground and fell on him. Inside the car, the boy's mother screamed, her face twisted in horror.

Craig turned away. He didn't want to see. He quaked with nausea. He'd puke soon if he couldn't get some air. It was stifling in the car. And the bloodshed all around didn't help.

"Mum, switch on the radio – we should have it on."

"No, Craig, we're not listening – "

"Mum, I've just seen a kid being eaten. It's all around us. We've got to listen to the radio. They might tell us where to go, where it's safe."

Mum folded her arms. Dad switched on the radio.

A presenter was saying, "… and the authorities are designating areas where people should gather as quickly as they can – I repeat, as quickly as they can. The Army has been ordered out on the streets, and will be able to maintain order in some time. But meanwhile, please go to these points – "

And he reeled off some venues. Ibrox, he said. Celtic Park football ground in Parkhead, too. The Barrowlands ballroom on Gallowgate. The Carling Academy, he mentioned. And The Braehead International Arena on Kings Inch Road.

"Braehead," said Craig. "We're headed that way, near the airport – we can go there."

The presenter said, "If you are at home and are able to barricade yourselves in, do so, but if you cannot, or are out, please hurry to these venues as soon as you can."

"Where too, where's the nearest one?" said Mum.

"Airport, they said the airport," said Dad.

"Braehead," Craig said.

They ignored him.

Rage built up in his chest like it always did before he smacked someone or smashed a bottle over their skull, before he headbutted them.

This is how he felt – hot and sweaty and shaking.

His gaze flitted around. He wanted to throw open the door and breathe fresh air. He grabbed the bottle of soda and opened it and drank. The ginger was warm and sickly in his mouth. He gagged, couldn't swallow the sugary liquid, so he spat it out into the footwell.

Dad said, "What the hell d'you do that for, you bawbag."

"You want me to open the door and do it?" said Craig.

"No, and I don't want you to spit in the car."

"Fuck you."

Dad turned, and his face darkened. He unbelted himself.

"Terry, no," said Mum, grabbing his arm. Dad swivelled in the seat. Craig tightened his fists and screwed up his face.

"Come on, bastard," he said to his father.

Sam started shrieking. Mum yelled at Dad, tugged at his arm while Dad tried to lash out at Craig, who flailed.

At first, he thought the roar came from inside his head. He guessed it was himself getting angrier, the fury rising in him.

Then a vast shadow passed across the car, darkening everything inside the vehicle, and he and Dad and Mum all froze as the Sierra shuddered.

The lorry swept past them. It was the red and gold Scania. Driven by that guy called Art who'd leered at Sam.

71

The truck ploughed into the vehicle in front of Dad's car, a blue Honda. The lorry's wheels mashed the car. The HGV's engine clanked and the brakes screeched. Metal screamed and bent. The Scania swerved and sliced across the lanes, mowing through cars and vans. And then it straightened and barged through the cars up ahead, cutting through them like a speedboat through water.

Craig thought, *Wow!* But then he heard the screech and saw the sparks as the truck's massive trailer swung across the motorway, swishing cars and zombies out of the way like the tail of some colossal beast, and sweeping towards the Murrays' vehicle.

CHAPTER 11.
THIS ISN'T FILMS.

HOLLY said, "Are you all right?" and she stepped out of the shadows.

Vincent sighed with relief and leaned against the wall. He felt weak and dizzy. "Yeah, I'm okay. What are you doing here?"

"Came looking for you. Did you see anymore of them?"

He shook his head. "I don't know how they got in, but it's okay, now – I think. They're out there, though."

They listened to the zombies claw at the door. Heard the undead moan and growl and their teeth clack.

"What are they, Vincent?"

"They're zombies, aren't they."

"There's no such thing."

"What else would they be?"

"Maybe they're just people. They're sick or something."

Vincent looked at the band of daylight across the bottom of the door. Shadows flickered across the strip of light as the zombies pressed forward, making the wood buckle and creak.

He said, "Maybe that's how they start – by being sick. But they look like zombies to me."

"How do you know? You ever seen one?"

"In films, I have."

"But this isn't films. This is Beaumaris. How did those people who made the films know what they looked like if they hadn't seen any before?"

He shook his head. He didn't know how he knew they were zombies. They were, that's all. What else could they be?

"Let's go and have a look," he said.

They went back into the passageway. She stayed close behind him. He looked up and pointed to the slits in the wall.

"They're called murder slots," he said.

Holly squirmed. "Yes, that's nice."

"They were used to – "

"I can guess what they were used for, Vincent."

He flushed. "All right, there's no need – "

"I don't want to be here – I want to be back inside."

"Okay, okay – you go ahead, and I'll have a look."

Holly scurried off, and he watched her go. He leapt and grabbed the edge of the murder slot. Pulled himself up, his arms straining. He held his breath and peered through the slot.

His skin crawled.

"Jesus, it's like *Dawn Of The Dead*," he said.

Zombies prowled Castle Street. Cars crisscrossed the road. People were still trapped in some of the vehicles. Vincent could see they were screaming inside their cars. Zombies tried to pry open the doors, the windows. The people must've been cooking inside those vehicles. Zombies dragged a woman out of a sports car. She wore a short, red dress. The zombies tore chunks out of her.

Vincent held on to the ledge of the murder slot, his arms growing numb.

He looked away from the woman's destruction, hoping he'd not have to see any more suffering. But the town, that day, was saturated in torment.

74

His gaze settled on a boy being used as a tug-of-war rope by two groups of zombies. They wrenched at him until he came apart, and his insides poured out, attracting more zombies, who threw themselves on the pavement to feed on the guts and organs and blood. The boy wailed, despite being torn in two. Zombies dragged away the lower half of his body.

Vincent said, "Jesus," again, and this time it was a prayer. But he didn't think God or Jesus were anywhere around.

This was more like hell.

He poked his toes in grooves between the brickwork, and this eased the strain on his arms and his shoulders. He let out a breath and felt giddy. He blinked, looked out again across the town.

The zombies were everywhere.

He squinted and stared towards the Menai Strait. The sun glinted off its surface. Yachts scythed through the water. On the other side of the strait, the mainland crawled, as if the land were alive. But Vincent knew it wasn't.

The land was dead.

Zombies marched across the hills and through the trees. They prowled the roads and stalked the fields. Towns and villages were over-run. They poured down the banks and to the shore of the channel.

He let go of the ledge, whimpering. He stumbled back into the castle's inner ward. A cry started to rise up from his throat, a warning to everyone else. But his voice died, and he froze. Terror chilled his bowels.

The others had gone.

The inner ward lay empty.

They'd found a way out, or the zombies had found a way in and murdered them all.

He was alone.

The sun blasted down, and he feared he was getting heatstroke. His mind reeled, and he fell to his knees. His throat filled with bile, and he threw up on the grass, retching and jerking.

A hand settled on his brow, and he panicked, scurrying away.

"Are you all right?" said Holly

He tried to say something.

"We're indoors, over there. The chapel, someone said," she told him. "It's a bit cooler, out of the heat. What did you see out there? I'm sorry I went off. I'm really scared."

"That's… that's all right. I'm scared, too."

"What did you see? Is everything okay?"

He said, "No, it's not really okay."

Holly nodded as if she'd known that all along.

* * * *

"If we stay here, the authorities will come," said Oswyn.

"No one will come," said Vincent. He paced the floor of the chapel. They'd all gathered there. It was muggy and dimly lit. The lancet windows, set deeply into the walls, failed to cast much light. Vincent stopped pacing and said to them, "I've had a look outside, and no one's coming – I'm telling you."

The two men who'd been bitten lay on blankets in the corner of the chapel.

Andrew panted, sweat coursing off his body. His wife, Penny, comforted him. But he was dying. And Vincent had a good idea what would happen after he died.

Penny kept saying, "He needs a doctor – we need to get him to a hospital."

Gavin was a nurse, and he did his best with Andrew, and with Neil, too. Gavin had dressed his partner's wounded arm. But Vincent knew what was going to happen to Neil. And Neil knew it, as well. Vincent saw it in the man's eyes.

"What if they get in?" said Bella, one of the staff members who'd raced in ahead of the zombies.

"They won't," said Oswyn.

76

"They might," said Bert, whose wife fanned him with a newspaper.

Oswyn said again that they wouldn't.

Vincent said, "They know we're in here, and they're not going to go away till they get to us."

"The authorities will come," said Oswyn. "Please stop scaring people."

"I think people are already scared," said Gavin, mopping Neil's brow. Neil slapped his hand away and gave him a look. Gavin lowered his gaze and slumped next to his partner.

"Everything's going to be okay – as long as we stay inside," said Oswyn.

Vincent said, "I'm telling you, it's not – the town's over-run with zombies, and maybe… maybe the country, too. The whole of Wales. The whole of Britain."

"Stop bullshitting, sonny," said Bert.

"I'm not bullshitting, mate – and I'm not your 'sonny', either."

"So what are you saying, sonny? You saying those things out there are dead people come alive?"

"That's what they are," said Vincent.

Someone guffawed.

"So why did they start chewing on people?" said Bert.

Vincent shook his head. He didn't know.

Oswyn said, "No one knows anything at the moment. It seems dire, I admit. But we must trust that the authorities will respond."

"Mate," said Vincent, "the authorities aren't going to respond. My guess is there aren't any authorities left. I saw three police cars out there. They were abandoned. No cops in them. I saw a fire engine, and that was empty as well. Those things are all over the place – and I mean *all over*. There's not a patch of land or a street that isn't crawling with zombies. Thousands of them."

One of Andrew's children started crying.

"Now you've upset my daughter," said Penny. She went to her

child. Took the girl in her arms and rocked her, saying, "It's okay, Bryony, baby, it's okay."

Everyone glared at Vincent. His nape flushed. He thought what Boyd would do. Boyd would go to the pub and get drunk. Vincent licked his lips, thought about the taste of beer. A cold one in this heatwave. He simmered, turned away from their stares and walked off.

Holly loitered near the entrance to the chapel, her arms folded, her eyes red with tears. She said, "Vincent's right. He's telling you what he saw, that's all."

"But he's scared the children," said a redhead woman with two kids.

"As if they're not going to know." It was Gavin. He rose to his feet. "The girl is – "

"Holly," said Holly, "I'm Holly, and he's Vincent."

"All right," said Gavin. "Holly's right. Vincent's right, too. We saw what came in here. They weren't human."

"They looked human to me," said Bert.

A murmur went through the chapel.

Gavin continued:

"They attacked my boyfriend, and that gentleman – "

"Boyfriend?" said the Bert. "Jeez, are we all going to die of AIDS in here, trapped like this?"

"You fucking – " and Gavin went for him. Bert quavered. Two men stepped in and eased Gavin away.

"This is God's punishment."

They looked towards the voice. Bert's wife. Her name was Patty. Her head swivelled from side to side, taking everyone in, but her eyes were hidden behind her large, owl-eyes sunglasses.

She went on: "This is the end of days – it has to be. Isaiah said the earth shall cast out its dead, and Jesus himself, he told us the dead would be raised up. "

"Great," said Bert, "and I'm trapped here with a fag."

One of the men who'd held Gavin back said, "We won't stop him next time, mate."

Bert shut up.

Vincent said, "We've got to come up with a plan."

"Plan? What plan?" said Oswyn.

"We can't stay here."

"We can. I've told you. I've told you all. The authorities will be here in no time."

"Your name's Oswyn, yeah?" said Vincent.

Oswyn nodded.

Vincent shrugged. "Oswyn, mate. No one's coming."

"That's nonsense. There's always someone. There's always authority. They won't let things break down."

"Things already *have* broken down. And there's no one to put them back together."

CHAPTER 12.
ENDLESS CARNAGE.

"DAD!"

Craig shouted till his throat burned.

"Dad!"

His dad screamed. The engine revved. The trailer sheared towards them. Sparks flew as metal gouged the tarmac. Craig smelled burning.

Mum shook Dad and was saying, "Terry, for God's sake! Terry get us out of here!"

Dad rammed the accelerator. The car jerked forward. Slammed into the wreck of the Honda in front. The impact tossed Craig into the back of Dad's seat. Sam bawled, curled up on the floor now.

"We're going to get crushed," said Craig.

The trailer loomed, its shadow blocking out the sun. It creaked and groaned as it gnawed up the road and surged towards them.

It would smash into them and crush the car. Craig yelled out at the thought of dying like that. He hoped it would be quick and wouldn't hurt.

The Scania cab pulling the trailer ploughed forward. The trailer teetered and almost toppled, but then righted itself as the HGV churned through the traffic.

The trailer slashed past the Sierra. Craig screamed, and his family screamed. The rear of the lorry clipped the bonnet. Ploughed into a Transit van and mashed it against low railings that ran alongside the motorway. The Transit spun over the railings and smashed, cab first, into a car lot.

"Dad, there's a space, there's a gap," said Craig, seeing the breach in the traffic created by the truck.

Dad slammed the Ford into gear.

He swerved into the second lane, tyres skidding.

Other vehicles were doing the same, spotting a way through.

Mangled metal lay along the road. Oil and petrol poured from wrecked vehicles. The smell of fuel and tarmac saturated the air.

Flames erupted from some of the damaged cars. Smoke filled the M8. The smell made Craig's eyes water.

"Where are we going?" said Mum.

"After that truck," Dad said.

"But we want to go home, Terry."

"Home's back there. So are those things. Those – whatever they are. We're going this way."

"Going where, Terry?"

"I don't bloody know, woman. Anywhere. The airport. The Braehead International Arena. The pool at the Hotel Don Bigote in Palma Nova. Aye, why not. We get to the airport, we can get a flight, maybe. Get away from here. This country's gone to shite."

He drove into the smoke, and for a moment they saw nothing, and it grew silent.

But only for a few seconds. And then the noise erupted again.

And now headlights sliced through the smoke. The Ford's lamps showed the car up ahead. The smoke cleared, and the sun blinded Craig.

Dad said, "Jesus Christ," and shielded his eyes.

Craig blinked, his vision adjusting to the sun's glare, and he looked behind him. The smoke swirled and thinned and wafted upwards to reveal the carnage they'd left behind.

It looked like a bombsite. Mangled and overturned cars everywhere, some of them on fire. Bodies, mutilated and charred, lay strewn across the motorway. Some had limbs missing. Some had their bellies ripped open, and their insides snaked out across the tarmac, the guts sizzling in the heat.

Zombies skulked out of the dwindling smoke. They pounced on any human fool enough to be wandering around. They fed on the broken bodies, finding those who were still alive but too injured to move. Tearing the flesh apart with their teeth, they shovelled organs and chunks of meat into their mouths.

One zombie scurried away with a leg. Two others chased after it. The first zombie started gnawing at the meat. The other two tried to grab at the limb, but its possessor swiped at them with its free arm, still tearing at the meal.

And then it tripped over a bumper torn from a car. Its grip on the leg loosened, and the limb rolled away and one of the chasing zombies pounced on it. The second chaser went on all fours, biting at the meat and the creatures tussled over the meal.

The first zombie now rose and stood and sniffed the air.

It ignored the two zombies eating its catch. It didn't seem to care. The zombie's head snapped from side to side, as if it were trying to catch a scent. It scurried away between the ruined cars.

Craig looked away, his mouth open. It was like *Resident Evil*, but for real. And it wasn't fun.

Mum said, "My God, Terry, where are you taking us?"

"In the direction we were going, Helen."

The Scania that had cleaved a path for them headed down the motorway, weaving through abandoned vehicles and dead bodies.

"It's endless," said Mum. "What on earth's happened?"

"Zombies, I told you," said Craig.

"Shut up," said Dad.

"Stop telling him to shut up, Terry."

"Well, the lad's talking nonsense."

A dozen vehicles followed the Scania as it weaved its way along the snarled M8, southbound.

In the opposite carriageway, vehicles were headed north. Their occupants looked terrified.

Drivers on both sides of the motorway faced a difficult task. Discarded vehicles blocked their way. Dead bodies cluttered up the lanes.

Zombies prowled the M8, too.

They scrabbled through wreckage, scavenging for food. They swarmed over broken-down vehicles trying to get at the terrified people inside.

The convoy drove past an over-turned bus. Zombies scuttled all over it like crabs. They found an opening, a broken window, and poured through it into the bus where they attacked the passengers.

Craig looked to his right, towards the city. He wondered if there was anyone left alive in all the tower blocks and terraces. Smoke billowed from the heart of the city. Flames flickered in the distance. Glasgow shimmered under a blanket of heat.

Craig shut his eyes. He didn't want to think about what was happening. He wondered where Nacker and KP were. Jex and Mikey. And Hallie. Yeah, Hallie. With her golden hair and her green eyes, and the way she turned her head away, but not her eyes, which made him fizz.

They did it two months ago, and he'd pined for her since. But it wasn't cool to brood over a girl. You had to let the bitches do the chasing. You had to let them ring you and then you'd say, "Yeah, I'm not bothered, I'm not up for that, I'm busy with my crew," and then swagger about when you heard they'd been weeping.

But he found it tough. Hallie wasn't a caller. She wasn't a weeper, either. And then he heard she'd slept with Jex. Craig shrugged his shoulders at the news. But in his chest, his heart wrenched.

"But she still likes you, Craig," her friend Lacey had said.

He'd said, "I don't give a fuck," but he did.

And he did now more than ever.

His felt sick for her. His chest hurt with missing her. He remembered how beautiful she was, feeling the grief churn inside him at the thought of maybe never seeing her again.

He opened his eyes and blew air out of his cheeks, and Hallie's image flitted from his mind.

Christ, he thought, *she might be out there. She might be alive and scared. She might be dead. She might be –*

"We're stopping."

Craig jumped.

It was Dad who'd spoken, and he spoke again:

"We're stopping. Why the fuck are we stopping?"

"Terry, for goodness' sake, don't use that language with the children."

Craig ground his teeth – *I'm not a fucking child* – and leaned between the front seats.

Up ahead, the truck had veered across the carriageway and come to a halt. The cars behind it slowed.

Craig eyed the bodies on the road. Half-eaten carcasses of men, women, and children. Swarms of flies already hovered over the remains. Crows flapped away as the cars slowed and stopped. A dog raced off with something red and wet in its jaws.

Craig's face twisted. He imagined the stench. He'd never smelled a dead person, but he'd got a whiff of a dead badger once.

Him and KP and Nacker had found it near the river. Its belly ripped open, its guts rotting. Maggots squirmed in the gore. Flies droned over the body. The stink had made Craig puke, made his eyes water. The lads had rolled the body into the river. Watched it float away. The smell had lingered, and Craig threw up again.

He thought of that now, and the memory brought hot liquid up into his throat. He retched.

Mum looked round. "Are you okay, Craig?"

He nodded.

"You look really pale, sweetheart. And your eyes are red."

"I'm okay," he said.

"Drink some ginger."

"I'm okay."

"You sound croaky."

"Mum, I'm – "

"The lad said he's okay," said Dad.

"I'm only asking him."

"He's fifteen – don't baby him, woman."

"Maybe if I had, he wouldn't be in… " She trailed off and put her face in her hands, sobbing.

Dad tutted and cursed.

Craig felt bad. He looked at Sam. She cowered in the footwell, terrified. For a second, he felt love swell in his heart for his sister. He wanted to wrap his arms around her and tell her everything would be all right.

But then the car stopped with a skid of the tyres, and he stowed the love away and straightened.

The truck driver leapt down from his cab.

It was Art. The guy who'd offered Craig a drink. The guy who'd smiled at Sam. He carried a police baton. The type you whipped out to extend. A zombie darted towards him and without glancing at the creature, he swung the baton and cracked open the dead thing's skull.

CHAPTER 13.
REALITY BITES.

VINCENT led them up to the walkway that ran along the top of the inner wall.

Behind him came Gavin, and following him, the two men who'd prevented him from attacking Bert: a bodybuilder called Simon and his brother Mark. Oswyn came too, and he muttered all the way, complaining that this was ridiculous.

They stood on the wall in the blistering heat and looked – over the street and The Green towards the Menai Strait and beyond, at a land of walking dead.

"I'd say we're fucked," said Mark. He lit a cigarette.

"Christ," said Simon, "my wife and kids are in here. What am I going to tell them, eh? What's Sandra going to say? This'll panic them."

Oswyn whimpered.

"See, mate," Vincent said to him. "There's no one coming."

"I... I still don't believe that. I can't. Oh my God."

"What do we do?" said Simon. He ran a hand over his crew cut. Looked at his hand, then flicked it. Sweat sprayed from his fingers. His pale, muscle-packed arms were already reddening in the sun. "I mean... our families... our kids... "

Vincent saw the fear in the man's eyes. Fear for his kids, his wife. Simon had no idea how he was going to protect his family, and for a man, that had to be terrifying.

Well, it would be if you were a proper father and husband – not like Vincent's dad.

Drunk all the time but still a laugh, though. Always joking, always ganging up with him and Boyd against their mum, who'd be battling to get Dad off the booze. She'd scream at him and throw things at him.

Boyd was ten years older and gone by then. Living with some bird in Wood Green.

Mum finally had enough and came here, where she'd been born. Dragged Vincent along.

Wales, he'd thought. *Fucking great. Full of sheep and shaggers of sheep.*

But it was all right. There were drugs, there was booze, and there were girls – so everything was okay.

"And what'll happen to" – it was Simon again, glancing at Gavin now – "your friend, and to the guy who got – got eaten up?"

They looked at each other. Vincent could see what they were thinking. All of them, apart from Oswyn, who's eyes flitted over the other three, his brow knitted.

Mark said, "Will it happen?"

"W-will what happen?" said Oswyn.

Vincent shrugged.

"Will what happen?" said Oswyn again.

Gavin looked at him and said, "Will my boyfriend die and then wake up? Will that other man – "

"Andrew, I think his name is," said Vincent.

"Yes, Andrew." Gavin glanced at the zombies. They were prowling around. Some scratched at the walls of the castle now, trying to climb up to get at the men. "Will they be like them after they die?"

"Die? They're not going to die, surely," said Oswyn. "I mean, your – your friend, he only has a bite to his arm."

"Andrew's bad, though," said Vincent.

"But what are you saying?"

"We're saying, Oswyn," said Mark, "that Andrew and Neil might die and wake up again."

"Wake up?"

"The walking dead," said Mark. "Like those things out there."

"Dead? They're not dead. They're just – "

Oswyn scanned the zombies.

They were bones with rags of skin on them. *Some of them must've died hundreds of years ago*, thought Vincent. He wondered how long it took for a body to decay, to become dust.

Oswyn said, "This is impossible. The dead don't become alive again."

"They're not really alive," said Vincent. "They're undead. They're between alive and dead. You can't kill them like you kill ordinary people."

"The head, you've got to go for the head," said Mark, lighting another fag. Simon scowled at him and rolled his eyes.

"What are you talking about?" said Oswyn.

Simon said, "Like in the films. Shoot them in the head."

Oswyn's voice went high-pitched: "Films? We're not in films. This is real."

A yacht rocked on the river.

Zombies rose up from the water, crawling into the vessel.

Aboard, a man and woman in swimsuits screamed.

The yacht rolled. The zombies swarmed on deck. They attacked the couple.

Vincent turned away. He said to Oswyn, "Did you see that?"

Oswyn kept staring out towards the yacht. His mouth opened and closed.

CHAPTER 14.
LONDON EYE.

THE red van shot across the road and mounted the pavement and mowed down the zombies.

The impact sent the creatures flying, and they flapped like rags in the air.

The driver leaned out of the window and said to Carrie, "Get in the back," and the panel door slid open on the side of the van.

Carrie gasped. Two men armed with shotguns stared out at her. The older one, grizzled and rough looking, raked her up and down with his eyes. He said, "Nice one," and then the driver said, "Get in, then."

She threw herself into the van. The grizzled man aimed his shotgun out of the door. The blast made Carrie's brain rattle in her skull. A zombie's head disintegrated. The creature collapsed. But more of them spilled forward.

The grizzled man reached across Carrie and slid the door shut and then said to the driver, "Go on, Sawyer, do what you're paid to do."

The van screeched off, and Carrie tumbled in the back, and the two men with her laughed. She looked at them. The grizzled one smiled, showing yellow teeth. He had a neck as thick as a tree stump. A film of sweat glistened on his sun-beaten face. The other guy was young – a teenager maybe. He had red hair, and freckles peppered his chalk-white cheeks.

The driver asked, "Are you all right?"

The grizzled man said, "Keep your eyes on the road, Sawyer."

The van swerved. Carrie felt it bump against things in the road and knew what they were.

And the one called Sawyer said, "They're all over the place."

The grizzled one said, "Shut up and drive."

"Who – who are you?" said Carrie.

"Doesn't matter," said grizzly.

"Are you okay, Miss?" said the driver.

"Where are you going?" she asked.

"Haven't a clue," said the driver.

Grizzly nudged the back of the driver's seat with the stock of his shotgun. "Sawyer, you just drive."

"I need to get to Wood Green," said Carrie. The youth licked his lips, and his hand kept opening and closing on the butt of his shotgun.

The driver asked, "Why Wood Green?"

"My daughter's there."

He stopped the van.

"Sawyer, keep driving," said the grizzly.

Sawyer twisted in his seat. His eyes flashed. They were jungle-coloured, Carrie noticed. Sweat trickled from his crow-black hair. He was about thirty. Some would say he needed a shave, but Carrie didn't think so. She thought he looked fine, and for a few seconds got lost in his stare.

And then he said, "Is she safe, your daughter?"

Carrie held out her phone. "I – I don't – " Tears threatened to come again.

"Sawyer," said the grizzly, "get the fuck moving."

"Where are we?" said Carrie.

"Big Ben," said Sawyer.

"Where are you going?"

"Look, sweetheart, never you mind that," said grizzly. "Shouldn't have picked you up in the first place. It was this romeo here. He should've had his eyes on the road, not some bird."

Sawyer said, "What's the address?"

She told him, and he typed it into the TomTom.

Grizzly said, "Hang on a fucking, wanking minute, Sawyer – "

Sawyer said, "We can't leave her daughter. Would you leave this wally behind?" and he jabbed a thumb at the youth.

The youth bristled. "He's not my dad, he's my Uncle G – "

Grizzly slapped the teenager. "No names, you prat."

"You've already told me *his* name," said Carrie, talking to grizzly, looking at Sawyer. "Are you bank robbers?"

"Not anymore, we're not," said Sawyer.

"That's not your decision," said grizzly.

"All right," said Sawyer, "you find a bank that's safe to rob."

Grizzly murmured something.

"I need to get going. Are we going?" said Carrie.

"We're headed south," said grizzly.

"Home, Uncle G – Daddy?"

"Daddy?" said Carrie, and then she started yanking at the handle. "Okay, if you can't help me, let me out here."

Sawyer said, "No, you can't."

"Yes she can," said grizzly and slid open the door for her.

The dead stopped and turned to look. She gawped back at them. For a second, Carrie and the zombies stared at each other. Her gaze swept over them. She saw hordes of them crossing Westminster Bridge. In the distance, the Hungerford Bridge, too, seemed overrun by a sea of figures.

She didn't think they were human.

The dead darted towards the van.

Carrie screamed.

The grizzled man swore, and the youth said, "Shut the door, shut the door!"

Grizzly slid the door shut, and Sawyer sped away. The acceleration tossed Carrie about in the back. She felt every thump as the van careered through the zombies.

"Wrong way, Sawyer, wrong fucking way," said grizzly, rocking around in the back of the van.

Carrie clambered into the front and sat next to Sawyer. He smiled at her. She didn't smile back. She seatbelted herself in. She looked out of the window, and her blood froze.

"Look – look at that," she said.

Grizzly swore and told her to get in the back.

But she ignored him. Sawyer slowed the van.

"Christ," he said, eyes on what Carrie had seen.

Grizzly poked his head between them and said, "What's the fucking – "

And he saw it too.

The London Eye crawled with zombies. They'd clambered all over the 440ft-high observation wheel. They looked like ants swarming their prey. They swung on the pods that contained frantic, terrified tourists and tried to smash their way into the capsules. The wheel rocked under the weight of the zombies. Carrie had never seen it tilt so much.

She felt panic race through her veins. Her heart thumped, and she put a hand to her breast.

"I want to go," she said.

The van moved, and the image slid away, and in its place there came clear blue skies and a blistering sun.

"Mother of God," said grizzly, and slumped in the back.

Carrie studied her surroundings now. Cars were strewn across the road. Some were still going, speeding along. A bus lay on its side. Zombies squatted on it, scooping gore into their chomping mouths.

They drove past Waterloo Station. Carrie's eyes fixed on a man wearing a grey suit. He was mid-thirties. His clothes were torn and his hair ruffled. He stumbled out of the station and spoke into a mobile phone. He looked around frantically with wide eyes. From the station concourse behind him came three figures. They hurtled into the street and ploughed into the man. They dragged him to the ground and buried their faces in his body, and Carrie saw blood spurt from him as he thrashed against the attack. One zombie drove its hand into the man's torso and wrenched out a rib. The man arched his back in agony.

Carrie raised a hand to her mouth, and she felt the blood leave her face. The van glided past. The man's fright-filled eyes fixed on Carrie, and he reached out a hand towards her. His pain-warped mouth seemed to be begging her for help.

The scene passed, only to be replaced by other similar sights.

Carrie came out of her daze to hear the grizzly man telling Sawyer he was going the wrong way.

The older man jammed his shotgun into the driver's neck and said, "Right, that's it, Sawyer – I'm not being nice anymore. Around we go, or I'll deck the fucking dashboard in your brains, loverboy."

Carrie stayed still and looked at Sawyer from the corner of her eye.

Sawyer didn't flinch. Kept driving through the chaos. Eyes on the road. Speed at around thirty miles per hour. Zombies hurled themselves at the van. The vehicle jerked and bounced as it ran over the dead things.

"Sawyer, I swear – "

"We're going to find this lady's daughter," said Sawyer.

The grizzly man sighed. "All right, mate, if that's how you want it." He drew the gun away from Sawyer's neck. Carrie breathed out with relief. And then felt cold steel press into her cheek.

"Turn this van around, Sawyer – or I'll kill her."

CHAPTER 15.
SAWYER'S SACRIFICE.

SAWYER guided the van down a residential street.

"Park up here," said the grizzled man.

Carrie felt the cold barrel of the gun on her face.

She tried to stem the alarm coursing through her body.

"Not worried about getting a ticket?" said Sawyer as he drew the van up on the pavement.

"Fuck off, Sawyer," said the grizzly man.

"Uncle Gilbert," said the youth.

"Oh for Christ's sake, Nathan – "

"Now *you've* done it, Uncle Gilbert."

"Doesn't matter," said the grizzled man, or Uncle Gilbert. "We'll be off soon, leave these two fucking lovebirds to sing a pretty tune together."

"But Uncle Gilbert, right, I'm serious – you need to look at this, right."

"What?" said Uncle Gilbert.

"Have – have a look."

"I'm busy at the moment, son."

"Yeah, but you really need to take a look."

He went to open the back door, and his uncle said, "For Christ's sake, Nathan, don't do that."

Nathan leapt out. He was looking down a side street.

Carrie opened the door and threw herself down on the street while Uncle Gilbert looked the other way. Sawyer sprang out of the driver's seat.

The trio stood there, gawping.

A knot of maybe two-dozen zombies was crammed down a dead-end street. They were outside a four-storey block of flats.

A group of youths on the roof of the flats were lowering someone down on a rope.

The boy being lowered kicked and screamed.

The zombies reached up for the youngster. The youth squealed and thrashed about.

The zombies grabbed his legs. They pulled him down. He shrieked and begged the ones on the roof to help him. But Carrie heard the rooftop crew laughing.

The zombies tugged him down, and he went under them, like someone going under water – legs first, and then belly, chest, up to his neck and after that… he was gone.

Carrie heard the zombies growl and the boy shriek, and the kids on the rooftop pointed down and laughed.

Carrie doubled up and puked on the pavement.

A hand pressed against her forehead and brushed her hair away from her face. She heard Sawyer asking her if she was okay. She looked up into his eyes. He drew back her hair and ran his fingers through it, and she let him, liking his hands on her.

Gilbert's voice snapped her out of her shocked state:

"We've got to make a move."

Zombies were running down the road towards them. Sawyer yanked her to her feet. He scooped her up in his arms and tossed her in the back of the van.

Gilbert tried to stop him, but Sawyer punched him in the face and told him to get in the van or get eaten. Gilbert stumbled into the van, followed by Nathan.

Sawyer started the engine and drove forward, ramming into a car. He reversed at speed, straight for the zombies.

Carrie watched through the rear window.

The dead charged for the van, and when it hit them, it jolted, and they fell, and the wheels ran over them.

She gritted her teeth, the sounds of bodies breaking under the tyres making her cringe.

The van rattled as more zombies slammed into it. Carrie stared into the face of one creature.

The dead eyes. The snapping jaw. The pasty skin. The creature had long, stringy hair, and a wound strapped its scalp, from ear to ear. Carrie saw its brain in there, milky white.

Who was he?

How long had he been dead?

She looked into the zombie's eyes, but then it was gone. Dragged under the wheels as Sawyer reversed.

He handbrake-turned, and the van whirled round, tyres screeching. Carrie was tossed about in the back, and she bumped into Gilbert and Nathan.

Sawyer straightened the van and drove it down the dead end.

Gilbert said, "Where the hell are you going?"

"Not letting those people die," said Sawyer, as another figure was lowered from the rooftop into the zombies below.

Gilbert, blood dripping from his lip, shouted for Sawyer to turn back. Nathan whimpered in the back of the van. Carrie watched as the girl dangled halfway between the roof's edge and the zombies.

Sawyer turned right. A steel door blocked their way. It looked like the entrance to an underground garage. He jumped out. Carrie wanted to call him back, but she had no voice. He went to the door and looked at it, trying to find a way to open it.

Zombies poured down the road towards the van.

Carrie screamed at Sawyer.

He told her, "Get in the driver's seat and take it in," and he pressed a green button on a unit next to the door, and the steel rolled upwards. "Now," he said as zombies closed on him.

Carrie jumped into the driver's seat.

She drove the van into the gloom of the garage.

She lost sight of Sawyer and yearned for him.

Come back, she thought, *come back and take me to Mya.*

In the underground lot, she stopped the van and got out. The dimly lit garage darkened further as Sawyer, still outside, heaved down the steel door. A zombie darted through into the garage just before he sealed the entrance.

When the light died, the creature appeared to slump. It kept coming, but seemed more lethargic. Saliva oozed from its mouth, and it groaned. It staggered forward on unsteady legs, looking like a drunk.

Carrie furrowed her brow, thinking.

She stepped back and studied the creature. It loped towards her, moaning and waving its arms, its head tilted to one side and its shoulders hunched.

Gilbert stepped out of the van. The zombie slewed towards him and grabbed him by the arms and opened its mouth. Gilbert yelled out, and the zombie bit him on the arm. Gilbert jammed his gun under the zombie's chin and pulled the trigger.

The shotgun blasted, and Carrie cowered, her ears ringing.

The zombie's head erupted, and the headless corpse slumped to the ground.

Blood poured from Gilbert's arm. "It bit me – it fucking bit me."

Nathan leaned out of the van's side door with his shotgun, his eyes fixed on the zombie.

Carrie ran to the door and banged on it, calling Sawyer's name. She pressed her ear against the steel. But all she heard were growls and moans.

The sounds of the dead.

Hope filtered out of her. She was lost now, confused. Had no idea what to do. Sawyer, although she'd known him only a few minutes, had been a beacon for her.

A light that could guide her to Mya.

Behind her, Gilbert screamed that he'd been bitten, and Nathan tried to calm his uncle down.

She had to do something. She couldn't pine here for a man she'd only just met. She strode back towards the van and headed for the lifts at the back of the parking lot.

"I've been bitten," said Gilbert.

"He'll turn into a zombie," said Nathan.

"Maybe it'll be an improvement," said Carrie, wheeling to look at them. She smelled rotten flesh and cordite. "I'm going up on the roof to help those people. You've got guns. Guns would be helpful in this kind of pressurized situation, but I don't know what you're like in a crisis. Anyway, since you can't go back out there, you might as well come with me."

She stomped off, making like she didn't give a shit but hoping they'd follow.

She got to the elevator and pressed the button. The elevator arrived and pinged open. Carrie cast a glance towards Gilbert and Nathan. They loitered in the dark near the van.

She stepped into the lift. Stared out through the door into the gloom. Closed her eyes and prayed – for Mya, for Sawyer, for Gilbert and Nathan to go with her.

The door slid shut. She opened her eyes. Dread filled her. She'd be alone up there with those kids. Kids who were feeding people to zombies.

The elevator was inches from closing when a blood-covered hand clawed around the edge of the door and held it open.

CHAPTER 16.
BURN HIM.

"OKAY," said Bert, the fat American, "it seems to me you need a king in this castle, and seeing as I'm the only one with military experience – "

Vincent looked at the Yank standing there with his belly thrust out and his LA Lakers cap canted back on his head.

"What military experience?" said Gavin.

"I was in the National Guard, sir."

"Okay, I was in the Royal Marines," said Gavin.

Bert gawped. Everyone looked at Gavin.

"You all looked surprised," he said. "There are queer soldiers, you know."

Bert was trying to say something, but he didn't seem to be able to get the words out.

"You still want to take charge?" said Gavin.

"As… as a matter of fact, I do," said the American.

Gavin smiled and said, "Fight you for it, big boy."

Bert bristled.

And then a voice said, "He's dead! Oh God, he's dead!"

It was Penny.

And again she said, "He's dead! Andrew's dead! Where are my children? Where are his children?"

"It's okay," said Bella. "They're… they're out of harm's way with the other children… oh goodness… "

They stared at Andrew's corpse, sprawled on the chapel floor. Penny sobbed over her husband's body, Bella attempting to comfort her.

Vincent caught Gavin's eye. He looked at Mark and Simon, and finally Oswyn. He read their faces, saw what they were thinking.

Holly caught his eye, and she knew what would happen, too, he could tell. Her look urged him to say something. But he waited for someone else to speak.

No one did. They goggled as Bella tried to pry Penny from Andrew. Penny wouldn't let go, holding on to him, wailing.

Vincent braced himself and said, "I'm really sorry to say this, but we've got to get rid of him."

Everyone looked him. *Shit*, he thought.

Penny, her face puckered with grief, said, "What did you say?"

Vincent swallowed. Holly squeezed his hand. He glanced at Gavin, who gave him a nod.

Vincent cleared his throat: "We think… we're pretty sure… that if you get bitten, if you… you die… you're going to come back as a… as one of them."

Penny's face darkened. Bella cried out. Bert roared with anger. Roger the footballer shouted, and his orange-skinned wife gasped.

Gavin said, "Vincent is right," and he glanced at Neil, who was glazed in sweat.

"So what are you saying we do?" said Bella.

"We've got to get rid of… of his body."

Penny's face contorted with hate, and she lunged towards Vincent. Bella held her back.

"Where are the young 'uns, Roger, where are they?" said Teena, the footballer's wife. "I don't want them to be hearing this rubbish."

"They're outside playing," said Roger and, with his glare fixed on Vincent, added: "You saying, lad, that we have to... " He trailed off.

"What are you saying, sonny?" said Bert.

"Good grief, this is dreadful, dreadful," said the man in shorts and socks and brown leather shoes. His name was Derek, and his tall, thin wife was called Claudette. She was outside in the vestibule, shouting in French at her phone and hitting it against the wall. Derek wringed his hands and shuffled from foot to foot. "We have to find a solution, a better solution – "

"Come up with one, if you can, mate," said Vincent.

Derek frowned, and his eyes sought out his wife.

Vincent nodded to himself. No one had an answer. He knew the truth, and it meant they had to get rid of this man's body.

They lapsed into silence. Vincent looked at them all in turn.

Bert's wife Patty spoke up.

She said, "The boy is right. The poison is in the body. The soul is corrupt. The man will rise as a demon and infect us."

"Not exactly what I had in mind, but you've got the right idea," said Vincent.

"Don't you realize?" said Patty, her head swivelling again, eyes hidden behind the sunglasses. "This is our doom. Isn't that true, Bert?"

"Yeah, I guess it is."

"Burn him," she said.

Penny gasped, and her legs buckled. Bella supported her.

"Burn him," said Patty again. "Isn't this what you were saying, boy?"

"I'm not a boy," said Vincent.

"You are a boy, and you were brave enough to speak the truth.

You've spoken the truth from the beginning. The only one."

He felt uncomfortable receiving praise from Patty. He gripped Holly's hand.

Patty went on:

"There's only one way. It must be burned. The poison in it destroyed by fire."

"Wait," said Gavin.

"You be quite, sodomite."

"Shut up, witch," said Gavin.

"You've brought this on us. We should burn you, too."

"What?" said Gavin.

Vincent said, "We have to get rid of Andrew, right. But we should discuss how."

Penny shrieked. "What are you saying? You're talking about burning my husband's body. You bastards. I've got children, here. Andrew's children. His babies." She shook with rage, Bella clutching her tightly.

Patty ignored Penny and said, "I've said how – burn him."

"Yes, Patty," said Vincent, "but I don't think – "

"Burn him," she said, "burn him – burn him – burn him – "

"Burn him," said someone else, "burn him," and then another voice chanted, "Burn him, burn him, burn him."

Penny shrieked. She tore free from Bella's grasp and threw herself across her husband's body. And by then Bella had also started to chant, "Burn him, burn him… "

Holly nuzzled up to Vincent. He could feel her shake, and he shook too. This was going badly. He glanced around. Now Mark was saying, "Burn him, burn him," and when Vincent looked into Simon's eyes, he saw that the bodybuilder was moments away from joining the chorus.

Bert lumbered forward. Mark followed, as did Derek. Bella stepped ahead of them, and eased Penny away from Andrew's body. She struggled, screaming at them to stop, Bella comforting her and telling her everything would be okay.

Bert, Mark, and Derek hoisted Andrew's body off the floor. They ferried it out of the chapel. Penny wailed, collapsing in a heap.

Patty followed, as did Simon and Oswyn.

The chanting droned on. It had become a low hum, almost imperceptible. Vincent looked at Holly and then at Gavin, who was comforting Neil.

The men carried Andrew out into the inner ward. Patty followed like some high priestess, waving her Wales baseball cap above her head and leading the chant of "burn him, burn him".

And then Vincent heard something else. A change in their demand. Something that made his insides turn icy.

Someone had started chanting:

"Burn *them* – burn *them* – "

CHAPTER 17.
FEEDERS.

KAYLEE Connor lashed out at Jared as he tried to loop the rope over her head.

She said, "Jared, no – please," but Jared laughed and slapped her arms away and tried again to get the rope around her waist.

Kain and Reece held her arms, and they were laughing too. Everyone was laughing. Cackling and braying as they got her ready for the game they'd been playing.

Kaylee cried, and she wanted to pee. Fear made her shake. She'd seen what had happened to Gimbo and Lucy. They'd been lowered into the zombies, and she'd had to watch them being eaten alive.

Jared's crew, all fifteen of them, had been at Kain's all night smoking and drinking. Kaylee had tried to get back with Jared, only for him to say he was with Hayley West now. It had been Kaylee's sixteenth birthday, and she thought getting back with him would be a nice birthday present since she hadn't got any gifts or cards, or "happy birthday, Kaylee," from her mates.

"But if you love me, you can suck me off, if you want," he'd said.

So she did. Right there in the kitchen. With three others watching and laughing, like they were laughing now.

After she'd finished doing it to Jared and wiping her mouth, he cuffed her across the head and called her a whore. He took Hayley West, who'd been watching, upstairs. Kaylee had started to cry.

Reece had come up to her and pretended he liked her. He said if she did to him what she'd just done to Jared "I'll tell him how cool you are, babe, and he'll take you back, you see".

So she got on her knees for Reece as well.

She was a bit drunk and a bit stoned. After it was done, she felt empty inside. She felt like she'd been used, like she was rubbish to them. And when Hayley West and Jared came downstairs, Hayley West smirked at Kaylee and said, "I've just given him a *proper* blow job – the way he likes it."

At eight-thirty in the morning, Jared and Kain had decided they would go out for breakfast. Some of the crew went home, and there were ten of them left. They wandered the streets. Kaylee lingered at the rear of the group, with a headache and a line of cold sores that really stung.

They were loitering around Waterloo. They scanned the commuters. Jared had been talking about slapping someone so Kain could film it, and post the video on YouTube. He was eyeing up a victim when the zombies came from nowhere.

The gang ran like everyone else ran. Zombies attacked anyone they could get a hold of. Dragged them down. Two or three zombies pouncing on one human. And then, just like the movies and the video games, they started to eat the people.

And the people cried, and their blood sprayed, and their guts poured out, and soon Kaylee was seeing disembowelled and dismembered bodies everywhere.

Jared and Kain ran, and the others followed, so Kaylee, sobbing and shaking with terror, followed too.

Zombies had swept through the streets. Hundreds of them. Cars skidded and brakes screeched. Kaylee smelled rubber as tyres smoked along the tarmac. Vehicles smashed into buildings, into other vehicles. Zombies crawled over the cars, trying to get at the people inside.

Kaylee raced after the crew. Her chest tightened. The taste of tobacco and booze soured her throat.

They ran for ages, it seemed, and came to an estate. Redbrick buildings. Ugly, like the ones they lived in.

Kaylee stopped and puked and then got going again, the bitter taste of vomit in her mouth.

She saw the guys swing into an underground garage. She followed. Jared was pulling down the garage door, and the zombies were chasing her, and she screamed.

He grinned at her and tried to pull it down faster, but she dived and rolled and cried out at him.

He laughed and went into the darkness of the garage, leaving her to sob.

The door behind her rolled and rocked as the zombies pushed against it, trying to get in.

She rose and followed Jared into the darkness.

It had been baking hot when they got up on the roof. The sun glowed very powerfully today. Hotter than Kaylee had ever known it. She saw Jared and Kain and the others looking over the edge of the building.

They could see Waterloo Station from here, and they could see towards the South Bank. She saw the London Eye, and it looked like it was crawling with insects. Kaylee shivered. She didn't think they were insects, those things creeping over the wheel. She knew they were zombies.

"Look at this shit," said Jared.

A pack of zombies, maybe twenty or thirty, had crammed down the dead end street. The dead things snarled up at the gang. They clawed at the bricks, trying to climb up.

"Come here, babe," said Jared to Hayley West, and she went to him and snuggled up to him. Kaylee's skin flushed and something churned in her belly. She wanted to be sick again. Jared kissed Hayley West and put his hand up the back of her skirt and groped her backside.

Then he shoved her off the roof.

Some of the others gasped.

Jared howled with laughter and watched her fall.

Kaylee saw her fall too.

Saw the shock on Hayley West's face as she plunged into the zombies. Saw them swarm over her and writhe as they tore at her body, eating her.

Kaylee quaked as Hayley West screeched. The zombies pulled her apart, and throughout the ordeal, her face, beautiful even if it were twisted in agony, remained untouched.

Jared did high-fives with Kain and Reece.

Lucy started crying. Gimbo said he wanted to go home. Gimbo was slow, but Jared had always let him run around for him, though he treated him like shit. Now Jared said, "Go find some rope, Gimbo," and Gimbo went and came back in ten minutes or so with a length of rope. Handed it to Jared, grinning.

Jared headbutted him.

When he was down, Jared and Kain tied the rope around Gimbo, binding his arms to his side.

Then they lowered him off the building into the zombies. Lucy cried and screamed, and then they did the same to her.

Then they looked for someone else.

Kaylee, terrified, turned away, scoped London. The streets crawled. Smoke rose in the distance. She could see really far because of the weather – the fantastic summer weather.

Then she heard her name:

"Kaylee Connor."

A cold fear swept through her veins.

She turned her head slowly, and there was Jared and Kain and Reece leering at her.

Jared said, "Plenty of meat on her."

And they came for her. Gave her no chance to run. Put her on the floor. She screamed and begged for them to stop. They laughed and tried to loop the rope over her shoulders and around her waist. Gimbo's blood and Lucy's blood soaked the rope.

Now Jared had the rope around her, and he tightened it until the cord bit into her belly.

"Lift her up," he said.

Kain and Reece hoisted her off the floor, over their shoulders. Kaylee thrashed and screamed. She clawed at the rope. But it was tight around her and slippery with blood.

"Down she goes, and do it slow," said Jared. "Feet first so they can take bits off her. Let her see herself being chewed up." And he laughed again as Kain and Reece took her over to the side of the building, and she saw the ravenous zombies looking up at her, their mouths agape, their faces stained with blood and their hands coated in gore.

CHAPTER 18.
MAKING A MEAL OF
CARRIE.

"AREN'T you going to do anything?" said Carrie.

Gilbert watched as the youths hoisted the girl over their shoulders and carried her towards the edge of the building.

"Nothing to do with us," he said. "Let's just watch the show."

Carrie glanced up at the grizzly man before looking at Nathan. The youth sweated. The sun took its toll on his pale complexion. His skin reddened in the heat.

She'd been grateful to see the men stepping into the elevator moments earlier. At first, she'd thought the hand that appeared on the door had been a zombie's. It had been Gilbert's, and she'd sagged with relief.

But now that relief had been replaced by anger.

"What about you?" she said to Nathan.

He said nothing, squinted at what was going on.

Carrie looked at the youths. They were baying and laughing. The girl screamed and struggled. They were going to lower her over the edge, like they'd done with the others.

Carrie snatched Gilbert's shotgun, and before he could do anything, she marched towards the group, the gun's stock jammed into her side.

She pulled the trigger. A jolt of pain jarred her ribs. She was thrown to the ground. Her ears rang, and her vision blurred.

The youths ducked and scattered. The two boys dropped the girl. She slammed down on the ledge and hung there, legs dangling over the side.

A tall youth with close-cropped blonde hair and pale skin glowered at Carrie. He swaggered towards her, fury creasing his face.

She panted for breath. Her side hurt. She got to her feet, unsteady. She tried to pull the trigger again, but it wouldn't work.

The youth grinned. "You want to be fed to them fucking things, bitch?"

Carrie backed up. She looked over her shoulder to where Gilbert and Nathan had been – but they were gone.

She fished into the pocket of her skirt.

The youth came closer.

Two other boys were striding over, too. One in a hoodie, the other in a vest that showed his muscles.

The blonde reached for her, growling.

She got the perfume out of her pocket and sprayed him in the face. He shrieked and reeled away, groaning and flapping his hands near his eyes. He jigged around the roof, screaming, rubbing his face.

The other two faltered and gawped at their mate.

Carrie said, "Don't come any closer, or you'll get it, too," but she didn't know how that would help her save the girl hanging off the ledge.

The boys knew that. The hoodie said, "What you going to do with that, slag – make me smell nice?"

The hoodie and the vest-boy laughed.

The blonde youth squatted, rocking back and forth, rubbing his eyes.

The hoodie rushed her. She yelled out and sprayed. He smacked the bottle out of her hand. He slapped her across the face. Carrie's cheek stung, and she saw stars.

Hoodie and vest-boy grabbed her and sneered and spat. She cried and lashed out, swinging her fists, catching vest-boy on the jaw.

"Hold her," said the first youth, getting up, his eyes red.

Hoodie and vest-boy held her. The first youth stomped over, blinking, tears streaming down his cheeks. Carrie struggled but they were big and strong. Fear made her cry. The blonde kicked her in the stomach and the air was knocked out of her. She bent double, and they let her drop. The pain shot through her, and she writhed there in the dust and the litter, crying and thinking of Mya and cradling her belly.

"I'm pregnant, you bastard," she cried.

The blonde said, "Like I give a shit who fucked you, whore."

Hoodie said, "You smell nice, Jared, man."

"Fuck you," said the blonde. "Get this bitch and her fucking baby over there. Fucking lunch and dessert for them fucking zombies."

Someone grabbed her hair, and it felt like her scalp was on fire. They dragged her towards the ledge.

CHAPTER 19.
THE ANDREW-ZOMBIE RISES.

THEY continued to chant, "Burn them, burn them... " as they carried Andrew's body out to the castle's inner ward.

Vincent held Holly's arm. They watched from the chapel.

A head popped round the entrance. It was the girl who worked there, the younger one named Catrin. "What... what's going on out there?" she asked. "The kids, they're really upset."

Vincent said, "Where are they?"

"We're up in the sleeping chamber, just round the corner. It's quiet and a bit cooler. What's happening?"

"Who's there?"

"Me and Sandra and the kids. Why? What's wrong?"

"Stay there, okay?" said Vincent.

She asked what was going on. He told her. She sobbed and had to rest a hand on the wall to steady herself.

Vincent told her, "Go back up there to the kids. Don't let them see you cry. And don't say anything, right."

Holly said, "I'm scared... scared of how they were... the American woman... they... they looked like they were... enjoying it too much... "

"We should go out there," said Vincent. "Or they'll think we're… " He trailed off, not wanting to think about it. He asked Gavin, "Are you coming?" but Gavin said he'd stay with Neil.

"How is he?" Vincent asked

Fear paled Gavin's face. "One bite, Vincent, that's all. Look at him. He's… he's dying. And they'll want to burn him too. What did we start, here? Why did you suggest it?"

"Gavin, we had to. You know we had to."

"I can't bear it. Losing him like that. Maybe he'll be all right. We can… we can find antibiotics or something."

"We haven't got time, mate."

Gavin started to cry. Vincent stood there, watching. But Holly drew him away and led him down the staircase, out into the inner ward.

The moment he stepped out into the sun, Vincent felt his whole body slow. The heat was overwhelming. Sweat filmed his body. Thirst gravelled his throat. They'd need a water supply quickly, or people would suffer heatstroke, dehydration. He had his bottle of water, which he was rationing, but that wouldn't last another hour between him and Holly.

A pint, that's what I need, he thought.

The men had laid Andrew's body at the centre of the inner ward.

Simon and Mark lingered nearby. Derek sat crossed legged on the grass, taking notes. His wife wavered about as if she were drunk. She ranted in French, trying to get a signal on her phone.

Roger told his sons, "Bobby, Jack, you listen up now, lads. I want you to watch this, right. You two, you might have to do this soon enough if things get bad, so you watch and learn. Time to be men, lads. Right?" Teena smoked a cigarette and took photos of Andrew's corpse with her disposable camera.

Bert leered at Vincent and Holly and said, "Come on, you two, come watch the bonfire."

Holly said, "This isn't about entertainment – we *have* to do this, don't we."

113

"That might be true, love," said Roger, "but it will be fun as well. Keep the boys entertained, at least. Better than fucking X-Factor. Strictly Come Burning, how's about that?" He cackled. "Hear that, Teena, Strictly Come Burning?"

"Aye, that's a good one, love," said his wife. "You're a comic, you are."

Bobby and Jack hissed with excitement.

"Where are those people?" said Patty.

And then Oswyn and Bella appeared from a doorway in the eastern wall. Oswyn carried a red fuel can.

Roger said, "Here they come, look: Tweedledum and Tweedle-dumber."

Vincent's bowels chilled.

"You store fuel here for the apocalypse, Oswyn?" he said.

"Lucky I do," Oswyn answered. "You never know when someone'll run out of petrol – or when you'll have to burn a body."

He presented the can to Patty but she said, "What do you expect a lady of my age to do with that, sir?"

"Well… you wanted it," said Oswyn.

"Jesus, give it here," said Simon. He snatched the can from Oswyn and then unscrewed it. He tipped the container. The fumes shimmered. He eyed his audience and said, "I'm not doing this for fun, right. I'm doing this because I think we have to. If we don't, this guy, he's… well, he's going to turn into one of those things outside. I don't want anyone" – he glared at Patty – "to have bright ideas, all right. We only do this when we have to. When they're definitely dead, okay?"

A murmur rippled through the spectators.

Simon poured the petrol over Andrew's body. The fumes hit Vincent's nose. He screwed up his face. Patty turned away. Bert gritted his teeth.

Holly said, "That stinks," and Vincent thought, *You wait till the flesh starts to burn.*

Simon backed away from the body, pouring a trail of petrol as he went.

Teena said, "You want a light, love?"

Simon glowered at her. Mark, Zippo in hand, stepped forward and said, "Let me, mate."

The fumes rose off Andrew's body and made the air ripple.

Holly buried her face in Vincent's shoulder. "I can't watch this. It's disgusting."

Mark crouched and flicked open the Zippo.

Andrew sat up and bit Mark's cheek.

Mark screamed, blood spurting from his face.

Simon staggered away. Patty ran, shrieking. Screams tore through the inner ward.

Mark put his hands over his face and howled. Blood poured from between his fingers.

The Andrew-zombie sprang to its feet, rage on its dead face, pieces of Mark's cheek in its mouth.

Everyone ran back towards the south gate, towards the chapel.

Vincent shoved Holly and told her to go.

"You too," she said, but he stared at the zombie.

"Go, Holly," he said.

Simon charged the zombie. The creature hurtled to meet him. They barrelled into each other. They tumbled across the grass. The zombie leapt to its feet, dived for Simon. Pinned the muscleman to the ground. Simon screamed and lashed out.

Vincent gawped with horror.

The zombie fended off Simon's blows. Rammed its head into Simon's face and chewed off the man's nose.

Simon screeched. Blood fountained from his face. The Andrew-zombie thrashed its head from side to side, Simon's nose in its teeth. And then it chomped on the meat, blood and bone spraying from its jaws.

115

Simon squealed and bucked, tossing the zombie off him.

Mark, on his knees, said, "I've been bitten, I've been bitten," as he tried to hold his face together.

Simon crawled away, blood gushing from his mangled face. He screamed, his whole body shuddering.

The zombie pounced on Simon again and bit him in the back of the neck, tearing away flesh.

Vincent glanced around. Everyone had retreated back to the south gate, but they were watching. They couldn't take their eyes off the carnage.

The Andrew-zombie buried its face in Simon's nape, and Vincent saw that it was feeding.

Simon moaned, and his movements slowed.

The zombie savaged the back of Simon's neck.

The dead thing, covered in blood now, stuffed its fingers into the open flesh and dug around.

Mark got up and reeled.

The zombie yanked Simon's spine out of the wound. It spooled out and uncoiled like a spring. Simon twitched and gurgled.

Vincent heard the screams from behind him.

Mark swerved along like a drunk, the skin hanging off his face like a rag.

The Zippo glistened in the sun.

Vincent darted for it and snatched it off the grass.

The zombie snarled at him, and with Simon's spine in its hand, it raced towards him.

Vincent yelled out in horror as the Andrew-zombie attacked.

He flicked the Zippo's wheel, once, twice, three times, but nothing happened. He smelled the fumes. He felt queasy. The blood-covered zombie charged, teeth chattering.

The Zippo lit. The flame flickered. Vincent cried out. The zombie shot forward. Vincent tossed the lighter. Dived away.

He heard the whoosh of the zombie going up in flames and felt the heat sear his back.

The creature moaned, and Vincent dared a glance.

The zombie stumbled around, flapping and staggering. It was a pillar of flames.

Sandra had raced out and screamed Simon's name.

Bella and Catrin held her back.

The Andrew-zombie wheeled about the inner ward. The grass caught fire. Vincent stamped out the flames. The smell of burning flesh made him heave.

The zombie toppled over, hit the ground face first. Ash showered from its body. Flames spat. Black smoke billowed. The odour made Vincent retch again, and he nearly choked.

The zombie crawled towards him, its charred face showing rage. Vincent gawped at the creature.

The milky-white eyes were empty and dead and stood out in the blackened face.

Vincent stared into them.

The Andrew-zombie finally succumbed. It slumped, burying its face in the grass. Fire ate its body, and smoke from the carcass bulged into a dark cloud above the castle.

Vincent came out of his trance when Oswyn sprayed the zombie with a fire extinguisher.

He looked at Vincent after he was done and said, "You… you can't let it burn here. There's health and safety to think about."

Vincent wanted to laugh, but it came out as tears.

CHAPTER 20.
GOD'S HOUSE.

"YOU can't burn my husband," said Sandra, shaking with panic. She wore a green vest top, stained with blood, and grey shorts. She had legs like tree trunks and was heavy around the waist, but Vincent guessed she was probably very pretty when a zombie hadn't just killed her husband.

"Sandra," said Mark, holding a cloth to his cheek, "we've got to – you saw what happened to Andrew." He couldn't speak properly because of the hole in his face, and you had to concentrate to understand his words.

Sandra stared at him and said, "How can you say that? He's your brother."

"He's dead, Sandra. Dead, and likely to be alive again soon. But not as Simon – as something else."

"What am I going to tell Hettie and Maisie?"

Mark lowered his gaze.

Bert told Mark, "You are right, my friend. He was your brother. But what about you? You got bitten, too. You'll change."

Gavin said, "We don't know that. We only know that if someone's killed, they... they change. Not if someone's just bitten."

"Well, your lady friend over there," said Bert, gesturing towards Neil, "doesn't look like he'll be alive very long."

"You know what, I hope you get bitten," said Gavin. "I hope you get bitten and I hope you feel yourself die and change. I hope you feel the human in you slip away – if there is any human in you. You're probably a zombie already, since you've got no brain cells."

"Can we stop calling them that?" said Oswyn.

"What do you want to call them?" said Gavin.

"They're… they're sick, that's all."

"So sick they want to eat us," said Gavin

"I… I don't know, Gavin, I'm only… I'm only trying to avert panic till the authorities come – "

"You've not done a very good job, mate," said Gavin. "Oh, and if they do come, will you say we burned Andrew – with *your* petrol?"

Oswyn squirmed.

Bert said, "So what about that one?" indicating Simon's body outside on the grass. "Are we burning him? You want to do it, kid? You did a good job on the other one."

The American chuckled and Vincent glared up at him. Holly put her arm over his shoulder. He could still smell burning flesh. Smoke from the Andrew-zombie's corpse wafted into the chapel where they'd all gathered again.

"Leave him alone," said Mark. "He did the right thing."

"Hey, you won't be saying that at lunch-time – you'll be wanting to *eat* him," said Bert.

"Why don't you shut up, you fat bastard," said Sandra.

Bert gawped at her. A gasp went through the chapel, echoing off the walls. Patty hissed and said, "We're in a sacred place, you blaspheming harlot."

Sandra seethed. "You shut up, too. I've lost my husband. My kids are up there, the kids whose dad you've just burned. Do you want to tell them? What should I say? What should I say?"

"The truth, that's what you should say," said Patty. "The truth about your dreadful mouth, young lady. I've never heard such language. That's the language of the gutter. The language of the devil. And spoken in a chapel, too. God's house. That's why we are doomed. Why *you* are doomed."

"I think we should stop sermonizing," said Vincent. "Maybe start thinking about how we're getting out of here."

"Well, we're not," said Patty.

"Why do you say that?" asked Vincent.

"Because it's the end of the world. This is where we are all destined to die. Whether some of you join my husband and I in paradise, is another matter. We don't know yet. But we are all here to die, and that's that."

"I'm not," said Holly. "I don't want to die here."

"Neither do I," said Gavin.

"I might die here, but I don't want to," said Mark.

"We're not going to die," said Oswyn. "We're safe here."

Vincent sneered at him. "And you've been in a zombie invasion kind of situation before, have you?"

"No, Vincent, I haven't – but I trust the authorities."

"The only authority we can trust," said Patty, "is our Lord, Jesus Christ, and he has brought upon us judgment day. We must do what he wants until he is ready for us. We must keep burning the poisoned and the corrupt." She swivelled her head in Sandra's direction. "And we start with your husband, missy foul mouth."

CHAPTER 21.
DIE FOR THEM.

THE man who'd called himself Sawyer accelerated the London bus into the estate.

He passed people packing belongings into cars. He passed people who were covered in blood, running along the streets. He passed bunches of zombies huddled around human remains, feeding.

One of the dead caught his eye, and they looked at each other, Sawyer seeing the white, empty eyes. The zombie opened its jaws to growl at him, and he saw the blood-filled mouth.

After he'd shut the garage door on Carrie and the other two, he'd got down to surviving.

He could've gone with them into the garage. But Carrie had to get to her daughter. He could help her do that by holding off the zombies. It would give her time. Okay, she was stuck with Daddy and Sonny, or whatever their names were. But he hoped they wouldn't abandon her. He didn't know that for sure. He'd never met them before last night. But he had faith that people stuck together when there was trouble. He had to believe that.

That was the only way Carrie would get to her child.

He had no one. When he died, no one would cry. And there was no one to live for, either. So he could do the right thing for the first time in his life. Fight for someone who really had something valuable to protect. Die for them too, if he had to. And that would be it – all over.

The family name dead.

Him, the last of his line, gone.

His dad had died of cancer in jail. His mum, he didn't know. His older brother was HIV positive, and his middle brother was in jail for life – 40 years.

Just me, he thought as he had faced the zombies outside the underground garage. He hoped Carrie would wait for a while, then make a run for it – and not get involved in the murderous game taking place on the roof.

He'd watched the rooftop gang lower the girl into the zombies. But he couldn't do anything for her. He had a fight on his hands, fending off the undead. Then he'd run. Back down the road. Zombies chasing him. Growling and moaning as they pursued him.

He'd found the bus near Waterloo Station. He'd pulled the dead driver from the seat. The man had come apart in his hands and slithered in pieces off the bus. The vehicle smelled of meat. But he got into the driver's cab, managed to start the double-decker. The engine coughed, and he'd looked around, worried the noise had drawn out the zombies.

But there was nothing. The streets were still. Dead bodies piled everywhere. Crows pecking at the flesh. Dogs sniffing at the meat. Rats scurrying out of drains and down the alleys. Flies buzzing in clouds over the carcasses.

He'd driven back, weaving slowly through abandoned traffic, past dead bodies.

Now, back in the street where he'd left Carrie, he saw the

zombies crammed down the dead-end.

They craned their necks and reached out their arms, waiting for the next feed.

He could see a woman on the ledge. She was fighting with a man, struggling.

And he recognized her.

Carrie.

He belted himself in. Slammed the accelerator.

The bus rattled and rumbled. The engine churned.

Up ahead, the youths on the roof had overpowered Carrie. They lowered her, head first, towards the zombies. She struggled, and the rope around her ankles swung her like a pendulum.

He sped into the road. The way was narrow. Too narrow for a bus. The vehicle's sides scraped along the buildings. Sparks flew. He heard metal clank and tear.

The zombies didn't turn to look as the bus hammered towards them. They were fixed on the flesh.

Carrie's flesh.

He gritted his teeth. His hands sweated on the steering wheel. The blue boiler suit stuck to his back. He was soaked through, perspiration streaming down his body.

He tensed and gave a roar.

And ploughed into the zombies.

The bus crashed into the dead-end. The impact jerked Sawyer forward. The seatbelt chewed into his chest and shoulder. The vehicle mashed the zombies against the wall. They erupted, spraying the cab with blood and gore. Churned up zombies coated the windscreen. Pieces of them slithered down the front of the bus. Blood seeped through fissures in the glass.

Sawyer groaned, pain in his chest and neck.

The smell of death filled the bus, and it turned his stomach.

A zombie's face was pressed flat against the glass. As Sawyer unbuckled himself from the seat, he stared into the dead thing's

123

bulging eyes.

He looked back up the bus. The vehicle had concertinaed. He squeezed himself through the door. Clambered up the narrow gap between the side of the bus and the wall. Guts and blood covered everything. He had to wade through limbs and remains, but he managed to hoist himself up on the roof of the bus.

Carrie crouched there, unwinding the rope from around her ankles. She looked at him through a mask of blood and said, like she was pissed off, "You nearly took my head off."

CHAPTER 22.
DO UNTO OTHERS.

SAWYER scrambled on to the roof of the bus and scowled at her. "Bloody hell, I'm really sorry I rescued you. I'll be more careful next time I drive a bus at a bunch of zombies who were about to eat you."

Carrie's heart thundered. The bus had whipped past her head. She'd felt it tug at her as it shot by. It had smashed into the wall and crushed the zombies, spraying her with blood.

Before she could say sorry and thanks, the blonde youth she'd sprayed in the face with perfume jumped down from the building and landed on the bus. His knees gave with the impact, and he fell on his face, sloshed about in gore.

Carrie didn't give him chance to get to his feet. She dived at him. Landed on his back. Pinned her knees to his flanks and rained blows on his head. He cried out and managed to lift up, piggybacking Carrie. She punched and slapped him round the head. He wheeled, trying to dump her.

He shouted two names: "Kain, Reece – "

Hoodie and vest-boy bounded off the roof, on to the bus. Hoodie went for Sawyer, who said, "You don't want to be doing that, son."

Sawyer threw a punch that struck the youth on the jaw and sent him reeling across the roof. Vest-top faltered, seeing his mate so easily dealt with. Carrie caught glances of Sawyer while trying to claw out the blonde's eyes.

The rest of the group were shouting and screaming from the rooftop. Carrie craned her neck and looked at them. The girl they'd been planning to feed to the zombies before Carrie had now got to her feet and was staring down from the roof.

Sawyer bounded towards vest-top.

The blonde tipped Carrie over his head. She bounced on the bus's roof. Tried to get up but slipped about in the blood. The blonde raged, his eyes on fire. Carrie scrabbled away, sliding around in the gore. She looked up the street and gasped.

More zombies streaked towards them.

She turned, looking for Sawyer. He was fighting with vest-top, delivering punches to the youth's gut.

The blonde came at Carrie again. He raged at her. His friends up on the roof egged him on. Urged him to toss Carrie to the zombies.

The bus quaked as the dead horde slammed into the back of the vehicle.

"They've come for their dinner," said the blonde.

Carrie glanced towards Sawyer. He'd knocked out vest-top and was kicking the floored hoodie, shoving him towards the edge of the bus.

Carrie crawled away as the blonde strode towards her. Behind her, she heard the zombies growl and moan. She heard them claw at the bus. She heard their teeth chatter.

She'd slid herself right to the edge. She had no strength left, and she panted for air. Her limbs felt heavy, and blood and sweat coated her body.

The blonde smirked. He saw her as easy meat. She looked over her shoulder. The zombies drooled and reached up for her.

The blonde got ready to kick her off the roof of the bus. He quickened his pace. Swung back his leg. Belted out a laugh. His friends encouraging him.

Carrie spun on her backside away from his kick. She scissored his balancing leg between the both of hers. She rolled sideways, towards the ledge, forcing him forward. Toppling him off the roof of the vehicle.

The blonde waved his arms. His eyes went wide. He tipped over the side of the bus. Carrie kicked him in the backside as he went. He screeched and plunged headfirst into the zombies.

Carrie had a quick look and saw the zombies part. The youth hit the ground in the space they'd created. He stared up at her, horror in his eyes. The zombies swarmed over him. They jerked and jostled as they devoured the blonde.

She rolled away from the side.

Two girls on the roof were screaming and pointing at Carrie, calling her a murderer.

The hoodie crawled towards her now, Sawyer kicking him in the backside. She looked at Sawyer's face and it showed nothing. No rage, no effort, no fear. He kicked the hoodie off the roof, and the youth shrieked. She didn't look where he fell. She stared into Sawyer's eyes. He looked back at her, and they fixed on each other for a few seconds.

Then he wheeled and went after vest-top.

He grabbed the youth's neck and forced him forward. Carrie watched open-mouthed as Sawyer shoved him off the bus.

Carrie hadn't taken her eyes off him.

He saw her staring, and he told her, "They would've done the same to us. Do unto others, Carrie. They're the ring-leaders. Without them, that lot up there are nothing."

He gestured to the roof of the building.

The youths screamed and cried. There were four boys up there, but they weren't bold enough to take on Sawyer.

He was right. They'd lost their pack leader in the blonde lad, and his enforcers in the hoodie and the vest-top. The girls were still accusing Carrie of murder.

Then one girl leapt over the edge of the building, onto the bus. She was the one they were going to chuck to the zombies before Carrie intervened.

"If you're going, I'm coming with you," she said, looking from Sawyer to Carrie.

Sawyer tutted and spun round. He ran towards the building on the other side of the bus. He grabbed the ledge and heaved himself up.

Standing on the ledge, he looked down at Carrie and the other girl and said, "Come on, then."

Carrie and the girl looked at each other and then at Sawyer.

He said, "You'd better get a move on, because those things are learning to climb."

Carrie glanced down. A zombie levered itself up using the gap between the wall and the bus. It forced itself upwards with its arms and legs, almost like a spider.

CHAPTER 23.
THE SWARM.

MUM panicked and grabbed Dad's arm, saying, "Don't go out there. You can't go out there, Terry."

Craig went to open the back door.

Mum turned, her face ashen.

"Craig, stay where you are," she said.

Drivers were getting out of their vehicles and shuffling towards Art, who stood smoking near his truck, blood dripping off his baton. The drivers glanced around, watching out for zombies. Art looked cool and untroubled.

Dad got out of the car. Mum screamed and reached out, trying to pull him back inside. He leaned in and snarled. "Shut up, woman, it's fine. If we see anything, I'll get back in the car. I'm not hanging around outside with those hungry fucks around."

Craig leapt out of the back. Mum bawled his name. He ignored her shouts and strode after Dad, towards the knot of drivers gathered near Art's Scania.

Craig's gaze flitted around, looking for zombies. Fear shook him, but he tried to control himself. He didn't want them to think he was just a kid.

"Hello again," said Art to Dad and Craig.

"What's going on?" said Dad.

"We can't go any further," Art said.

The drivers and passengers mumbled.

Art went on:

"We've got to go back."

"Back where?" said a woman wearing a bikini top and cut-off jeans.

Craig saw Art's eyes rake over the woman.

"Back to where we came from, Miss."

"But that's where… where those things were headed," said Dad.

"Aye," said Art, " and that's" – he threw a thumb behind him, gesturing south – "where there are more of them. Take a look."

They peered between the Scania's cab and trailer. Craig felt the heat. It was hard to breathe. He smelled sweat and fuel. A hand fell on his shoulder. He gasped and wheeled. It was the woman in the bikini. Craig gawped at her cleavage and turned away, looking straight ahead again.

The woman at his shoulder cursed, and he heard Dad say, "Christ almighty!"

Some of the others swore too when they saw.

Craig couldn't close his mouth. The sun glared and made the world hazy. But he could see the M8 snaking away into the distance. Cars choked the highway for miles, and bodies lay everywhere. Crows flapped and croaked above them, swooping down now and again to rest and peck at carcasses. Clouds of flies droned, blotching the blue sky. They hovered around the bodies, landing and lifting, landing and lifting in billows.

Craig held his breath. Someone gasped behind him, and he heard another voice say, "Holy, holy Jesus, save us… "

Sweeping over the horizon, from east to west, came a swarm.

Heading directly towards them, the dark canvas washed north across the terrain.

130

It rippled and rolled like a wave.

It swamped everything in its path.

It was a torrent of death.

It was zombies.

Thousands of them.

The walking dead.

The hungry dead.

"Coming straight at us," said Craig, but his voice came out as a rasp. He felt himself begin to cry, and he stifled the tears. He turned to look for his dad, found him, and he saw terror in his father's face, too.

"Dad, what are we going to do?"

Dad said nothing.

Art answered:

"We head north. Find a haven."

"What do you mean?" said a bare-chested man, whose torso was roasted red by the sun.

Art scowled. "I mean, we find our place in the country. Cross to one of the islands. I mean, we do something and not wait here to be eaten. That's what I mean." He stared at them, his eyes swivelling from face to face. He spat and curled back his top lip. His earrings glittered in the sun. He said, "I'm going, so I don't know about any of you lot."

They were quiet for a few moments, everyone thinking. Craig looked at them all, two-dozen people with furrowed brows, chewing nails, whispering to partners and mates.

A scream pierced the stillness.

Craig jerked.

The crowd scattered.

The corpse twitched.

The crows pecking at its eyes flapped away.

Craig's belly twinged, and he stepped away from the truck, ready to make a run for the car.

The corpse convulsed.

The woman in the bikini said, "What is it?"

Art climbed back into his cab. "It's getting worse, that's what it is."

Three other bodies, their wounds glistening in the sun, the smell rising off them, began to tremble now.

Craig said, "They're waking up."

The bare-chested man said, "What?"

Dad said, "Come on, lad," and grabbed Craig by the sleeve.

The corpse sat up.

Screams jolted Craig.

And then the three other dead bodies rose too.

The crowd scattered, racing back to their vehicles.

"Oh Jesus!" someone cried. "There are more of them. They're getting up, for Christ's sake!"

Craig held his breath. Dread clutched his heart.

A half dozen bodies, killed by zombies less than an hour previously, were becoming alive.

And as they sat up, their guts spilled from ripped bellies. Their eyes swung along their cheeks, hanging there on ribbons of flesh. One creature had lost its lower jaw. But it was still intent on feeding, from the looks of things. Someone slapped Craig across the head.

"What are you doing?" he said.

His dad said, "I'm giving you a clout, you rockit. Don't stare like you're staring at tits, get a fucking move on back to the car."

Dad ran, his shoulders heaving as he struggled to breathe. He wheezed, sounding like a punctured tyre. Craig raced after him, his lungs burning.

If this was what life would be like in zombieworld, he'd have to get fit, and he blurted out a half-laugh-half-cry at that mad thought.

Getting in shape for the zombieworld challenge.

Everyone ran now, making for their cars.

The zombies shook off their deaths quickly and found their feet. They developed from stuttering forward on stiff legs to bolting after their prey.

The woman in the bikini shrieked as she sprinted back to her car. Craig gawped at her bouncing breasts.

Two zombies closed in on her.

Craig shouted and caught her eye. Fear contorted her face, and her mouth twisted in terror as the zombies brought her down. She hit the ground and yelled, a guttural noise coming from her throat. The zombies crawled over her, ripping into her with teeth and hands.

She stared at Craig, and his guts twisted.

She screeched and covered her head with her hands, but more zombies had joined the fray now and chomped at her fingers, biting chunks from her scalp.

The woman writhed and shrieked.

The zombies flayed the skin from her back.

Blood gushed from her mutilated body.

She was still alive and still making a dreadful noise when Dad shoved Craig into the car and slammed the door.

Silence fell, and Craig stared ahead, seeing nothing but blood.

Blood everywhere: on the windscreen, all over the road, streaming down Dad's face as he opened his mouth, making the shape of Craig's name.

And then his Dad disappeared, and in his place came the woman's warped face, terror in her eyes, pleading for Craig to save her.

He quaked and choked on puke, spluttering. The silence broke, and Dad was shouting his name, telling him to pull himself together, and there was no blood on his dad's face or on the windscreen, and Craig threw up in the footwell again.

He shut his eyes and kept his head down there, between his knees.

In the car, Sam shrieked and Mum wailed, and Dad was saying, "Holy Jesus! Holy Jesus!" over and over.

And the face of the woman begging Craig to rescue her etched itself into his memory.

CHAPTER 24.
ANGELS OF DEATH.

THEY burned Simon's body in the castle's inner ward. Fire charred the grass. The smell of roasting flesh filled the air.

Vincent and Holly watched from the south gate, standing in the archway. Patty and Bert, Bella and Catrin, Derek and Claudette, and Roger and Teena and their twins formed a circle around the bonfire.

The twins were yelling and braying, shouts of "Burn, you bastard zombie, burn," rising above the crackle of flames.

"We're turning savage," said Holly.

"Yes," said Vincent, feeling the heat of the fire on his face.

"And how long has that taken?"

"About as long as it would take to roast a chicken."

"Vincent, do you think we had a choice, though? I mean, they'd come alive if we didn't."

"Some of us shouldn't be enjoying it so much."

Vincent watched Patty and her congregation. Teena took photos. Her twins pulled faces at the bonfire.

"And if those zombies outside can smell human meat, that" – Vincent pointed to the tower of smoke rising from the carcass, wafting over the walls of the castle – "isn't going to help. That'll give them an appetite."

Patty turned and looked his way. She said, "They are hungry enough already. These creatures have the mind of Satan, remember – that makes them clever, clever, clever."

Vincent shook his head. "I think they're dumb. There's just a lot of them, that's all. They herd after food, and I don't know if they hunt by smell or sight. No one knows."

"I might be able to tell you in a while."

Vincent and Holly turned to find Mark leaning against the wall. He looked ill, his skin pale and blotched, the blood on his face caking.

He went on:

"I'm scared silly, though. I've got a kid. The thought of not seeing him again tears me apart. And my nieces are up there. They've already seen their dad die. Christ, my ex is going to go ballistic with me."

"I don't think she can blame you for a plague of zombies," said Holly.

"She'll give it a try." He ran a hand through his hair. The colour had drained from his face.

Vincent knew Mark'd be like Neil, soon: gasping for breath, unable to move.

And they would die and come back as zombies.

Vincent needed to get away from the odour of burning flesh, and he headed for the stairs that led up through the south gate's walls.

Holly said, "Where are you going?"

"Up top, along the walkways."

"Nothing I said, I hope?" said Mark.

Vincent didn't answer.

"Can I come?" said Holly.

They made their way up Gunners Walk. It was a flanking wall to the left of the castle's entrance. Not open to the public, Vincent and Holly had to vault down from the south gate tower and make their way along a joining wall. They hurdled metal barriers warning visitors that entry was prohibited, and mounted the Gunners Walk. From this jutting partition, troops stationed at the castle would fire at rebels, or hurl stones at them, or pour hot oil over them.

That's what we need, thought Vincent as they made their way along the walk: *weapons*.

Holly faltered and tugged at him, and he saw why.

The zombies wallowed in the moat below, raking at the walls when they saw Vincent and Holly.

They snarled and growled, and their teeth gnashed.

They crammed the street and The Green, right down to the water's edge.

Hundreds of them. Maybe thousands.

"They all want to eat us," said Holly.

Vincent scanned the mass of undead.

His gaze fixed on a figure – one zombie amid the hundreds.

It was the woman in the short red dress who'd been dragged out of the sports car. Dragged out and eaten. Parts of her, anyway. Like the right side of her face, which was a nothing but blood and bone, now. The dress hung down and showed where the zombies had eaten her left breast. A wound showed ribs beneath the pale flesh.

The red-dress zombie glared up at Vincent from across the road, fury etched on its face, hate even. Or perhaps it was just hunger.

Vincent shuddered.

The creature shoved its way through the horde, trying to get to the front. Trying to get closer. But all the zombies were doing that. Pushing and shoving and barging towards the food – towards Vincent and Holly.

"They're unaware of each other," said Vincent.

Holly whimpered. She was tucked into the crook of his arm. He felt her quiver.

He went on:

"They're just single organisms. They don't belong to anything apart from themselves. Look. They're not pack animals. They're not a society or anything. They're broken down, Holly. They're just us broken down."

"I want to go," she said.

He turned to lead her back down.

"No, Vincent."

He stopped and looked at her.

She said, "I want to go from here. I can't stand this. I'm too scared. I want to be with my mum."

She gazed up at him and sobbed, and he thought she was lovely, and it made his heart heavy to think of her in this hell.

They looked into each other's eyes, and he bent his head to her, and she craned her neck.

The zombies growled and clawed and washed forward in waves, trying to get at them. The creatures clambered over each other. They were trampled and crushed. They were pressed down under the waters of the moat. They hurled themselves at the castle walls, against the door in the Gate Next the Sea.

But Vincent and Holly ignored them. For him, there was only her.

They kissed on Gunners Walk, surrounded by the dead.

* * * *

Back in the chapel, Vincent told them, "We've got to think of a way out of here." Holly stayed close to him. They held hands. His heart knocked, thinking about her. He wanted to get out of here with her. Try to find somewhere safe, a place where there weren't any zombies.

138

Oswyn raised his hand and was about to speak, but Bert interrupted saying, "The authorities are *not* coming, my friend."

"The only authority left is Jesus Christ – and he's on his way," said Patty. "These are the signs."

"No one's coming," said Vincent. "Only the zombies. More and more of them. They know we're here. And they'll wait till we die of starvation, or till they can find a way in."

"Or till we're stupid enough to go outside," said Sandra, her eyes red from crying. She sat with Penny.

Widows together, thought Vincent. He shuddered, thinking about them having to watch their husbands being burned. Penny had witnessed her husband rise from the dead, too.

And then they had their children to worry about. Vincent looked at the kids: Penny's daughters, Annalee and Bryony. Sandra's Hettie and Maisie. They were all under ten years old. And they all looked terrified. He pitied them, and sensed the dread they must've been feeling

Gavin said, "I think if people want to leave, they should be allowed to – but some of us have to stay here." He dabbed Neil's brow with a damp cloth.

"Some of us don't have a choice," said Mark. His face had paled further. Dark circles ringed his eyes, and the colour seeped from his lips.

"I vote we stay till the afternoon," said Roger. The white nylon of his England football shirt had darkened with sweat.

"I vote that, too," said Teena.

"That's no surprise, is it," said Derek.

"Here, mate, what's that supposed to mean?" Roger said.

Derek swallowed. "What I mean is, your wife is hardly going to disagree with you."

"We're a team, mate, that's why," said Roger. "Team Bidden. Me, the wife, and the lads."

"Aye, you keep out of it – look after your own business, bloody MP or whatever you are" said Teena. "Appears to me you can't."

Derek glanced towards Claudette. His wife smoked in the passageway just outside the chapel. Roger and Teena's twins lingered nearby, watching her. The boys whispered to each other.

Trying to beg fags from Claudette, thought Vincent.

He looked away and told them, "We can't stay here. We'll die."

"We'll die out there, too," said Derek.

"I keep telling you all, it is perfectly safe in here," said Oswyn. "This castle has repelled many an attack over the centuries. I'm sure we can hold out for a few hours."

"Why do you think someone's coming?" said Mark.

Oswyn stared at him. "Because someone *is*."

The sound of helicopters made them stop. They looked at each other as the noise grew louder. Everyone dashed for the door. They shoved and barged down the passageway.

Outside in the heat and the light, they craned their necks and waited. They could hear the churning rotors, but there was nothing to see.

Then Derek pointed to the east and said, "There, over there."

And they swept in. Six helicopters, black like angels of death.

They came closer, flying in formation: one in front, then two, another two, and one taking the rear.

"See," said Oswyn, "I told you they were coming."

"Why would they send six helicopters for us?" said Vincent.

"They didn't know how many of us there would be," said Oswyn.

The droning grew louder as the 'copters approached.

"If they're coming to rescue us, they'd better be making their descent soon enough," said Roger.

"They're not coming to rescue us," said Holly.

The helicopters whizzed overhead. Roger and Teena started to wave and shout. Oswyn scurried back and forth, waving his arms above his head.

140

The helicopters flew west.

Vincent and the others stood in silence. Only Oswyn spoke saying, "They'll be back… they'll be back, you'll see… they'll be back… "

Apart from his shouts, the only sound was the drone of the zombies outside the castle.

Oswyn quieted and lowered his gaze, and Vincent caught his eye.

Oswyn said, "They – they should have stopped for us."

"Why?" said Vincent. "Why should they stop for us? Do any of you think the government, or the authorities, or whatever, give a shit about us? They don't. Not about us, not about anyone else in our situation. All they care about is their own necks. I bet you, *I bet you*, who was in those helicopters – I bet you that was the prime minister and his cabinet. I bet you. No one's going to look out for us except us, do you get that?"

"Jesus is looking out us, young man," said Patty. "If you are saved, that is."

Vincent shivered with fury. "Sorry, but I can't hang around for Jesus."

Patty continued:

"Jesus has waited two thousand years for you, little blasphemer. Can't you wait a few more hours for him? You can be saved, you know. Saved like my husband and me. You can all be saved. Come to Jesus, and he'll protect you. Come to Jesus through me." She stretched out her arms. Tears trickled down her face from behind her owl-eyes sunglasses. Then she said, "I am the way. The only way to life. Without me… you will die."

CHAPTER 25.
INVASION.

KAYLEE led them down the staircase. The building was dark. Condensation dampened the walls in the stairwell. They were slippery when Carrie rested her hand on the plaster. She turned her nose and looked at her hand and stopped, her legs not moving.

Sawyer asked her if she was okay.

She held out her hand to him, wanting him to look.

He said he couldn't see.

"Blood," she said. "On the walls."

"Come on, we've got to get going."

Kaylee had gone ahead. Carrie could hear the girl's footsteps echo up the stairwell.

"Come on, Carrie," he said again.

Minutes earlier, they'd been standing on the roof. The sun had grown hotter. No breeze blew. It was still and sweltering.

The youths from the building across the street had gone. The zombies had given up trying to clamber to the top of the wrecked bus. They'd marauded back down the street.

From where they stood, Carrie had been able see over Lambeth. She could see Waterloo Station. The Thames beyond it rippled in the heat. Big Ben poked out over the high rises, and she could make out the Parliament buildings.

When Carrie said, "We've got to get going," Kaylee had asked, "Uh, where are we supposed to be going?" The girl wore a short blue dress. Her legs were covered in scratches and cuts. Make-up streaked her face and blood stained her dark hair.

Carrie had told her Wood Green, and the girl said, "You're never going to make it, sweet."

Carrie had bristled. "My daughter's there, I'm going." She looked at Sawyer. "Are you going to help me or not?"

She'd stomped off towards the door marked exit. She wrenched the handle, but it wouldn't open. She looked over at Sawyer and said, "Well?" He kicked down the door, and when they were about to scoot into the stairwell Kaylee had cried out:

"Oh shit, look at that."

Carrie stopped and turned and saw Kaylee gazing to the north.

Carrie asked, "What is it?" but then she saw and it made her insides melt.

Zombies swept down from The Strand into Embankment, flooding across Blackfriars Bridge and Waterloo Bridge.

"Hundreds of them," said Kaylee.

"Thousands," said Sawyer.

They looked like an army invading the city. Storming through the streets. Destroying everything in its path.

Now, in the stairwell, Carrie followed Sawyer.

She thought about the army of the dead. Where had it come from? Had it swarmed London from the north? That meant it had swept through Tottenham. Torn through those streets – *her* streets.

Mya's streets.

Mum, there are zombies outside the house.

She quickened her pace. Came right up behind Sawyer, and shoved him in the back. "All right," he said, "all right."

When they stepped outside, the heat slowed Carrie again. She felt faint, but kept going, wavering down the road.

Kaylee peered through car windows. She glanced around. Crouched and picked up a brick. Hurled it at a car window, smashing it to pieces. Carrie flinched. The car's alarm wailed.

Zombies shot round the corner. A pack of a dozen. They came at pace, but they were clumsy, bumping into one another.

One of them tripped and fell, and the others trampled it. The creature staggered to its feet, turned round like a drunk, and regained its balance. The zombie clawed at the air and came racing after the others.

"You can't drive," said Sawyer as Kaylee leapt into the driver's seat.

"Yes I can."

Carrie opened the back door and dived in. The car was a red Peugeot.

"How old are you?" said Sawyer.

"Doesn't matter, does it," said Kaylee.

"Okay," he said, "get on with it."

"Hurry up," said Carrie, seeing the zombies race towards them. "Hurry up, Kaylee."

Kaylee hotwired the car. She looked small in the driver's seat and had to crane her neck to see over the steering wheel. She revved the engine.

The first zombie tossed itself on the bonnet. Blood-tinted spit sprayed from its jaws, splattering the windscreen. The creature had half a face, the other half a skull. Split right down the middle like the Batman villain, Two-Face.

Kaylee rammed the accelerator. The zombie rolled over the roof of the Peugeot. She ploughed through the other undead, scattering them.

Carrie twisted in the back as the wheels crushed zombies. She looked through the rear window at the trail of blood and gore.

A zombie cut in half under the tyres crawled after the car. But Kaylee floored the accelerator, and soon they were on Lambeth Road.

Carrie said, "How do you kill them?" and she told them what she'd seen through the back window. The half-zombie still alive, its face twisted with rage.

"You shoot them in the head," said Kaylee.

"How do you know that?" said Sawyer.

"Films and video games, innit," she said. "You can crush them with buses, too."

Carrie told them how she'd killed one outside Westminster Abbey, knocking its head off.

She tried calling home again. She got a weak signal, and the phone rang, but kept cutting out. She ran a hand through her hair. Blood and sweat made it greasy.

"Any luck?" said Sawyer.

"I can't get through."

Kaylee said, "I couldn't get through to my mum, either. I ain't seen her in ages, yeah, but I just thought... And then I tried some of the crew."

"Which crew?" said Sawyer.

"Crew you just killed. Jared, the blonde guy. He was like my man, yeah. But he discarded me, see. And then he pushed his new girlfriend, Hayley West, off the roof earlier, and I thought he'd want to go out with me again. But then he was going to... "

She trailed off.

"You're a good driver, Kaylee," said Sawyer. "Keep on the Blackfriars Road, over the bridge."

"So what do you do then?" Kaylee was asking Sawyer.

"I rob banks."

"Cool."

"No it's not."

"You been inside?"

"Yeah, too often."

"What's it like?"

"It's shit, Kaylee."

They drove on. Abandoned cars crisscrossed the lanes. Trucks lay on their sides. A bus had ploughed into a building on the corner of Stamford Street and Blackfriars Road. People staggered around, covered in blood.

Others were looking for loved ones, shouting names. A woman held a framed photograph above her head. The picture showed a girl, aged five or six. Blood smeared the image. The woman cried out:

"Nancy! Nancy! Has anyone seen my Nancy?"

Partly eaten bodies covered the road and the pavements. Clumps of gore were scattered everywhere, and Carrie saw limbs, too. A leg. An arm. A head.

Flies darkened the air over the flesh. Other scavengers were already searching for easy meals. Dogs fought over bones. Rats buried themselves in disembowelled bodies. Birds flapped around, cawing, swooping down and grasping chunks of flesh in their claws.

"Do you have a gang?" said Kaylee.

"No. I was freelance. People came to me. I worked for men who put gangs together." He glanced over his shoulder at Carrie. "By the way, you see where Laurel and Hardy went earlier?"

She didn't answer him. "I can't get through," she said and began weeping.

Sawyer reached over the back seat and laid a hand on her shoulder. "Hey, it's all right," he said.

"Well it's not, is it."

"We'll get your daughter."

"Yes, but what will she be like? Like that?" she said, indicating a mutilated corpse. Two crows perched on the carcass, pecking at the shredded flesh.

They crossed Blackfriars Bridge. Kaylee weaved the Peugeot through a maze of abandoned vehicles.

Through her tears, Carrie saw the dome of St Paul's and the

gherkin-shaped Swiss Re building. She wondered if there were anyone left in there. If there were anyone left anywhere.

* * * *

"Hear that?" said Kaylee.

Sawyer said he did. Carrie did too. It was gunfire.

"Maybe we're fighting back," she said.

"Yeah, maybe," said Sawyer.

They'd stopped on Ludgate Circus, the main link between the cities of London and Westminster. Kaylee stopped the car on the crossroads. Wrecked vehicles had turned the road into an obstacle course. A black cab had gone through a shop window. Smoke billowed from the taxi. Bodies were strewn across the road. Birds, mostly crows and seagulls, picked at the human remains.

A pack of rats streamed out of a drain.

Carrie gasped.

The creatures were as big as cats, their fur wet from the sewer. They scurried towards a headless corpse. Carrie looked the other way.

"Where to?" said Kaylee.

Up ahead, from where the gunshots came, lay Farringdon Street. To the left ran Fleet Street. A right turn would take them down Ludgate Hill.

"Go up Farringdon" said Carrie, thinking the girl was asking directions.

"I mean, do you want to head towards the shooting?"

"I want to go towards my daughter. If there's shooting, there's shooting."

Kaylee looked at Sawyer. "What do you think?"

Carrie flushed with anger. "We're going to get my daughter."

Sawyer said, "We don't know who's doing the shooting. We don't want to a walk into a scene from Death Wish – vigilantes taking potshots at anything that moves."

"Okay, it's decision time. The lines are open. The numbers are on the screen. Which way?" said Kaylee.

Carrie said nothing. She had no voice. She began to shake as she stared at the crowd marching down Ludgate Hill, and she tried to say something. Warn Sawyer.

The crowd thronged. Maybe a hundred people armed with baseball bats, meat cleavers, tyre wrenches, hammers, and saws.

She found her voice:

"I think we should go."

Rage bubbled in the crowd. Carrie sensed it and saw the fury in the eyes of those leading the horde. They were men, mostly. In suits and ties. But their clothes were tattered and bloodied. They'd been fighting, she could see. But fighting what?

Carrie could hear the rumble of their footsteps. The noise grew louder.

"They're… they're alive," said Kaylee. "They're… not zombies. They might help us, man."

Sawyer said, "We should get going. They don't look like the helping sort."

Kaylee put the car into gear and shot forward, the wheels spinning.

A roar came from the crowd. The men leading it pelted down Ludgate Hill towards the car.

The Peugeot shot up Farringdon Road. The tyres shrieked and left a trail of smoke in their wake.

* * * *

Five vehicles, including a BMW and a VW Camper van, followed Art's Scania north on the M8, cutting through Glasgow.

They weren't the only convoy. Others travelled south. Craig saw a fleet of vehicles slice across a field. A line of lorries with foreign words on their trailers careered down a slip road, headed into the heart of the city. But many people weren't going anywhere. They stayed with their cars or wandered the carriageways, or gathered in groups.

Craig and his family listened to the radio as they followed the Scania. The radio crackled, but they got some voices coming through. The towns were riddled with zombies, said a voice through the interference at one stage. Many thousands had been killed, according to the broadcast. And now the recent dead appeared to be rising up, too.

"Bollocks," said Dad to that, still denying what the killers were.

He coughed, and Mum said, "My God, Terry, that sounds awful now. You shouldn't have strained yourself. You'll be coughing up blood if you're not careful. I don't want the kids to see – "

Dad flapped a hand at her and grunted.

"What do *you* think they are?" said Craig.

"Bollocks."

Mum said, "It's – it's drugs or something, you'll see. Or some disease. You know, they warned us about a swine flu epidemic last year. They said it would get worse."

"This is not flu, Mum. It's an invasion of zombies."

"You don't know that, Craig. You don't know anything. No one does at the moment."

Craig tutted. He tried to get a signal on his phone again. Tried ringing Nacker, KP, and then Hallie. Seeing her name in his contacts directory made his belly trill.

But then the excitement dwindled and became something heavy and black in his chest.

He'd lost her, he knew that. Lost them all unless they'd stowed themselves away somewhere. Unless they'd got to one of those safe havens the radio had mentioned earlier.

That was possible.

Anything was possible.

Craig mopped his brow. Sweat soaked his scalp. The car felt like an oven, and Craig thought they'd be roasted alive in here if they didn't get some air.

He and Sam had emptied the bottle of soda. The drink had been warm and sickly.

They drove north, crawling through abandoned traffic and past stragglers meandering the highway.

"There's no bodies," Craig said.

"What did you say?" said Mum.

"No bodies here."

"Well, sweetheart, that's a good thing."

To his left, Craig saw a dozen figures hurtle across playing fields towards a row of houses.

That's why there aren't any bodies, he thought.

They're all zombies, now.

The creatures weaved from side to side as if they were drunk, but they moved at speed.

"It's *not* a good thing, Mum."

"What do you mean?"

The small voice had come from the footwell. Sam peered up at him. Tears stained her face, and sweat plastered her hair to her head.

"I mean – " Craig began.

"No," said Mum, twisting in her seat. Her eyes blazed with fear. "No, Craig."

"You don't know what I'm going to say."

Dad said, "She does. She knows everything. She's like that fucking Derren Brown."

They ignored him, and Craig went on:

"Mum, you said it was a good thing there weren't any bodies – well it isn't."

She widened her eyes. "Be quiet, Craig."

Sam rose from the footwell and sat up on the seat. "No, I've got a right to know. I want to know."

"Sam, listen to me – "

"No, Mum. I want to know. Don't treat me like a kid. You can't

150

protect me, you know. I've seen what's going on." She looked at her brother. "Say, Craig… say what you were going to say. Say why it's a bad thing."

"It's a bad thing because the ones we saw being killed have risen up as well, now – that's why it's a bad thing."

Mum sobbed. "I don't want to hear this."

Dad grumbled.

Sam said, "You think if you get bitten you turn into one of them?"

"I think if you *die* you become one of them. Don't matter how you die. You can die by being run over or from a heart attack, or by being eaten – "

"For heaven's sake," said Mum.

"Thinks he's an expert now," said Dad. "That he's the fucking David Attenborough of zombies, or something."

Mum said, "Terry, please – "

Craig said, "I'm not. I'm just guessing from what I've seen, that's all."

Dad sneered at him in the rear-view mirror. "Think you're clever, eh?"

"I said I didn't, you rockit."

Dad growled. "Don't you fucking call me names you little shite, you little fucker."

"Don't give me a hard time, then."

"Should've given you a hard time from the kick off. You might not have turned out to be a useless layabout."

"I'm following in my dad's footsteps."

Dad slammed the brakes. The car travelling behind them skidded and swerved as it tried to avoid crashing into them.

The sudden deceleration tossed Craig forward, and he put his arm out, and it jarred against the driver's seat. Sam squealed and fell into the footwell again. Mum shouted at Dad, calling him an idiot.

Dad stopped the car. The vehicles following them swept by, and the driver who'd been immediately behind waved his fist and glowered at Craig.

Dad swivelled in his seat. Mum grabbed him and shouted. Dad's face twisted with rage. He reached over into the back seat.

Craig gritted his teeth. Dad grabbed his collar and pummelled him with swinging lefts.

Craig raised his knees to try to protect himself. He flailed at Dad's punches. Threw his own left hooks, clipping Dad in the arm and shoulder.

They swore at each other, Dad calling him a cunt, Craig crying but trying not to, calling Dad a bastard.

Mum clawed at Dad, and Sam shrieked.

The car rocked.

Dad punched Craig in the side of the head.

Stars erupted in front of his eyes, and the right side of his face went numb.

His head swimming, he thought he saw shapes outside. Dark figures swooping over the car.

The car shook, and the suspension creaked.

He and Dad must've been really going at it to make the Sierra jerk so much.

But then Sam cried and said, "They're all around us… they're all around us."

Mum screamed again and said, "Terry, you idiot, stop this and get us out of here."

The car pitched.

"They're trying to roll us over," said Sam. "They're *going* to roll us over."

Her screeching pierced Craig's skull.

Dad stopped beating him.

Craig fell back in his seat. His face hurt. His jaw felt swollen. Everything was blurred.

Dad faced front again, and Craig heard him cry out.

It was dark, shadows skipping inside the Sierra, and then the car filled with screams.

Craig came to, his head clearing, his eyes seeing properly again – and seeing the zombies clawing at the car, trying to pry open the doors to get inside.

The engine started and it whined and Craig's stomach lurched when he thought the car would break down and they'd be stuck here.

A dozen or more zombies surrounded the car. They scraped at the doors and the windows. They pressed their faces to the glass and their mouths left smears of saliva, like snail trails. Their jaws opened and closed. Sam had curled up into a ball again, her knees up, her face buried between them. Mum shuddered and was making a noise Craig had never heard before that must have come from deep inside her, where real fear lurked.

She'd cried before. Cried because he was a bad lad. She'd screamed too. Screamed at him when he came home pissed or when the cops brought him back, or when he gave the magistrates two fingers.

But he'd never heard a noise like this come out of his mother.

The car bucked forward and shunted zombies out of the way. More had clustered around the vehicle. They'd screened off the light, and now and again shafts of illumination sliced through the gaps between the shuffling bodies to blind Craig.

The Sierra stalled, and Dad yelled out.

He started the engine again and the car shot forward, jerking, bouncing over something.

The zombies at the front fell under the wheels, and Craig again heard bones crack and flesh pop.

The car jolted forward. The zombies held on. The roof buckled, and something hammered on it.

Dad slammed the breaks. A zombie flew off the car.

Dad accelerated forward. The zombie rose to its knees. The car thumped into the creature, crushed it under the tyres.

Craig looked through the back window.

A trail of twisted bodies lay on the highway. Dismembered zombies flailed, trying to crawl after the car. But the main group continued to chase the Sierra.

They couldn't keep up, though, as Dad weaved up the motorway.

After a few minutes, Dad slowed the car.

Up ahead, they could see the convoy, bearing left along the M80, now.

Mum cried. Sam sat up. Craig's jaw throbbed. He could taste blood in his mouth. He scowled at his father.

Dad said, "Don't you ever fucking speak to me like that again – or I'll throw you out of this car, I swear I will."

Tears welled in Craig's eyes. Hatred for his father coiled in his belly, and he wished the bastard was dead.

"Maybe I'll get out before you throw me out."

"Maybe you fucking should, you waste of fucking space."

* * * *

The Metropolitan Police had blockaded Charterhouse Street.

The gunshots came from inside the Smithfield Central Market.

Kaylee slowed the Peugeot down. Around fifty people clustered near the police barriers, watching what was going on. They looked ragged and roughed up. Police cars filled the road as far as the junction with Aldergate Street.

"We need to go left after the central markets," said Carrie, "and then up St John's Street."

"We're not going anywhere now," said Kaylee.

Sawyer said to Kaylee, "Cops aren't going to be happy seeing a fifteen year old driving, whatever state the country's in – get out and let me drive."

While they were swapping seats, Carrie got out.

Sawyer stood next to her. "Are you okay?"

"How are we going to get through?"

"I don't know."

Carrie walked towards the police barriers. The gunfire deafened her. The locals gathered at the barrier had their hands over their ears.

The shooting stopped.

A policeman wearing full-protective gear said, "It's all clear. They're all dead. File into the market."

The crowd shuffled towards the entrance to the market. They rolled into Carrie, shoving her along.

She complained, but a policeman told her to get moving.

She looked over towards the car.

Sawyer and Kaylee had been ordered out of the Peugeot. They were being frogmarched over. Sawyer held his hands over his head. Two armed officers walked behind them.

Carrie slipped free of the crowd. She barged past a policeman. She ran, and the cops shouted, saying they'd fire.

She threw herself at Sawyer, tossing her arms around his neck. He swept her up and swung her round. Her feet knocked into one of the policemen behind them. The officer reeled into the other copper.

"Go," said Sawyer.

They made a dash for the car.

Gunfire raked the road next to them.

Bullets chewing up the tarmac.

Sawyer slowed, hands out. Carrie hit the ground, knees first.

The crowd shouted.

A copper said, "You do that again, we won't miss," and forced Sawyer, Carrie, and Kaylee towards the crowd.

Carrie said, "What's going on?"

"It's martial law," said policeman.

"It's for your own protection," said another officer.

"The market is a designated safe haven. There's dozens throughout Central London, mostly."

"Central London?" said Carrie.

"The outskirts are lost," said the policeman.

"What about Wood Green?" said Carrie.

The policeman chuckled. "Tottenham's always been lost, love."

She bristled. She made eye contact with Kaylee and Sawyer. She read something in Kaylee's eyes.

"What was the shooting about?" asked the girl.

The copper said, "Some of those things – "

" – zombies – "

" – just got into the market, that's all. We were disinfecting the place."

Kaylee threw herself at the two cops. It triggered panic in the crowd. They scattered. The armed cops fired into the air.

Sawyer grabbed Carrie's hand, and they ran.

Gunshots and screams filled the air.

Carrie looked over her shoulder. She couldn't see Kaylee. She wanted to stay for the girl.

The crowd stampeded. The police fired over their heads. People screamed and cried.

Sawyer tugged on Carrie's arm. He dragged her down an alley, opposite the market. She didn't look back.

CHAPTER 26.
KIDS.

"DOES it work yet?" said Vincent.

Holly fidgeted with her iPhone. She shook her head. "I'm getting interference." She was trying to pick up a news channel. Making calls had failed. No signal came through. She'd logged into her Twitter account earlier, and found reams of Tweets about zombie attacks across Britain. Then her phone died and came alive again, and now she was becoming frustrated. "There's static, nothing else... so shit."

Vincent glanced at the group clustered around Patty and Bert in the chapel.

Bert looked bored. He fanned himself with his baseball cap. His belly strained at the buttons of his shirt.

Patty held court. Perched on a bench against the chapel wall with her congregation gathered around her. Among them was Claudette. She sat crossed legged on the floor, checking her mobile phone now and again. Vincent guessed if she got a signal from the Samsung before she got a signal from the Christ, she'd be re-converted to modern technology and leave superstition behind.

Bella knelt with her hands together, as if in prayer. She mumbled, eyes closed, swaying back and forth.

Brother- and sister-in-law, Sandra and Mark, were huddled there with Hettie and Maisie. Mark rocked from side to side.

Vincent knew the man was very ill, but he didn't know if he'd die. How were they to know what a zombie bite did to a human? They'd seen what dying did to a human – it got them resurrected.

Patty's Jesus would be pleased about that, he thought.

He looked at Mark and then at Neil. Would they turn into zombies? If they died, they would. But perhaps being bitten only made you sick. And then you got over it. He shook his head. He didn't really believe that. Vincent knew what was going to happen.

In a few hours, they'd have two zombies here in the castle.

Gavin attended to Neil. He told him he loved him and that everything would be all right.

But Vincent knew it wouldn't be.

Roger and Teena muttered with Oswyn and Derek near the chapel's entrance. They glanced around the room now and again, nodding towards certain people.

Vincent saw them gesture towards Holly. What were they up to? Something brewed that he didn't like.

"We've *really* got to think of a way out of here," he said to Holly. "I don't like what's going. We've got fucking Mother Theresa over there, and Oswyn and that lot are up to something, as well."

"What do you mean?"

"I mean people go mad in situations like this."

He offered her the bottle of water, and she shook her head.

"You've got to," he said.

She took the bottle and swigged. She grimaced. He knew the water didn't taste good. It was tepid, but they had to keep drinking. They sweltered here. The heat was relentless. And it would worsen, Vincent knew that.

"So hot," she said.

"I remember it like this in Egypt. My brother took me couple of years ago. Fifty degrees, it was. He was trying to get off the booze – again."

"Did he manage it?"

Vincent shook his head.

"You see him a lot, your brother?"

"No, not much. He's in London. He's got a kid with this girl. I don't know why she stays with him. She's really nice, and he's not."

"Maybe she loves him."

"I guess, but he's still no good. He just gets drunk all the time. And there's the little girl, you know. Mya's her name."

"That's nice. Is she sweet?"

Vincent shrugged. "Yes, she's lovely. I've only seen her a couple of times, though. Shy and quiet. Scared of the dark."

"Do you want kids one day?"

Vincent blushed.

Holly smiled – the first time in a while, and she really looked pretty, which made his belly flutter.

"What about you?" he said.

"Yeah, I want two – boy and a girl." She looked around. Heard Bobby and Jack making aeroplane and machinegun noises outside. "Wouldn't raise them like that, though. I'd be a good mum. Well, I'd try to be, anyway."

"I think you would be."

He leaned in and kissed her, and she kissed him back, and their lips stuck together for a few seconds before he drew away. The dryness in their mouths made their parting sting. He took a swig of water.

Holly lowered her head, and her shoulders sagged.

"I really hope we get out of here," she said.

"We will."

"Because, Vincent, you know, I really, really like you and keep thinking about us doing, you know, normal stuff together."

His belly fluttered. "Yeah, me too."

He was going to kiss her again, but then a wail echoed through the chapel and Vincent stiffened.

CHAPTER 27.
"LAST MAN-LAST WOMAN".

CARRIE and Sawyer worked their way back to St John's Street.

Partly-eaten bodies littered the roads, and they were beginning to smell. The reek of decay hung over the city. Flies droned over remains. Birds pecked at the gore, and rats skittered about.

"This is medieval," said Carrie. She wiped her face. Her throat felt like sandpaper. Sawyer had taken down the top of his boiler suit. He was bare-chested. She caught herself looking now and again, and swooned. She cursed herself, angry that she wasn't focused on Mya.

But seeing Sawyer's sweat-slick torso made her think of Boyd's scrawny figure.

Boyd.

How did that happen? she thought.

How did we *happen?*

She couldn't get Boyd out her mind. He'd attached himself to her tissue, to her cells. He'd entwined himself around her heart and wouldn't let go, even though she really wanted rid of him.

Boyd would never do this. He'd never risk his life like Sawyer was doing.

Boyd would've found the nearest pub and drank himself to death before the zombies or the police or the vigilantes got to him.

Anger towards him flared in her breast. The way he'd left Mya. Abandoned his daughter.

Mya.

Carrie quaked and started to cry.

Sawyer stopped and looked at her.

"It'll be okay," he said.

She apologized for crying, and he said not to.

"I'd feel the same way," he told her.

"I'm so scared for my little girl."

"I know. We'll find her."

Sweat filmed his face. His eyes glittered in the glare. He reached for her face and brushed a stray hair away from her cheek, hooking it behind her ear.

She turned away from him, feeling the guilt well up in her.

I shouldn't, she was thinking, *not now – not ever*.

They were in St John's Street on the junction with Skinner Street and Percival Street.

A bar called The Peasant stood on the corner. All its windows were shattered. A dead man lay on the pavement outside the front door. His belly had been ripped open, his insides scooped out. Blood raced down the pavement.

Carrie could see piles of dead bodies inside the pub, too. Mounds of dark shapes in the gloom.

She shuddered.

Sawyer's hand rested on her shoulder. She gasped, and gooseflesh ran up her flanks. She edged away from him and said, "No, I... I can't... I don't – "

Shame flushed her skin.

She sobbed again, but this time he didn't comfort her.

He moved off and turned his back and crouched.

She shuffled over to him and squatted.

She said, "I'm really sorry."

"It's 'last man, last woman' stuff, isn't it," he said.

She tried to smile. Her lips were chapped, and her face felt stiff, the blood caking on her cheeks.

He rose. "Let's get going. Find Mya. Then I'll leave you alone. You don't want to be mixing with my sort, anyway."

She stood and scoped her surroundings.

"So quiet now," she said. "Feels like we *are* the last two people on earth," and she looked him in the eye.

* * * *

PC Dermot Macey asked the girl, "What's your name?"

"Piss off," she said.

Macey's nerves jangled. He was soaked through. The heat today was intense. But the stress was even worse.

He jabbed the Benelli M3 shotgun in the girl's face. "Tell me your name."

"What's yours?"

He told her.

"Then I'm Kaylee Connor," she said, "and take that fucking gun out of my face. I ain't scared, right. I ain't half as scared as I've already been today. My ex-boyfriend tried to feed me to the zombies this morning, so this don't rattle me, mate."

"I'm scared," he said.

"Yeah, well, that ain't no fucking good, then, is it? Cops being scared of zombies."

"Move inside," he told her.

"I don't want to. I want to go after my friends."

"Them two? They're dead, love. Anyone who's not 'havened' by now will be dead by dinner – actually, they *will* be dinner. They're lucky we didn't shoot them."

163

"Are they?"

Maybe not, thought Macey. Like he'd told her, they were dead now for sure.

Zombie meat.

He tried not to think about it. This girl had nearly caused a riot. A distraction tactic so her two mates could leg it. And because of that, Macey and his colleagues had to open fire. Not something they'd been keen to do, even if it was into the air – just warning shots.

Macey's team, and other units from the Met's authorized firearms squad, had been mustered at 8.40 a.m. – but by then, it was too late.

They had no clear orders, and no one knew what was going on. Troops ponced about, too, and the cops and the soldiers were fighting over bragging rights.

"Who's running this fucking show?" was the million-quid question.

No one, was the answer.

And it showed.

The zombies – or whatever they were – massacred thousands in the first few minutes. As the team drove through London, Macey's sergeant had handed down the orders: "We've got designated safe havens for civilians. Our job is to get 'em into those safe havens. Anything that looks dead, kill it. Any citizen disobeying... " He'd trailed off and swallowed, his eyes skipping over the team.

And they'd all stared back.

Macey didn't have the stomach to shoot unarmed civilians.

"I'd like to see the bastard politicians who give us these orders blow a terrified mum to bits just because she wanted to go looking for her kid," Macey's mate Davison had said, the sweat rolling down his face.

Macey's team were deployed at the Smithfield Central Market on Charterhouse Street.

When they got there, the sergeant said, "Barricade the road. Gather all the civilians. File them into the market, pronto. Kill any zombies. Lockdown. We stay inside till it's safe."

"And when will that be, sarge?" Davison had asked.

"Don't know, Davison. Phone a friend. They might know. I don't. I am the weakest fucking link. Get out there and save some lives."

They'd tried their best.

The civilians were in a state. One of the armed officers who'd been in the Army and served in Bosnia had said, "They're like refugees, man. You wouldn't know the difference between this lot and the ethnically cleansed sacks of humanity I saw over there."

The people came, and they wailed for loved ones lost in this armageddon. Mothers weeping for children, brandishing photos of them, asking, "Have you seen her, have you seen her?" Husbands howling for missing wives. Children orphaned in the onslaught stuttering around, their faces and their clothes soaked in their parents' blood.

A team of paramedics checked everyone for bites. Anyone wounded by a zombie were ushered down a side road. Macey knew that a juggernaut waited there, and the infected would be piled into the trailer and then driven off.

"Where are they taking my wife?" a grey old man had asked, sobbing.

"To the hospital," the paramedic had said, the lie creasing his face.

Those who were separated from loved ones by this apartheid were the first to protest, and Macey had feared that he, or one of his colleagues, would be forced to shoot someone.

But there were only minor scuffles, the refugees to weak to mount any revolution against the segregation.

"They're going to be checked over, that's all," said the paramedic through a loudspeaker. "You'll be reunited once they get the all-clear. This is a very difficult time, and we're trying to protect you."

I can still see you're lying, Macey had thought.

Now he told this girl, Kaylee Connor, "You need to forget about your friends. They nearly cost you your life, you know. We've got orders to shoot dissidents."

"Dizzy what?"

"Anyone disobeying orders. How old are you?"

"Fuck-off years old."

"Don't be like that, love. We're only doing our best. I got a daughter about the same age as you. Fifteen, yeah?"

"Whatever. Let me go after them."

"Move inside, Kaylee."

He glanced around. The last of the civilians were being herded into the market. Before Kaylee and her friends had arrived, causing trouble, Macey's mates had been killing zombies. The monsters had broken into the market. A few civilians had already been havened there. *Havened: fucking jargon*, thought Macey. Not very havened, were they. Not havened enough from the zombies who got inside and attacked them. Davison had led a team into the market to cleanse the area. And then Kaylee and those other two turned up.

Neverending, he thought.

"Make me," she said.

"I'm asking nicely."

"I don't think that's nicely."

"Well, what would be nicely?"

"Nicely would be to get out of the way, let me go after them two."

"Why do you want to die, Kaylee?"

"Why do you want to live, copper?"

He gawped. "Because... because of my children and my wife."

"They're dead."

His heart froze. He looked around. He'd tried to call them

166

earlier, but got no answer. He licked his dry lips.

"Come with me," she said. "We'll find your family and my mates."

He knitted his brow, thinking.

"Come on, pigsty," she said. "Bring your gun."

A voice snapped Macey out his thoughts:

"Get her inside. That's the last of them."

Macey turned. The sergeant stood at the barricade. His Benelli was slung over his shoulder.

He scowled at Macey. "Didn't you hear me? She's" – and he shouldered his shotgun – "stop her, stop her!"

The girl brushed past Macey, knocking him off balance. She sprinted across the road, directly towards the sergeant.

Macey said, "No, Kaylee, come back."

She glanced over her shoulder, five yards away. "You won't shoot me, will you. You can't, you've got a kid, my – "

The gunshot deafened Macey. He smelled cordite, and his ears rang.

Kaylee lifted off her feet and folded as if she'd been hit in the back by a massive weight. She flew through the air and came down in a heap, blood sprinkling from her body as it hit the pavement.

The sergeant gawped, his unfired shotgun jammed into his shoulder. He dropped the weapon and raced over to the girl, crouching over her, saying, "Christ, she's dead… oh Christ… "

Macey slowly turned.

Davison stood there, smoke filtering from the M3's barrels.

For a moment, the coppers stared at each other.

And then Davison said, "Following orders, mate. Don't blame me. It's those bastard politicians."

He walked away.

CHAPTER 28.
THE LEXINGTON DEAD.

BLACK smoke billowed in the northwest of the capital.

"That's Pancras International," said Sawyer.

They stood on Rosebery Avenue, on the corner of Amwell Street.

The smoke scudded like a threatening cloud over London.

Sawyer and Carrie stood in silence.

Sirens blared. Gunfire barked in the distance. They could hear screams. Helicopters sliced across the cloudless sky. Half a dozen choppers hovered around the pillar of smoke. Flashes of light sparked from the undersides of the helicopters.

"They're firing," said Sawyer. "Over there, too."

He pointed towards another group of helicopters.

"That's near Euston Station," she said.

"That's where they are."

"Who?"

"The people. The areas of quarantine."

"But – but why are those helicopters firing at them?"

"They're not. Where there are people, there are zombies. The zombies go where the food is. Those 'copters are firing at the dead."

They walked up Amwell Street, staying on the pavement, keeping alert. There were remains everywhere. Mutilated corpses. Carcasses shrivelled in burned out cars.

The body of a woman lay trapped under an overturned bus. Innards spooled out of her mouth. Her eyes had popped out of their sockets, and her head had swollen to twice its size.

Rats and birds scavenged the dead. A fox hurried across the road carrying an arm in its mouth. Cats, their fur stained with blood, chewed on chunks of meat. Dogs fought over human bones.

They'd walked for a few minutes when Sawyer said, "We need a car. This heat's a killer, and I've left my factor 50 at home."

Carrie was thirsty. "Should we get some water? What about over there?"

A bar called The Lexington stood on the corner of Pentonville Road.

They walked towards it, and when they came to the entrance, Sawyer peered into the gloom. The power was out, so it was dark.

"Can you see anything?" she said.

He said he couldn't. They sneaked in.

A rotting smell hit Carrie as she entered. Tables and chair were overturned. The mirrors behind the bar were shattered. The floor glistened and was slippery. Carrie held her breath, knowing what she was stepping in.

"Be careful," said Sawyer.

"Extra," she said.

Shattered glass sprinkled the bloodied carpet. Rats scurried through the bar, stopping to sniff as Carrie and Sawyer approached.

Carrie's heart quickened, and a cold sweat ran down her spine. Sawyer held her hand. His grip felt wet and hot. She turned to look over her shoulder. Wished she were out in the light.

Sawyer hissed, and Carrie's skin tingled with fear.

"What?" she said.

And then she saw.

A middle-aged woman wearing an apron lay on the floor. A bucket and mop stood beside her. The woman's throat had been ripped out.

"Let's get water and get out of here," said Sawyer.

They hurried past the woman. Carrie vaulted the bar. She found a carrier bag. She opened the fridge. The electricity had died, so no cool air rushed out to brush her face. She piled bottled water into the carrier bag. She took one bottle and drank it, tossing another over the bar to Sawyer.

Someone groaned.

Carrie froze and looked up at Sawyer, who leaned on the bar.

She said, "I take it that wasn't your belly rumbling."

He shook his head.

Carrie rose and looked out across the drinking area.

The cleaning lady sat up and groaned again.

"She's alive," said Carrie in a whisper and made to leap the bar, go to the woman. Sawyer grabbed her. She looked into his eyes and saw fear in them. She said, "What's the matter?"

"She's not alive, Carrie. She's dead."

The woman opened her mouth, and black goo oozed out.

She turned her head to look towards Sawyer and Carrie.

"I think we should go," said Sawyer.

Carrie crawled over the bar, shaking with terror, eyes fixed on the newborn zombie.

Sawyer grabbed Carrie's arm and led her towards the door.

The undead cleaner moaned and waved her arms at them. Carrie and Sawyer backed towards the door, keeping their eyes on the zombie.

Carrie saw something move in the corner of her eye.

She swivelled round.

Sawyer kept backing up, headed straight for the man in the doorway.

"Sawyer, you need to stop right there."

He halted and slowly turned towards the door, and the man standing there shuffled into the gloomy pub.

He snarled at Sawyer and Carrie.

Half his face had been chewed away to reveal arteries and meat. His jaw snapped open and closed, and saliva drizzled from his mouth.

Carrie lunged for a chair. Hoisted it above her head and went for the male zombie. Smashed the chair across its skull. The creature sprawled.

Carrie tossed the chair at the female zombie as she was rising.

She didn't wait to see if she hit the creature. Wheeled and ran out of the bar with Sawyer. The sun blinded her for a moment, her eyes adjusting after being in the dimly lit pub.

She and Sawyer turned to look and saw the cleaning-lady zombie shuffle towards the exit.

"They came back to life," she said, and then: "Why are they dopey?"

The zombie loped out into the sun. It stopped and straightened. The creature's brow furrowed with rage. The lips curled into a snarl.

The zombie shook itself down like a dog.

And bolted towards them.

"The sun," said Sawyer, "they're quicker in the sun."

Sawyer headed straight for the zombie.

"Sawyer, what are you doing?"

The zombie darted towards him.

"Don't let it bite you," said Carrie.

The thing came at Sawyer, its hands clawed.

Sawyer punched the zombie in the face, and it staggered backwards.

He kicked it in the belly, and it doubled up.

He picked up a broken bottle and smashed it across the back of the zombie's skull.

The thing fell face first to the ground. Sawyer stomped on its head.

Carrie flinched with every stamp and turned away when the skull caved in and what had been inside it spilled over the road.

She didn't turn round till he touched her arm.

She looked at him and saw over his shoulder the mess he'd made.

The zombie's head was mashed.

She took his hand and led him away.

"Wait," he said. He trotted across the road to a BMW. The passenger door stood open. "There's a key, come on."

They got in, and Sawyer started the engine.

"Christ, it stinks," she said.

The warm air held the hint of decay, as if something had died in here.

"There's blood on the back seat," she said. "And a – "

She reached over and grabbed the box file perched on the seat. The name John Shaw was printed on the front of the file.

She opened it and found a wallet. In it she found money and credit cards. The cards were embossed with the name John Shaw or Mr JT Shaw.

She found a photograph. A family portrait taken in a studio. It showed a man with blonde hair and a red-haired woman, with two kids – a girl and a boy, teenagers.

They wore smiles. Carrie felt a jolt of grief shoot through her, and she touched her breast. She thought of Mya, and her energy sapped.

She looked at the photo and thought about something.

The man looked familiar to her.

But she didn't know a John Shaw.

She looked up to think, and in the side mirror, as Sawyer drove away, she saw the male zombie from The Lexington stumble out into the street.

172

And when the sun struck it, the monster seemed to be amped.

It came racing down the street after the car.

Carrie watched open mouthed.

The zombie gained on them. It weaved from side to side. Waved its arms and chattered its teeth.

Sawyer accelerated away.

But Carrie kept looking at the zombie till it dwindled in the distance.

The zombie had been John Shaw.

CHAPTER 29.
NEW DEAD, OLD DEAD.

GAVIN rocked back and forth, wailing, as Sandra comforted him.

"He looks dead to me," said Derek, crouching over Neil's body.

"Can you make sure?" said Teena. "Check his pulse or something. Here, let me. I did First Aid at my factory." She shoved Derek out of the way and crouched next to the body, placed her finger on Neil's neck. She waited a few seconds. "Yes, he's dead."

"Burn him," said Patty.

Gavin said, "No, you bitch, you leave him be."

"Burn him," said Patty again.

"We've no choice," said Bella.

"It's the only way," said Bert. "We know what's going to happen to him. He's going to wake up wanting breakfast. We've got to burn the body. You all know that."

Sandra ushered Gavin away, and she glanced over her shoulder. "Do it, then, do it now," she said. "Children, come with us. You twins, too."

"No," said Teena. "Don't you talk to my boys. They stay. They watch and see."

Sandra tutted as they filed out of the chapel, up into the sleeping chamber where Penny and Catrin had taken refuge with Penny's kids. Mark stumbled after them, fear in his eyes. He knew this would be his destiny, and Vincent pitied him.

"Come on, gentlemen," said Bert.

Vincent, Derek, and Roger ferried Neil's body out into the inner ward. Patty, Teena, Claudette, and the twins followed. The men laid him on the charred grass where they'd burned Simon.

"There you go, lad," said Roger.

He handed Vincent the petrol can.

Vincent looked at the jar, then at Roger, and curled his lip.

He said, "That's kind of you."

Roger shrugged. Vincent tutted.

He shuffled over to the body.

Neil's face was green and swollen. The blood had blackened around the wound on his arm. His carcass festered in the heat.

Vincent unscrewed the jar and the fumes filled his nose. He felt dizzy for a moment. He went to pour the fuel over Neil but then remembered something. He looked over his shoulder at the others. "Any of you got a lighter, then?"

He was looking at Roger at that moment and when Roger's eyes went wide and his mouth dropped open, Vincent knew something was wrong.

And he knew *what* was wrong, too. He just didn't want to think about it. And he didn't want to turn round and find out.

Derek took a backward step. Patty's hands flew to her mouth. Claudette pointed and shrieked. The twins gawped.

Vincent held his breath and slowly turned his head.

Neil had sat up.

* * * *

Carrie thought about John Shaw as they drove: his life, his family, his world.

A cold feeling spread across her chest.

She asked Sawyer, "What did you do? Before all of this."

Sawyer drove slowly through the ruined city.

"I did everything your dad wouldn't want a boyfriend to do."

"Are you a robber?"

"I've robbed."

"What have you robbed?"

"Everything, anything."

"Banks?"

"Tried, but they're impossible these days."

"Post offices?"

"They're better."

"What about the people?"

"I don't think about it. I'm the driver, so I don't go in."

"What if I'd been in one of your post offices?"

He glanced at her. "I'm not proud of it, you know. It's not the life I chose."

"Yes it is."

He stopped the car near a church. He looked at Carrie. "So you think we can choose our lives? What can we choose, Carrie?"

"We – we can choose what we do. Like I can choose, now, whether to go" – she stuttered, finding it difficult – "and find Mya or to – to *not* go and find her. . . "

"And do you regard that as a choice? Would you choose *not* to go and find your daughter?"

She thought about it. Bit her lip and stared at her hands. It wasn't a choice, was it. She realized now.

Sawyer said, "It's biological, Carrie. You protect your young. It's not a choice. It's a demand."

"And – and this" – she gave him a hard stare – "this robbing, this is a demand on you, yeah?"

"Yes, it is. It's a means to survive. My family did it, I did it. I wanted to be part of the family, so I had no choice. See?"

She did, but she wasn't sure. "You… you still have a choice about whether you terrify people."

He gazed out across the street. The heat rose in waves from the asphalt. He said, "I had no choice where I was born or who gave birth to me. I'm just a slab of DNA, of genes. Everything is written into me."

"But you can rewrite it."

"I don't know"

She thought about Boyd. His dad was a boozer. His granddad was an alcoholic.

"I hope we can," she said.

"We're no different to these things, Carrie, these zombies. They've no choice. They're just following their instincts. Following their DNA."

"But what DNA? They're human."

He said nothing as he stared out at the church. He got out of the car.

Carrie said, "Sawyer, no – we've got to – "

But he was gone, bounding over the low wall and into the church grounds where he stood and stared.

Carrie got out of the car and went to stand by the wall. She was ready to ask him what he'd seen, but then she saw it too.

"It's… it's been dug up," she said.

"Yeah, or burrowed out of."

The church green had been gouged. It looked as if it had been turned inside out. The soil had erupted out of the earth. Mounds of dirt lay everywhere.

Carrie climbed over the wall and stood at the edge of a pit. She saw down into the earth. Furrows and tunnels ran through the ground. She saw bones too, jutting out of the soil.

She shook her head. "What is it?"

"They've woken up, haven't they." He turned to look at her. "All the dead. The dead from centuries ago. They've just got up."

"All…"

"The dead from yesterday. The dead from last week, from last year. From ten years ago. From a hundred years ago. If there was anything left of them, they dug themselves out of their graves, Carrie. Dug themselves out and started to eat us."

"There was never a graveyard here."

"They must've buried people here. Maybe not recently, but they must have. They always did, didn't they. The dead go with churches."

Carrie shook her head. She tried to find words but none came. She backed away from the ploughed earth.

CHAPTER 30.
ART ATTACK.

"WHERE are we going?" said Mum through the window. It was only open a few inches. They'd stopped at a BP garage on the A80, Cumbernauld Road. Cars cluttered the dual carriageway both ways. A housing estate lay on the opposite side of the road. Blood smeared the front of a house, the grey pebbledash now sprinkled scarlet.

Art leaned out of his cab, elbow on the windowsill. "Continue along the Cumbernauld Road here for a few miles, join the M80 and head towards Perth and Stirling. That'll bring us to the M9 and then the A9 – and we go north."

"But those things, those... those creatures... they're everywhere," said Mum.

"Aye, well we'll just have to be places they're not."

"Are you hearing anything on your CB?"

"My CB, missus? No, nothing. Just a lot of crackle. Seems the heat's affecting communication. Radio's hit and miss, too."

Sam asked to go to the toilet, but Mum said no. Told her to use the empty soda bottle. Sam complained, saying she'd not do it in a bottle in front of Craig.

"Well, you can hold then," Mum said, turning her attention back to Art.

Dad smoked in the car. The odour gave Craig the itch, and he asked his dad for a fag.

"Fuck off," said Dad.

"Fuck off yourself."

Mum said, "Can you two stop being childish?"

"He's trouble," said Dad.

"He's only following his father's example," said Mum.

Dad said nothing. Puffed on his Silk Cut. Coughed now and again.

Sam whined. "Mum, I want to pee."

"It's not safe to get out of the car."

"I've got a toilet here in the cab," said Art.

Mum craned her neck to look up at him.

Sam squirmed in the back seat. "Mum, I've got to go."

"Let her go outside, piss in the forecourt of the garage – there's none of them zombies around," said Craig.

"Piss off, Craig," said Sam.

Craig tutted.

Mum said to Art, "Are you sure?"

He said he was.

"Craig, go with your sister?"

"What?"

"I said, go with your sister."

"Mum," said Sam, "I don't want him to come with me."

Craig stepped out of the car, and the silence made him shudder. You'd usually hear traffic on a road like this. But there was nothing except for a dog barking in the distance and the croaking of crows.

"Hurry up, kids," said Art.

"Go on, stupid," said Craig and shoved Sam on to the step. She reached up and Art grabbed her hand, and she climbed into the cab. Craig clambered up and saw Sam scrabble across the lorry driver, his hand pushing at her backside.

Art winked at Craig. The cab smelled of fags.

Sam disappeared between the curtains behind the seats. Craig climbed past Art and into the passenger seat.

"You got cigs?" he said to the trucker.

Art offered him a tin. Craig took it and rolled himself a fag. He looked round the cab. You could see for miles.

"Great view, eh?" said Art. "Panoramic, front and sides. I can see what's coming from miles around."

Craig nodded and studied the cab. The black dashboard curved, and it made Craig think of being a pilot, and he said, "Looks like a plane."

"Aye, it does – and feels like you're flying sometimes."

A photo of a woman was pinned to the dashboard.

"Your wife?" said Craig.

"Depends," said Art.

"On what?"

"Many things, laddie, many things. How old's that sister of yours?"

"Twelve. Thirteen next month."

Craig put the roll-your-own between his lips, and Art leaned across to light it for him with a match. Craig sucked in the tobacco, and it got rid of the itch. He coughed and then breathed the smoke into his lungs. It made him dizzy, but it felt good. Relaxed him after everything that had gone on. A toilet flushed.

He glanced at Art.

"Good truck, then. Got it all," said Craig.

"Oh aye, sleeper cab in the back – room for two. Got a microwave, fridge, and a toilet. Could live in here, see. I do, tell the truth."

"Who's Porter's, then? On the trailer?"

"Meat-packing firm down in Berwick. I was headed down there to collect some stock, distribute to restaurants in Perth. Guess they'll not be needing the meat, now. Plenty of human flesh about, eh?" Art cackled.

181

"So what do you think is going on?" said Craig.

"End of the world, looks like to me, laddie."

"Never thought it would end."

"Bound to end sometime. Now's as good a time as any."

"That's shite."

"Is it?"

"Yes, it is. I got lots I want to do."

"Have you, laddie? What exactly?"

Craig shrugged. "Usual, you know."

"What? Fuck all with a bit of fuck all in between?"

"Guess so."

"Get in to trouble, do you?"

"Aye, with my mates, Nacker and KP. We nick cars, mostly. Bit of burgling."

"Think it's decent to steal other people's stuff, eh?"

Craig shrugged.

"Don't you think about what they're losing, those people?" said Art.

"They got insurance."

"That makes it all right?"

Craig curled his lip. "I don't know. What's that got to do with it?"

"You want to do the right thing, don't you?"

"No." Craig smoked. The cigarette tasted good. He looked out of the window, straight up the A80.

Art said, "Tell you what, laddie, if you stole anything of mine, I'd cut your balls off."

Craig glared at him. "You'd have to find me first."

Art's eyes flashed. "I'd find you, laddie. I'd find you, all right."

Craig's belly squirmed, and he thought for a second the trucker would lunge across at him. But then Sam's head popped out from between the curtain.

Art smiled and said, "How was that, missy?"

Sam tutted and rolled her eyes. She clambered over and tucked herself next to Craig. "Are we going back, then?" she asked her brother.

"Drive with me if you like?" said Art.

Sam looked from Craig to Art and back to Craig. Her face was stiff, and her lips tight.

"You go back if you like," Craig told her.

"Both of you stay," said Art and started the engine. The cab quivered with the power of the engine. Sam jumped in her seat. Art leaned out of the window and spoke to Mum, saying, "They're riding along with me for a while to give you a break, okay?"

He didn't seem to wait for an answer. Rolled the big truck off the forecourt and out on to the road. Craig leaned out of the window and looked back. The other cars followed.

Art said, "There's that jerry can behind the seat, there. Have a drink."

Sam and Craig drank a lot. The can held a gallon, and they nearly emptied it.

"Don't worry, kids," said Art. "Got a barrel in the back there. Did you have a nice piss, doll?"

"Jesus," said Sam and folded her arms.

Craig frowned at Art.

"You want to sit next to the window, Sam?" he said to his sister.

Sam sneered at him. "You what?"

"I said, do you want to sit next to the window? Get some fresh air."

"What's up with you being nice to me? What do you want?"

"Swap with me," he told her, and he rose from the seat and tugged her across, ignoring her complaints. Craig glanced at Art, folded his arm, and scowled.

Art grinned at him and winked.

Sam stuck her head out of the window.

"Oh, that's cool," she said. "That's really cool."

The truck ploughed along the A80. The abandoned traffic thinned. The northern sky was blue, cloudless. Craig had his feet up on the dashboard. He glanced at Art now and again. And Art glanced back, winking when he caught Craig looking.

Craig thought about what the man had said:

I'd find you, laddie. I'd find you, all right.

Most of the time, him, Nacker, and KP escaped the cops. They could outrun everyone. But there was something about the way Art had said it, something about the fire in his eyes.

Craig shivered and thought that maybe for the first time he should take someone seriously.

Parents, teachers, social workers, police, magistrates, judges – he didn't worry about what they said.

They were all rockits who didn't understand Craig, didn't get what he and his mates were about. All those nuggets, they were looking to stop him and the guys having a laugh.

That was the only point in life, having a laugh.

Anyone stood in your way was the enemy.

And everyone who tried, they couldn't do anything about it, anyway.

But maybe Art could, he thought. *Maybe he was for real.*

Craig glanced at him again before folding his arms and leaning back on the headrest. He shut his eyes and felt the heat on his face. The sound of the engine hummed, and he drifted away.

He thought he'd only shut his eyes for a few seconds.

But he woke up with a start, not recognizing his surroundings anymore, with Sam screaming and Art looming over him, brandishing the police baton.

CHAPTER 31.
VINCENT'S BEEN BITTEN.

VINCENT yelled out and tried to stagger away. The Neil-zombie lunged forward, teeth bared, jaws snapping. The creature's hand closed around Vincent's ankle. He screamed and tried to yank his leg away, losing his balance.

He heard Holly shriek his name.

He teetered, the Neil-zombie clawing at him, trying to get up off the ground.

Vincent tugged his ankle free. He lurched.

The zombie sprang to its feet and loped after him, baring its teeth.

Vincent cried out, stumbling away.

The zombie snarled and charged at him.

Vincent swung the petrol can. The fuel spilled, splashing over his clothes.

The can whacked the zombie across the temple.

The creature staggered away, wheeling like a drunk.

Vincent smelled of petrol. The fumes made his eyes water.

"He's been bitten, burn him," said Patty.

Terror clogged his throat. He couldn't breathe. Claudette handed Derek a lighter. Derek shook with fear and scuttled towards him.

"You've been bitten, lad," said Roger.

"I haven't, Jesus. I haven't," said Vincent, panic racing through his veins.

"He blasphemed," said Patty, her voice a screech.

The Neil-zombie found its feet. From the corner of his eye, Vincent saw it charge again.

"Come on, lad," said Bert. "You're bitten."

"I'm not fucking bitten."

The Neil-zombie closed on him. He swung with the can. Clunked the creature in the skull again. Sent it tottering towards Derek, who screamed.

The zombie reacted to the noise. Steadied itself and faced Derek, snarling.

Vincent raced forward and smashed the creature across the back of the head this time. It stumbled away again.

"Give me the fucking lighter," said Vincent.

He yanked it out of Derek's grasp. Whirled to chase after the zombie. But the creature was lumbering towards him, five yards away.

Vincent lost his balance, tottered backwards. Terror melted his guts. He was going to die. The zombie'd have him – any second. He dropped the petrol can. Raised the lighter. Ready to flick the wheel, ignite the flame. Burn the zombie and burn him, too.

Just like Patty wanted.

Maybe he had been bitten. He just didn't know it. He was so scared he thought he was going to piss himself.

He screamed, the zombie so close he could smell it. He got ready to light the flame.

Holly's roar gave him a start.

She whipped by, brandishing something long and sharp, like a spear.

She headed straight for the Neil-zombie and thrust the spike into the middle of its face.

Blood spurted from the mutilated features.

The nose, the eyes, and the mouth imploded, and sunk into the creature's mug.

The spike burst out of the zombie's nape.

Holly roared and drove her weapon into the zombie's face once more, then shoved the creature.

She dropped to her knees. The zombie staggered around, its arms flapping, blood spurting from its disfigured face.

It made a keening noise, sad and desperate to Vincent's ears, and then slumped forward, twitched, and became still.

Everyone stood frozen.

They stared at the Neil-zombie.

Vincent shuffled over to Holly and hugged her.

"You stink of petrol," she said.

CHAPTER 32.
THE BREEDING AND FOOD
PROGRAMME.

VINCENT had to stand there naked while Bert and Roger looked over his body.

He'd gone to the toilets and tried to wash the smell of petrol off his body. His shirt was ruined. Stank of fuel and gore. He'd put his combats back on and then the men had walked in. He thought for a minute they were going to attack him.

But Roger said, "We want to check, lad, that's all."

So he let them check. Dropped his pants and stared at the tiles on the wall while two men studied his naked body.

When they were happy he pulled up his trousers. He swore at the men and stormed out of the bogs.

"He's clean, Patty," said Bert back in the chapel.

"Clean," said Vincent. "Makes it sound like I'm diseased or cursed."

"It *is* a curse, young man," said Patty. She looked crazier than ever. Her eyes hidden behind those sunglasses. Her eye mascara smeared down her cheeks. Sweat glistening her face and her neck and her scrawny old arms.

"We've got to start thinking about how we're going to cope, here," said Roger.

Everyone looked at him. He stood with his wife and Derek, and the twins.

"What do you mean?" said Oswyn.

"What my husband means is," said Teena, "we've got to think about things like... the human race."

"The human race is doomed," said Patty. "However, some of us can be saved. The rapture is close."

"Might be," said Teena. "But we're not there yet. We might be the last people on earth, for all we know."

"And if we're trapped in here for much longer, like, we've got to think about food," said Roger. "Seriously think about food."

Vincent narrowed his eyes, trying to imagine where Roger and Teena were headed. He had the feeling it was somewhere unpleasant.

"Roger's always thinking about food, aren't you, love," said Teena. "But, really, there's something else needs mentioning." Her gaze flitted over them, and she swallowed.

"Tell 'em, Teena," said Roger.

"All right, then... " She made a face. "Right, most of us here are of a breeding age, and we should – "

A gasp went through the chapel.

"There are children here," said Sandra.

"Well take them out then," said Derek, and they waited while Sandra ushered the children away.

"What about yours?" said Oswyn.

"Bobby and Jack stay," said Teena.

Gavin said, "Christ, I know where you're going with this, and it's crazy, it's madness – "

"Hey, keep the trap shut, homo," said Roger. "This don't concern you, at any rate. You... you haven't got the will, mate."

Gavin got to his feet. Vincent urged him to calm down.

Teena went on:

"We've got to make a little community here, is what we think. We might, in a few days, weeks, have to think about stuff like this. We have a responsibility, see."

"No, we don't," Vincent said.

"You shut your trap, lad," said Roger. "You can't keep her to yourself, you know," he added and pointed at Holly. "You share her with the rest of us."

"What the fuck are you talking about?" said Holly.

"I'm talking," said Teena, "about our responsibilities. You, love, have to think about the future. You can have your boyfriend there, fine. But you've got to strengthen the gene pool, like. Spread yourself around a bit. Me too, like."

Holly's eyes bulged, and her mouth gaped.

"You're off your heads. The sun's got to you," said Vincent. "This hasn't broken down yet, Roger. We've should be thinking about getting out of here, first. Surviving."

"This is *about* surviving," said Derek.

His wife said something in French.

Derek said something back in French.

"Talk English in England," said Roger.

"We're not in fucking England," said Vincent.

"You're crazy to talk about sex at a time like this," said Bella. "We're going to die here. We've got no food, hardly any water."

"We was coming on to food," said Roger. "Anyone of you seen that film *Alive*?"

No one said anything.

Vincent did think of saying something, but he didn't have the words. He guessed that's how the others felt, as well, as they gawked at Roger.

And then Teena said it out loud:

"We might have to eat our dead."

"Devil's work," said Patty. "Sex and death, the devil's work. You are cursed, madam, and you shan't curse us. We are the saved, and we'll stay saved."

Teena said, "You're not saved, you mad old bat. Can't you see? We've got to make plans. We're stuck here, and this might be our cave, like. For the rest of time. So we've got to think of food and breeding. It's our responsibility."

"We can't eat the dead. They're poisoned. We might be infected," said Bella.

Teena and Roger's eyes ranged the group.

Derek looked away.

Roger said, "I mean, we have to kill people to provide food. That's why we've got to seriously think about breeding, like. We've got to think about how we get food."

Bella fainted.

Holly said, "Oh God. You want us to have sex with each other and then eat the babies."

Patty rose to her feet and jabbed her finger at Teena. "You will burn in the lake of fire for this, madam."

Teena said, "Shut up, fucking Blair Witch Project." She turned to Holly and said, "I'm not saying that, love, but we've got to think about it."

"Can you not think about it out loud, then," said Holly.

"There's no need to be thinking these things at *all*," Oswyn said.

Vincent said, "We're only a couple of hours into this and already we're talking about killing each other for food. What are we going to be like tomorrow? The next day? What we've got to do is think of a way out of here."

"And how do we do that, lad?" said Roger

"I haven't got a clue, but at least I'm not suggesting we eat you, Roger. "

191

"Even if we get out of the castle, where do we go then?" said Derek.

Claudette had gone off somewhere again. Vincent noticed her just outside the chapel, in the passageway. The twins were there. Plumes of cigarette smoke clouded the doorway. Vincent could smell tobacco. He just shook his head and answered Derek: "I don't know, do I, but we've got to try."

"Seems to me like we have differing opinions here," said Roger. "We have our American friends here believing, well, believing we're facing the end of the world."

"The return of Christ," said Patty.

Roger ignored her and went on:

"We have Oswyn, who thinks the government is coming to rescue us. Now that's bollocks, and we know it."

Oswyn blushed. Roger continued:

"We have this young fellow" – pointing at Vincent now – "wanting to get out of here. And me and my wife, and Derek, wanting to plan for a future that might see us living here for a few years. Seems to me we should vote on which idea's the more sensible."

Teena said, "Our idea sounds the best to me – we should go with that."

"Ah, democracy in action," said Gavin.

Holly said, "You think I'm being some kind of baby machine?"

"It's not about choice, is it, love," said Teena. "It's about what we have to do to survive. And I told you if you'd listen, it's only something to *think* about."

"Well I don't *want* to think about it," said Holly. "It's already in my head and now it'll be there forever. Like some stain I can't get out."

Teena craned her neck. Her orange skin glistened. "Right, don't think about it then, Hannah fucking Montana. Let the grown-ups do the thinking. You just do as you're told when the time comes."

Holly sobbed. Vincent put an arm around her. He felt her shudder. He said to Teena, "This is why you shouldn't open your mouth before consulting your brain cell."

Roger squared up to him. "Don't you talk to my missus like that, lad. I'll smack you round the head."

Anger flared in Vincent's chest. The fat ex-footballer swaggered towards him.

Derek stepped between them and said, "We fight among ourselves, we're dead – we're dead before we decide anything."

Vincent and Roger eyed each other for a few seconds before backing off.

"You're all doomed," said Patty. "Doesn't matter what you do, what schemes you hatch, what plans you formulate, you are not saved – you will burn in hell. Hell is a real place, and you" – she pointed at Teena – "you should be telling your children, your twins. Putting the fear of God into them. That's the only way they'll be saved."

Vincent looked around. He couldn't see Bert, who was usually a puppy at his wife's side.

Sandra, back from the sleeping chamber where she'd taken her children, said, "You're scaring us all."

Patty said, "You should be scared, missy. You know where your husband's gone? He's gone to that lake of fire. He's being tortured for eternity. You should all be scared – "

"We are fucking scared," said Vincent.

Patty glowered at him. "Dirty, dirty mouth. I'll cut your tongue out if you speak like that again."

"Who'll cut my tongue out?"

"Maybe I will, maybe we *all* will," said Roger.

A knot of fear tightened in Vincent's belly.

Roger gave him a hateful look. Derek too. Even Mark, who stood nearby nursing his damaged face, his skin paling, managed to glower.

Teena stood at the door and shouted for her twins:

"Bobby, Jack – where are you?"

"Wh-where's Claudette?" said Derek.

"I saw her giving fags to my lads earlier, before I stepped in," said Roger. "If she's doing that, I'll have her, Derek."

Derek blustered. He nudged his glasses up his nose. His brow glistened with sweat.

"Where did you buy her, Derek?" said Roger.

Derek's mouth opened and closed. He had something to say but couldn't say it. His eyes flitted around the room, and he seemed to shrink under everyone's gaze.

Roger folded his arms and sneered, "Tall, leggy thing like that wouldn't want to marry a short, tubby, four-eyed twat like you – unless he had a fat wallet. You got a fat wallet, Derek?"

Derek bristled.

Roger continued:

"How much she cost you? Found her on t'internet, did you? Russian, is she?"

Derek said, "She… she… she is Belgian, if you must know. Not French, as some of you have said. And not Russian."

"Weren't they cowards during Word War Two?" said Patty. "That's what my father used to say. Said they rolled over for Hitler. Godless heathens."

"Cowards and slags, eh?" said Roger.

Roger and Teena cackled.

Gavin said, "Leave him alone – you bloody mullet-haired twit."

Roger minced. "Look at Danny la Rue over there."

Gavin swept across the room in a flash and decked Roger with a right hook before the ex-footballer could protect himself. The Yorkshireman slumped. His wife screeched. Gavin backed away. A murmur went through the chapel.

Teena squealed. "He's killed my husband."

Roger groaned and lifted his head.

Teena leered at Gavin. "I'll sue you, you bloody queer."

"Sue me, then." Gavin turned and walked back to his spot. Sat down against the wall and rubbed his fist.

Teena helped Roger to sit up. She fussed over him. He swatted her away. His face was red – with shame, Vincent guessed, as he felt Holly pressing up against him.

He said, "You okay?" and Holly said no she wasn't.

"We're stuck here, Vincent. We're never getting out, are we?"

"We will."

"How? I can't see how. Teena might be right, you know. We'll have to start again – I might have to sleep with men here, make babies – Jesus – " She gagged, and Vincent held her.

He stroked her back. He wanted to say it would be all right. But that would be a lie. He guessed it wouldn't be. He felt useless. Useless to Holly, and to the rest of them. No one had listened when he'd said:

We've got to think of a way out of here.

But they were right not to.

He didn't have a plan, did he?

He had nothing.

He was twenty. He was no one to them.

A shriek came from outside.

Holly said, "Oh God, not more of them."

CHAPTER 33.
ALONE.

ART slashed at Craig with the baton, his face twisted with rage.

Craig screamed and threw himself backwards against the door, raising his legs to protect himself.

The baton whacked into his knee. The pain flashed like an electric shock. He shrieked.

Art struck again, snarling as he whipped Craig's thigh. A stinging sensation raced up his leg as if someone had thrown acid on him.

His shouts of anguish mixed with Sam's panicked voice, yelling in the truck's sleeper cab.

Craig kicked out, striking Art in the chest. The trucker grimaced and swatted Craig's legs away.

And Craig said, "What the fuck are you doing?"

Art struck him again, this time across the forearm. Pain raced up Craig's arm.

Art curled back his lip and said, "Get out of my truck, laddie."

"Just ask us to leave, there's no need to – "

"*You*, laddie, not your sister – just you." He rained blows on Craig, striking him about the legs and arms.

"Sam, Sam," said Craig.

"Craig, Craig," he heard her screech, and then she burst out from behind the curtain, her face white with terror. "Craig, he tried to rape – "

Art backhanded her across the face, and she slumped back behind the curtain.

Craig, arms and legs stinging from Art's attack, lunged forward. He rammed his shoulder into the lorry driver's ribs.

Art gasped. Slammed his elbow down on to Craig's back. Once, twice, three times. Craig shouted in pain. Art shoved him backwards. The man, thin and bony, was strong – stronger than Craig. Art punched him in the face. Craig saw stars.

"You getting out of my cab, laddie?"

"Why, what do you – "

"I'm not explaining to you. You get out, or I kill you."

He struck Craig again. Craig's head swam. He felt weak and couldn't raise his arms to protect himself.

"Sam, what about, Sam?"

"I said, she stays."

"What – what do you want with her?"

Art grinned. "She's mine now. The world's changed. It's like *Mad Max* out there, laddie. It's the apocalypse. You got to get a hold of your life, see. Take responsibility. A man's got to have a woman. A woman to build a new world with. Your sister, she's ripe and ready."

"She's twelve, you fucking pervert."

Art's face darkened. He struck Craig across the collarbone with the baton. Craig screamed, the pain making him sick.

Art said, "Nature doesn't count years, laddie. She's female, and that's it. Times are changing, and age won't mean a thing in the world that's coming."

Art leaned over and threw open the door. The heat poured in. Brilliant light filled the cab, blinding Craig. Art booted him between the legs and shoved him out.

Craig yelped and fell headfirst out of the truck. The world spun. He heard the door shut above him before he hit the ground.

He bent double and rolled into a ditch.

He lay there, head spinning, body aching. Pain pulsed through him. He wanted to lie here and sleep for a while and dream the anguish away.

The truck rumbled and rolled off, and Craig watched it head down the road.

He sat up too sharply. Pain slowed his movements, and he gritted his teeth and groaned, waiting for a few seconds. After a moment, the pain dimmed.

He scanned his surroundings.

Fields carpeted the landscape, some of them scorched, others lush in the soaring temperatures. The smell of blood and manure mingled in the air. The carcasses of cattle and sheep dotted the landscape. Birds circled, swooping down now and again to rest on the remains and peck at them. Clouds of flies rose and fell from the cadavers, and their hum wafted across the pastures.

On the side of the road up ahead stood a cluster of buildings. They looked like offices. Beyond them, the road went into a roundabout. A sign told drivers to follow either exit for the M80 – one took you south, the other north. That's where they'd come from in Art's truck. He remembered swaying in the cab. That must've been when they circled the roundabout.

Then he looked over his shoulder in the direction Art had taken Sam.

It was rural down there, and rural made Craig's belly twist. He liked concrete. He liked tower blocks. He liked noise. He scoped the land, and the panic intensified.

Where was he? How far from the Cumbernauld Road, from Mum and Dad, was he? Where had Art brought them? And where was he taking Sam?

He crouched, trying to steady his breathing. He peered down the road in the direction Art's truck had gone. The road crested over a railway bridge, and in the distance he saw houses.

He rose and stumbled towards the roundabout, hoping it would show him the way back to the Cumbernauld Road.

He got his phone out and dialled his mum's number. Nothing. He tried again and failed, then tried to text her. But the phone warned he didn't have a signal.

Where the fuck had the signal gone, then?

And where was your mum when you needed her?

And your stupid dad?

He looked around, fright racing through him, turning his blood cold, making his skin crawl.

He felt vulnerable. The road provided no cover. Zombies might swarm over the fields at any moment.

His lips were chapped, and sweat coated his body. The sun beat down, and he felt as if he were staggering through a desert in need of a drink.

He headed for the roundabout. Cars choked the lanes. They'd been abandoned.

He hobbled on, his legs pulsing with pain, his arm and shoulder throbbing.

If he got through this, if the world became right again, he promised himself he'd behave. He promised he'd never steal cars again, or break into people's houses and nick their computers and their DVDs. He promised never to drink or smoke fags or weed, or sniff glue. And he pledged not to fight anyone without being threatened first.

He promised to be better.

He didn't know how he'd do it, because this was how he thought he should behave. It was how his dad had behaved. How everyone he knew behaved. But there had to be a different way.

"If I get out of this," he said, as if there were someone listening who could make a judgment. "Only if I get out of this."

He stopped and looked at the waste ground to his left, where the buildings stood. They looked prefabricated. He held his breath when he saw that one of the structures was a school.

The Richmond Fellowship School, it said on the side.

In the distance, he saw housing estates, and he swallowed, fearful that any kind of human settlement would inevitably draw zombies.

Or that the humans had *become* zombies, by now.

Cars filled the parking lot. A red Mitsubishi Shogun, the sun splintering off its paintjob, caught his eye. Fifteen years old. Good condition. The bumpers gleamed. Tarpaulin covered the back, thrown over what appeared, from their shapes, to be sacks.

Craig clambered over the fence and down the slope into the lot.

He touched the Mitsubishi and hissed, drawing his hand away. The surface was baking hot. He peered through the window. Tried the driver's side door. It opened. He smiled. Climbed in and settled into the driver's seat.

It was hotter in the truck than it was outside, and he burned his arse on the seat.

He settled down and traced his hands along the steering wheel, adjusted the seat and rested his feet on the pedals, and for a moment he forgot where he was, his instincts taking over: the car thief in him.

Craig peered under the steering wheel. He yanked off the ignition panel, and it came away with a crack.

The noise made him flinch, and he looked across the car park.

But there was no one to hear.

Only the dead.

A chill rinsed his veins.

He blew air out of his cheeks and returned to the panel, trying to go about his task quietly.

He hotwired the car. The engine coughed and came to life.

Craig sat up and shuffled about till he felt comfortable. He said, "Yes," to himself. He revved the Mitsubishi.

"Yes!" he said again, louder this time.

His hands perspired on the steering wheel, so he wiped them on his trackie bottoms.

He was still drying his hands and thinking how far Mum and Dad and the rest of them had got to when he saw the figure stumble out of the building, his white shirt soaked with blood and sweat.

Craig's first thought was: *Zombie*.

But he saw that the figure carried a shotgun.

And he was raising it.

Aiming it straight at Craig.

His chest tightened. He rammed the truck into reverse. The gears clanked. He floored the accelerator. The engine whined and the Mitsubishi weaved backwards across the parking lot.

The gun fired and Craig ducked. Pellets peppered the vehicle.

Craig headed straight for the entrance. He clipped another car. Metal screeched. Craig gritted his teeth.

The gun went off again.

Craig gawped at the man.

He was stumbling forward, now. He was saying something, his mouth moving.

The man jabbed his finger at the Mitsubishi.

Sparks flew off the truck's side, and Craig swung it into the road and rammed it into first and hammered down the road, blowing air out of his cheek. He sped away, back down the Cumbernauld Road, his mind fixed on finding his mum and dad and the convoy.

He glanced in the rear-view mirror. The man scrambled up the slope and waved after Craig, then fell to his knees.

The man grew distant, becoming a small, curled up smudge. But not distant or small enough that Craig couldn't see him put the shotgun in his mouth and fire, his head erupting in a red cloud.

Craig stared ahead and felt sick and tired. The road stretched out before him. The image of the man's head erupting repeated in his head.

What was the guy saying? Why had he pointed at the Mitsubishi?

Probably threatening Craig for nicking his truck. He'd had enough of that. Furious owners chasing him while he raced away in their cars.

He glanced in the mirror again. Opened the windows to let some air in. Shuffled in the seat, making himself comfortable. He started to breathe steadily and to feel better. He looked in the rear-view mirror.

Behind him, the road lay cluttered with cars.

The tarmac glistened in the heat.

The tarpaulin shuffled in the breeze.

Eyes on the road ahead, he drove on. He tried the radio and got static, although a voice broke through now and again, but he couldn't make out what it was saying.

He thought about the man pointing at him.

He thought about the empty road.

The glistening tarmac melting in the heat.

The tarpaulin shuffling in the –

His bowels turned icy.

– breeze…

What fucking breeze? he thought.

There was no breeze.

Not a whisper.

He heard them before he saw them, and hearing them made him not want to look.

He was shaking and couldn't stop himself.

They growled and scuffed about.

He dared a glance in the rear-view mirror.

The woman zombie, in a short floral dress covered in gore, wavered in the back of the truck, crouching and scowling at him. The creature bared its teeth, its jaws snapping open and shut.

Two more zombies rose up from beneath the tarpaulin.

CHAPTER 34.
WAR ZONE.

"CAN you hear that?" said Sawyer, and he slowed the car down.

"Come on," said Carrie.

They were on Drayton Road. Residents, laden with boxes and suitcases, spilled out of their terraced homes. They packed their belongings into cars. Women wrapped in blankets carried babies. Children cried and staggered around, half naked. Men armed with hammers and knives kept watched.

It was like a war zone.

Something you'd see reported on the news from Africa or Afghanistan or Iraq.

Not Islington. Not London. Not Britain.

Some of the people had blood on their faces. Some had wounds on their bodies.

Bite marks, thought Carrie.

"They'll change," she said.

Sawyer said nothing.

"Change like the man in that bar, like the woman."

He stopped the car and said again, "Can you hear that?"

She rolled down the window. The residents' crying and wailing became louder.

But there was another noise.

The sound of a crowd. Its murmur rolling through the streets.

Where was it coming from?

He turned the car round and headed down Benwell Road, driving past more terraced housing.

No people here. Blood on the streets. Gore sprayed across cars. Human remains littered everywhere.

The Emirates Stadium rose above the redbrick terraces.

Carrie thought about the two-fingered salute her father had taught her, and it brought tears to her eyes. She shouted at Sawyer, asking what he was doing.

"I want to see what's going on," he said.

"Okay, why would you want to do that?"

He said nothing. The drone of the crowd grew louder.

"This is where Arsenal play," he said.

"I know, I can smell it."

"What do you mean?"

She said nothing, shook her head.

They crawled along and reached the junction with Queensland Road. On their right loomed the stadium. Carrie's mouth dropped open.

Zombies surrounded the football ground.

Thousands of them, like a crowd waiting to go in on a Saturday afternoon.

They crammed the road, swarming forward, trying to get at the stadium.

A helicopter rose from inside the Emirates and shot off in a westerly direction.

Carrie and Sawyer stared at each other and then Sawyer said, "They go where the food is."

Carrie gasped. Her belly churned. "There are people in there."

"Like in St Pancras. Euston. The O2. Wembley Stadium. It's what I heard on the radio this morning. These are havens."

Carrie turned on the radio.

He said, "No," and tried to stop her, but the radio came on and the static crackled and Carrie realized what she'd done.

A half-a-dozen zombies at the rear of the horde turned. Their empty eyes fixed on the car. Their tongues lolled. Blood bubbled from their mouths.

They were in various states of decay. One was a walking skeleton, ribbons of flesh flapping from its bones.

"Sorry," said Carrie in a whisper.

Sawyer slammed the car into reverse.

The zombies swept after them.

Carrie screamed. The creatures chased the car. Streaked down Benwell Road. Waves of undead swarming towards them. She didn't know how many. Hundreds, maybe, peeling off from the mass of undead crowded around the stadium.

Sawyer spun the car round. The tyres screeched and smoke puffed up, blinding Carrie for a moment. She smelled rubber and petrol. She could see nothing but smoke, and the zombies poured through it.

Sawyer tossed the car through the streets, reaching Drayton Street again. The zombies continued to tail them. They pounded down side streets now, closing off Sawyer's exits.

Sawyer and Carrie drove past the terraced houses, past the refugees they'd seen earlier packing their cars.

And Carrie screamed.

"What? What?" said Sawyer.

"You're leading them towards those people."

The zombies ploughed after them, sweeping along the road.

And the residents who'd been preparing their escape saw what was coming.

They dropped their boxes and their clothes and their suitcases, and scooped up their children.

Carrie screamed.

"We're killing them, we're killing them!" she said, clawing at Sawyer. "Stop the car, stop it!"

Sawyer fought against her, trying to control the BMW.

The car lurched across the road.

Clipped parked vehicles.

Bumped over dead bodies.

Carrie yanked at the steering wheel.

The car careered into a wall.

The impact tossed her across Sawyer's lap and knocked the air out of her.

Without thinking, she opened the door and tumbled out of the car.

Sawyer tried to grab her. "No, for Christ's sake, Carrie."

She staggered away from the car.

The zombies flooded Drayton Park.

They mowed down the refugees, swamping them – a tide of undead drowning the living.

Carrie's legs buckled.

A boy, aged six or seven, face and naked torso covered in blood, stood frozen in the middle of the road as the zombies flocked towards him. At the child's feet lay a corpse.

"No," she heard Sawyer say, "don't, don't – "

But she was gone. Sprinting down the road. Towards the boy.

Towards the zombies.

She was so scared, seeing the dead flood towards her, towards the child.

Her lungs burned. She sobbed, thinking she was going to die.

She heard someone running behind her and thought for a second she was being pursued by the dead.

But she looked back and saw Sawyer, his face dark.

The boy fell to his knees and bowed his head over the cadaver.

Praying, thought Carrie, *praying and waiting.*

The zombies swept towards the boy. Hundreds of them. Carrie screamed. She didn't know if she'd make it. She panted for breath. Her body felt weak.

She smelled the zombies, every gasping breath she took sucking their odour into her lungs.

Decay and rot and death filled the air, the heat making it worse.

She reached the boy and grabbed his arm. His skin felt cold and clammy.

He turned to look at her, and his blank eyes fixed on her, and his open mouth showed the meat he'd bitten from the corpse at his feet.

CHAPTER 35.
FAMILY OF ZOMBIES.

SO now Craig had three zombies in the back of the truck.

The other two that had just got up were – or had been – girls, one about sixteen, the other Sam's age.

The older girl wore a white dressing gown open down the front. But Craig didn't see skin. He saw ribs and organs. Her chest and belly had been ripped open. But now she was living again.

The younger girl wore Sindy PJs, pink, smeared with blood. Half her face was missing. She stared at Craig with an eye set in sinew and muscle and bone.

The mother zombie lunged forward, smashing into the cab's back window.

"Oh fuck," said Craig, and revved the engine, speeding up.

The mother zombie stumbled backwards and fell out of the Mitsubishi. The creature hit the road and rolled and bounced.

The daughter-zombies took no notice.

They were fixed on Craig. Fixed on eating him.

The older one reached around the cab, its arm snaking in through the open window.

The zombie snarled and clawed at Craig. Its fingers brushed his cheek, and he leaned away, screaming.

He glanced to his left.

The younger zombie had clambered down on the footrest on the passenger side and was trying to climb in through the half-open window.

Craig said, "No, oh Christ," as he fumbled to find the switch that would close the window – then realizing the truck didn't have electric windows.

He slammed the breaks.

The truck skidded, smoke hissing from the wheels.

The zombie sisters flew off the Mitsubishi.

They soared down the road, hitting the tarmac.

They lay there for a few seconds, and Craig stared at them.

He didn't know what he was waiting for, what he expected to see. And when the sisters lifted themselves off the ground and glowered at him again, he knew he should've got going once he had the chance.

Quaking with fright, Craig floored the accelerator.

The PJ-zombie rushed towards Craig, and he thought the creature was playing chicken with him.

You'll lose, he thought, and ploughed into the child-zombie.

Its body wheeled up the bonnet and thumped into the windscreen. A crack spread across the glass. The zombie rolled over the roof of the truck and bounced off, hitting the road, rolling along behind the vehicle.

Craig whooped as he saw the twisted body writhe and try to get up. His eyes off the road, he lost control. The steering wheel pulled. He gasped as the truck swerved.

The tyres squealed as he hit the breaks. He slowed the Mitsubishi, bringing it under control, puffing with relief.

He brought the truck to a halt, the engine grumbling.

He glanced in the mirror.

"Oh shit," he said as the older girl-zombie came barreling down the road after him. The dead thing's white, bloodstained robe flapped like wings as it leapt on the back of the 4x4, clambered over the roof, and slid down the windscreen.

Craig cursed again and shoved the vehicle into gear, sped down the road towards a bridge.

The zombie clawed at the cracked glass. It left smears of spit on the windscreen as it tried to bite the window pane.

Craig reached the bridge, the road rising slightly. He handbrake-turned the 4x4. Smoke rose from the screeching tyres. The vehicle wheeled. Craig was tossed around. The zombie went flying off the bonnet, over the bridge.

Craig whelped again, saying, "Yes! Yes! Yes! Who's the fucking zombie killer?"

He was now pointing in the direction of the roundabout again.

The younger zombie was still alive. Its legs were twisted over its head, and one of its arms had been dismembered.

But the thing still snarled at the approaching Mitsubishi.

"Bye, bye," said Craig.

The vehicle bumped and jerked, and then the road smoothed out. Craig glanced in the rear-view mirror. A trail of blood and guts and Sindy PJs smeared the road.

He blew air out of his cheeks. His heart pounded. He wiped his brow and felt relief wash over him.

And then he saw the mother zombie hobble up the road towards him.

"Oh Christ," he said.

It looked like it had a broken leg, the limb warped as it dragged it along. But injuries didn't trouble the zombies. You had to crush them. Smash their skulls. Destroy their brains.

Just like in the movies and in the games – shoot them in the head.

"Come on," he said, and floored the accelerator.

He ploughed into the zombie at 80 miles-per-hour, cutting it in two. Blood and gore splashed across the windscreen, seeping into the cracks.

He kept going, careering around the roundabout and skidding to a halt near the man's body. He kept the engine running and leapt out. Flies rose off the suicide's cadaver. The guy's head was gone. A rat scuttled away from the viscera on the tarmac.

Craig grabbed the shotgun, got back in the truck.

He drove back into the parking lot and sat in the vehicle for five minutes, panting, his head spinning. He stared at the building and thought about things, wondered if what he wanted to do was sane or not.

He decided it probably wasn't, but he should try. He needed food, he needed water.

He stepped out of the truck, his throat dry, his hand slick on the shotgun.

Flies hummed, their drone constant. Dogs barked in the distance. A dozen crows perched on the roof of the building, watching Craig. He glanced around, feeling vulnerable.

He said to himself, "What are you doing, Craig?"

And then he entered the office building.

CHAPTER 36.
JEZEBEL CONDEMNED.

TEENA had gone from orange to purple. "She were on her knees, giving him a blow job – and my boys were there, just there, watching – and smoking her fags." She quaked with anger. Roger had to hold her back. She was gunning for Claudette.

"Is this true, Bert?" said Patty, a quiver in her voice.

Bert tugged up his shorts. A slab of white belly showed where he'd unbuttoned his shirt. The block of fat hung over his groin. Vincent wondered how Claudette had got her face in there to do what Teena had accused her of doing.

Bert leaned against the wall of the Gunners Walk. Below him groaned a sea of zombies. There were fewer of them out there now, though. Perhaps they'd moved on, looking for easier prey.

Vincent swallowed, nerves tight. The zombies snarled up at him. Some of them were walking skeletons, ancient things somehow risen from their graves. Others were dressed in hoodies, in policemen's uniforms, in Hawaiian shirts, in butchers' aprons, and in… short, red dresses.

She was here again, the girl he'd seen dragged from the sports car. Blood streaked her blonde hair. Death had ripped her open and paled her skin.

Patty's voice broke his trance:

"Bert, did this Jezebel tempt you?"

"She did, Patty," said Bert. "The whore came up to me, got into my head. Said she could – could take me to heaven."

Bella and Oswyn restrained Claudette. The Belgian woman thrashed about and screamed. Derek glowered at her, his face dark. Oswyn said, "You know, we're not… not even supposed to be here on the Gunners Walk. This is closed to the public," but everyone ignored him. "You over there, you're too near the edge. Catrin, you should know better."

Mark, Gavin, and Catrin glanced at him, then turned their attentions back to the zombies swarming in the street.

Patty spoke to Teena:

"What did you see?"

"What I saw was this slag sucking off your husband, with my lads watching."

Bobby and Jack sat crossed legged on the walkway. They frowned, but now and again they nudged each other and giggled before Roger snapped at them, telling them to shut up or he'd kick them off the ledge so the zombies could skin them.

Teena went on:

"She made them watch, I'm telling you." She scowled at her boys. "What did she make you do?"

The boys looked at one another and then at their mum. One of them – Vincent couldn't tell the difference – said, "She made us watch, Mum. Forced us."

Claudette screamed. Vincent heard her say, "He pay me – he say he had helicopter coming – I be first on – room for four only – "

Bert's mouth opened and closed. His eyes widened, and his face reddened. "That's – that's a lie – "

"Do you have a helicopter, Bert?" said Vincent.

"We do," said Patty, "but it's in the States and no good here."

"How would she have known you had a helicopter unless Bert had told her?" asked Vincent.

They glared at Bert.

He squared his shoulders and said, "Of course I told her. We were conversing. I said – I said we had a helicopter, of course."

"Did you promise to save her first?" asked Vincent.

"Who are you, kid? The judge?"

"No, Bert, I'm just asking."

Teena broke in:

"My boys don't lie. We know what happened. I'm their mum. I screamed when I saw her there on her knees. I went mad. What would you do? She's a slag and a pervert. She was poisoning us."

Patty said, "She might have cursed us all."

"Aren't you going to stand up for your wife?" said Vincent to Derek.

Derek said, "Not now she's had another man's cock in her mouth." He folded his arms and turned his back. Claudette shrieked. Oswyn and Bella fought to hold on to her. The woman railed against Derek, making accusations Vincent couldn't make out but they involved her husband's penis.

"Cast her down."

Vincent froze. Had he heard Patty right?

She said it again:

"Cast her down."

Jesus Christ, no, thought Vincent. Holly gripped his arm, and he heard her take a sharp breath.

Bella said, "But Patty, we – "

"She's poison, and unless we cleanse ourselves, we'll all go to hell. We'll burn in the fire. Cast her down."

No one moved.

Claudette gawped at Patty.

Silence fell for a few seconds.

Teena screeched and raced forward. Her breasts bounced, and her belly wobbled as she charged.

Bella and Oswyn backed away, Bella's mouth making the shape of "No, no", her head shaking.

Claudette screamed.

Teena shoved her in the chest.

Dread contorted Claudette's face, and she tottered backwards.

Vincent shouted and reached out.

Claudette toppled over the edge.

She shrieked.

Vincent heard himself shout, "No!" and grabbed for Claudette, but she'd fallen.

He looked her in the eye as she plunged into the zombies, and they reached for her, and she fell into them, and they swarmed forward.

Claudette hit the ground, and the zombies smothered her. Vincent saw nothing of her, other than a glimpse now and then – her face twisted in pain, her leg kicking out, her belly torn open.

But if he couldn't see her, he heard her.

And the screeching that came from her as she was dismembered knotted Vincent's guts.

* * * *

"I intended to divorce her, anyway."

Vincent lifted his gaze to Derek.

The guy had just watched his wife being eaten by zombies.

Vincent fumed. "Might save you some money, then."

Derek mumbled and wrote in his notebook.

Vincent was about to say something else when Mark shouted, "There's no way you should get away with that," at Teena.

Roger squared his shoulders. "Maybe we should throw you over the wall as well. You're already half-zombie."

216

Holly said to Derek, "Why are you saying that, now? How can you be so cruel?"

Derek said, "I met her in Brussels, right, if it's anybody's business. I was an MEP, she was… well, she danced at this club. She was a prostitute. I paid her for the first few times. And I kept on paying. And I was still paying her."

"Once a whore always a whore," said Patty. "The Jezebel gene was in her, you see."

Her lips were pursed, and she fanned herself with a magazine. Sweat oozed from beneath her Wales baseball cap.

"She was desperate to get out of here," said Derek. "She was really panicking and had been trying to get in touch with her – her boyfriend."

"Boyfriend?" said Holly.

"This guy, this bodyguard she'd met over in Brussels. She couldn't get a hold of him to come and get her. She hated me, anyway. She would've been willing to do anything to get out of here. I think your husband *did* offer her a helicopter ride for a blowjob, Patty. One thing, Claudette never, *ever* gave it away for free. She *always* demanded something in return. That's why I'm skint and we're holidaying in Anglesey and not Antigua."

Bert leapt to his feet. "How dare you. She – your wife – she raped me, practically raped me."

"And let my boys watch." Teena looked wild. Make-up streaked her face. Her hair was tangled and messy. "She was a pervert, a sick pervert, and deserved to die. That's what Patty said. Patty knows what God thinks, don't you Patty?"

Patty nodded.

Teena went on:

"Perhaps we should listen to Patty, I say. She knows what God wants, and God wanted that slag dead."

"How do you know that?" said Vincent.

"Patty says so."

217

"How does she know?"

"She knows."

"That's only you saying that, Teena," said Vincent.

"Patty says it, too."

"And I say it," said Roger. His mullet had flattened on his head.

Gavin said, "We've just witnessed a murder, do you realize this? And we have the murderer here."

They all looked at him. He stood, arms folded, near the entrance to the chapel.

"It weren't murder," said Teena. "Patty spoke to God, and God told her, *Kill the bitch*. Isn't that right, Patty?"

Patty nodded.

Oswyn held his hands up. "Before we end up at each other's throats – "

"Too late," said Gavin.

Oswyn continued:

" – we should get some water, we really should. We can fill bottles and jars with water from the bathrooms."

"I'm not drinking bog water," said Teena.

"You might have to drink your own piss if we stay here much longer," said Vincent. "And mine too."

"Roger," said Teena, "Roger, do you hear what he says? He says I have to drink his piss, Roger."

"We'll see," said Roger. "Where's this water, Ossie?"

Holly, still pondering Derek, said to him, "You were an MEP?"

"I was. Labour. North-West of England. No one knew me, of course. No one knows their MEP."

"What happened?"

"I was caught with Claudette. The MEP and the lap dancer. A News Of The World sting. I lost my seat."

"Were you in love with her?"

Derek furrowed his brow. "Of course not. She was a trophy wife. Beautiful women like that don't marry men like me unless there's money or power or some other luxuries involved."

Holly looked at Vincent, and he saw the gloom in her eyes. He put his arm around her. He glanced around the chapel.

Patty perched on the remains of a stone bench next to her husband. They both sweated. She stared ahead, not making eye contact with Bert. Vincent guessed she didn't entirely trust his account of the incident with Claudette. Bert didn't look like the sort of man who'd be forced to do anything he didn't want to do. However, the American *did* look like a bloke who'd make demands – and if he didn't have them met by his wife, he'd go elsewhere.

Bella sat on the ground with Catrin. The younger woman had her head in her hands. She rocked back and forth, whimpering.

Mark leaned against the far wall with Sandra and the children. The kids were quiet. Playing games with stones they'd found. No computers here, no Playstation or Wii. Mark looked sick, his skin pale and clammy, his eyes red-rimmed. Sandra had taped gauze to his cheek, but blood was seeping through.

Teena, Roger and their twins, were outside in the inner ward. Roger played football with his boys. Vincent could hear him:

"Bidden on the ball for England, Bidden through the defence…"

How could he do that, minutes after his wife had killed someone?

"…Bidden strolling through the defence… "

You only played for Doncaster Rovers, thought Vincent.

And that had only been for five years, till he got too fat and too drunk after a knee injury forced him to quit the game.

Oswyn and Gavin were huddled near the vestibule. They whispered. Oswyn slashing his hand up and down as if making a point. Gavin's gaze skipped around the chapel.

Vincent's belly groaned.

We shouldn't be loitering in groups, he thought, *we should be sticking together*.

It was how they'd survive.

He got up to say that when Teena screamed from outside.

As he raced out with the others, Vincent thought, *Where's Derek?*

He got his answer.

Roger shouted, "No, no, no, for Christ's sake, no!" and raced to the castle's entrance at the Gate Next the Sea.

Teena said, "He's trying to open the gate."

Vincent stopped and looked towards the entrance, and his skin crawled.

Derek unbarred the wooden door.

He heaved it open, the hinges squealing.

From outside, hands slid through the gap between the wall and the door. They clawed and scrabbled.

The door screeched open.

Light poured into the passageway from outside.

The first zombie stumbled into the castle.

And there were dozens more behind it, waiting to stream along the bridge and through the open door.

CHAPTER 37.
THEY'LL GET US ALL.

THE boy lunged at Carrie's face, his jaws snapping. She punched him in the nose and reared back.

The zombies hared towards her. They were ten yards away. They snarled and growled and salivated, their faces dark with fury.

The boy came again, his milk-white eyes fixing on her.

Carrie screamed, lost her balance. She was going fall in a heap and be swamped by the dead.

They'd eat her alive.

The boy was on her. She threw her arms over her face.

A boot flashed in front of her eyes. Cracked the boy on the skull. The zombie child's neck whiplashed. The creature staggered away and fell into the path of the undead sea sweeping towards Carrie. They trampled the boy-zombie, tripping over him, stomping on him.

Hands grabbed Carrie from behind.

"Come on," said Sawyer, and he hauled her to her feet, and they legged it.

The zombie stampede shook the road behind her. The undead throng roared. They sounded like they were gaining on her and Sawyer. But she wasn't going to look back and check.

Sweat greased her body. She felt sick. But she kept running. Her legs were heavy. Her lungs felt like rags flapping on a washing line.

Sawyer angled off the road and into someone's front garden.

The front door of the house stood open.

Sawyer raced into the building. He hauled Carrie inside and shoved her down the hallway. He kicked the door, and as it swung shut, Carrie saw the zombies pour down the path. The door closed and quaked as the dead rammed against it. They growled and moaned outside. Their dark shapes fluttered behind the pebbled glass.

Sawyer took her hand, and they went through into the kitchen. Boxes of breakfast cereal stood on the table, along with two plates of bacon and eggs. Flies fed on the food.

"It's like the Marie Celeste," said Sawyer.

Carrie's belly rumbled. She retched at the sight of the food.

Sawyer kicked open the back door. They went out into the garden. A child's swing stood in the corner. Children's clothes hung on the washing line. Toys were strewn across the lawn. The partially eaten body of a toddler lay in the rose bushes.

Carrie stiffened at the sight, and she backed away.

"Come on," said Sawyer, grabbing her hand.

"It's a… it's a… child… "

"Don't look," he said.

But her eyes wouldn't come away from the child's remains. The carcass held her gaze. And even as Sawyer towed her across the garden, she twisted her head to see.

With a brick, Sawyer smashed the padlock on the back gate, and kicked it open. Out in the alley, he looked both ways.

He grabbed her arms and put her against the wall. She thought he was going to kiss her. She parted her lips for him. She panted and was hot with fear, but her crazed mind told her she wanted this.

But then he said, "Stay there," and he clambered up the fence of the house backing up on the alley. He stayed there for a few seconds, scanning the gardens.

Carrie's legs almost gave, and shame rose up in her. She expected a kiss. Wanted a kiss. Wanted him against her, pressing her to the wall. Needed his strength against her.

Hormones, she thought, *my hormones going crazy.*

She lay a hand on her belly and thought of her baby.

Pull yourself together, she told herself.

And she cleared her mind. Discarded the debris that had been piling up in there all day. She had to be focused. She had to be cool, in control. She couldn't depend on Sawyer for everything. He might not be around, anyway.

Sawyer said, "Come on, don't daydream," and he helped her up.

They dropped into another garden. There were toys here too, scattered across the backyard. Rats scurried through an overturned wheelie bin. A pair of legs in shorts poked out of the tub.

"Oh God," she said. "Look."

"I see."

"He must've climbed into the bin, tried to get away."

"Come on, Carrie, don't loiter."

They crossed the garden to the opposite fence.

"They'll get everyone, won't they," she said. "They'll get those people who think they're safe, those people in the Emirates Stadium. The O2. Wembley. Everywhere. Sawyer… Sawyer – "

He stopped tugging her and faced her. "What?"

"They'll get us all."

He didn't say anything.

"They will, won't they?"

"Maybe," he said. "But the least we can do is make it difficult for them, eh? Come on."

They leapt from garden to garden, finally breaking through a garden gate and entering an alley. Carrie had kept her gaze ahead, trying to ignore the corpses in the gardens.

"All those bodies – the baby, the man in the bin," she said now as they cowered in shade, taking a breath, "they'll wake up. Just like… like John Shaw."

"Who's John Shaw?"

She told him and then said, "They're killing people, Sawyer, and then those people, they're… they're becoming zombies, too. Soon… soon this county will be nothing but zombies. We can't stop it, can we."

He opened his mouth to say something.

A rumble rose in the distance, growing louder.

The ground shuddered.

Carrie only half noticed. She felt weak and desperate. She said again, "They'll get us all. There's… there's no point… " Her chest hurt, and she slumped against the fence. Weariness overwhelmed her.

The rumble grew louder. It sounded like vehicles.

"You should be ashamed," he said.

She looked up at him.

"You know, I've got nothing to live for. Nothing, no one. My family is gone. My brother's in jail for murder. My dad died in prison. My mum… " He shook his head and then went on: "You've got a little girl out there. If she were my little girl, I wouldn't rest. I'd go and go and go till I found her, till I knew. Till I knew if she was alive or dead or… whatever. I'd look for the rest of my life. I'd scour the earth for her."

He stared at her and then made a dismissive noise and turned away.

She kept looking at him. At his chest and arms, slick with sweat. At his jet-black hair, down to his shoulders. At his coarse, unshaven cheeks. At the man in him. The rough, physical, brute in him. The prince in him, the knight in him.

"Where do you find your strength?" she said.

His eyes blazed. He came to her and lifted her by her arms, and she gasped.

"Don't you want to live?" he said.

Tears welled, and she nodded. "But I can't see how."

"Me neither, Carrie, but I'm going to find a way. I'm going to find a way till there's no way left to find."

She fell into him, and he held her. She pressed her head to his chest, and she could hear his heart, its beat like a shield to her. The world trembled. The noise was deafening now, a shudder coursing through the earth

"What would I have done if you'd not been there?" she said.

"You'd have been okay, is my guess."

"I wouldn't, would I."

"Where were you going when we found you?"

"Off to get Mya."

"That's right. Without me. On your own. Come on."

"Jesus," she said, furrowing her brow, "what the hell is that noise?"

CHAPTER 38.
ZOMBIES VS. ARMY.

THE ground shook.

Carrie and Sawyer ran up St Thomas's Road. The houses here seemed abandoned too, like everywhere else. A pub called The Auld Triangle stood on a junction. Its windows were shattered. The doors quivered on their hinges as the streets rumbled.

Carrie stopped. A woman and a child stared down at them from the third-storey window of one of the houses.

Carrie and the woman looked at one another for a while. The woman cried and hugged her child. There was desperation in her face. The ground floor window had been boarded up. The windows on the second floor were blacked out. Someone had pinned dark curtains up to block the light. Or to stop anyone seeing inside. *Blackouts*, she thought.

Her granddad had told her about them. "Pitch black," he'd say, "and you'd hear nothing except for the sirens telling you the Germans were flying overhead, dropping bombs."

Hearing his voice in her head made her think about her mum again. She'd thought about her in the alley moments ago, when she considered abandoning Mya.

She shuddered with horror now at the thought.

But she wondered if this was how her own mum had felt when she walked out on them.

Carrie had been five. She'd asked Dad where Mummy had gone. Dad had tears on his face and said Mummy had gone away for a while. "A while" turned out to be for good, forever.

Granddad hadn't been so vague.

He'd said, "She's abandoned you, little flower. She's gone and turned her back on the child she carried." He'd shaken his head and tutted. "Cold woman. Cold, cold woman."

"Wait," said Sawyer now.

They crouched behind a car.

They looked up the road. Up there lay Finsbury Park. *Open ground*, thought Carrie. On a day as beautiful as this, the common would be teeming with people. But not today. Today, blood and gore would stain the grass. Zombies would prowl The Pit, the basketball courts, and the flower gardens.

Engines growled. The city quavered. Buildings seemed to shake, their doors and windows rattling.

The first vehicle appeared at the top of a road.

"Army," said Sawyer.

The tank churned down the street. Mashed a car that had been left in the middle of the road. Metal clanked as the vehicle was crushed under the caterpillar tracks.

Another tank loomed into view and tailed the first vehicle over the flattened car.

Soldiers followed, marching behind the tanks.

Their boots hammered a rhythm on the tarmac.

Carrie felt the road judder. The tanks growled, four of them now rumbling up the street.

Sawyer took her hand and led her out into the road.

They stood and waved at the soldiers.

The first tank clanked to a halt.

The soldiers swept forward and kneeled in a line across the road, aiming their guns at Sawyer and Carrie.

Carrie sensed something behind her. She glanced over her shoulder. Her heart nearly stopped.

Sawyer said, "What are they – "

Carrie said, "Look," and he did.

And he saw what she'd seen:

The zombies who'd chased them from the Emirates Stadium had swarmed through the streets.

A wave of them washed up St Thomas's Street towards Carrie and Sawyer.

Hundreds of them, fifty yards away and shifting.

"Run," said Sawyer, and they ran towards the soldiers.

A voice on a loudspeaker said, "Get off the road or we will shoot you!"

Sawyer and Carrie veered left. They scrambled over the wrecks of two cars that had ploughed head-on into each other. The metal felt hot under Carrie's hands. They leaped over a low wall and into a garden.

The zombies filled up the road. They mowed forward, heading straight for the soldiers.

An explosion rattled Carrie's bones, and she threw herself to the ground. She peered through her fingers.

The blast had gone off in the middle of the zombie horde. The detonation threw up a geyser of concrete, metal, and flesh.

But the zombies kept coming. They swarmed through the smoke thrown up by the explosion.

"Sawyer," said Carrie.

"I know," he said.

She couldn't hear him very well. Her ears rang.

Sawyer smashed the rippled glass of the front door with his elbow, but Carrie didn't hear the window shatter.

He drove his hand through the jagged glass, not being too careful. Shards sliced his knuckles, and blood oozed from his skin.

He threw open the door. Carrie rose from the ground. The zombies swerved towards her.

"In," said Sawyer, "in," and she dived through the door, Sawyer coming after her.

A zombie lunged into the house.

Sawyer threw himself at the door. Slammed it on another zombie's arm. Slammed and slammed till the arm sheared off and clumped on the hallway carpet, the fist opening and closing like a clam.

The zombie inside the house raced after Carrie as she ran upstairs.

She tripped on the steps, and rolled on her back.

The zombie staggered up towards her. It was female. Blood and meat matted its blonde hair. A flap of skin hung from its cheek. The creature's shirt had been torn open down the front, and the breasts ripped away. Carrie saw inside the chest cavity. The ribcage contained nothing but chunks of meat and offal.

When the zombie had been human, its organs had been devoured. It had been sliced open and pulled inside out.

And now it wanted to do the same thing to Carrie.

The zombie towered above her.

Carrie kicked the thing in the ribs. They cracked. The creature grunted and flew down the stairs. It crashed into a coat stand.

Sawyer raised an umbrella and Carrie's reeling mind thought, *Where did he get that from? It's not raining.* And then she screamed and Sawyer drove the pointed end of the umbrella into the zombie's face.

Carrie flinched as a geyser of black fluid spurted from the creature's head.

The zombie squealed and scrabbled at the umbrella. It kicked about and its skirt rose, and Carrie saw the clammy, green-tinged flesh of its thighs.

Sawyer, driving down on the umbrella, looked up at Carrie, and dread filled his eyes.

CHAPTER 39.
DEREK LETS THEM IN.

VINCENT didn't think. He just ran at the zombie.

The creature, wheeling into the castle grounds, steadied itself. Another one bundled in through the open door, and then a third, both losing their balance.

Vincent charged. The zombie had seen him coming and bared its teeth, drooling as it rushed at Vincent.

The creature lunged. Vincent ducked. The zombie stumbled, arms lashing the air. Vincent hurdled the other two zombies. Hurled himself against the door with a cry. The impact jarred his shoulder and made him see stars. The door slammed shut.

Vincent, head swimming and pain wracking his body, leaned against the door.

Derek cowered in the corner.

Vincent said, "What do you think you're doing?"

Derek said nothing.

A shout drew Vincent's attention.

Gavin grappled with the first zombie. They wrestled their way out into the inner ward.

Someone screamed, "Don't let it bite you! Don't let it bite you!"

The other two zombies were getting to their feet. Vincent's bowels quivered. He was caught between the door and the zombies.

They rose and swivelled and saw him.

He grabbed Derek and said, "Come on, we've got to fight our way out."

Vincent looked for a weapon.

Behind him, zombies scoured at the door, trying to get inside.

"Don't let them bite you," he said to Derek.

The zombies ploughed forward.

Vincent's knees almost buckled, and if he'd fallen, he'd have been dead.

But he found strength from somewhere. *More like desperation*, he thought, as he grabbed the zombie by the collar.

Vincent held the snapping jaws away from his throat. He wheeled round, dragging the zombie inside the castle. The creature snarled and foamed at the mouth.

"Derek," he said, "Derek," hoping the man could cope with the other zombie.

Vincent spun out into the sun's heat again. It was sizzling. He rasped for breath, tussling with the zombie.

He was sick with hunger and fear. The smell of the zombie turned his stomach. They whirled and whirled, and that made Vincent dizzy.

He saw the other people, gathered in the inner ward. They screamed and shouted. Gavin, on the ground, struggled with the first zombie. Roger loomed over it, a plank of wood raised over his head.

Vincent wanted to puke. He kicked the zombie in the balls, but it didn't flinch. Jaws snapping, face creased with rage, its instinct to bite and to eat was overwhelming.

Vincent twisted, hitching the zombie on his hip in a judo-style throw. He flipped the creature over his side. Dropped it on the ground and stamped on its skull.

"Derek," he said, "where's Derek?"

The zombie grabbed Vincent's leg. The face was crushed, mashed by Vincent's boot. But the creature's impulse was still to bite, despite all its teeth being broken now.

Vincent yanked his leg away and kicked the thing in the face.

Roger bounded over with his weapon. He'd sorted Gavin's zombie. Smashed the creature's head in with his plank of wood. Now he started on this one, thumping its already broken skull.

Vincent took one look at the twitching zombie and then raced back to help Derek.

He froze.

Stared into the shadows surrounding the entrance.

Something moved in the shade

"What's the matter, Vincent?" said Holly behind him.

He didn't answer.

He waited, his nerves cord-tight.

A shape lumbered out of the shadows, staggering forward.

Holly screamed.

Vincent said, "Oh, shit."

It was Derek, blood staining his white shirt, his hand clasped across his throat.

"I'll be okay," he said, his voice a croak.

"Derek… where… where is it?"

The zombie shot out of the shadows and pounced on Derek, forcing him to the ground. The creature tore at Derek's nape, biting into the skin. Derek bawled and thrashed.

Vincent remembered a zombie plucking Simon's spine from his body. He didn't want to see that again. The sight was already seared in his mind for good.

He shot forward and booted the zombie in the head.

The creature rolled away, but righted itself sharply and was up and springing towards Vincent.

Roger's plank caught it full in the face. It floundered, unsteady on its feet. Roger chased after it. Smashed its head into the castle wall with his plank. The skull burst. The zombie slumped, leaving a trail of brain, blood, and bone on the wall.

Vincent glared at Derek with dread rising in his chest.

The man rose, wavering. He was covered in blood, his skin glistening with it, his shirt soaked through. "I'll be perfectly all right, you know," he said, and he cackled. "Perfectly all right... perfectly all right... we will all be perfectly all right... when... when we're zombies... "

* * * *

They burned the zombies' remains. The smoke, black and stinking of death, billowed over the walls.

"You think these fires are like beacons to those things?" said Gavin.

The smell of burning flesh clogged Vincent's throat. "I don't know. They don't seem that bright. They're not organized or anything. You know, like vampires."

Gavin arched his eyebrows. "You have experience of vampires?"

"You know what I mean. Our perception of them. What we read in books, see in films. I mean, who could've guessed that the zombie films were all pretty accurate – they're like that in real life."

"I had hoped those movies were made up, myself."

"They probably were. But maybe, I don't know... " He trailed off, thinking about things. His head throbbed, and he grimaced, touching his brow.

"What were you going to say?" asked Gavin

"I was going to say, perhaps we know what they're like because our ancestors might have come across them. And, you know, that information is encrypted in our brains, in our DNA. So, then, we know what they're like. And those filmmakers, writers, whatever, knew because we're coded with the knowledge – we just don't

233

know it. I mean, we *know* zombies are real now. So if they're real today, they must've been real" – he shrugged – "ten thousand, a hundred thousand years ago."

"Don't you think *we* made them?"

"What do you mean?"

"Nuclear power. Environmental damage. Science gone wrong. Some mad professor somewhere. We've made diseases, haven't we? We've made so many things that can kill. Why not these things?" Gavin gestured at the charred remains. "They might've come from a lab, for all we know. Man-made monsters. Just a handful of them to begin with. But then it becomes an apocalypse."

"I saw them come out of the water. From under the river. The first ones. The ones that were just bones. They looked like they'd been dead a long time. Maybe they were in a graveyard under the river. Maybe they'd been buried at sea and swept in by the tide. Then they rise up. Like all the others."

"But how?"

Vincent looked up at the sky. It was a cloudless, blue canopy. The sun flared down relentlessly. "Maybe it's the heat," he said. "They said on the radio this morning that it had never been this hot in Britain."

"So the dead come out for a tan."

"I don't know."

They lapsed into silence and watched the bodies burn.

After a while Gavin said, "Things are going to get bad in here."

"I know."

"People are losing their minds."

"Some have already lost them."

"We've got to be careful. Patty's winding people up. Sticking the spoon in and stirring. She's got Bella and the younger girl on board. Oswyn, too. If she gets Teena and Roger, we're looking at a real split, an 'us against them' thing going on."

"What about Mark and Derek?"

Gavin said nothing.

"They're going to die," said Vincent, "and they're going to get up again. And we'll have two more zombies dancing around the place."

"Got any suggestions?"

Vincent thought about it. He didn't want to say it, though. But Gavin told him to go on, it was okay.

"We might have to kill them, Gavin. Kill them before they die."

Gavin stared at him, and for a moment Vincent thought he'd said the wrong thing.

But then the older man said, "You are right. But we can't, can we. Not even now, not even under these circumstances. Murder, when it comes down to it, is murder."

"Only in law, Gavin. Doesn't seem to be much law out there, now, if you ask me. I mean, Teena killed Claudette. She's not going to get arrested and fingerprinted and DNAed, is she."

Gavin said nothing.

They watched the smoke climb over the walls.

After a while, Gavin spoke: "Truth is, we're no better than those zombies out there. Actually, we are worse – far, far worse."

They were silent again.

Then a small voice behind them said, "Vincent."

He turned and Holly stood there. She was shaking, and her skin looked like chalk. She stared at him with fear in her eyes.

His guts tightened. "What is it?"

She said, "It's that crazy Patty woman."

* * * *

"They are saved, now," said Patty.

She stood before the alter table. Mark and Derek kneeled either side of her. She rested her hands on their heads. They were like dogs squatting next to their mistress.

235

Derek's wounds coagulated. Blood stained his shirt. He'd paled considerably since Vincent had seen him last. His tongue, fat and blue, lolled out of his mouth.

Mark looked no better. The colour drained from his eyes. A milky film coated the iris. The flesh around his face wound blackened.

He's turning, thought Vincent.

Gavin said, "What do you mean, 'saved'?"

Patty said, "I mean, faggot" – Vincent sensed Gavin bristle – "that Jesus has cleansed them of sin. Their souls are safe, now."

Gavin's face coloured. Vincent laid a hand on his shoulder. "Come on, mate," he said, but Gavin shrugged him off.

Bert said, "You turning the boy now, fag? Making him a sodomite, too?"

Gavin glowered. "Maybe I'll turn you, fat man. Maybe I'll put your gut on the floor, arse up, tear off your pants and mount you."

Bert quivered and took a backward step.

Gavin went on:

"But I think you'd like it, fat man. I think you'd like mine up your arse, right there inside your bowels, wouldn't you."

Bert clutched his breast and tried to say something, but he only blustered.

"Threats of sodomy from Satan's ejaculation," said Patty. "Ugly words in God's house."

A tug at his sleeve made Vincent start. He gasped, looked behind him. It was Holly, her eyes wide with fright. She gestured for him to go with her.

They made their way up to the Gunners Walk and surveyed the area.

"They're going," said Holly, indicating the zombies outside the castle. "There's fewer of them."

She was right. Their numbers had dwindled. But there were still hundreds, maybe, lingering on the road and The Green. When they saw Holly and Vincent up on the flanking wall, they stormed forward.

Vincent shielded his eyes and squinted, trying to see across the Straits to the mainland.

There might be fewer zombies here, but across the water they trawled the landscape, moving back and forth in search of food. Hundreds of them rippled over the countryside on the other side of the channel. They clambered up the hills and crested their peaks. They roamed the fields, the mountains, and the roads, looking for the one thing that sated them.

Meat.

Human meat.

"Things will never be the same, will they," she said.

"I'm – I'm sure they will."

"You're lying to me, now." She looked up at him, and through her tears, she smiled. "Are you still showing off, trying to get me to sleep with you?"

Vincent blushed. He drank some water, warm from the bottle. But at least it dampened his sandpaper-dry throat.

She spoke again:

"You know when we were standing by the water's edge earlier this morning?"

He nodded, remembering – just. It seemed like ages ago.

"I said I wanted a hero, wanted a man to be brave. Wanted a prince or a knight."

He nodded again.

"Okay, this is a really cheesy line… but I found one."

He stared into her eyes, and they shone, and her pupils flared.

She went on tiptoe, and her dry lips brushed against his, and he put his hands in the small of her back and pressed her to him.

He bent down to kiss her, and their lips were hard and dry against each other. But it didn't matter. Her lips didn't matter.

It was the *whole* of her that mattered.

From her eyes to her heart, her skin, her hair, her voice, and everything she did and the way she did those things.

She led him from the Gunners Walk, and he was dizzy. They descended the stairs and went from sunlight into gloom, and finally came to a guardroom.

Set into the wall was a sleeping chamber – a platform of stone, that was all. But fine for them.

The sun streamed in through the opening, but Holly and Vincent stepped out of its glare, and they sat together in the chamber, not taking their eyes off each other.

She put her arms around him. "I think this is the most romantic place I've ever been."

She drew him down on to the stone.

CHAPTER 40.
CRAVE.

OUTSIDE, the war began.

Carrie cowered in the corner of the front bedroom, hands covering her ears. Sawyer crouched near the window, peeking out through the lace curtains. He flinched now and again as the tanks fired their shells, as the soldiers raked gunfire into the zombies. Despite trying to block out the noise, Carrie could still hear the muffled explosions, the dulled blasts.

Sawyer looked at her, and his eyes were wide. He scuttled over and held her.

She drew her hands from her ears, and the noise made her flinch. Screams and shouts filtered from the street. Gunfire and explosions rattled the window.

She looked up into Sawyer's face and said, "What's happening?"

He shook his head.

She held him tightly and cried into his bare chest, and her hands moved up and down his back, tracing his muscles.

His arms were powerful around her. Her insides quailed. She bit her lip, trying to stifle her desire. It was unwelcome, but she couldn't stem its flow.

She looked into his eyes again and groaned.

He bent his face to hers, and they kissed, and she clawed his back.

Her hands slid down his damp skin and found the waistband of his boiler suit, and she pushed the material down, putting her hands inside, feeling him naked underneath.

She crawled backwards and up on to the unmade bed, and he came too, and together they pushed her skirt up her thighs and then he touched her between her legs, and she arched her back and moaned, and he slid her underwear aside and moved onto her, and she clamped him between her thighs. And then, reaching down she found him hard, and she cried, shame and desire filling her.

"Please," she said, her voice a hiss.

She eased him to her and she moved towards him and he went into her and she stiffened and wheezed and threw back her head, and tears came to her eyes.

He moved on her and in her, and she moved under him and around him.

Outside the war went on.

Smoke filled the air. Made a fog that hid the sky.

The smell of burning and gunpowder blended with sweat in Carrie's nostrils.

Her insides seared now, and sweat glazed their bodies. He'd pushed up her T-shirt and handled her breasts, and she clutched handfuls of his hair and pulled his face to hers to kiss him.

She reached down and with her fingers made herself come, and he pushed harder into her as she cried out, and as she flagged under him she let him hammer at her and loved the way his face twisted as he climbed and climbed, and his muscles tensed, and his mouth opened in a gasp, and when he shuddered, she felt him come inside her.

They lay on the bed. The war outside faded. Carrie hoped the right side had won.

She closed her eyes and said a prayer, asking forgiveness for this lust when she should have put Mya first.

She cradled Sawyer and loved his weight on her, the feel of him withering in her, and wanted it to be like this for a long time.

But she didn't have a long time.

With him still inside her, the fire in her body smouldering, she said, "We have to go."

CHAPTER 41.
GOING AFTER SAM.

IN THE office building's reception area, Craig found a vending machine crammed with chocolates and crisps.

He smashed it open with a hammer he'd found in a toolbox behind the reception's counter. He piled the sweets into a cardboard box.

Also behind the counter, Craig had discovered a box of cartridges for the shotgun. The man must've been preparing a last stand. Craig wondered who the guy was. Did he work here? And if he did, why did he have a gun with him at work?

He might've been the boss, and he used it to shoot lazy workers, he thought.

He smiled and bit into a Mars bar. The sugar spiked his blood, and he shuddered. It made him dizzy for a moment, and his vision blurred, so when the zombie came through the door at the back of reception, Craig was off balance.

The creature snarled, hands clawed. Tears of blood ran from its milky eyes.

Craig yelled and stumbled, tripping over a chair.

The zombie charged.

Craig raised the gun, pulled the trigger.

Click... click click click...

He screamed.

The zombie closed on him.

He swung the empty shotgun. Clipped the creature across the cheek. The zombie went spinning.

Craig headed straight for his supplies – the confectionery, the cartridges. Grabbed the box and ran for the exit. Glanced behind him. Saw the zombie shake its head and fix on him again.

"Fucking bastard," said Craig and legged it for the door. He shouldered it open and stepped outside. The heat nearly decked him, it was so powerful. He slowed, and squinted across the parking lot. He trudged towards the Mitsubishi, huffing and puffing, his chest tight.

The door clattered behind him, and the zombie growled.

"Oh fuck shit," he said, not looking back, running till his legs were heavy.

The 4x4's door stood open. Craig dumped the box and the gun on the seat. Clambered in. Shoved the box over to the passenger side, spilling chocolate bars and crisp packets all over the floor.

The zombie hurtled towards Craig. He slammed the door shut. The creature thumped against the side of the truck and wheeled away.

Craig grabbed the shotgun, snapped it open. The smell of oil made him cringe. He took two cartridges and slid them into the shotgun, shut the barrel.

The zombie came again.

Craig rolled down the window and poked the gun out of the vehicle.

When the zombie came close enough, Craig fired.

The impact tossed him across the seat, the stock slamming into his ribs and winding him. His ears rang, and he couldn't hear.

He groaned and sat up.

The headless zombie had crumpled to the ground, blood pouring from the stump of its neck.

Craig belted out a laugh, and he laughed so hard that tears rolled from his eyes and the laughter became crying, and he shuddered there in the driver's seat, his ears ringing, his belly churning.

After a few seconds, he mastered his emotions and told himself, *Sort yourself out, Craig.*

He eased the truck out of the parking lot and drove for the roundabout. He intended to get back on the Cumbernauld Road and follow the convoy, hoping he'd find his mum and dad.

But he thought about Sam.

Sam with Art. Art who wanted to…

He stopped the 4x4 and stared into space, thinking.

He'd find Mum and Dad. Bring them back here. And together they'd go looking for Sam.

And then he thought, *How long has she been gone?*

He looked at the gun.

He guided the Mitsubishi round the roundabout and headed along the road he'd seen was called Dewar Road – in the direction Art had taken Sam.

CHAPTER 42.
THE CITY OF THE DEAD.

"NO," she said and brought her hands to her face. "No, no, no."

She stepped back towards the door of the house again.

Sawyer stood by the gate, scanning the carnage on the street.

Smoke rose from the tanks. Craters rutted the road and chunks of concrete and tarmac were strewn everywhere.

Bodies lay all over the place, most of them dismembered, many of them soldiers. Limbs showered the pavements and the street. Blood coated the buildings, staining the bricks and smearing the windows. The Auld Triangle pub had gone, nothing but a pile of rubble now.

"Troops didn't stand a chance, did they," said Sawyer.

He was right.

The zombies must've marched on the troops. Carrie imagined they'd been like a suicide squad. An undead kamikaze army.

She pictured them ploughing forward, their frontline being blown away. But then the second front swept in. Maybe those had been scythed down as well. But the third wave was already swarming forward, storming through the carnage, shearing into the troops.

A zombie crouched on top of a tank. It spooned intestines from a corpse into its mouth.

Sawyer strode out of the garden and picked up an automatic rifle from the pavement.

The zombie saw him coming and sprang off the tank and came at Sawyer, snarling and baring its bloodied teeth.

Carrie thought Sawyer would shoot it, but instead he swung the gun like a baseball bat, clattering the zombie on the jaw.

The creature wheeled away.

Sawyer pursued it. Whacked it full in the face with the gun. The zombie collapsed in a heap. Sawyer stove its head in with the weapon.

After he was done, Sawyer panted for air, and he looked up at Carrie. Blood flecked his face.

"Come on," he said.

She went to him, and they waded through the gore. Rats scattered, and flies rose up in clouds, disturbed by the trespassers.

And Carrie realized that's what they were.

Trespassers.

This wasn't their city anymore.

This was a city of the dead.

A city of scavengers.

Of rats and flies and dogs.

The rivers of blood dried up, and Sawyer and Carrie came to the end of the road and turned right into Seven Sisters Road and then up Stroud Green Road, and passed Finsbury Park.

Carrie's vision of the place had been right.

Blood stained the grass. Bodies baked in the heat. Dogs fought over dead flesh. Zombies picnicked on human remains.

"Jesus," said Sawyer, his voice shaking with fear.

"I'm scared," said Carrie, "I'm scared that you're scared, now."

"I've been scared since nine o'clock this morning, Carrie."

"I don't want you to be scared. I need you to tell me everything will be all right."

He said nothing. He kept walking, and she walked after him. His head moved back and forth.

"What are you looking for?" she said.

"I'm looking for a car that's drivable."

Carrie shivered with fright and started to sob. She felt disgusted at what they had done together in the house. Ashamed that she'd loved it so much when her daughter was out there.

Please be alive, Mya, she said to herself.

Please be alive and forgive me.

They glanced down a residential street off Stroud Green Road. More bodies, more abandoned vehicles, possessions scattered all over the street. Carrie guessed the locals had been fleeing, trying to take anything they could with them. But their escape was foiled. A swarm of zombies had probably attacked while they were lugging their belongings to their cars. Killed them all. Killed them and left them to rot and cook in the sun, left them there to rise up and join the ranks of the undead.

Sawyer asked which way, and she said, "Up there," and they strode up Woodstock Road.

"We shouldn't have done what we did," she said.

He stopped and glared at her but said nothing.

"It was wrong, Sawyer."

"I don't understand."

"No, you don't. You don't have a child out there somewhere. It was wrong, I shouldn't have – "

His face darkened. "Too late now."

She shook with anger, and she tried to say something but didn't know what to say. It *was* too late, he was right.

Too late for Mya.

She fell to her knees and put her face in her hands and let the shame consume her.

After a few moments, she sensed him looming over her, and she looked up and could only see his silhouette in the sun.

"I wanted you," she said. "I wanted you so much, but it was wrong, that's what I'm saying. I'm not saying I didn't want to, you see. Just that…"

She stared up at his dark shape for a few seconds, and then he reached out his hand, and she took it.

He lifted her to her feet.

"Forget it," he said. "Forget it happened."

And he turned his back on her and walked on.

CHAPTER 43.
THE PIT.

"AND where have you two been?" said Patty when Holly and Vincent came back to the chapel.

Holly said, "That's none of your business."

"Sex, that's where they've been," said Bella.

Holly glared at the woman. "Do you remember what that is?"

Bella bridled. "Don't you think we should be trying to do more useful things than sex?"

"Such as?" said Vincent.

"Such... such as praying... We've been praying."

"You pray?" said Vincent.

"We should all pray," said Oswyn.

"You too?" said Vincent. He looked around the chapel. Only Gavin was missing. Roger snored in the corner. The twins were outside. Vincent could hear them yell and laugh. Teena smoked in the doorway, snapping photos with her Kodak. But everyone else seemed to be in Patty's thrall. She was turning them.

They found Gavin smoking in a passageway. "I gave up two years ago when I met Neil," he said. "But I am weak. Always carry a pack of ten with me for emergencies." He took another drag. He coughed and spluttered. "I think we can deem this an emergency."

Holly said, "What are you doing here?"

"Well, God's back there, and God doesn't really like gays."

"It's scary," said Holly. "I don't like what's happening. Patty's spreading her poison. Even Mark and Penny and Sandra are joining her now."

"Mark doesn't know where or who he is at the moment," said Gavin.

Vincent said, "He'll change. Him and Derek."

Gavin dropped the cigarette butt. "Not according to Patty. They're saved now."

Vincent said, "We've got to do something. We can't sit around, waiting for someone to save us – no one's coming."

Vincent peered into the alcoves off the passageway. He thought about something and then said to Gavin, "Have you got a lighter or matches?"

Gavin handed him a disposable lighter. He edged into an alcove and saw what looked like two small, square cavities in the floor. He lit the lighter and studied the structures he'd found.

You could sit on these, he thought, *your bum cheeks on either side of the bricks.*

"What is it?" said Holly.

"Latrines," he said. "There's loads of them throughout the castle. Back-to-back cubicles."

"Nice," said Gavin, "I've been having a fag where they used to do some medieval cottaging."

Vincent lifted his leg into the latrine and stamped. Nothing happened. The earth was solid and damp. He stamped again. The ground gave a little. His blood quickened. He stamped again, harder this time. He felt the ground loosen under his foot and the earth hollowed. Again he slammed his boot down on the soil and

250

it cratered, falling away. He stamped again, with all his strength. The ground gave. Debris rained down into an abyss. The smell of decay wafted through the hole in the ground, and Vincent gagged.

"Oh God, what is it?" said Holly.

Gavin's eyes widened. "I know what it is."

Vincent breathed, his nose growing accustomed to the odour. He said, "Me too. It's a sewerage system."

"Clever bastards, all those years ago," said Gavin.

Vincent went on:

"There's a pit under the walls where all the shit and piss dropped from the latrines. Channels led from the pit, feeding the muck, you know, *out* of the castle… "

"Out?" said Holly.

"Out," said Gavin. "Out through thousand-year-old piss and shit. Out into the river."

"But… but we don't even know if they're still open," said Holly.

Vincent looked at her. "No, we don't."

CHAPTER 44.
LOST CHILDREN.

HELEN told him, "We have to go back."

Terry said nothing. Stared ahead and drove on.

Fear coiled in her belly. Her children were gone. She put her head in her hands and started to cry.

Terry said, "We've got to keep going," his voice low and quiet.

"My children," she said.

"What can we do?"

"What any father would do."

His knuckles whitened on the steering wheel. Blood pulsed at his temple, and his nostrils flared.

She said, "You hate them, don't you. You hate us all."

"Shut up. Sam's safe. She's with that fella. Craig, he can… he can… fuck off. He's a bastard, an ungrateful bastard."

Her anger boiled over. "He's his father's son, that's what he is, Terry."

"He's no son of mine, that bastard."

"You don't think? Is that what you're saying?"

He glowered at her. "You came to me soiled, you slag." He looked at the road again. "No reason for that not to continue."

Her throat locked, and she thought she'd suffocate. She coughed, nearly puked. She panted for air, the shock of what he'd suggested knocking all the breath out of her.

She grabbed at the wheel. "Stop this car, stop this fucking car and go and look for our children."

"Get off me, you bitch." He swiped at her. The car swerved. Clipped an abandoned ambulance. Careered across the carriageway. The car behind honked its horn.

Terry swore at Helen. She screamed and clawed at him, her eyes burning with tears.

He punched her in the face. Her head knocked against the side window. Everything went black for a moment. She came to and moaned, cradling her throbbing head.

"Sit still, woman," he told her.

"I want my kids."

"Which ones, eh?"

"I want my kids, Terry."

"Shut your mouth. It's guilt you're feeling. Guilt for leaving her all those years ago. Now you want to swathe them in fluff when lashing them in chains would've been better, I'm telling you. See what your softness has done to Craig? Turned him into a... I don't know what."

She was too weak to fight back but managed to say, "I didn't love him enough," and she cried.

What Terry had said was true: she'd abandoned her child twenty-two years ago, when the girl was five.

But Helen was only twenty and couldn't face it. Couldn't face another night without sleep. Without seeing her mates. Without having a night out.

She wasn't ready to be a mum, and the kid would be okay, wouldn't she, with her dad and his family. All close knit.

Helen's boyfriend – the dad – was only nineteen and a brickie, but he wanted to join the Army.

"You can't leave me with the kid," she remembered telling him, screaming till her throat burned and her head hurt – just like they burned and hurt now.

She recalled weeping in the kitchen of that grotty, smelly, damp-stained council flat, begging him not to sign up. Trying to feed the kid, the kid sullen, refusing her Sugar Puffs. And Helen going nuts with him for his Army dreams and with their daughter for not eating.

The night he was going to join up, she left. Her head ready to burst. Her lungs so tight she couldn't breathe.

She'd packed his old Adidas school bag. Black leather with the handle chewed by his dog. Stuffed her belongings into the satchel while he was in the pub with his dad.

And she did a runner.

She'd looked at her daughter, wrapped up in the pink, rose-patterned blanket with Dandy the doll in her arms. Like the blanket, Dandy had been Helen's, had been Helen's mum's, and her mum's mum's. It was some kind of link, she'd supposed, something to connect her to the child long after she'd gone.

Helen had thought about saying bye-bye, blowing a kiss that had no meaning and saying, "Have a good life, chicken," and walking away.

Instead, she'd turned her back without a word and walked out. Took a bus to town. Found her way to Euston and caught the 7.25pm to Glasgow, reaching Scotland at past midnight, where it was cold and dark, the rain chucking it down.

The cold nights continued. She barely remembered sun – not like today, the heat intense. She remembered the drunks, menacing her, plaguing the station. And men offering her drugs, saying, "Come with me, babe, get you a place."

They offered her booze, and they asked her for sex, and she gave it now and again for money to buy food. She hadn't wanted to and promised herself never to fall into that life.

Her great-grandmother, they said, had been a prostitute, and a client had murdered her during the First World War.

But needs must. And when you're hungry, you do what you have to, and thinking about it now made Helen feel sick.

Her memory resurrected those sneering faces, their scoffs and their curses. Their grunts and groans and dirty talk from all those years ago swilled about in her mind, and her body remembered how they felt, heavy and wet, between her legs.

The images swirled, and a face appeared.

Clive Redman.

He rose like an angel from the debris and promised her that Jesus cared. He took her in and married her, and all she had to do was sleep with him. Spent ten years with him, finding God and then losing God when the urge for booze clawed at her again.

And where there was drink, there were rotten men.

Rotten men like Terrance George Murray, a thirty-year-old unemployed docker, who was handy with his fists and his tongue. A dark-haired, smooth-talking, hard-living Scot who made her insides fizz.

She tried to better herself. Passed some O-Levels. Found a job at the supermarket, where she was now an assistant manager.

Craig came along, and then Sam.

And life was… shit.

It had always been shit.

She'd hidden the shit behind a veneer, that was all. Thought she was better than she was. Thought she could *be* better. But Terry had said it:

She was soiled.

She was a mother who'd abandoned her child.

The face of the five year old dreaming on the mattress came to her now. The thumb sucked. The eyes screwed up. The body, wrapped in the pink blanket spattered with roses, twitching now and again.

Carrie, Helen thought.

Carrie, where are you?

And she came apart, slumping in her seat, sobbing and shaking and breaking down.

And all Terry had to say was, "Pull yourself together, woman."

CHAPTER 45.
NO LIGHT AT THE END.

"BE CAREFUL, Vincent, please," he heard Holly say as he lowered himself down through the latrine.

The hole was only wide enough to squeeze his body through. For a moment, he felt panic rinse through his veins as the opening tightened around his belly. But then he inched himself down. He reached up, and Gavin grasped his hands. His head went into the opening. The smell hit his nose. The darkness engulfed him.

Gavin said, "How are you doing?"

"It… it stinks."

"That's thousand-year-old poo, for you."

"You… you can let me go."

Gavin let go of his hands. Vincent dropped. He held his breath, thinking for a second he'd misjudged the depth of the pit. But then his feet hit soft, sludgy ground.

"See anything?" came Gavin's voice from above.

Vincent looked around. He blinked, trying to adjust his eyes to the darkness. He felt something rise from his belly, and he gagged, hot liquid filling his throat. He threw up.

Holly's voice echoed down into the pit:

"Vincent, are you okay?"

"Yes, yes, I'm fine – just the smell – it's rank."

"Can you see anything?" asked Gavin again.

"Oh, hang on, I'll try to find a light switch – no, Gav, it's fucking arse-dark in here, mate, okay. Give me a minute."

He stayed where he was for a few moments, getting used to the gloom and the smell.

And then he began thinking:

He'd read about the pits under the castle and how they had to be emptied through channels. Everything he'd read told him the channels were now blocked. But even if they weren't, even if he found one open channel, where would it lead?

If he found an open channel and crawled through it, and then popped his head out only to find he'd come out in the moat, he'd be dinner for the zombies.

What he needed was a route down to the water's edge. They could commandeer a boat. Abandoned vessels bobbed on the Straits. If they could get to one of them…

The zombies could swim, though. He recalled the couple attacked on their yacht.

We have to try, though, he thought. *We can't stay here. We can't go out into the street. We have to try.*

Vincent looked up. He'd dropped ten, maybe twelve feet down into the pit. Weak light shafted through the kicked-through latrine. He told Holly and Gavin to boot through the other cubicles.

They stamped, and dirt rained down and daylight speared into the gloom.

The pit became illuminated.

Moss crawled along the walls. Slime moistened every surface. Damp earth covered the ground.

Behind him, the pit stretched out into darkness – a long tunnel of blackness that made him shudder.

For a second, he thought he saw movement. A shadow flickering. He held his breath. Gooseflesh raced up his back. He waited for the zombies to lurch out of the dark. He couldn't move, his limbs frozen.

"Vincent," said Gavin, and then again: "Vincent."

"Christ," said Vincent, coming to.

"Are you okay?"

"Yes, fine. Seeing things, that's all."

"Seeing what?"

"Nothing, that's the problem."

He turned and stared ahead, blinking. Tried to figure out where he was. The wall before him faced south, he guessed. That's where he wanted to go. Right down to the river.

He trudged forward, his feet squelching in the grime.

He crept along the wall, hands moving over the sludge. The stink made him screw up his face. The air was muggy, and he could hardly breathe.

He crouched and shuffled along on his knees, pressing into the wall with his hands.

A familiar odour invaded his nostrils. He furrowed his brow and trawled his memory.

What is that, what is it?

He followed the wall, unsure of how far he'd gone.

Follow the filth, he told himself, *follow the filth down to the sea, down to the water's edge.*

The smell came to him again, stronger this time. It pierced the stink of decomposition that hung heavy in the pit.

What is it, what is it?

The wall was soft under his hands. His pulse pounded. He wiped sweat from his brow, smearing his face with slime.

He jabbed the wall with the palm of his hand and the soil gave, collapsing inwards.

He made a fist now and punched, gasping with every impact.

The wall crumbled. His fist slid through. He dug with both hands. Clawed at the soil. Dirt flying, showering his face, sour in his mouth.

Christ, he thought, *Christ*.

Vincent moled his way through the dirt, raking away the soil.

He cried out. Ran his hands around the edge of the hole he'd scoured out of the wall. It was circular – a pipe, a channel.

He dug his fingers into clay, thick and heavy.

He cursed again, gasping for breath.

He reached in, his arm going deeper, deeper, up to the shoulder, hand grabbing at air, at space.

He quaked with excitement and poked his head into the hole.

The darkness swallowed him. The channel pitch black. It was man-wide, just enough room to squeeze inside.

The odour filled his nostrils again. He breathed it in. The stench of ancient shit and piss. The damp odour of brick. The heavy smell of clay. The hint of seaweed.

Seaweed.

Adrenaline fizzed through his veins. He crawled into the channel without thinking. He had to press his arms out in front of his body and inch along using his elbows. He dragged himself into the tunnel, just a few feet, but all the way in.

The air was thin, and his lungs felt like lumps of lead in his chest.

He blinked into the darkness.

He stretched an arm and felt nothing. Nothing but space. Space to crawl.

He tried to move back.

But he didn't budge.

"Jesus," he said.

Panic squeezed his heart.

The channel pressed in on him.

He panted, thinking he was suffocating, kicking his legs.

Wriggled and cried out. But he couldn't move. He was stuck, and he thought he'd die here, jammed in a thousand-year-old sewerage system.

Then he became still.

He steadied his breathing, concentrating hard.

Don't panic, he told himself, *don't panic.*

He lowered his head and rested his brow on his forearms.

Waited a few seconds, breathing in the dank air slowly.

And then he backed up an inch.

And another inch.

He fended off the urge to retreat quickly. He'd get stuck again. So he snaked backwards, slithering gradually along the channel.

His feet had only been six inches inside the tube, but it took him a while – a few minutes, he guessed – to haul himself out.

"Where the hell did you get to?" said Gavin.

Vincent panted and stared up at Gavin's face.

"Trying to find a way out."

"And did you?"

Vincent didn't want to say that it might be dangerous and they might get stuck and die in old shit. He didn't want to take the little bit of hope he'd found and stomp on it.

"Might have," he said.

* * * *

Oswyn said, "You shouldn't have done that, because you might have damaged public property."

Vincent pulled a face. "Okay, report me."

"Those pits are dangerous."

"And this is safe, yeah?"

"It is until… " Oswyn trailed off. Vincent knew he was going to say, "until someone comes". But the castle official didn't look like he believed that anymore.

Patty filled in for Oswyn: "We're safe here until Jesus comes."

"I don't think Jesus is coming," said Gavin.

"Faggot blasphemer," said Patty.

"You call me that again, you hag, and I'll toss you over the wall, see if those undead puke on you."

A gasp rippled through the chapel.

Bert said, "Don't you talk to me wife like that, homo."

Gavin scowled at him. "I see, but it's okay for you to get a blow job off another woman, is it?"

"She tempted me – she was Jezebel," said the American.

Patty rose and pointed at Gavin. "And you are an abomination."

Gavin gave her the finger, and she hissed at him.

Vincent ignored Patty's ravings and said, "Those channels, they lead down to the Strait. If we can crawl through, we might be able to make it to a boat."

"Crawl through?" said Bella. "How far do we need to crawl?"

Vincent looked at Gavin who shook his head.

"Well," said Vincent, "just work it out – from the castle down to the shore."

"That's two hundred metres, at least," said Bella.

Vincent shrugged.

"We can't make it that far," she said.

"We've got to try, Bella," said Vincent.

"No, we should stay here."

"Excuse me, please."

They turned towards the voice. Sandra had her hand up. She looked ill, her skin grey and her eyes sunken. Next to her, nuzzled up to their mother, stood Hettie and Maisie.

Sandra said, "I… I'm really concerned about the children. They're scared, they're upset. I just think anything we can do to try and get out, we really should."

Patty said, "Do you want to lead those children to hell?" jabbing her finger at Hettie and Maisie, now.

"I think we're already in hell, Patty," Sandra said.

Patty said, "If you had Christ in your heart, woman, you would never feel the inferno. You would enjoy always the warm glow of Jesus's love. If you are not willing to let him into your heart, then Satan must have already taken up residence there, dear."

Sandra's eyes flared. "I have lost my husband. My children lost their dad. You have no idea how I feel, Patty, how utterly destroyed. But while I breathe, I will do anything to save my kids and" – she started to sob – "and if that means crawling through, I don't know, through the earth, I – I will do that."

Patty's head swivelled. She still had those sunglasses on. Her hold on the group was weakening, Vincent thought.

She said, "Satan is spreading dirt through you minds. He is tempting you out into his world where his demons prowl. Here is safe. Here is where Christ will come."

"And what if he doesn't?" said Gavin. "What if he comes where another lunatic is holed up? Where the Pope's holed up, maybe? Or the Archbishop of Canterbury? Or some mullah or Mormon? Or there's a bunch of loons where I live in London, the Church Of The Event Of Resurrection. Perhaps that's where Jesus will pop up."

"God is in my heart," said Patty. "I know that. I feel him. You feel nothing. Just Satan's dick in your rectum. Satan's come in your bowels. Vile, vile man. Vile, vile fornicator."

"If you were a man, I'd have broken your face," said Gavin.

"Yeah? We'll I'm a man," said Bert.

Gavin barrelled into the American. Bert, hefty as he was, didn't stand a chance. Gavin shoved him to the floor and then straddled him.

Vincent, thinking Gavin was about to batter Bert, prepared to dive in. But Gavin did something far worse than punch the American.

He kissed him on the mouth, instead.

Bert thrashed about, but couldn't dislodge Gavin.

Patty screeched. Oswyn and Bella yelled for Gavin to stop. Holly laughed, and Vincent looked at her, smiling. Vincent scanned the group, seeing how they'd reacted. Roger screwed up his face in disgust. Sandra laughed, holding on to her belly. Hettie and Maisie giggled. Derek vomited in the corner. Mark lifted his head, and Vincent looked at him to see what he would do – laugh or scowl.

He did neither.

His eyes were blank.

He was dead.

And now he was alive again.

Vincent shouted a warning.

Mark sprang for the children.

CHAPTER 46.
JAGUAR.

THEY walked through a ruined capital. The zombie apocalypse had ravaged the city. There was nothing untouched.

They saw the dead everywhere. They saw them killed, lying in the street, in shops, in pubs, in cars and buses, in houses.

And they saw them living.

The first wave had been skeletal, swathed in rags, skin rotting away and their hair long and grey. They were the old dead. The corpses that had been in the earth before today.

And now the second wave was rising.

Men like John Shaw. Women like the cleaner at the pub. And the boy near the Emirates Stadium.

They were the new dead.

And they were everywhere.

As they walked, Carrie and Sawyer saw them come awake. A carcass would jerk and then sit up. It would make a keening noise and shudder and then stagger to its feet. Its nose would twitch, sniffing the air. A roar would escape the new creature's throat, and its face would twist with rage. And it would hare off somewhere, smelling flesh or seeking out food.

The zombies usually moved in groups of around a dozen, no more than two-dozen. But most of them were gathered now around the venues where humans had been evacuated.

The zombies go where the food is.

Earlier, on Oakfield Road, a tree-lined residential street in Tottenham, they'd spotted a larger group of around fifty stalking towards them.

Carrie and Sawyer had slipped through railings. They'd cowered in bushes on a slope that led down to a railway line. She pressed herself against him, and he embraced her, and she felt his heart pound and his body quake.

He's scared, she'd thought, and tightened her arms around him saying, "It's okay, it's okay."

They'd watched the zombies shuffle past the railings, and dread had coursed through Carrie's veins.

They'd waited a few minutes and then rose nervously from their hiding place.

A train hooted and Carrie flinched.

The grumble of its engine grew louder, heading towards them from the west. The train appeared in the distance. Its surface seemed to be undulating, alive.

Sawyer said, "Christ."

Carrie squinted and shielded her eyes so she could see.

The train neared. It was a London Overground service. The hooter blew again.

Carrie's belly squirmed.

"Let's go now," said Sawyer.

But she couldn't move. Her chest grew cold, and her legs quivered. She could see why the train appeared to be rippling.

Sawyer grabbed her arm and said, "Now, don't wait. They'll see us, Carrie."

Eyes fixed on the train as it came closer, she reared up the slope, holding on to Sawyer.

The train shot by. Zombies crawled all over its carriages. Hundreds of them clambering on the coaches, trying to get at the passengers.

As the service passed, Carrie looked into the eyes of the driver. He stared up at her, his face pale and stretched in an expression of horror.

And as the train swept east, she saw the travellers inside. Clawing at the windows, their mouths making the shape of "Help! Help!" as they rode the Gospel Oak to Barking line.

"They're… they're going back and forth, Sawyer," she said.

"Come on, Carrie, don't look."

The train streaked under the railway bridge. A dozen zombies were splattered, and their remains sprayed back over the train.

"They're… they're trapped in the train."

Carrie quaked with horror at what she'd seen as they walked on. She couldn't cleanse her mind of the terror those passengers must have been experiencing. Riding back and forth on that line, their train crawling with zombies. They couldn't get out. The driver, his eyes telling Carrie more than she needed to know about his suffering, had to go back and forth, trying to shake off the zombies. They would go on and on, from Gospel Oak to Barking and back again. They would die on that train – of starvation, of thirst, of heat.

Carrie had to stop and throw up three times before they found themselves in Haringey, now, heading towards Hornsey.

It was only then, when she realized they had maybe three miles to go, that she'd been able to paint out the images of the train from her mind.

Carrie quickened her steps. She felt the draw of her offspring. She imagined Mya's scent on the air. She genuinely thought she could smell her daughter, was convinced of it, and rejected logic on the matter. She was desperate. She would believe anything.

And believing she could pick up Mya's odour convinced Carrie that her daughter was near, that she was alive.

"It's like those end of the world movies," said Sawyer.

She said nothing.

He went on:

"You know, when the streets are deserted. The human race wiped out."

"Maybe they are. Maybe we're the last."

"And the first, then."

She kept walking but glanced over her shoulder at him. "The first?"

"Like Adam and Eve. Starting again."

She felt something move inside her and remembered him. She placed a hand on her tummy and a shiver ran through her. She ignored her urges and cursed them for haunting her now.

Not when I'm so close to Mya, she thought.

She strode on, and a car raced down Inderwick Road.

Sawyer eased her towards the kerb.

The vehicle weaved towards them. It was a Jaguar, a black one. The sun splintered off its paintwork.

Something was attached to the bonnet, to where the Jaguar emblem would usually be. Something Carrie recognized when the car screeched to a halt ten yards away.

It was a human head.

PART TWO.

MELTDOWN.

CHAPTER 47.
NATHAN AND GILBERT.

"EVERYTHING'S going to be all right," Nathan told his Uncle Gilbert.

But Uncle Gilbert didn't look like he believed him. Uncle Gilbert didn't look like he believed *anything* anymore. He didn't look like he *knew* anything. He was slumped in the Vauxhall Vivaro's passenger seat. His face had the consistency and colour of that Copydex stuff Nathan used to plaster on Phoenix Lewis's chair at school, and then Phoenix would pipe up, "Look what fucking Nathan Briggs's done to my skirt, Miss."

Nathan would say, "Take it off and show us your fat arse, then," and everyone would burst out laughing and the teacher – whatever her name was, because Nathan never remembered unless they were hot – would say, "Please be quiet, please be quiet," and no fucker would listen.

Yeah, Copydex: that's what Uncle Gilbert's skin looked like. And his eyes were dark. And they oozed blood. And spit drooled down his chin. And he wheezed, his chest heaving. And his arm that the zombie had bitten in the underground car park where they'd gone with that bird and that Sawyer cunt had swollen and gone purple. And it reeked like it was festering.

Generally, things weren't looking good.

"Don't die, Uncle Gilbert," said Nathan, eyes flitting between his uncle and the A2, his hands sweating on the steering wheel. "We'll be in Dover soon. We'll catch a ferry to Calais. Get zonked on Frog wine, yeah? Shag some French birds. No zombies in France, Uncle. I'm sure of it. We'll be safe, there. Do some jobs. Tide us over. Don't fucking die."

The A2 looked like a scrapyard. Derelict cars and trucks all over the place. A trickle of vehicles headed in the same direction as Nathan.

Same plan, he thought. *Destination Dover.*

Get the fuck out of England.

An England plagued by zombies.

The undead prowled the A2. They mobbed vehicles, trying to find drivers or passengers stuck inside. Now and again, they stepped out in front of the van, but Nathan pinballed through them.

"You all right, Uncle Gilbert?"

Uncle Gilbert gurgled. His eyes were half-shut.

"I said this job would be shit, didn't I," said Nathan. "That geezer who called himself Sawyer, he wasn't to be trusted. I told Granddad, *Don't trust that geezer, Granddad*. But Granddad, you know what he's like – well, he's your dad, so you know – but you know what he's like. Stares at you with those blind eyes of his and you're sure he can see you, though he can't, and you feel them, those eyes, drilling into you. Blind eyes. How are you now, Uncle?"

Nathan got another gurgle.

This has been his first proper job. He was seventeen and had done burglaries before. An apprenticeship, Uncle Gilbert had told him. Now he was ready to qualify.

Uncle Gilbert had raised Nathan after his mum had died and his dad had been jailed. The pigs caught Dad and his gang while they were hijacking a truck carrying bullion. Nathan, ten at the time, remembered the word "grass" being used.

"That fucking grass," Granddad had said soon after. "I'll cut him open and eat his heart with ketchup smeared all over the bastard thing– I don't give a fuck if he is my son."

The judge sentenced Dad to fifteen years. Two years after he'd been inside, four prisoners kicked him to death. Revenge, a bloke told Nathan once.

"It was the blind man who did it," the bloke had said. "Your granddad. Your granddad killed his own son for grassing up the job."

Nathan wanted to ask the bloke what he meant, but he never saw him again.

Two months ago, Granddad had called Nathan in. "Time for you to lose your cherry, boy, so we got a sweet little job for you," the blind man had said. "High street bank. Your Uncle Gilbert'll be there to hold your hand, and we'll get you a good getaway driver."

The "good getaway driver" was the one who'd called himself Sawyer when Granddad said, "Not your real names, dickheads. Make something up. I don't give a shit. Do I look like I do? I can't *see* if I do, but do I?"

Later, after that meeting, Uncle Gilbert had told Nathan, "He made us choose fake IDs to protect you, son. He's got his eye on you, and as blind as he is, he sees better than any of us, I tell you."

Now, driving along a zombie-savaged A2, Nathan said, "I was right about that Sawyer geezer. Wasn't I right, Uncle?"

Uncle Gilbert coughed.

Nathan glanced at him and said, "Oh Christ."

Dark blood spurted from Uncle Gilbert's mouth. He twitched, making that nasty gurgling noise again.

"Oh my God," said Nathan.

He eyed his uncle, then looked at the road again. His uncle croaked. Nathan shot him a look and saw him arch his back, stiffening.

"Uncle Gilbert… Uncle Gilbert, are you dying, are you – "

Nathan should've kept his eyes on the road. He collided with an overturned police car. The van careened across the lanes, pitching and tilting, clipping other vehicles.

Nathan screamed, gripping the steering wheel, his stomach cartwheeling.

The impact made Uncle Gilbert flap around like a rag doll, blood spraying from his mouth and nose.

The van smashed side-on into the safety barriers in the central reservation. Nathan's neck whipped. Glass showered him. The world spun. He groaned, pain racing through him. His vision blurred, making everything ripple.

He came to, his eyes seeing properly again. He was saying, "Un-Un-Uncle Gil-Gilbert, are you – " just as he turned to check on him.

Nathan screamed.

Uncle Gilbert's eyes were dead and white. His upper lip curled back to show bloody teeth. He snarled at Nathan and snapped back and forth in the seatbelt, trying to reach his nephew.

Nathan scrabbled at the door handle. He looked through the shattered side window and froze.

They swept towards him.

Hundreds of them, piling down the A2. Hurdling over abandoned vehicles. Trampling human remains. Scattering rats and forcing crows to flap away from their carrion.

Nathan shrieked. He wet himself. The door wouldn't open. He gawked at his uncle-zombie. Rage etched the creature's face. It kept yanking, trying to free itself from the seatbelt.

Hands reached through the shattered window and grasped Nathan's head.

He hollered as they wrenched at him, twisting his neck.

He was saying, "No, no, no," in a high-pitched voice when the

Uncle-Gilbert zombie broke free and grabbed at Nathan's arm, biting into the flesh.

The pain was unbearable. But not as bad as the pain when the zombies twisted and pulled at his head till he was half-way out of the window, and they were able to start feasting on his face.

CHAPTER 48.
CM PUNK AND THE
"ZOMBIE KILLER".

A YOUTH with Braveheart paint on his face and a gold nose ring leaned out of the Jaguar's passenger side window. He wielded a shotgun and waved it at Sawyer and Carrie.

"Keep moving," Sawyer told her. They walked away, Sawyer wrenching car-door handles as he strode down the pavement.

Carrie heard the Jag start up again, and it crawled alongside them.

"Hey, are you living or dead?" said the driver. His bald head glistened with sweat, and the sun glittered off his wraparound shades. The words "zombie killer" written across his shiny forehead in black felt tip had smudged.

"At the moment, we're living," said Sawyer.

"Yeah, at the moment," said the driver.

Sawyer and Carrie walked on. The car rolled along after them. Carrie glanced at the men. The driver leered. The youth, a band of blue across his eyes, flicked out his tongue at her.

Carrie thought about something, then ran up to the car. Sawyer tried to grab her. She said to the driver, "Take me to Wood Green."

The car stopped. Carrie asked him again:

"Take me to Wood Green, please."

"Carrie, no," she heard Sawyer say behind her, and his hand was on her arm, trying to pull her away.

She jerked free. "Will you take me?" she said to the driver. "My daughter, she's there, you see. She's on her own."

The driver looked at her and then looked at Sawyer. He turned and spoke to the youth, both of them muttering and nodding. He looked up at Carrie and said, "Yeah, we'll give you a ride, doll."

"We're not taking CM Punk over there, though," said the youth.

"CM – who?" said Sawyer.

"You look like that American wrestler," said the youth.

"What he means is," said the driver, "you look like trouble."

"I'm not trouble."

"He's not trouble," said Carrie.

The driver shrugged. "It's you or nothing, doll."

Sawyer came forward. The youth leaped out of the car and aimed the shotgun at him. Sawyer stepped in front of Carrie and held out his hands. Carrie moved past him and said, "Okay."

"No," said Sawyer, "Carrie, you can't. I don't trust them."

"Hey, read this, sunshine," said the driver, running his finger across his forehead. "Says 'zombie killer' not 'human killer'. And see that?"

"I see it," said Sawyer looking at the head pinned to the bonnet.

"That's indicates ten kills – ten *zombie* kills."

"Your mother must be proud," said Sawyer.

"Get in the car, doll," said the driver, and Carrie didn't hesitate. Sawyer said her name, but she closed her eyes, shutting him off. She had to get to Mya. Nothing else was important. The car smelled of leather, and the seats were stained with blood.

The youth got back in the car, and the Jag sped away. Carrie looked through the rear window. They were leaving Sawyer behind as the car raced up Inderwick Road. An ache pulsed in her heart.

"Miss him already, doll?" said the driver. "Don't worry, we'll keep you company now."

The men cackled.

Carrie's head cleared. She realized her stupidity, what her desperation to find Mya had got her into. She lunged for the door.

The central locking engaged with a click.

"Too slow," said the youth, bug-eyed and drooling. Paint streaked his cheeks and matted his long, blonde hair.

The car turned up Tottenham Lane. A church stood on the corner. A sign declared Holy Innocents – Church of England. Fifty or sixty zombies were gathered outside, clawing at the building.

Carrie stared at the creatures as the Jag drove past.

The youth laughed in her face.

Carrie screamed and went for him. Clawed at his eyes. He shrieked as she scratched his cheeks.

The car swerved.

The driver shouted for them to stop.

Carrie ripped the nose ring from the youth's nostrils.

He shrieked, and blood sprinkled from his torn septum.

His hands flew up to his face, and he thrashed about.

He bumped into the driver.

The driver yelled out, twisting the steering wheel.

The car careered into a garden wall.

The impact tossed Carrie against the back of the youth's seat.

The click of the central-locking system disengaging snapped her into action. It must've have turned itself off when the car crashed.

She scrabbled for the door handle, managed to open it, and tumbled out of the car. She began crawling, hands finding the pavement sticky with blood.

The car door opened behind her, and the driver said, "Come here, you slag," and he grabbed her by the hair, lifted her head.

And she saw the zombies come for them.

The dead things hurtled from the church.

The driver, panic in his voice, said, "Now look what you've done. Get in the car."

Sawyer sprinted around the corner, directly into the zombies' path. He ran twenty yards ahead of the creatures. They saw him and quickened their pace, growling as they chased their prey.

The driver hauled Carrie into the car and slammed the door.

The youth leaned over the back seat. Blood and tears stained his face, the blue paint smeared.

He yelled and slapped her around the head and said, "I'm going to fuck you till you scream, you whore."

The car started. Carrie sprang forward. Grabbed the driver's face from behind, forcing her nails into his flesh.

"Get her off me," he said, screaming.

The youth bit her arm. She screamed, but wouldn't let go of the driver. She glanced over her shoulder.

Sawyer neared.

The zombies gained on him.

The car stuttered forward.

"They're coming – get us the fuck out of here," the youth said.

Sawyer, his upper body beaded with sweat, his face dark, hurdled over the car. His feet clanked on the roof. He leapt on the bonnet. The car jolted.

The youth grabbed his shotgun.

Sawyer jumped off the car, flung open the door. The youth swung the gun round, ready to fire. Sawyer dragged him out and knocked him flat with an elbow to the jaw, and then he got into the car and shut the door.

"Let him go," he told Carrie.

She released the driver's face and turned to look through the rear window while Sawyer shoved the driver out into the street.

Screams came from outside.

The zombies rammed into the car and swarmed over it. They piled into the youth and the driver. Carrie covered her eyes. She didn't want to see anymore. She'd seen enough of it: men being eaten alive, torn apart.

Sawyer clambered into the driver's seat.

The car rocked as the zombies tried to pry it open.

Carrie peeked through her fingers. The dead glowered at her through the windows, their jaws snapping.

The car shot forward, bowling the zombies aside.

CHAPTER 49.
CATTLE TRUCK.

CRAIG drove straight for the zombies. About a dozen of them crouched over a pile of gore. And when they heard the vehicle, they raised their heads from the meal. Blood smeared their faces and lathered their arms where they'd been digging into the corpse. They rose and faced the oncoming 4x4. They were fearless.

More like dumb, thought Craig.

They swept towards him. He put his foot down. Tightened his grip on the steering wheel. Ploughed into the first two. The impact shook the truck. The zombies sailed over a hedge and into a field.

Craig barrelled through the rest of them. Churned them up under his tyres. The truck bumped and jerked, zombies beneath its wheels.

Blood and gore sprayed as he mowed them down. The odour of rotting flesh filled the cab.

And then the road smoothed out.

Craig looked in the rear-view mirror. Bodies lay tangled and wrecked behind him. The blood glistened, and the flies billowed, a cloud of them falling on the gore.

Craig turned away from the carnage and stared down the road, towards the houses.

He shivered, thinking about what he'd find in that ghost town. No humans, probably. Just a population of undead. Hungry undead.

He tried his phone again, not wanting to go on with this on his own, needing support. But he failed to get a signal. He fiddled with the phone, gritting his teeth, sweating. The GPS worked, and Craig gasped with shock when he managed to connect to the internet. He just didn't expect it. Not today. The screen drizzled with static. But the search he carried out finally got him to the Sky News website.

He gawped at the screen. The phone crackled. An image played on the website.

Static sprinkled the screen again, and Craig grunted.

And then the picture cleared.

Craig watched glimpses of a city from the sky, the camera sweeping back and forth. He cursed at the sight, his belly twisting at what he saw.

Figures swarmed down streets, choking every alley, cramming the roads.

Was it London? He thought so. There was Big Ben and the Houses of Parliament. The hordes washed across Tower Bridge like ants – thousands of them.

And he knew they weren't human. He knew that before the voice told him:

"Ladies and gentlemen, those crowds you see down there, they are not human – they are not us. They are the undead, and they are now eating the living. It is estimated that tens of thousands died in the first wave of attacks that occurred across Britain this morning, and since… "

Static fuzzed the screen once more.

Craig tensed.

The voice broke through the interference again: "… could be witnessing the… of the human race… "

The "what" of the human race? thought Craig.

The end?

That's what the reporter meant, wasn't it.

The end.

The voice came again: "Sky News will stay on air as long as we are able. Our Skycopter will bring you these horrifying pictures from above London. Although we have lost contact with many of our correspondents, we know this to be the scene throughout Britain. Communications have been disrupted by this incident. Naturally, when the... the zombies first struck it caused panic, and this resulted in thousands upon thousands jamming the phone lines and... "

The phone crackled again, and then the voice returned:

"We have no official news yet from the rest of the world. Communication seems to have been affected by this... this outbreak. However, social networking sites such as Twitter have hinted at zombie attacks in the United States, Australia, the Middle East, and South Africa. The question asked by many here, by you at home and in the safe havens, I'm sure, is, *What caused this? How did it happen?* By the time this is over – if it ever will be over – we might not have an answer. We might never find out."

The picture died. Craig wept. He didn't want the world to end. His life had been fun, and he wanted that to continue.

He put the Mitsubishi into gear and rolled into the town, driving past estates of new housing.

No sign of life. No humans. No dead, either.

The town seemed to have been dumped on waste ground. The land surrounding it looked charred and scorched.

And then he thought about the cities. Their streets swarming with zombies. London. Manchester. Birmingham. Edinburgh. Aberdeen. Glasgow...

Nacker. KP. Hallie. All of them in Glasgow. Zombies surrounding them. He shuddered. Maybe it was best to be here, out in the country, where there were fewer zombies. Fewer people, too. Maybe they could start again. Maybe he could survive.

But how would he do that?

He always thought he was tough and fearless. The lads called themselves soldiers. Their gang was an army.

But we know fuck all, he thought. *We're not soldiers.*

Soldiers could survive. They could live off the land. Eat insects and shrubs. He couldn't, could he? Nacker couldn't. KP couldn't. They'd have to find a McDonald's. They'd have to find beer and fags.

How could they live like soldiers?

How could anyone eat bugs?

How am I going to survive? he thought, entering the housing estates now, his eyes flitting around.

I'd rather eat human than bugs, he thought, and remembered the story he'd heard about those rugby players from Chile whose plane crashed in the Andes years ago. They ate the dead passengers, didn't they.

It was only meat, wasn't it? Humans are only meat.

He wondered what it was like to be a zombie with a craving for human flesh.

Maybe it wouldn't be too bad. So he decided that if things got desperate, he'd lie down somewhere and let them have him.

He moaned with anguish at the thought.

The pain of being eaten alive would be awful. He'd seen it happen and heard the victims scream, their flesh being ripped away by teeth, by hands.

And he imagined how that would feel.

He put his hand in his mouth and bit on the fleshy part between his thumb and forefinger.

And he kept biting, teeth scoring the flesh.

He had to stop. It hurt too much. Teeth marks formed an arc on his skin.

"That's nothing, Craig," he told himself, "nothing to being chewed by a zombie."

A zombie wouldn't stop when it hurt. It would bite till it was through your flesh, and then rip you to open, eat your insides, snap your bones – and you might still be alive when it was feeding on you.

And not just one zombie: three, four, five of them at you, taking chunks out of you. Tearing off strips of meat. Scooping out guts.

He whimpered, and his skin goosefleshed.

Maybe being a zombie would be okay – he wouldn't know better.

But becoming one – that was the horrifying part.

He'd have to stay human. He'd have to eat bugs. He'd have to –

A dismembered leg draped over a road sign reading Whiteford Road. Rows of redbrick, detached houses with driveways and little lawns out front stood apparently empty. Blood coated pathways and smeared windows. Cars had been left with their doors open. Cases lay on the pavements, clothes spilling out of them.

He drove round the corner and saw the first zombies. They were dead. Mutilated and crushed. Blood and entrails everywhere. A trail of them led along the street. For some reason, it reminded Craig of the Hansel and Gretel story his mum read to him when he was small. In the story, the kids laid a trail of breadcrumbs to guide them out of the forest. This was like a twisted version of that story with body parts replacing the bread.

He inched out of a junction – and hit the brakes.

Down the road, Art's Scania mounted the pavement. Half a dozen other trucks were parked across the road, blocking a crossroads.

Craig narrowed his eyes and listened.

He heard voices in the distance, men laughing.

Holding his breath, he stepped out of the Shogun, careful not to make a sound.

284

He was shaking, gripping the shotgun tightly. He sneaked down the road, skirting the cars that lined the pavement.

The men's voices grew clearer. He heard bottles clinking. A gun fired, and Craig flinched. But the men laughed louder.

Craig ducked behind a car. He peered between two lorries. A group of truckers lounged in the front garden of the house on the corner of the crossroads. They sat on wooden benches, had their feet up on garden tables. They were drinking. A green Heineken bottle glinted in the sun as a fellow in a stained, white vest lifted the beer to his lips.

Craig rose up, craning his neck.

He opened his mouth in shock: the guy in the vest was Art.

The lorry driver leaned against the garden fence, talking to another man, both of them guzzling beer.

Craig checked the shotgun. His hands shook with fear. He wiped his palms on his shirt to get rid of the sweat. But once he'd done that and started checking the gun once more, the perspiration came out of his hands again. He dried them a second time.

He unhinged the shotgun's break-action and slid cartridges into the breech, then latched the barrel again. He tapped his pocket, making sure he had the extra shot.

And then he crouched behind the car, frozen.

He had no idea what to do.

What are you planning, Craig? he thought.

Crash in there, shooting?

He didn't stand a chance. They were armed, too. And they were probably better with guns than he was. And where was Sam? Maybe she wasn't here at all. Maybe Art had raped her and killed her and dumped her body.

The thought of her dead tightened his chest.

His bloody sister. Pain in the neck. His little sister. Love for her burned in his breast. Tears welled at the thought of her being abused and murdered by Art, by those men.

And Craig recognized, for the first time, what he was feeling: *Empathy*.

That's what the anger management counsellor had called it. *Empathy*.

He hadn't known at the time. He'd never experienced it before. Never thought how others felt. He didn't give a shit, to be honest.

Whatever, he'd said.

"Do you know what empathy is, Craig?" the AM counsellor had said and crossed her legs so her skirt went up a bit. And he'd smirked and had a look, and she'd scowled and stood. Sauntered over to get water from the cooler. She'd sat back down and kept her legs together then, her knees tight, her skirt locked around them

And again she'd asked, "Do you know what empathy is?"

And he'd said, "I know what cunt is," and he'd poked his tongue out and flicked it around.

She'd told him his behaviour wasn't particularly mature, was it. Mature?

Stupid word for toeing the line.

Craig said, "Don't give a shit. I do what I want." Like Nacker did what he wanted. Like KP, too.

Fuck off to mature.

He'd told her, "I don't give a shit about anyone, 'cause no one gives a shit about me."

"I understand how you feel," she'd said.

He'd smirked again and said, "Yeah, I feel like this," and pantomimed squeezing a pair of breasts with his hands.

She'd got up then and rang the bell, and two burly blokes came in. "I'm sorry, Craig, but you can't behave like this," she'd told him. "There are recriminations. You can think about what you've done now, and we'll talk again in an hour."

And they took him back to the cell, despite him struggling and even crying.

But during those sessions with the counsellor and her legs, he'd not understood empathy.

Until now.

Here, in this blood-soaked, zombie-ravaged housing estate where a gang of truckers were maybe holding his sister hostage.

Of all the places, he thought. *Of all the places to… grow up.*

But all that didn't help him think up a plan.

What *did* help was seeing the sun splinter off one of the vehicles. It was a cattle truck with ventilation slits in the side.

And poking through those slits, clawing at the air from inside the lorry, were dozens and dozens of hands.

CHAPTER 50.
NO SALVATION.

SANDRA screamed and tried to scoop up Hettie and Maisie as the Mark-zombie lunged for them. But she stumbled and bumped into the kids. They fell down, shrieking. Sandra lost her balance, tripping over her feet.

The children screamed for their mum.

And their Uncle Mark, now a zombie, darted after them.

Vincent threw himself at the creature. Shouldered it and sent it reeling into Patty. Patty and the zombie hit the floor in a bundle. Screams echoed through the small chapel.

Vincent dashed forward. Reached for the Mark-zombie. The creature scrabbled like an animal trying to right itself. The mouth snapped and the hands clawed at Vincent.

The zombie got a hold of his arm.

Vincent tried to pull it free, but the zombie had him. It frothed at the mouth, its jaws gaping, going in for the bite.

Vincent cried out, the creature's teeth inches from his arm. He kneed the monster in the face. The zombie grunted and loosened its grip. Vincent pulled free. Grabbed Patty and dragged her to safety and hoisted her to her feet. He shoved her towards Bert, who spread his arms and backed away, as if he didn't want to touch his wife.

The zombie launched itself at Vincent.

Gavin and Roger picked up the alter table. They charged at the zombie. Slammed the table into the creature's midriff, and it went flapping across the chapel.

"Smash the table up and use it as weapons" said Gavin, and he and Roger threw it down on the stone floor.

The wood splintered. Jagged timber scattered. Vincent clutched a sharpened stake. Wheeled round to face the zombie.

The creature had found its feet again. It fixed its blank, dead gaze on the nearest human – the nearest food source.

Sandra shrieked.

She was saying, "Mark! Mark, it's me, for God's sake! Mark!"

The zombie sprang for her.

Vincent lunged and drove the sharpened table leg into the zombie's ear. The stake pierced bone and brain. The creature writhed. Blood shot from the wound.

The zombie snapped its head from side to side. Clawed at the stake. Yowled like a wounded animal. Foamed at the mouth, the saliva pink with blood. It whirled around the chapel.

Sandra screamed, and the children shrieked.

Gavin and Roger, brandishing weapons from the broken table, battered the zombie around the head.

Sandra shouted "No! No!" but they didn't listen.

Vincent turned away. He caught Holly's eyes. She cowered in the corner. Flinched with every thud as the oak crushed the zombie's skull. He watched her until she became still, until silence fell. Nothing to hear except for whimpering children and panting men.

Vincent took his gaze from Holly.

The Mark-zombie's remains lay on the floor. Its head was pulped. The skull had split, and brain matter oozed out.

Vincent glanced at Patty, and anger flashed in his chest. "I thought he was saved," he said to her.

Derek rose and said, "I thought I was."

* * * *

They burned Mark's remains.

The carcass sizzled and cooked, spewing black smoke. A dozen crows perched on the walls of the inner ward. They croaked, waiting for the corpse to cool.

"News has spread that there's easy pickings here, eh?" Vincent said to the birds.

The crows watched.

"They'll be the only things left alive," said Gavin.

"What do you mean?"

"Scavengers. Crows. Rats. Cockroaches. Dogs, maybe."

"And zombies."

"I wonder what happens when the food runs out. When there are no more humans left for them to kill and eat. I wonder if they starve."

"Maybe they eat each other."

They said nothing for a minute.

And then Vincent asked, "So you think this'll wipe out humans, then?"

"Well, I'm not known for my optimism, that's true, but I don't hold much hope for humanity, no."

"So do you think there's a point in us trying to get out?"

"Really, no. But it keeps us busy. I don't have much to live for now, but – "

He trailed off, biting his lip.

Vincent felt uncomfortable, but he thought he should say something. "How long… you know… you and Neil?"

"We'd been together ten years. We got married last year. This is sort of our honeymoon. Sailing around the coast of Britain." He put his head down and sobbed, his body shaking. Vincent put his hand on the man's shoulder.

Gavin said, "I want you to… "

Vincent squirmed.

And then Gavin dug in his pocket, brought out a bunch of keys. He filed through them, showed one to Vincent and said, "It's for our boat. She's called Flower Of The East – don't ask. She's down there, just floating on anchor. You'll see her. She's got an outboard motor, and it's padlocked. You'll need the key. Take the key. Take the key, Vincent."

"No, no – you'll – you'll need to – to skipper her when we… "

"Take the key, mate," said Gavin, and shoved it at Vincent.

"Gav, you're coming with us."

"In-fucking-case, okay. Can you do this for me?"

Vincent looked at the key. "What… what if I don't… "

"You pass it on. Just pass it on. Just make sure someone – anyone apart from those religious zealots – gets out of here."

Vincent took the key. Gavin threw his arms around him. Vincent held his breath. Gavin laid his head on his shoulder and cried.

Up on the walls, the crows croaked.

And waited for everyone to die.

CHAPTER 51.
CHOICES.

"I AM going to die," said Derek, his arm laced around Hettie's throat. "I am going to die and then get up and eat you – that's what's going to happen."

"Please let her go," said Sandra.

Maisie shrieked, seeing her sister in the stranger's grasp.

Penny had come down from the sleeping chamber with Annalee and Bryony, and they were squealing too.

The shrieks echoed around the chapel. They'd brought Vincent and Gavin back inside, Vincent tucking the key of the boat into his pocket and trying not to think about it. Trying not to think about Gavin not making it.

"We can't survive this, don't you see?" said Derek. "You should've let them come in when I opened the door. It would've been done with, then. Over. We'd have been killed, and that would've been the end of it. But you, you" – he glared at Vincent – "It was you. You interfered. I would've died. But now I'm bitten, and I *know* I'm going to be one of them, and Jesus, I don't want to *know* that. I just wanted to be dead and be done with it."

Panic laced his voice, and perspiration streamed down his face. His gaze skimmed around.

Gavin said, "What do you want us to do, Derek?"

"I wanted you to let me die. But you... you" – eyes settling on Vincent again – "you messed things up, and now... now I just have to wait as things get worse and worse and worse."

Vincent sneered. "I'm sorry for saving your life."

"You didn't save it. You extended it, that's all. Extended it into suffering and dread. Do you know how scared I am? I *know* what's going to happen to me, and do you know how terrifying that is?"

Vincent flushed. "But you were going to kill yourself. You were going to die. What difference does it make?"

"I planned to die on my own terms. Not like this. Not slowly, my mind slipping away, forgetting who I am, who my family is. I have children, you know?"

Vincent felt ashamed.

Derek went on:

"Three children. The youngest is ten. I haven't seen them in two years. My wife took them away when we split, when Claudette and I met... when that bloody scandal broke. I was planning to see them again. Make contact. Now I won't, will I. I never will."

"But you wouldn't have anyway," said Holly. "You were going to kill yourself. You were going to let those things come in here to kill us, too."

Derek quavered. Blood caked around the wound in his throat.

"I was going to die with my children in my head. I'd prepared myself. Don't you get that? My own terms. Waiting there at the door, my kids in my thoughts. Now, I won't know them. I'm already forgetting their faces. They're fading from my memory. Like Polaroids in reverse. And as for killing you – I was doing you a favour. You're going to die anyway. All of you. Those undead things out there will either kill you, or you will starve to death in here. Either way, it won't be pleasant."

"You should've let us choose how we die, Derek," said Vincent.

Derek's face twisted with anger. "And you should've let me choose how I die."

Silence fell. Vincent's shoulders slumped. Maybe Derek was right. Vincent had denied him the right to die in his own way.

But then Patty said, "The young man was right. He had to make a choice. If you don't like what he did, then I'm sure he is sorry. You can't always choose when to die. You can't choose when to live, either."

Derek said, "You told me I was saved."

She lowered her gaze. "Maybe I was wrong. I hope I'm not, for my own soul. But maybe I'm wrong. Maybe you're doomed, Derek, and that's that. I think the truth is, we are all doomed."

Derek slumped. He loosened his hold on Hettie, and she raced into her mother's arms.

Vincent didn't know what to say. He looked at Patty and nodded, because that was all he felt he could do.

She said to him, "You had a scheme, young fellow. Maybe a way for us to get out of here."

"Well... um... "

"Share it with us."

He told them what he'd found in the pit and explained what he had in mind:

"So if we can make it through, there are boats – there's... there's Gavin's boat – floating out there. We can sail off somewhere – "

"Where?" said Derek. "And am I allowed to come?"

Vincent thought for a moment.

Then he said, "I suppose we can't leave you."

Roger said, "We bloody well can. He's not coming on a boat with me and my lads if he's about to acquire a taste for flesh."

"You and the kids?" said Teena. "What about me?"

"You and all, woman. You know what I'm saying. He's not coming with us."

Vincent said, "We can't leave him. Not while he's alive."

"We'll fucking kill him, then," said Roger.

"Execute away, Roger," said Vincent. "Or your wife maybe? She can do it. She's already killed once. Derek's wife. Why not make it a couple?"

Teena said, "Don't you talk to my husband like that, lad."

"Oh, fuck off," said Vincent.

"Hey!" Roger marched forward. But Gavin stepped in front of him. Roger looked straight at Gavin. Fear spread across the ex-footballer's face. He broke eye contact and retreated.

"Are we going to do this, or not?" said Vincent.

"Is it safe?" said Bert. He cowered in the corner with his wife. They both looked deflated. Bert had been shamed by the Claudette incident, and by Gavin's kiss. Mark coming back from the dead had shaken Patty. It had dampened her religious zeal.

"I don't know," he told Bert. "I can't tell you that."

He said nothing, and waited for someone to speak. They pondered his words.

Bert spoke again:

"We're safer here, is my opinion."

"For now, maybe," Gavin said. "But we don't know what'll happen. We don't know how long we can last. We don't have much food – chocolate bars, crisps. And not much water."

Oswyn rose from his seat. "I still say we should stay, wait for the authorities. I'm convinced they will come."

"There's no authorities, is there," said Catrin.

Oswyn glared at her.

She went on:

"You've been saying that for hours, but there isn't any authorities. There's no one, Oswyn. Everyone's either dead or stuck like us."

Oswyn scowled. "Catrin, I don't think you should – "

"I think she's right," said Vincent, cutting Oswyn off. "No one's coming to save us."

Teena said, "I think our idea's a good one, then. Stay here and start a new life."

"You're off your trolley, darling," said Gavin.

"Don't you darling me, you fucking shirt-lifter. Tell him, Roger, tell him not to darling me."

But Roger didn't say anything. He wasn't going to challenge Gavin. Not again.

"You're pathetic," Teena told her husband and stomped off, taking the twins with her.

The others waited for Roger to follow his family. But he stayed where he was. He said, "Best one of us Biddens stays here and listens to you lot. Don't want you buggers running off without us."

* * * *

Vincent, Holly, Gavin, Patty, Oswyn, Roger, and Bert stood on the Gunners Walk, looking down across The Green towards the Straits. The zombies massed. They flooded forward, surging towards the castle. They clawed at the walls, snarling up at the seven humans staring down at them.

"There's fewer of them, now," said Roger. "Maybe we could make a run for it. Saves having to crawl through dark and shit."

"Still too many," said Patty. "Far too many."

"And where does your tunnel come out?" said Bert.

Vincent shared a look with Gavin. The truth was, they didn't know. He said, "Down there somewhere."

Bert's eyes widened. "Down there?"

"I told you, the pipes must've channelled the sewerage from the castle down to the river. There must be an exit."

"But that was hundreds of years ago, Vincent," said Oswyn. "I'm astonished you found your way into the pit. We thought they

296

were closed, inaccessible. And I cannot believe that any of the channels are open. Not the whole way, surely."

Vincent said nothing.

"You don't know much do you, lad?" said Roger.

Vincent said, "No I don't. I don't know anything. But we're getting sick in here. The heat'll kill us, or the zombies will kill us, or starvation or thirst – or we'll kill each other – "

"Man can go forty days without food," said Patty.

"Man wouldn't feel too good if he did, though," said Gavin. "Vincent's right. We're dead if we stay."

They looked down at the zombies in the moat. The creatures were sodden. They tried to clamber up the wall.

"This heat doesn't slow them down, does it," said Holly. "You'd think they'd flag after a while. Just seems to make them stronger. Where d'you think the rest of them have gone?"

"Gone looking for food, is my guess," Bert said. "Looking for more of us – ones of us who are not holed up in a castle."

"Bert was right," said Roger. "We are safer in here."

"But where do we get supplies?" said Vincent.

Roger looked out over the town and squinted. Sweat poured down his face. His skin was terracotta in colour.

"I don't know, do I. You seem to be the one with the bright ideas," he said to Vincent and then looked at the others. "Maybe we'll have to start eating each other, just like me and the wife suggested earlier. I know it were mad, but this is a mad world we're living in. I don't want to eat any human, but if it meant I lived, well… " He shrugged and loped off.

"Maybe he's right," said Oswyn.

"What?" said Vincent. "Have each other for breakfast?"

"Are you going to do the killing, Oswyn?" said Gavin.

"Killing?"

"Well, yes," Gavin told Oswyn. "Unless you're suggesting we eat each other *alive* – just like those zombies down there are

297

doing. I don't think that'd be palatable, personally. You'd have to do some skinning, as well. And gutting. You ever gutted an animal, Oswyn?"

Oswyn blustered and shook.

They were quiet, everyone thinking about things. Mulling over Vincent's escape route, maybe. Or brooding on Roger's scheme for cannibalism.

Vincent said, "So what do we do?"

Bert stared over the town, which was teeming with zombies. "Let people choose. Let people make their own judgments. If they want to go with you, then that's okay. If they don't, let them stay."

CHAPTER 52.
THE SEVEN.

"I MUST go back, please," said Helen Murray.

They'd barely made twenty miles, and the going was slow. Abandoned vehicles clogged the roads, and the convoy had to thread its way through the gridlock. Not much of a convoy by then, really. They'd lost two vehicles on the way. One had been over-run by zombies and the other had disappeared. Shot down a slip road when no one was looking, Terry had said.

Now, they'd stopped at a service area on the M80 and were raiding the garage for fuel, food, and water.

There were seven of them:

Terry and Helen. A six-foot-seven drag queen named Gary, or Greta Tease, as her flyers declared. His manager, Duncan, who shouldn't have put a shirt and tie on that morning, because the sweat had made the material transparent, and his flab showed through. Three American teenagers – Dayna, Ryan, and Jaime-Ann – were also part of the convoy. They were touring Europe in a VW camper van that had been owned by Dayna's grandfather in the Sixties. Her rich daddy had flown it over especially for Dayna and her friends to trek the continent – just like he'd done in the 1980s.

They were nice kids, and Helen pined for Craig to be like them. She thought about her children and sobbed, realizing she'd been a bad mother. And now she'd lost them all – Craig, Sam, and Carrie.

Helen had always harboured hopes of a reunion with her first child, her abandoned child. A reunion and forgiveness. But not now. Not with the world falling apart.

"It looks all clear out there," said Dayna. The girl, a slim, pretty auburn-haired cheerleader-type, peered through the door of the service station.

Helen told Terry again, "I must go back."

He munched on a pasty. Crumbs rained from his mouth. He spoke while he ate: "Why's that, huh? For them? Nah! They're fine. They're safe, I'm telling you. It's for the best. You want to go back for you, Helen. To make yourself feel better. For abandoning them."

"I haven't abandoned them – you have."

"It's in your nature. You abandoned the first, and you'll abandon these two."

"I want to go back."

"Aye, I said – for yourself, not for them."

"For them, you bastard – "

"Excuse me." It was Gary. "Are you two all right over there?"

"Fuck off, queer," said Terry.

"Excuse me, darling, I'm not queer, I'm camp," said Gary, hands on hips, mincing.

Terry tossed the pie's wrapper aside and squared up.

Gary baited him:

"But I know quite a few lovely boys, if you're that way inclined."

"No," said Helen as Terry strode towards the tall man.

Duncan stood in Terry's way and held out his hands. "No, please, we mustn't fight among our – "

Terry headbutted him. Duncan slumped. Gary gawped and reared away. Ryan rushed forward. Muscles rippled on the American boy's lean, bronzed frame, and Helen caught herself looking a little too hard at his body. Ryan blocked Terry's way and said, "No, sir, please. Please don't," and then he looked over his shoulder at Gary: "You too, sir, please. Let's try to get along."

"I'll cut your cock off," said Terry to Gary.

Ryan said, "Hold it, sir, please," and held Terry back.

Duncan groaned and sat up, blood streaming from his nose.

"My children are out there," said Helen. "I've got to go back."

"Yours are the ones Art took in his cab?" said Gary.

Helen nodded.

"I'm sure they'll be fine," said Gary, helping Duncan to his feet.

Dayna, at the door with Jaime-Ann, said, "Hey guys, we have to make a move. I can see those things. Please."

Helen and Gary went to the door. He was amazingly tall. She glanced up at him, craning her neck. And then she looked outside and held her breath.

Seven zombies prowled through the car park. They headed for the garage. They peered into cars, drooling.

Dayna said, "Please, we must leave now."

Helen glanced over at Terry. He was drinking Carlsberg from the cooler cabinet. The smell of beer wafted over to her and it sparked memories: Terry staggering home, raging. Barging into the house and threatening her, calling her a slag. Lunging for her and striking her, Helen hitting him back, and whole thing escalating into a brawl.

No wonder Craig had turned out like he did.

"Oh my God," said Jaime-Ann, her cowboy hat casting a shadow over her face. "Ryan, we've got to go." She opened the door as the zombies stalked the garage forecourt – and twenty more appeared in the distance, cresting the slope separating the service area from the motorway.

Jaime-Ann opened the door.

Gary said, "No!" and lunged for the girl.

Ryan rushed past him, shoving him out of the way, and tried to grab Jaime-Ann.

But she was out of the door.

Helen put her hands to her face and opened her mouth to scream, but no sound came from her throat.

The heat seared her face. The zombies growled and quickened their pace.

Dayna, screaming, stormed out after Jaime-Ann.

Ryan followed.

Jaime-Ann was half way to the VW when a zombie caught her.

The creature and the girl struggled as more undead surged towards them and towards Dayna and Ryan.

Gary screamed for them to come back inside.

Helen felt panic race through her.

"Shut the door! Shut the door!" she was screaming, and she threw herself against it.

Jamie-Ann stumbled and collapsed in a heap, the zombie on top of her. It bit into her arm. The girl squealed.

Dayna charged and kicked the zombie in the head. The creature fell away.

Dayna grabbed Jaime-Ann and dragged her to her feet. Her arm poured blood. She screamed, her face sheet-white.

Gary opened the door and raced out. His long, thin legs carried him quickly across the forecourt.

Ryan wrestled with a zombie, trying to keep the monster's teeth away from his face.

Gary grabbed a bucket and slammed it across the zombie's head.

More zombies poured into the forecourt now, sweeping down from the motorway.

Dayna and Jaime-Ann stumbled towards the garage building.

"Open the door," said Duncan.

Helen went to open it.

Then something hit her. Something heavy that sent her staggering. Her head swimming, she turned.

It was Terry.

He'd barged into her and slammed the door shut.

He stood there, not opening it.

The kids wailed and screamed outside, banging on the glass.

"We can't let them in – she's infected," he said.

Duncan said, "Open the door, you bastard."

"Shut your face, or I'll smash it again."

The girls clawed at the door and begged for someone to open it.

The zombies flooded the forecourt.

Gary pulled Ryan away, and they ran for the garage door now, too, the zombies corralling them.

Terry said, "We're safe here," and he stared into Jaime-Ann's tear-stained eyes. "They can't get – "

Helen smashed him over the head with a Coke bottle. He sagged and hit the floor, knocked out for a few seconds.

Helen dropped the bottle and opened the door.

The girls spilled in, their shrieks filling the garage.

Gary shoved Ryan ahead of him. They stumbled through the door, pushing Helen aside. They all tripped over each other, scattering shelves, skidding along the tiled floor.

The door stood open and unattended.

The zombies were ten yards – seven yards – five yards away.

Helen's innards turned into liquid. Fear froze her to the spot. They were coming in.

Helen screamed. Found strength somewhere. Threw herself at the door. Slammed it shut, slicing off a zombie's fingers. She felt the impact as the other monsters rammed the door.

She shrieked, tiptoeing around the twitching digits.

Ryan locked the door.

303

Zombies surrounded the garage. They pressed their faces against the windows. Spit and blood smeared the glass. Their hands tapped and clawed, trying to get at the food inside.

Jaime-Ann screamed. Blood soaked her arm. Dayna tried to comfort her.

Ryan said, "We need to disinfect it *now*."

"See what you've done, you bitch."

Helen cringed and turned towards the voice.

Terry rose. His face darkened. Blood dribbled from his hairline where she'd struck him.

He said again, "See what you've done? You've murdered us all. You've murdered us. See her?" – he pointed at Jaime-Ann – "She'll turn. That girl will turn. She'll turn and infect us all."

CHAPTER 53.
THE BISHOP.

SAWYER nudged her awake. She blinked, and the sun's glare blinded her for a few seconds. A sour taste in her mouth made her grimace. Gore and blood streaked the car's windows, and she remembered where she was, then.

She sat up in the back seat. She leaned forward, saw the shotgun lying on the passenger seat. The car had stopped, and Sawyer stared ahead.

A dozen men blocked the road. They were gathered near vehicles – trucks, mostly, and pinned to the bonnets were heads.

Just like the head on the Jag's bonnet.

"Where are we?" she said.

"Hornsey Park Road."

Close to home. Close to Mya.

"They're… they're human, aren't they," she said, regarding the men.

He said nothing.

"What are they doing?" she said

"It looks like a road block – or a checkpoint."

"Are they soldiers?"

"They're not soldiers."

Sawyer had stopped the car at the junction of Turnpike Lane and Hornsey Park Road.

On the corner stood a lighting and china shop called Angelo's. Human remains lay outside the store.

On the other side of the road, a tower block painted sky blue cast its shadow across abandoned vehicles.

The men and their cars blockaded the route at the junctions with Clarendon Road and The Avenue. From what Carrie could see, the men had guns.

"This isn't good, is it," she said.

"I don't think it is, no."

"We should go. Go back up Turnpike Lane, then we can – "

"Hey there, Brogan," said a voice.

Carrie froze. She turned her head slowly. A bearded man wearing a pair of football shorts and an Arsenal bobble hat – and nothing else – came towards the car. Sweat poured down his chest, over his heavy belly. He carried a handgun, and an airhorn was clipped to the waistband of his shorts.

The man leaned to peer through the Jag's bloodstained window

Sawyer kicked open the door, smashing the man in the face, and he slumped to the ground.

Carrie leapt out of the Jaguar.

Sawyer pounced on the grounded man. But the fellow snatched his airhorn and let off a blast.

Carrie flinched.

The men in the blockade ran towards her.

"Don't move," said the bearded man, pointing his gun at Sawyer.

"Can you shoot that thing?"

"Do you want to find out?"

"Carrie," said Sawyer, "get back in the car and drive – go."

306

The bearded man smiled. "You do that, darling. Just do that. And I'll shoot your boyfriend, here."

"Go, Carrie."

Carrie didn't move. "I'm staying with you."

"Ah, there's love for you," said the bearded man and got to his feet, his belly quivering.

His companions approached, four of them, all armed.

The bearded man said to them, "That's Brogan's car. Brogan and his son."

The armed quartet parted, and a man wearing a stained, white vest and a priest's dog collar stepped forward. Tattoos of religious icons covered his thin arms. He nudged his sunglasses up his nose and spat.

He said, "Where's Brogan and Barry?"

Sawyer said, "Who are you?"

The bearded man stepped forward, jabbing his pistol at Sawyer, and said, "You answer the bish', you fucking – "

The man with tattoos interrupted him and said, "It's all right, Fred, let me answer the man. I'm Gordon Drake, my friend. I'm a bishop of the Church of the Event of Resurrection."

"Never heard of you," said Sawyer.

"No, we're new. These are days for new religions. The old ones didn't work, did they. See where they got us?" he said, and made a gesture with his arm. "We come to God in different ways, now."

Carrie said, "I'm going to find my daughter. She lives in Wood Green – "

"Shut up," said Drake. "Women don't talk."

"What did you – "

"I told you to shut up, darling," said Drake. He swivelled his head towards Sawyer. "Now, Mr Brogan and his lovely young son, Barry… whereabouts would they be, my friend?"

"They've converted to another religion," said Sawyer.

Drake smiled. "I know where they are: they're dead, ain't they." He put a finger to his temple. "I can read minds, see. I can see the truth."

"God speaks to the bish'," said Fred, the bearded man in the Arsenal hat.

"Which god?" said Sawyer.

Drake knitted his brow. "The god that says you and your bitch killed them, and killing humans carries a grave sentence."

"Please," said Carrie. "Let us go. My daughter, she's six, and she's on her own – "

"And she'll turn out to be a mouthy cow like her mother, if you ask me," said Drake. "Better she be eaten, made into one of those devils. Then we can cut her head off and stick it on a stake, eh?"

The men laughed.

"You bastard," said Carrie.

The laughter stopped.

Drake hissed. He wheeled and strode away.

"What shall we do with them, bish'?" said Fred.

"Burn them," said Drake as he walked off, "and don't call me 'bish'"."

CHAPTER 54.
YOU'RE A FOOL, BERT RIPLEY.

VINCENT threw up his arms and said, "That's crazy – you can't do that."

"Can't? Why 'can't'? You can't stop us," said Teena.

"But it's madness. You're committing suicide."

"No more suicide than going through those tunnels – by heck, you don't even know if they're clear or not. They might be clogged up with the shit of old kings and peasants, for all you know."

"But, Teena, you can't go – "

"I'm not." She folded her arms. "My husband is. And Oswyn, and all. They're going."

"And us, Mum," said one of the twins.

"Shut your gob, Jack. You and Bobby are staying here."

"You can't get further than the bridge, I'm telling you," said Vincent. "You won't even reach the road."

"We'll have to see, won't we," said Roger.

"Stupid, that's what it is – crazy, stupid," said Vincent.

Roger scowled. "And as the wife said, as stupid as crawling

through old filth."

Oswyn spoke then:

"There are vehicles out there. If we can get to one of them, we can get help."

"From your authorities, Oswyn?" said Vincent.

"There has to be someone out there."

"There is, but they'll want to eat you before helping you." Vincent blew air out of his cheeks. He looked into Holly's eyes and wondered what she thought. She tried to smile but didn't pull it off. The sun had scalded her brow.

He held her hand. It was clammy. But that didn't matter. Holding her hand, however wet and sticky it felt, made everything all right for a moment. A moment when this wasn't happening. When there weren't zombies roaming around. When Teena wasn't proposing a breeding programme. When Roger wasn't on about eating people. When Patty wasn't predicting the apocalypse.

When there was only Holly and him.

The pair of them left the chapel, wended their way along the wall passages. The walkways wormed through the castle's inner curtain walls. Hundreds of years ago, they'd have been used to link the towers. Now they provided Vincent and Holly with privacy. They sat on the stone floor, backs against a wall.

The mugginess made it hard to breathe. Vincent wanted a drink. He shut his eyes and imagined himself supping a cool lager in the Victoria's beer garden. That'd be fine, just now.

Holly hugged him, pressing her face to his chest.

"I'm scared of the tunnel, Vincent."

He stroked her hair. Her scalp was damp with sweat.

"So am I," he said.

"That doesn't help, does it." She looked up at him, and her mouth quivered into a makeshift smile. "My knight in shining armour shouldn't be shitting himself."

"Well, he is."

He kissed her, and her lips were dry, and she smelled of sweat, but he liked that. It was familiar to him. It was Holly's smell, Holly's touch. Even if she'd been an ugly old hag, he'd still kiss her – because she was Holly.

He shook his head. His mind reeled. He felt dizzy and sick. All kinds of things went through his mind, spiralling and crisscrossing and tangling together. It made him light-headed, and he thought he might be suffering heatstroke.

Holly furrowed her brow. "You okay?"

He gasped. "I'm fine. Hot, that's all."

She didn't say anything. He tried to relax, focusing on her, now.

Then he said, "I can't make you come, but I won't go if you don't."

He looked her in the eye. In his head, he wanted her to say, *I'll come with you.*

But he'd said it now – said he'd stay if she stayed. Gave her a get-out that she was bound to take.

And he *would* stay, too. He wasn't just saying it. No matter how desperate he was to get out of here, he'd stay if she stayed.

Stay in this old place and die with her.

"I'll come with you," she said, her voice very small and weak.

* * * *

"You're a fool, Bert Ripley," said Patty. "You're a fool, and Jesus doesn't love a fool."

"I have to do this, Patty. I can get a car. Maybe I can get to a phone that works and call Mike in California, and he can arrange the helicopter or something. I'm doing this for you, honey."

"No you're not," she said. "You're doing it for yourself. You're doing it because you feel guilty about letting that woman take it in

311

her mouth. *That* is why you're going. You are running away, Bert Ripley, and Jesus knows it." Patty shivered, and tears streamed down her cheeks. "This is foolishness. You will die. And unless they eat every piece of you, Bert – and there's a lot of you to eat – you will likely rise up from the dead again and come looking for me."

"I won't do that, Patty. I'd still be scared of you, then."

She ran up to him and grabbed his shirt and shook him, and said, "For God's sake, Bert, don't go out there."

He gestured to Holly, who came and ushered Patty away.

The three men stood by the entrance.

"If you're going," said Vincent, "run as fast as you can for the nearest car. There's a BT van near the railings. You've got to chance it that the keys are still inside. Get in, and slam the doors."

He grabbed Holly's hand, and they went up to the Gunners Walk to watch.

"The bridge is clear," Vincent shouted, and then to Holly he said, "But I don't know how long it'll be like that."

They heard the creak of the wooden door opening.

Vincent shook with fear.

Holly said, "They're going to get killed, aren't they."

Zombies prowled the street. They turned and looked towards the castle. They snarled, their faces creasing. They began to drool, their mouths making that biting motion. They propelled themselves into the castle grounds. Thronged along the path that led towards the bridge. Churned through the moat.

They know, thought Vincent. *They know the gates are opening.*

Terror flushed his veins.

"Oh, Jesus!" he said. "They know! They know!"

CHAPTER 55.
KILLER.

CARRIE wriggled, trying to loosen the nylon rope. She and Sawyer had had their hands cuffed behind their backs, and then they'd been tied to chairs.

Sweat poured off her, dripping to the floor. The room, empty apart from the wooden chairs they'd been bound to, smelled of damp. Cobwebs hung across the blacked out windows. Mice droppings peppered the sill. It was like an oven in here, and Carrie felt as though she were being baked alive.

When he'd left them tied to the chairs, Fred in his football shorts and Arsenal bobble hat had said, "Get ready for your big performance. You're the main event, see. The X-Factor."

Carrie thrashed. The handcuffs cut into her wrists. Nothing moved. Nothing came undone. She was stuck fast. She threw her head back and sobbed.

"It's okay," said Sawyer.

She looked straight at him, and his eyes narrowed and glittered like they'd done when he was on the bed with her.

Something stirred inside her. And again the shame rose up in her belly, and she squirmed. She looked away.

"What is it with you?" he said.

She didn't answer.

He went on:

"You're all over me in that house but now it's like I'm against you or something – like you want to get rid of me. Do I make your skin crawl?"

She shook her head and flicked it to clear the hair from her face. She licked her lips, and they tasted salty.

"It wasn't you, it was me. I felt dreadful, not because – not because of what we did but" – she blushed – "the circumstances… it's Mya. She's out there and I – I – I behaved like some slut."

"We couldn't have gone anywhere, Carrie. We were stuck in that house."

"We could've not… done it. *I* could've not done it."

"Did you want not to do it?"

"Not… not that… we… I shouldn't have… not I didn't *want* to, oh God… I shouldn't – "

"Oh for fuck's sake – "

"What?"

"You can go your own way when we find Mya, all right. You won't see me again. I'll leave you to it. You can pick up the next guy, bed him too, see if he helps you."

"You bastard," she said.

She jerked her chair towards him. Kicked him in the shin.

He flinched and said, "Ow, ow," but she kept kicking.

Her chair rocked. She kept missing his legs, kicking at the chair legs instead.

He shouted at her to stop.

Carrie ignored him. Anger pulsed through her. She pitched on the chair. She toppled over. Gawped and felt herself fall and could do nothing. Her shoulder slammed to the floor. Pain shot through her arm, up into her neck.

The chair splintered.

She loosened herself from the ropes.

"Carrie," he said, "roll away," and she rolled away, freed from the chair.

Footsteps came down from outside. They both looked at the door, then at the wrecked chair.

"You've got to get the key off them," said Sawyer.

"Me?"

"Yes, you. Get your hands out in front of you. Can you slip them under your arse?"

"What?"

"Try, Carrie."

The footsteps approached.

She sat and lifted her legs. She eased her arms down, her hands slipping under her bottom, her bottom rising off the floor.

She slid her handcuffed wrists passed her knees. Scooted them down her legs, under her feet. Sat there staring at her hands as if she'd never seen them before.

"Impressive," he said, not sounding like he meant it. "Now get a move on – someone's coming."

She rose off the floor and went to stand behind the door.

"What do I do?"

The door opened and a voice was saying, "Last supper coming up," and Carrie smelled burgers.

Sawyer made a face at her.

Fred came in and stopped, and he looked at Sawyer.

Carrie stared at the back of Fred's head. He had a thick neck and the skin peeled on his bald pate.

Sawyer said, "Smells nice."

Fred said, "Where's the – "

Carrie looped her hands over his head.

The chain on the handcuffs bit into his throat.

She pulled, forcing her knee into his back.

He dropped the tray, and it clattered, and food and drink spilled.

315

He backed up, forcing her against the wall. He squashed her, and she balked at being so close to him, squirming and crying.

Fred lurched away and clawed at the chain. She held on and wrenched, choking him. He gurgled, and she shut her eyes, not wanting to think what she was doing.

Mya, she thought, *I'm doing this for Mya... Mya... Mya...*

Sawyer kicked Fred's legs from under him. The man stumbled and toppled on his face. Dust rose from the floorboards when he struck them. Carrie fell on top of him.

Fred croaked and squirmed. He scrabbled his legs across the floor. Carrie held on tight, pulling.

She looked up at Sawyer and said, "How long am I suppose to do this?"

"Till he's dead."

Her bones chilled, and for a second she slackened her grip. Fred coughed and tried to roll over on his back. Carrie bucked, losing her balance.

Sawyer said, "No," but it was too late. Fred rolled quickly and shoved Carrie away. His face was purple. Saliva poured from his mouth. A gash collared his throat where the chain had dug in.

"You bitch," Fred said, his voice like sandpaper.

He went to get up but Sawyer booted him in the face. The man sagged.

Carrie, without thinking, grabbed a knife that had fallen from the tray.

She raised it and, realizing what she was doing, tried to stop herself. But she couldn't. The blade arced downwards towards Fred's neck, and it sank into his nape, hitting something hard, which Carrie knew was bone. She gritted her teeth and shut her eyes and drove the knife into the muscle and sinew and gristle.

Fred convulsed. He rolled over again, tossing Carrie off his back. His mouth gaped, and blood came up from his throat. His eyes bugged, and his face had purpled. He twitched and clawed at the back of his neck. He spluttered, and blood sprayed from his nose.

Carrie couldn't move. Sawyer spoke to her. Something about keys. But her eyes wouldn't leave Fred.

He arched his back and gasped.

Carrie smelled piss.

He wilted and became still.

"Carrie, the key," said Sawyer.

But she still stared at Fred.

"The key, Carrie."

She said nothing.

"Carrie – "

She found her voice then:

"I've killed him."

"Get the key."

"I've killed him. I've killed him."

"The fucking key."

"Oh my God, I've killed him."

"You killed him for Mya, Carrie. The key."

* * * *

Carrie unlocked Sawyer's cuffs then gave him the key. She kneeled on the floor, drained of energy.

"Come on," he said, "let me," and he unlocked her cuffs. He kissed her brow. "It was him or us, Carrie. Him or Mya."

"Don't say that."

"It's true. They'd've killed us. They'll still kill us if we don't get out of here."

The corridor was dimly lit. They waited and listened. Muffled voices came from behind a door.

317

"Can you hear what they're saying?" she asked in a whisper.

He put his finger to his mouth and then led her past the door. As they went by, she heard someone say, "…burn that pair…" and she moved past the door, her guts quailing.

A fire exit lay at the far end of the corridor. Sunlight spilled in through the gap at the bottom of the door. She wondered what time it was. They'd taken her phone before tying her up, so she had no way of telling the time. It still felt early to her, though. She hoped she was in time for Mya. Hoped her daughter had gone down into the basement, into the darkness she feared. The darkness that made her cry. The darkness that made her cry for her –

"Mummy… "

Carrie's heart stopped.

She wheeled round.

"Mummy," said the blonde girl, "the devils are getting away."

The child pointed at them, scowling.

Carrie stared at the girl.

A woman appeared behind the child.

The woman screeched.

CHAPTER 56.
ZOMBIES UNLEASHED.

CRAIG crept alongside the HGVs, eyes fixed on the hands poking through the vents in the cattle truck up ahead. The thought of those people crammed into the trailer made his skin crawl.

As he sneaked along, he noticed that all the trucks had their cab doors open. It was probably to release the heat. Most of the vehicles would have had air-con. But the temperatures today were intense. And getting into the driver's seat after the door had been shut would've been like stepping into an oven. Any fresh air that could be circulated was going to be helpful

Craig reached Art's Scania. He stepped up on the footrest and peered inside the cab. He felt the heat wash over his face and it made him squint.

Craig whispered Sam's name but no reply came. He glanced through the windscreen at the truckers. They boozed in the garden. Beer cans and bottles littered the lawn. The men laughed and joked, and two of them wrestled on the grass, the others tossing cans at them.

Craig shuffled away from the cab and checked the other trucks. The sun scorched Craig's back as he leaned into the cabs to inspect them. It was like being in a furnace. Sweat drenched him. His insides were baking. And by the time he crouched next to the cattle truck, he could hardly breathe for the heat.

A bad smell came from the lorry's trailer. He looked up at the hands dangling through the slats. He tried to speak to those inside, but he got no answer. They seemed lethargic and weak. The heat must've been severe. He didn't know how anyone could be alive in there.

"Are you okay?" he said.

No one said anything.

The hands were pale and bony, draped like rags in the sun.

"If you can hear me, my name's Craig, okay? I've got a gun here. I'm going to let you out so maybe you can help me. Rush those guys, aye? Rush them and we can all get away. There are loads of you, so we should be fine. My sister's in the house, right. I think she is. But anyway, that Art bastard, he tried to kill me, so I'm having him, okay?"

They said nothing. A rattle came from inside the truck. Someone shuffling about. He wondered if they were hostages like Sam. And then he thought she might be in there, and a chill ran down his spine.

He called for her, but again no answer came.

Why are these bastards kidnapping people? he thought.

They didn't give a shit, did they?

The counsellor had told him, "Adults have empathy, Craig. They care. They want the best for other people."

Bollocks, he told himself now.

Not the adults he'd known.

They looked after themselves. You looked after your mates, maybe. Your family. But not just any old rockit.

These truckers didn't give a damn, so why should he?

He'd release those hostages in the truck because they'd create a diversion. He wasn't doing it to help them. He wanted to make that clear in his head to anyone who might have been listening to his thoughts.

"For me," he told the people in the truck, "I'm doing this for me, not you."

He scuttled to the back of the truck. He smelled rotten meat in there. He furrowed his brow, thinking. Were they living with a dead body?

And then he thought, *Did that mean they were zombies?*

No, because they would've gone crazy when they saw him and smelled him.

He laid the gun down and then unlatched the trailer door. The door loosened. He rolled away the bars from either side. Eased the door down. Strained as the weight pressed on him.

He lowered the door, nearly dropping it, trying not to let it clank on the tarmac. He shut his eyes, fighting the pressure in his arms. Inched the door down, and rested it on the road.

He panted and looked at the figures inside the trailer.

They lurked in the darkness, glowering at him.

Craig blinked, unable to make them out.

The men in the garden laughed.

"Are you coming out?" he said to the figures in the trailer.

They stayed where they were, wavering.

But then, the front few shuffled forward. And something came undone in Craig's belly.

He picked up the gun and backed away, a cold sweat coating his back.

The first three figures lumbered down from the trailer, and the ones behind scuttled forward from the shadows inside.

The sun sliced across the trailer door and the figures stepped into its glare.

And the moment the light struck them, they stiffened. Their brows furrowed. Their eyes widened, and Craig looked into them.

Into dead eyes.

Into zombie eyes.

"Oh fuck," he said.

The creatures caught by the sun darted forward.

Craig wheeled and stumbled and ran, looking over his shoulder. More zombies loped out of the truck, and when they stepped into the light, they transformed from slugs to sprinters.

The sun energized them.

He ran, the zombies chasing him.

He hared around the truck and headed straight for the garden, and the men saw him coming.

"Jesus holy fuck!" Craig heard one of them say when he saw the zombies sweep from between the vehicles.

Art said, "You little bastard," as Craig raised the shotgun and fired at the men, forcing them to dive for cover. The impact jarred Craig's injured ribs and threw him to the ground.

Heaving for breath, he found his feet and hurdled the garden wall. The men scattered. The zombies swarmed into the garden. Craig fixed on the house's front door. It lay open. He raced towards it. Screams filled the air and the zombies mobbed the truckers.

Craig entered the dimly lit house. He shut the door. He smelled beer. The air was muggy. Shouts and screams came from outside. Someone rapped on the door, and Art's high-pitched voice said, "Jesus, laddie, help me! I helped you! Help – "

And Art screeched.

Craig raced upstairs, shouting Sam's name.

Clothes littered the first bedroom he entered. The window was shattered, and the curtain drenched in blood. He bounded across the landing into the second bedroom. Craig nearly screamed. A woman, her body coated in blood, lay sprawled on the bed.

He mouthed, "Sam," but he knew it wasn't his sister. Shaking, he backed out of the room. Kicked open a third door, terrified of what he'd find. Held his breath as the door swung open.

Boxes of booze filled the room. Crates containing bottles of beer and cider were piled high. Six-packs of Carlsberg and Stella Artois were heaped on the bed.

Craig's shoulders sagged. From outside, came screams.

And then, through the cacophony, he heard someone shout his name.

Sam!

He raced to the window. He leaned out and saw Sam standing on top of Art's cab.

"Craig! Craig, help me!" she said.

Small and blonde, her clothes stained and her face dirty, she looked like what she was – a child, his baby sister.

"Hold on, Sam," he said.

He scoped the garden and the street. Zombies devoured the truckers.

He looked at his sister again and a sense of hopelessness came over him.

How was he going to rescue her?

But however useless he felt, he said, "Hold on, I'll get to you."

She cowered on top of the gleaming red and gold Scania. The truck stood like an island in a sea of zombies. They rippled and washed against the cab, making it rock.

He stared at her and saw the desperation and the fear in her eyes, and then he scanned the undead and thought, *I can't save her – she's going to die.*

CHAPTER 57.
THE TRIO'S ESCAPE BID.

VINCENT had known from the beginning that Roger, Bert, and Oswyn weren't the best choices for this mission.

Roger had been a professional footballer who'd retired early with a knee injury. He was in his late thirties, and carried a belly around that would make a darts player proud. And he couldn't exert himself too much without resting his hands on his thighs and puffing.

Oswyn was a lump of lard. A white-fleshed, soft-bellied mound of human that wobbled when it moved.

Bert had age and weight against him. Over sixty years old, for sure, he was a big man – six-four, maybe. Unfortunately, he was six-four around the girth, as well.

The trio huffed and puffed along the narrow wooden bridge that led from the Gate Next the Sea, the entrance to the castle.

Ahead of them lay an iron gate that dangled on its hinges. Something had rammed into it, knocking it askew. The zombies could've easily poured through that gap. But instead they attacked from the men's right, flooding from the booth where you paid to get in, tearing along the path, wading through the moat.

And for that, Roger, Bert, and Oswyn should've been grateful. But not for long. Vincent could hear Oswyn wheeze as he ran – or tried to run.

Holly said, "They're not going to make it."

The zombies on The Green and down by the water's edge had sensed the trio's presence, and were streaking towards the castle.

"How do they know?" said Vincent. "Those down there, how do they know?"

Were they wired? he thought. *Were they linked in some way?*

He'd not seen evidence of that. What he'd seen were thousands of individuals going it alone.

He leaned over the Gunners Walk.

He shouted at the men to run.

Roger found an extra yard. He hurtled past Oswyn. Bert lagged behind.

He was dead, Vincent knew it.

Screams came from the Gate Next the Sea. The others watched through the murder holes.

Roger clambered through the broken gate into the road.

The BT van had mounted the pavement and ploughed into the garden opposite the castle.

That's where Roger was headed. The other two struggled to keep up. Vincent yelled out in desperation. He fixed on Roger again, bounding across the road.

Go on, he urged the man, *go on*.

But there were too many zombies. They swept towards the men. They growled, their jaws snapping open and shut, desperate to bite into something. Some of them appeared uncoordinated, wavering from side to side, arms flailing. Others stormed towards the men like guided missiles, knowing their targets.

They weren't like the zombies in the *Night Of The Living Dead* movies, those lumbering things, nor were they quite as synchronized as the hordes in the film *28 Days Later.*

They were worse. They were much, much worse.

They were real.

Roger made it to the BT van and dived in. A zombie clawed at him and grabbed his leg. Roger kicked it away. He slammed the door shut. Scrabbled around in there, probably trying to start the van.

Vincent shook with horror. Holly shrieked next to him and squatted, hiding behind the wall, not wanting to see.

Bert screamed.

Five zombies dragged him to the ground.

Patty's cries came from the Gate Next the Sea.

Bert writhed and screamed. The zombies tore chunks from his arms, his legs, his neck. They shoved one another out of the way, fighting over the best cut of human meat. More creatures barrelled into the fray. They smothered the American. All Vincent could see of him was his foot, clad in a Nike trainer, twitching.

Oswyn screeched. He'd made it out into the street, but there was nowhere to go. Zombies blocked his way.

Vincent sensed the man's terror.

Roger started the van. He swung the vehicle around, shearing through the flowers, churning up the soil.

Zombies clambered on the bonnet and then slid off and fell under the wheels, and Roger mashed them, their bodies breaking and twisting.

He drove at Oswyn.

"Go on, Oswyn," said Vincent. "Run, mate, run."

Oswyn trundled, chest heaving. His shirt flapped open. His belly juddered. Zombies corralled him. He shrieked.

The van ploughed into the undead, scattering them.

Oswyn threw himself at the van. The passenger door flung open. He crawled in. His backside and legs hung out of the door.

A zombie latched on to his thigh. Another one grabbed his foot.

Oswyn kicked them off. The van skidded on The Green. Wheels tearing at the earth and spitting up dirt. Scattering the undead.

Running over them. Blood coated the van's rims and its wheels.

Roger drove clear of the zombies and slowed, long enough for Oswyn to clamber in, shut the door.

The zombies, more of them now, those from the shore, from the town, pelted towards the van.

Roger raised his fist as if to say, *We'll be back for you* – or that's what Vincent hoped he was saying. Maybe he was saying, *Fuck you, you bastards, we're off.*

The van headed west, up Castle Street. Vincent stared after it long after the vehicle was out of sight. The engine hummed in the distance. The gears clanked. Vincent listened till there was nothing to hear.

Nothing apart from the zombies tearing Bert to pieces.

Nothing apart from Patty wailing.

CHAPTER 58.
STAYING OR GOING.

PATTY said, "I told him, I told him he shouldn't do this – I told him," and she whined and rocked back and forth.

Sandra tried to comfort her.

"I feel really sorry for her," said Vincent.

Gavin stood with him in the shadow of the north wall. "You shouldn't be. She would've had us all killed in the name of Jesus."

"I know. She's just scared, that's all. Fear makes us mad."

"Maybe she's just scared for now. Once she gets her Jesus mojo back, she'll be wanting to stone me to death again."

They fell silent. Eyed the others as they sprawled around the inner ward. The children huddled together in a circle. Even Jack and Bobby. They'd mucked around all day. But not now. Not with their dad out there.

Vincent said, "We should do this, now."

"You reckon?"

"We have to. It's three o'clock. It'll take, I don't know, a good couple of hours to crawl through. Maybe more. I've never crawled through a sewerage pipe before." He shuddered at the thought. "We don't want to be doing it when it's dark. Easier to see those things in daylight."

Gavin moaned.

"What's the matter?" said Vincent.

"The thought of those narrow channels. We don't even know how wide they are. Jesus, they might not even be clear. We could get stuck in there. Fucking hell, that shits me up more than those zombies do, I'm telling you."

"Me too. And Holly. She's claustrophobic, and that makes me sick, thinking about her in any distress."

"You know, we could wait."

"Wait for what?"

"For Roger and Oswyn."

Vincent thought about that.

Gavin shrugged. "That's what the others will want to do."

Vincent bit his lip.

"You look worried, mate," said Gavin. "What could you possibly have to worry about on such a lovely fucking day?"

"I'm only twenty, Gavin. I work in a pub. I don't have to make decisions like this. Life and death stuff. The only decision I make is when to get up and what to have for breakfast."

Gavin said, "Breakfast. A fry-up. Black pudding, fried bread. Milky tea, three sugars." He fanned his face with a sheet of pink paper.

Vincent said, "What is that?"

Gavin looked at the paper. "It's our wedding service."

Vincent grimaced. "I'm sorry."

Gavin smiled. "I think we should talk to the others."

"Yes, okay. But… but what about him?" said Vincent, gesturing.

Derek had curled up into a ball against the west wall. He shivered and groaned.

Vincent went on:

"He'll be dead soon. And then… "

329

* * * *

Teena said, "We're bloody well staying and waiting for my bloody husband, that's what we're doing."

"What about everyone else?" said Vincent. No one said anything. "Okay, who wants to go now, and who wants to wait?"

He looked at them all in turn. No one spoke. And they couldn't look him in the eye, either.

Teena shuddered with fury. "Come on you bastards, say you're staying."

"All right," said Gavin, "I'll go first. I want to stay and wait for Roger and Oswyn."

Vincent gawped at him.

Gavin raised his shoulders. "I just think we should give them a couple of hours, that's all. Then, I vote we go."

Anger flared in Vincent's breast. He'd thought of Gavin as a mate, an ally. And now he was lining up with the others.

But maybe Gavin was right. Maybe it was worth waiting for a while. He just didn't know.

He looked at Holly and said, "What about you?"

Holly's eyes flitted around. She folded her arms. "I – I don't – don't know."

"Well," said Bella, "you've got to make a decision, love."

"No, she hasn't," said Vincent. "She can wait. Anyway, what about you?"

"I vote wait," Bella said, "and so does Catrin."

"Can Catrin speak for herself?" asked Gavin.

"Not really anymore." And Bella turned and everyone followed her gaze to where Catrin sat, swaying back and forth, singing to herself.

"Patty?" said Vincent.

The sun glinted off her sunglasses. "I want to leave."

Vincent nodded, pleased he had a supporter, surprised at who it was.

330

He asked Sandra and Penny. Sandra said stay, Penny said go, adding, "I've got two kids, and they're not going to die where their dad died. I want to do everything I can to save them."

Sandra said, "My children saw their dad die here, too. But I think we should at least wait a couple of hours."

"Okay," said Vincent. He looked at his shoes. "Settles it then. Most of you want to wait."

"Only for a couple of hours," said Gavin. "We should give them a chance, you know."

Vincent nodded. "I'm just worried about the dark, that's all."

"It's light till nearly nine," said Bella.

"I know, but I don't know how long it'll take to crawl through, and then by the time we get through... " He trailed off. Shook his head. *No point in arguing*, he thought. They'd made their decision. "Okay, a couple of hours."

They were quiet for a few minutes.

And then:

"What about me?"

It was Derek, huddling in the shadows near the west wall.

He spoke again:

"No one wants to know what I think?"

"Couple of hours ago you wanted to kill us all," said Vincent.

"I still have a view, though – and it's the same. We're all going to die. But I think we should go. So if I'm allowed, Vincent, I'd like to come with you when we're ready."

Vincent chilled. He didn't want an almost-zombie near him or Holly.

Not in those tunnels.

CHAPTER 59.
DEVILS.

TERRY glowered at them, his cheeks red. Pointing at Jaime-Ann, he said, "We've got to get rid of her, I'm telling you." He drank again. On his fourth can, now.

Helen squirmed, the shame rising up from her belly to clog her chest. She wanted to tell him to be quiet, to stop drinking. But she felt a duty towards him, to be the supportive wife.

Dayna, comforting Jaime-Ann, said, "She's not going anywhere."

"She'll turn. I'm telling you, you stupid hen, she'll turn. You saw them change out there on the motorway. One minute they were dead. Next minute they got up, bright as day, hungry as fuck."

Dayna rose and scowled. "Don't you call me names, okay?"

Terry flapped a hand at her. "Oh fuck off, cow."

"Hey, fella," said Ryan.

"Don't talk to me, you fucking child, or I'll make you look like the elephant man, pretty boy."

"You think you're tough?" said the American youth. "You're just a drunk old man. You shut up before I slap you down."

"Please," said Helen, the shame bursting out of her now. "Please don't argue. Terry, stop drinking, please. Stop being like this. You've... you've got to drive."

"Oh shit, yeah," he said, "I forgot about the zombie police out there. Ready with their breathalyzers. 'Excuse me, sir, could you blow into this while I eat your brains, thank you.'"

Gary said, "We need to think of something." He was staring out into the forecourt. About fifty zombies were out there now. They were pressed up against the windows, scowling and salivating at the humans inside.

Helen tried her phone again, ringing Sam and Craig. But she got no signal. "Does anyone know why the mobile phones don't work?"

"No one knows anything, love," said Duncan, nursing the bloody nose Terry'd given him.

Gary said, "I do know we need to be thinking about how we get out."

Terry said, "Don't need queers telling us what to do."

"Or drunks," said Gary. "And, darling, I told you – I'm straight. I like women. Like your missus."

Helen saw Terry bristle and told him, "Leave it," and he did, hunching his shoulders and mumbling something.

Dayna said, "We've got food here to last a while. If we wait till they go away, we can make a run for it, get back to the vehicles."

Helen shivered and wrung her hands. "They might not go away. My children are out there."

"I'm sure they're fine," said Gary, his smile not enough to console her, but she tried to smile back.

"I've been a bad mother – "

"Aye, that's true," said Terry, now onto his fifth drink.

Helen snapped. "And you've been a worse father."

His face darkened. "Don't talk to me like that in front of these strangers."

"I just have."

"That's true," said Dayna. "She just has. But your parental skills aren't a priority here."

"No, getting rid of her is," said Terry, jabbing the bottle at Jaime-Ann. Sweat glazed her ashen face. Her eyes were red and watery. She rocked back and forth, cradling her wounded arm. Dayna had washed and dressed it with materials they'd found in the garage, and Terry said to Dayna, "Your nursing's not going to do any good, lassie. Mind you, a fucking doctor's probably caused this plague. Science gone to hell. Think they can change the world. Think they know everything. What do they know, huh? Fuck all is what they know. Look at it. Fucking look."

Dayna cocked her head to one side. "And what do you know, Mr… "

"Murray, it's Murray. It's *Mr* Murray, too."

"Okay, Mr Murray. What do you know?"

"I understand we're dead if we don't either kill your friend or chuck her outside with her kind."

Jaime-Ann cried out, and Dayna crouched next to her friend, hugging her.

"You bastard," said Ryan.

"I'm telling the truth, and you lot, you can't face up to it."

"Keep it to yourself," said the youth.

"Look, sonny, I'm not about to keep anything to myself when my life's in danger. I'm in a sharing mood when I'm threatened. You see?"

"What about your wife? She in danger?" said Ryan.

Terry grumbled.

"And your kids. They're out there, yeah? What are you doing about that, big man?"

"It's none of your fucking business, son. My kids can look after themselves. They always have. Been brought up that way. It's the way we do it, here."

"And look where it's got us," said Helen.

She sobbed, and gathered herself, continuing:

"You are a stupid, cruel man, Terry. A fool, a bully, a drunk. You've got the devil in you, and I should've seen that right at the off. I've been a useless mother to those children, but you've been a worse father. You've turned your son into yourself. You're turning our daughter into a drinker at twelve. When this is done, when it's over – we are too."

Terry laughed. "This won't be over till we're dead, woman. Till death do us part. And with those things outside, that's how it's going to be. You're stuck with me – even as zombies. And my guess is things'll be just as exciting as they've been for the last sixteen years." He drank again, beer drizzling over his chin. He rocked with laughter. "Idiots. You're all idiots. You and the rest of them."

* * * *

Sawyer clutched Carrie's arm and said, "Come on," as the woman continued to shriek, and the child said, "The devils are getting away."

They raced for the fire exit.

More voices behind Carrie now, saying, "They're getting away!"

Footsteps flooded the corridor. Men's voices filled the air, angry and loud.

Sawyer hurled himself against the fire exit. The door burst open. The sunlight poured in. Carrie blinked and stumbled down the metal stairs leading into a courtyard.

Shapes rippled in the glare. She couldn't make them out, but she kept going, following Sawyer. And then he stopped, and she bumped into him.

335

Her eyes adjusted, and she blinked again and found herself staring into Gordon Drake's grinning face.

Carrie craned her neck and looked round, trying to work out where she was. The building where they'd been imprisoned appeared to be a community hall. Graffiti festooned the prefab structure. The words warned of God's wrath and vengeance.

Carrie and Sawyer were now in the car park at the rear of the building. Beyond it, towering over wasteland, stood two gasometers. Carrie squinted and stared up at the imposing constructions. The sun made it difficult to see, but sacks seemed to be dangling from the frames. Smoke billowed from the pieces of cloth, and she was about to ask what they were.

But her mouth went dry, and her throat locked.

"Decided to join us, then?" said Drake. About forty or fifty men, women, and children horseshoed around him. They were all looking at Carrie and Sawyer. A dozen men guarded the entrance to the car park. They were armed.

Drake said, "Ah, I see you've spotted them, then," noticing that Carrie's eyes were fixed on the gasometers. "See them burn and dangle for their sins. See their souls drift away, never to settle. See where you will be."

A voice behind them said, "They've killed Fred Stanwyck."

The woman who'd screamed and the child who'd pointed stood outside the fire exit.

"Murderers three times over," said Drake.

He jutted his chin towards Carrie and Sawyer.

Three men slipped from the crowd

Sawyer shielded her as Drake's men stalked forward.

"She's the evil one," said the girl. "Her, her down there," and again pointed at Carrie.

The girl's mother said, "Come away, princess, we'll watch her burn later – watch God kill her."

CHAPTER 60.
BIG SHITE.

SAM screamed. The zombies clustered around the Scania. Some tried to clamber up the truck's front grille, but they fell back. They tried to scale the cab from all angles, but they couldn't grip on anything. The zombies that fell back or slid to the ground were trampled by the other undead, who then used them as a step to reach higher up the cab. And as more zombies fell underfoot, the higher the tide of bodies became.

A forest of arms scraped at the cab's windscreen now.

Craig yelled his sister's name, despairing.

He aimed the gun out of the window and blasted the zombies with both barrels. A shower of blood sprayed up as the pellets ripped through flesh. It did no good, but it made him feel better. Cleared his mind for a second. Long enough for an idea to ignite.

A chestnut tree towered over the garden. Its branches reached towards the house. The previous owners had clearly not bothered to prune it back. And when Craig stretched, he could grasp a branch.

Beyond the tree, a dust-coated black truck had been parked up on the pavement.

He re-loaded the gun. Strapped a belt he found in the first bedroom around the barrel and the stock, and then slung the weapon over his shoulder.

Sam continued to scream.

Craig rushed to the window again and looked at his sister and thought, *Even if I get to her, what can I do?* And then: *Do it – do something in your life that's worthwhile.*

Quaking with fear, he grasped the branch with two hands and swung out of the window. He whelped and drew attention to himself. Zombies clawed at the tree, snarling and showing their teeth.

"Oh shit," he said, thinking, *What if I fall?* and the thought made him go weak.

He scrabbled through the tree, twigs tearing at his face and arms, ripping his clothes.

Leaves rained down on the zombies below as Craig crawled along the branches. He rocked and wobbled, panting with terror.

The zombies below had started to climb the tree now, digging their fingers into the bark and hauling themselves up.

Craig said, "Oh shit," again and scurried along a branch, tearing his arm. But adrenaline killed the pain. He came out of the tree and the branch bowed and he screamed as he dipped down towards the zombies. They reached for him, their hands inches from his face. The branch arced upwards again, Craig's belly wheeling.

The branch slowly stopped bouncing up and down, and Craig held on, gasping.

He glanced down. They waited for him to fall, their teeth chattering.

"No, no," he said as the zombie tide rose around the Scania.

He willed himself to crawl along the branch.

"Don't look down, don't look," he told himself.

He crept along the branch, and it creaked.

Craig moaned in horror.

The branch sagged, and he screamed.

He set his gaze on the truck parked on the pavement, not far out of reach.

"Craig, be careful, you're falling," Sam said.

The branch cracked.

Craig cried out and threw himself towards the truck. For a moment, he hung in mid-air, and time seemed to drag. He flailed, convinced he was falling into the sea of hungry dead below him.

But his hand closed on the truck's roof rack. Dust rose from the cab and made Craig's eyes water and his nose itch. He sneezed and spluttered.

Sam said, "You made it, you made it, you... look out!"

Hands closed around his legs.

He bawled and kicked and dragged himself upwards, arms straining, wrenching himself out of the zombies' grasp.

Craig shuddered and lay on the truck's roof, panting.

Sam screamed again.

"Please, Craig, please hurry!"

She stood on the Scania's roof. The cab rocked as the zombies rolled against it, wave after wave of undead, rising all the time as they used the fallen zombies as steps.

Now, he thought, *now*.

Exhausted, he hauled himself to his feet. Bounded across the lorry's trailer, his feet clanking on the metal.

The edge of the trailer approached. He gritted his teeth. His legs had been sapped of strength, but he kept going. Leapt off the truck, bicycling his legs. Landed on the roof of another truck that was scrawled with foreign writing.

He rested for a couple of seconds, taking deep breaths.

"Hurry, Craig," shouted Sam.

Christ, he thought.

The zombies were piling up around the Scania.

He stood again with a groan, his thighs aching.

He leapt off the truck on to a Mercedes van. The roof buckled. The zombies barged the vehicle, and it pitched, Craig swaying. He crouched to stop himself falling off. The zombies rammed the Mercedes, made it feel to Craig like he was on a boat. They raked the van, the noise putting Craig's teeth on edge.

Sam kept screaming his name, and he was going to tell her to shut up, but he didn't have the energy.

He peered across to the Scania. Peeked over the edge of the van into the gulf of zombies between the vehicle and the Scania.

He'd have to leap the chasm. Dive through the cab's open window. The gap was barely seven feet, but to Craig it seemed like seven miles.

"What are you going to do?" said Sam, her face creased with fright, tears streaming down her cheeks. She crouched on the roof of the Scania as the zombies welled and surged around the cab, making it rock.

"Craig, please hurry."

Seven feet, he told himself. *Nothing.*

He rose and took a few unsteady steps along the roof of the wavering Mercedes, the zombies still shoving against it.

"Okay," he said. "Okay."

He took two steps back. Sucked in a breath. Ran towards the edge of the van and jumped. Again, his legs wheeled in mid-air. Fear clutched his heart. The zombies leapt at him as he flew over them.

He fell half-in, half-out of the Scania's window, landing on his belly, the impact winding him. He rolled into the cab, groaning. Crawled into the driver's seat and settled himself in. The zombies clawed at the glass, grabbing for the sills of the driver- and passenger-side windows.

"Yes," he said. "Yes, I fucking did it, you see?" and he put the gun aside.

The key dangled in the ignition. Well, why would Art remove it? He'd only been yards away, boozing. *Who was going to nick the fucking thing?* thought Craig.

"I am," he said, starting the engine.

He thought about Art's warning – *if you stole anything of mine I'd cut your balls off* – and he laughed. "I'd like to see you try," he said.

Sam screamed.

"Hold on to the roof rack," he called out to her.

"Craig, no – "

"Hold on to the roof rack. I need to get us away from here."

The engine roared. The truck felt huge. The steering wheel like the wheel of a ship. He didn't know if he could drive this thing. The size of it, the weight. The trailer long and heavy behind.

He rammed it into gear and ploughed forward, sucking zombies under the great wheels.

He whooped, swivelling the eight-wheeler around, crushing zombies, feeling them pop under his tyres.

He ploughed through the sea of undead, heading back up the road.

Sam screamed on the roof, and that was good – he liked to hear her scream, because it meant she was still there.

It meant she was safe.

He drove up the road. He glanced in the side-mirrors. The zombies gave chase, but as he picked up speed they lagged and dwindled, losing touch.

He noticed the Mitsubishi Shogun parked on the side of the road. He thought about stopping to get the water and food. Glancing in the mirrors, he saw the zombies were still on his tail. *Too close*, he thought, *too close*, and he carried on driving.

When he got to a roundabout leading to Dewar Road, he stopped and told Sam to climb down off the roof and get in.

She shook, her eyes red with tears, sweat coating her. Her hair appeared glued to her scalp. She'd sometimes spend hours in front of her mirror, preening. Usually if there was a hair out of place, she'd have a tantrum and not go out. If she saw herself now, she'd go mental.

"Are you all right, then?" he asked

"What do you think?"

"Uh… you want a hug or something?"

She looked at him and nodded.

He shifted over and wrapped her up in his arms, and she felt small and frail, and she cried and shivered in his embrace, and he shut his eyes, listening to her heartbeat drum.

And he said, "I love you, you little cow."

She spluttered. "Yeah, love you too, you big shite."

CHAPTER 61.
THE NEED TO BELIEVE.

VINCENT manned the Gunners Walk, waiting for Roger and Oswyn to come back.

He kept asking Holly what the time was, and she kept saying, "Five minutes later than when you last asked me."

He chewed his nails and paced up and down.

"They won't come, Holly."

"How do you know?"

"Where is there to make it to?"

"There's got to be somewhere. Somewhere out there."

He cocked his head. "You'll believe anything if you believe that."

She glared at him. "It's the only thing that's keeping me together. Believing we can get out of here, survive. Take that away, Vincent, I'm going to fall apart. I need to hope, that's all." She folded her arms and gazed over to the mainland.

The hills crawled with zombies. You couldn't make the creatures out, but the land rippled and undulated, and a dark wave washed over the fields.

Holly said, "Do you believe in God, Vincent?"

He shook his head.

"I do," she said.

"Okay."

"You know why?"

He shook his head again.

"I believe in God because I *need* to. Thinking there isn't one" – she trembled – "scares me. It's like hanging over a deep, dark pit with nothing to grab on to. Without God it's meaningless – and a long way down. And I just can't deal with that. I need to believe, see?"

He thought for a moment and then said, "You think God would let this happen? If he did, he deserves a god Asbo. He's made a fucking hash of things. I mean, you weren't into all that Patty stuff, were you?"

"No, that was crazy. That wasn't God."

"She'd say it was."

"Yeah, well – not my God." She looked up at the clear, blue sky. Blistering heat poured down. The sun scorched the earth. Vincent baked.

He took her arm and led her to the far end of the walk and flung out his hand saying, "Look at that, just look," and they gazed off across the Strait, over on to the mainland, the hills shimmering in the heat, crawling with monsters.

"Zombies and chaos, that's all," he said. "That's all there is, Holly. Them and us and just these walls between us – just these fucking walls."

She sobbed, and he cringed with shame.

He said, "I'm trying to be honest."

"Well, I'd prefer if you'd lie to me, then."

"I'm saying we can't depend on… on other stuff, other people. We can't depend on Roger and Oswyn, we can't… can't depend on God. We've got to do this ourselves, Holly. Only us can get us out of this. Christ, you wanted a knight or a prince, didn't you?"

344

"I want someone to say it'll be okay."

"You won't get that. Anyone says that to you, they're lying."

"Then lie to me, Vincent. Tell me Roger and Oswyn'll be back with help. Tell me God will see us through because he won't let us suffer. Tell me."

She shuddered and sobbed – with dread, most likely.

"Holly… "

She stopped crying and looked at him, waiting.

He stared right at her and said nothing. Because he had nothing to say. She might have been right: it was better to hear comforting lies instead of cruel truth. But while it might be better, it wasn't right.

"Well?" she said, her brow furrowed.

"If I tell you things are okay, it could kill you, Holly. Kill us all. Telling the truth, though… the fucking scary, nasty, cruel truth… that might just save us." He paused and regarded her face, etched with grief and rage. And he said, "They're not coming back. We have to decide."

CHAPTER 62.
LOSING SAWYER.

HANDS taped behind his back and kneeling in the car park, Sawyer said, "So you've founded this religion in the past few hours, have you? Done all this, all this killing."

Drake smiled. "God's always been here, my friend. He decided to show himself today, that's all. And these people, my flock, they knew that to survive this holocaust, they needed a messiah – and here I am."

Carrie seethed. "Let me go! My daughter, you bastard, my daughter!"

"I told you, woman. Don't speak."

"Or what, you… you… you fucking joke-Jesus?"

Drake flinched as if he'd been slapped.

"Pig language," he said, "from a skank's mouth."

"What are you going do to me, anyway? You're going to kill us, so what does it matter what I call you or if I talk?"

And she shrieked, thrashing her head from side to side.

A man said, "Has she got devils in her, bishop?"

Drake said, "She has. She's full of devils, this one."

"You're off your rocker, mate," Sawyer told Drake.

"Am I?" said the bishop.

"Why are you doing this?"

"I'm doing it because God tells me to. God tells me to cast out demons. To burn the devils. To heal the world. He wants a sacrifice, you see. He wants to be pleased. He might allow us to live, then. Guide us through this hell on earth. Give us the key. Give *me* the key"

Carrie said, "I've got to find my daughter."

Drake ignored her.

"Did you hear me?" said Carrie.

He glared at her. His eyes burned with hate. But Carrie refused to be cowed by him.

"You can give me the evils all day, but I want my daughter – you hear me?"

Drake stepped towards her and now she did flinch, thinking he would hit her.

He leaned towards her and said, "Hear me, skank – skank who spawned your offspring – hear me and know that you will burn, *burn*, for God – your dirty, skank body will melt in the flames and your dirty, skank soul will be sucked down into hell. There will be nothing left of you." He turned his back. "And anyway, your offspring has probably been eaten by these cannibals."

Carrie shook with rage.

Drake walked away saying, "I'll be back in an hour." He climbed the stairs back into the hall and the people filed in after him. When the car park had cleared, Carrie saw two women tied up like her and Sawyer. The women kneeled on the melting asphalt. Two armed youths had been left to watch the prisoners, and Carrie eyed the boys now.

"Don't look at her because she'll curse you," said one youth to the other.

Sawyer said to one of the women, "Who is this nutter?"

"He's some local fundamentalist." She was a redhead in her early thirties, her make-up smeared and her clothes torn. She said her name was Dani, and her mate was Joss.

Dani said, "They've run the church here for years. They made a lot of noise about sin, but they were harmless – well, we thought they were."

"And they just took over?" said Sawyer.

"Looks like it, mate," she said. "Me and Joss, we'd been out last night, got drunk. By the time we'd got up, couple of hours ago, everything was pear-shaped, weren't it. Zombies on the streets, Drake on his soapbox."

"They must've been hoarding guns," said Sawyer.

"Like that David Koresh in Texas," said Joss.

Dani said, "That's right, waiting for the end of the world – and it looks like they were on the button."

"How did they take over?"

"There was no one else to take over was there, mate," said Dani. "They just ordered everyone into the mission hall here. That Drake fella, he started preaching. Told everyone they had minutes to decide – join him or die. He promised them salvation, and if they hadn't believed in God before, now was the time to start. Well, when you've got zombies running around eating people, you start thinking maybe all that Revelation stuff was right after all."

"And did you believe?" said Sawyer.

"What does it look like to you?"

"What happened?"

"They started herding people who mocked Drake, or said fuck off to him, out of the mission hall – and then did *that* too them." Dani threw her head back, gesturing towards the gasometers. "Now it's our turn."

"I think I'd prefer to get chomped by them zombies," said Joss, an older woman, overweight and stuffed into a mini-dress.

"I dunno," said Dani. "I dunno. Makes me want to piss myself. So scared thinking about it. Burning alive or getting chomped on by the zombies." She looked at Carrie and Sawyer. "You two know what this is all about?"

Carrie shook her head.

"Where d'you come from?" said Joss.

Carrie told them, leaving out the part about Sawyer being a bank robber. Not that it mattered anymore. People could be anything in this anarchy – bishop or bank robber.

Dani said, "It's a wonder you got through the roadblocks. They've got them both ends. This is like their little kingdom. They kill zombies, pin their heads – "

"We've seen," said Carrie.

"They say you killed Fred Stanwyck, too," said Dani.

Carrie felt ill.

Dani continued:

"Fred was a local councillor. Not involved with Drake and his nutters till this morning. Then he joined the winning side. Joss here's known him for years."

"Years," said Joss, and winking at Carrie added: "Good on you, girl, switching his lights out."

Carrie blushed with shame.

Dani said, "Survival. It's fair enough.. You or him."

Carrie said nothing.

"What's your man, there, doing?" said Dani.

Carrie looked at Sawyer. He had his head bowed. Sweat dripped from his nose and glistened on his body. She thought about him being her man, and she was about to say that he wasn't. But then she said, "He's thinking. He's always thinking."

He raised his head and looked at her.

"I'm done," he said.

Carrie felt a chill in her veins.

"Done with what, doll?" said Dani. "Done thinking?"

He looked straight at Carrie. "I'm done."

His shoulders slumped, and the fire had gone from his eyes – and she understood what he'd meant.

She was losing him.

She tried to say no but only managed to shake her head.

She looked at the youths keeping watch. Two boys with guns sitting on the stone wall, having a fag.

Then she looked back at Sawyer and willed him to save her again. Save her like he'd saved her all day.

But she saw that he wouldn't. Not anymore. It had left him, now: the strength, the passion.

You're on your own, she thought.

She wanted to call him a coward, but he'd been the bravest man she'd known. He'd endangered himself throughout this journey.

And what did he have vested in it?

What was he fighting for?

Nothing.

He did it for me, she thought. *All for me*.

Her unborn child came to mind. How better it would be if it were Sawyer's and not Boyd's. A father who would fight for his young.

Carrie rose.

"Hey, back on your knees," said one of the boys, wearing a red FCUK T-shirt. He stood from the wall and flicked his cigarette aside. He aimed the gun – an old pistol, it looked like to Carrie. The weapon appeared too heavy for him. The other boy gawked.

Red-T-shirt stepped forward. "Did you hear what I said?" He licked his lips. His eyes flitted towards the hall.

"You can't call for help," Carrie said.

"W-what?"

"You can't call for help. He wouldn't respect you."

The other boy, a tall, rangy, bag of bones, came forward now. He aimed his weapon, and his arm shook. He said, "Tell her to get back on her knees, Skip."

"Skip, is that your name? Skip," said Carrie to the red T-shirt.

Dani and Joss stood up now, Joss with a little trouble since she was heavy.

"What's your name?" Dani asked the bag of bones.

"Don't matter," he said. "Get back down on your knees. Kneel before God, yeah."

"You believe in God?" said Carrie, looking into Skip's eyes.

He said, "I'll call for help."

"How would that look? The two of you with guns, and you can't control four dossers who've been tied up. How would that look? Drake'd hang you from that gasometer. He'd burn you."

From the corner of her eye, she saw movement. For a second, she thought it was zombies. It wasn't.

Sawyer bulled forward and shouldered Skip in the ribs.

Bones cracked, and the boy was lifted off his feet by the blow. He went flying into Bag of Bones, and they dropped their guns.

Sawyer stomped on Skip's head. The boy's skull cracked on the tarmac. Joss threw herself across Bag of Bones.

Her stomach smothered his face and chest. Dani threw herself across his belly. He writhed, and his muffled screams came from under their bodies. They lay on him and squashed him.

Sawyer was at the stone wall, his back to it. Raking his hands back and forth. Rage warped his face as he tried to shred the tape that bound his wrists. They came loose. He stared at Carrie, his arms outstretched after they'd sprung free from their bonds, and he looked like some kind of Jesus.

His muscles rippled and sweat drizzled down his chest.

He had come back to her.

351

CHAPTER 63.
PARENTS.

CRAIG drove the truck up the M80, eyes scanning the landscape. He'd unlatched the trailer and left it at the roundabout outside the town. The cab on its own felt much lighter, and it gave Craig a sense of power to be in control of such a big machine.

"It's like a mega pile-up," said Sam, gaze drifting over the abandoned vehicles littering the motorway. The chaos made the going slow, Craig never getting over twenty or thirty miles per hour.

Now and again, they saw zombies. Packs of them hurtling across fields, racing along the motorway. And every time they glimpsed them, Sam flinched.

Craig told her, "It's okay. They can't get us."

"They're horrible, Craig. I was so scared back there. I've never been so scared."

"Did… did Art… did he hurt you?"

She blushed and shook her head. "He slapped me and then told me to stay in the back of the truck, quietly. He… he told me to do as he said or he'd… he'd" – she blubbed, but then gathered herself – "he'd feed me to them, Craig – he said he'd feed me to the zombies."

She blew her nose and went on:

"I knew what he wanted to do, I knew. Him and his mates. They already had a woman. One of the other men brought her" – *the one in the bedroom covered in blood*, thought Craig – "and Art brought me, Craig. And they were all there for that. For me, for that woman. I'm not a baby. I know what they were going to do."

They were quiet for a while, and then Sam said, "Are we going to find Mum and Dad?"

"Do you want to?" he said.

He liked driving the truck. The roads empty, no one telling him what to do. If they found Mum and Dad, Craig'd be in the back of the car again – with Sam. It would be like before. Mum and Dad bickering, not knowing what to do. Him in the back, simmering.

Sam said, "What do you mean?"

"I mean, they're a pain."

"They're our parents."

"Yeah, what does that mean?"

"Means they love us, you nugget."

"Huh! Think they love me? Think our dad loves me?"

"Mum does."

"Yeah, there, you said it – Dad doesn't. I hate him too."

"Dad's dad. He's still that, though. Still our dad. We've got to find them."

"They didn't come find us."

"They didn't know where we'd gone."

"They could've come looking."

"You don't know, Craig, they might've. And they might be in trouble."

"Or they might be dead – or undead."

Sam's face twisted with shock, and she cried out, "No! Don't say that!"

"It might happen, Sam. There's a decent chance."

The sun raged. The air con in the truck blasted cool air through the cab. He could stay here like this, just drive. Who needed parents? They'd done nothing for him.

He checked the petrol gauge and bit his lip.

"What's the matter?" said Sam.

"Nothing."

He thought about pulling over, but the slip road was full of zombies, and they crammed the forecourt of the service station, as well. Congregated there, as if gathering for food.

And he thought, *Where there are zombies, there are humans.*

"Craig, look," said Sam.

He glanced towards the service station and said, "What?"

"It's – it's our – "

And then the fireball filled the sky and blinded Craig, and he swerved, the Scania's breaks screeching, and the truck ploughed straight for the central reservation.

CHAPTER 64.
DIVERSIONS.

CARRIE, her body aching, jogged after Sawyer as he raced across the scrubland towards the gates that opened up on Hornsey Park Road. He had the pistols they'd taken from the youths tucked into the waistband of his boiler suit.

Carrie glanced over her shoulder. Dani and Joss trailed behind her. They huffed and puffed, sweat streaming off them.

Sawyer picked up a rock and hammered at the padlock on the gate. He growled as he smashed the lock, sparks flying off the metal. The muscles in his arms corded. He gripped the rock so tightly that his fingers bled.

The padlock snapped.

Out in the road, they looked both ways.

Dani said, "They cleared all the bodies away. Not like the rest of London, ain't it. I saw on the TV earlier, bodies everywhere. Killed by the zombies. You see those poor people trapped in Victoria Station?"

Carrie said no, she hadn't seen them.

Dani continued:

"It was rush hour. Thousands packed into the station. The zombies came up from the Underground, says Sky News. Poured out of the tunnels. The reporter was caught up in it. Hell of a stampede, it was. Screaming and shouting, sirens going off. And then you saw the zombies plough through the crowds, saw them bearing down on the camera. And – oh – that's it, all over… and they went back to the studio then, and the presenter, his face was like milk, I'm telling you."

They said nothing. Carrie pictured the chaos at Victoria Station. She thought about the pandemonium that had spread across London.

They walked in the shadows of the trees, trying to keep out of sight. Sawyer led the way. Carrie behind him. Dani and Joss taking the rear. Carrie's gaze skated around the streets. The smell of burning hung in the air. Somewhere, a baby wailed.

Joss said, "You know what's going to happen to all them dead ones, don't you?"

"Same as what happened to Trevor," said Dani.

Carrie asked who Trevor was.

Dani told her:

"He was this geezer who was bitten, see. Drake and his bunch took him in."

"Locked him in a cupboard," said Joss.

"Then," said Dani, "someone goes and checks on him. He lurches out."

"He's a zombie," Joss said.

"Like in the films," said Dani.

"This was just before they brought you in. They pinned Trevor's head on the bonnet of a Jag. 'Baldy' Brogan's Jag, 'cause it was Brogan who killed him."

Carrie thought about John Shaw. And then Boyd filtered into

her mind. Had he been killed? Was he a zombie? Was he in the house with Mya? Her chest tightened, and she quickened her pace.

Sawyer halted them.

"What?" said Carrie, not wanting to stop now.

He pointed up the road. A cluster of vehicles blocked their way. Men with guns loitered there, smoking and drinking.

"Listen, my darlings," said Dani. "You two've been good to me and my girl here. This is our patch, is this road. You've got to get on and save your little girl. We'll do a bit of a diversion for you, and you make a run for it. It's a bit of a Baldrick 'I've got a cunning plan' type of plan, but it's the best I can do."

Carrie said, "You've got to come with us. If you stay, they'll kill you."

Dani shook her head. "They caught us unawares, see. They won't do that again. I'll smash Drake's face in if he comes near me. They've got no balls, the rest of them. Come on, Joss. There's only six of the bastards."

Dani trundled up the road, Joss loping after her.

Carrie stared at them and then looked at Sawyer.

"What are we going to do?" she said.

"We're going to do as they say."

Dani and Joss wandered into the middle of the road. The women shielded their eyes from the sun. Heat rose up from the road in waves. Carrie could smell the asphalt smouldering.

The men shuffled forward. You could see the uncertainty in their movements. They didn't know what to do. They were ordinary blokes. Not soldiers. Not killers. They could aim a gun at zombies and shoot them. But ask them to kill humans, most of them found it difficult.

Carrie heard the men tell Dani and Joss to get back, and what did they think they were doing.

"Are we going to nick another car?" she said to Sawyer.

"Look at that."

357

She did, and saw them:

Zombies swarming down Mayes Road. Hundreds of them pouring from the Market Hall.

Dani and Joss screamed and wheeled away from the checkpoint. The men swivelled. The undead cascaded towards them.

Carrie heard something behind her. She turned. Drake and a group of men appeared from the mission hall.

Carrie grabbed Sawyer's hand and started to run towards the blockade, towards the sea of undead.

"They've brought hell with them," Drake said.

The men at the blockade fired at the zombies.

Drake and his gang fired from behind.

Carrie and Sawyer ducked and scuttled away, Carrie leading the way down an alley as gunfire and screams filled the air.

"Where are you going?" said Sawyer.

"I don't know, do I?"

He said nothing and followed her. The alley swirled with weeds. Litter peppered the undergrowth. An arm poked out of the high grass, rats gnawing at the flesh.

They ploughed ahead, Carrie ignoring the debris.

She dared a glance over her shoulder.

Her heart froze.

Zombies funnelled down the alley after them.

"Sawyer, they're coming."

"Move," he said.

She moved. Faster than she'd ever moved. Her legs hurt and her lungs burned. She thought about the baby in her womb. Something lit inside her. A desire to survive, to make this embryo live. It branded itself on her heart. A mark there, forever declaring this mother would die and kill for her children. It had always been in her. This lioness was in all mothers. But only now, with death on her heels, did it tattoo itself on her flesh. Only now did it become her gospel.

Sawyer fired one of the pistols over his shoulder.

"Did you hit one?"

"Even if I did, it's not making much difference."

"Shoot again, for Christ's sake."

He did, peppering the zombies with bullets till the gun was empty. He tossed it at the creatures. He drew out the other gun but didn't shoot this time.

They kept running and came out of the alley, into a terraced street. Carrie skidded on blood, almost losing her footing.

Human remains were dotted around the street. The houses had broken windows, and front doors were yanked off their hinges. Smoke rose in the distance, billowing darkly in the blue sky.

The heat was stifling.

Her body told Carrie, *No more*, but that stigmata notched on her heart pulsed and kept her going.

Sawyer ran past her then stopped and told her to come on.

He fired above her head, towards the zombies.

She looked back. A dozen creatures chased them. One wore the rags of a policeman's uniform.

They're waking up. All the dead are waking up.

And how many of them were there?

Thousands? Millions?

How long would it be before everyone in London, in Britain, was dead – and walking around looking for food?

"Go," said Sawyer, "just go and I'll hold them back."

"No – "

"Go," he said.

"I'm not leaving you."

"There's a bike – go."

The cycle lay in a front garden next to a legless torso.

Sawyer ran straight for the zombies and shouted her name, telling her to go: "Go get Mya. Save her. Get out of London."

She turned her back and ran and heard him yell, and there was gunfire – from behind her and from a distance, too.

359

She leaped over the wall into the garden.

She glanced behind her, crying.

The zombies raced after Sawyer as he ran back down the road. He'd got through them somehow, and they pursued him down the street.

She knelt next to the bike and kept her eyes on the zombies until they'd gone. She didn't want to look at the half-man lying on the grass. She grabbed the handlebars.

Relief washed through her veins.

A cold, clammy hand closed around her wrist.

CHAPTER 65.
TERRY ON FIRE.

RAGE brewed in Terry Murray's chest. They were all against him, as usual. And his wife was leading them. He glowered at her as she spoke to the queer. *Not gay – bollocks*, he thought.

"You listen to me, you bastards," he said, and they all turned his way.

He pointed at the girl with the bitten arm. "You want me to tell you again? That one will change. She'll be like those bastard ugly things out there, and she'll want to eat you. Even you, you fucking queer. And you, too, muscles-for-brains."

The American lad glanced at him. Terry didn't like the look of the boy. The youth did have muscles. But that meant nothing. Where did biceps the size of Aberdeen get you if someone cracked a bottle over your skull?

Terry's head swam. He felt sick. The heat dried his lips together, glued his clothes to his skin.

He swigged from the beer again. Tore the wrapping from a pork pie and took a bite. He chewed, his stomach grumbling and aching.

He glanced outside. The zombies pressed their faces against the window. And there were even more of them gathered in the forecourt, lingering, waiting for food.

At the moment, they lumbered about and reminded Terry of those zombies in horror films from the 1960s and 1970s.

But he knew that once they got a whiff of human, they'd turn wild.

They could shift, those things. And he didn't want them chasing after him. He'd never make it. No breath in his lungs to run anymore. All he could do these days was throw a few punches. And unless he decked the bastard with his first flurry, Terry knew he'd be done for.

Getting old, he thought. *Old and useless.*

And fucking dying, too.

He watched the zombies and thought about things.

Something coiled in his belly. It was cold and slithered in his guts, causing him to shudder. It was a sensation he'd rejected in the past. It was fear.

For himself and for… for his kids.

He drank more beer to wash away thoughts of Craig and Sam. He didn't want them in his head. Having them there made guilt well up in him.

He shook his head, clearing his mind.

So what? He was only doing what his dad had done to him. Frank Murray'd let him get on with it and had only given him a slap if he stepped out of line.

Stepping out of line meant getting in the way or getting caught, of course. Getting caught stealing booze or fags from his dad, usually.

"Don't nick from your own," his dad would warn him, and Terry had passed the same message on to Craig:

"Take from others, not from your mothers."

Mother, thought Terry now and looked at Helen. He'd fancied her once, but the fire had dimmed.

He'd not stayed faithful, but who did? It wasn't possible. Not with women throwing themselves at him in the pub. Or falling towards him after too many drams.

Now Helen, looking like she thought she was in charge, said, "We've got to do something," and she was looking at him like he had the answer.

The fat one called Duncan, who Terry had decked earlier said, "We can't go out there, that's for certain."

Terry lit a cigarette. The American girl, the one who'd not been bitten – pretty thing, dark hair – said, "Do you mind not smoking?"

"I do mind," he said, growling. He sucked in the smoke. It charred his lungs, and he coughed. Coughed till it burned his chest and his throat.

"That's what you get," said the pretty girl again.

And the American lad said, "You'll die doing that."

"He's dying already," Helen said. "He's got lung cancer. The poison is in the body. Eating him from the inside. He's got a small chance, they say. It's not close to the windpipe yet. But not much if he doesn't stop smoking. Have you, Terry?"

He coughed up phlegm, and he would've normally spat it out, but there was something in their eyes that shamed him.

He pulled a handkerchief from his pocket, put it to his lips, and rolled the phlegm out of his mouth into the stained cloth.

"Everybody dies," he said.

"Not in agony, though – coughing up their lungs in blood and phlegm," said the drag queen. "Same thing killed my dad. It was ugly."

"Yeah? Well if you think that's ugly, you should see someone get eaten alive out there by those things."

"We can try to run away from those things. You can't run away from what's killing you, mate," said the drag queen.

"So what," he said.

"You won't be brave when it happens," said Helen, and he looked her in the eye. She stared right back and didn't blink.

"Don't be bold with me, woman," he said, but she ignored him and continued to stare.

His dad's words came to him:

"You can't let them know they're the boss, or you're hen-pecked and nagged all day, all night, and they can tell you 'No' when you want your oats, and no woman should say 'No' to her husband. It's not fucking Christian."

Terry tensed, the desire to spring at her overwhelming. But he didn't move and glared instead, trying to threaten her in that way. But all he saw in her eyes was derision, hate, and – worst of all – pity. And he felt something melt inside him, something hard and cruel. And he knew she'd beaten him. His power had been doused. He had nothing left.

He took a last drag of his fag and then stubbed it under his boot.

"Right, you cunts," he said.

He strode behind the counter and turned on the pumps, all of them. Their drone made the zombies in the forecourt jerk.

"What are you doing?" said the drag queen.

"Don't talk to me, half-man, half-lipstick."

"What're you up to, man?" said the American youth.

"I'm doing something, son, that's what – doing something. Jesus Christ." His dread grew. "Jesus Christ."

Helen said, "It won't make you a hero, you know. It won't make things better."

"Who gives a shit?"

"You're not going out there, are you?" said the pretty American girl, her brown eyes wide and making Terry want to flirt with her, say dirty things in her ear, make her come with him.

But he didn't.

He didn't have that urge now.

Odd, that, he thought. He was always up for it.

Things change, though.

"You're a tasty little cake, aren't you," he told her. "But the funny thing is, I'm not interested."

"You bastard," said Helen.

He went on:

"The apocalypse must make men lose their sex drive. Well, it's the end of the world, after all. And nature wants to clear away the debris. Cull the shitty species. Make humans extinct. Can't have studs like me going around breeding."

He chuckled.

"It's not funny," said the American youth. "You can't talk to her like that."

"Shut your face," said Terry.

He grabbed a fire extinguisher from behind the counter and slung it over his shoulder.

Heavy bastard, he thought. *How're you supposed to lug it around to put out a fire?*

He found another fire extinguisher in the corridor leading to the toilets and draped that one over his left shoulder. He gritted his teeth. The straps bit into his flesh, spreading pins and needles through his neck.

"Out of my way," he said, and Helen and the drag queen moved aside. He looked at her, hoping to see a glimmer of love there. Respect, even. But there was nothing.

He shrugged. "I guess I don't deserve anything, do I," he told her.

"I'm not sure that you do," she said, but she was crying.

Kind words lurked in his head, and he'd wanted to say them. But he failed to usher them out. And instead he told her, "Don't go shagging around."

"I'll come with you."

He turned towards the voice.

365

It was the bitten girl. Her eyes were sunken and her skin ashen.

"You look like shit," he said.

"I'm dying," said the girl, "I can feel it. And I don't want to be a monster. I want to do something."

"No, Jaime-Ann," said the pretty American girl, but Jaime-Ann got to her feet and said, "I'm going, Dayna. Don't make me stay here and become one of those." She sobbed and quaked.

Terry said, "If you're coming, come."

He handed her one of the extinguishers, and she grimaced at its weight. She was thin and weak, and Terry didn't know if she'd be able to hold it. But she said she'd be okay, and she hugged her friends, and they cried.

Terry looked to Helen again. This time she nodded and bit her lip, and then she turned her back.

"Aye, there we are, then," he said, blinking because his eyes were welling up. He sucked air through his teeth. "Open the door quickly," he said to the American youth, "then fucking shut it quickly, too."

The youth nodded.

"Now!" said Terry.

The youth unlocked the door, threw it open.

The zombies darted for the entrance.

Terry roared and let off the extinguisher.

Foam gushed from the pipe, coating the zombies.

They reeled and staggered, blinded by the spray. Terry ploughed through the door, roaring, spewing the foam.

Jaime-Ann screamed behind him and charged out, spraying the zombies.

The undead dashed towards them, but Terry and the girl sprayed the creatures, confusing them. The zombies wheeled and stumbled, tripping up and trampling over each other. There seemed to be hundreds of the bastards, and it made Terry's balls shrink.

Fuck, I'm scared, he thought, *I'm really fucking scared.*

He reached the nearest petrol pump. Yanked out all the hoses. Pressed the handles, and petrol and diesel spilled out. The fumes made him dizzy.

The fuel gushed out over the forecourt. He soaked zombies with it. He glanced towards Jaime-Ann. The zombies weren't bothering with her. He thought, *Shit, she's one of them.*

She tugged the fuel lines out of the pump.

"Are you still there?" said Terry, swivelling, spraying petrol from another pump now.

"I don't know," she said, and held two pumps like handguns, shooting the fuel out over the zombies and the cars.

"You'll be all right."

"I don't know… " She dropped the pumps and looked at him. "I'm… I'm going… "

Her eyes rolled back and became empty and white.

"Oh fucking hell," said Terry.

Petrol fumes rose, making everything undulate. The odour sickened him. He emptied another pump. The zombies slithered around. They slipped and sloshed in the fuel.

Terry shrieked and reached into his pocket, fished out the Zippo.

Jaime-Ann snarled and dashed towards him. She clamped her teeth into his neck. The pain shot through him. He staggered away, the Jaime-Ann-zombie attached to his throat, ripping away the flesh.

More zombies skated towards them across the lake of petrol and diesel.

Terry and the Jaime-Ann-zombie fell, splashed about in fuel.

He moaned as the fumes and the pain in his neck made his gorge rise.

The Jaime-Ann-zombie tore away the flesh, and blood pulsed from the wound.

Terry weakened. Shadows loomed. Zombies fell on him. They pinned him to the ground. Sank their teeth into his body.

He squealed in pain.

He said his mother's name.

He flicked the Zippo's wheel, and the fire engulfed him.

CHAPTER 66.
CRUSH.

CARRIE screamed and yanked her wrist free, scuttling backwards.

The half-man reached for her, its face pale and creased with rage.

The eyes were dead and white, and the mouth bubbled with saliva.

The zombie twisted itself round and began to slither towards her, gnashing its teeth.

Carrie lunged for the bike. She hefted it up on its wheels.

She felt the zombie's hand brush against her leg. The touch sent shudders through her. She cried out but didn't look. Mounted the bike. Started to pedal, tears streaming down her face.

Carrie cycled till her chest burned.

She came to High Road, which usually teemed with shoppers.

She stopped near a Lloyds Bank. The sign dangled drunkenly. Cash had spilled out of the ATM and now fluttered along the pavement.

She looked up and saw the Shopping City sign on the flyover bridge across the road.

To her right stood a WH Smith.

Her heart stopped.

Bodies filled the store. They were pressed against the glass, hundreds of them tangled together. It seemed as if they'd been jammed in there, body on body on body, till there was no space left – but they'd still shoved more in.

Her eyes scanned the corpses rammed against the windows.

A woman looked back at Carrie – and moved her mouth.

Alive.

Carrie dropped her bike and rushed forward, gasping for breath, terror rinsing her veins.

The bodies were meshed together.

"Oh God," she said.

The woman's mouth moved again. It was about the only thing she could move. Carrie read the horror in her eyes. And then more of them tried to move. The pressure had warped their faces, but they could twitch a cheek or an eyebrow, bend a finger.

Carrie dropped to her knees.

She imagined the suffering in there.

These people had fled the street and piled into the shop looking for a safe haven.

And found hell.

She noticed now limbs poking out from the lattice of bodies. A hand opened and closed. A finger wriggled. A foot trembled.

Carrie laid her hand on the glass, over the woman's hand, and the woman mouthed, "Help me, please," her face distorted.

Carrie rose and went to the shop door, tried it. It was locked – by the youth crushed against the glass. His key in the lock. His legs broken, twisted terribly behind his neck. One eye hanging out of its socket, squished to jelly against the door. Vomit dribbling down from his gaping mouth.

The boy wore a WH Smith nametag.

Dillon.

Carrie wrenched the door but it wouldn't budge.

Other eyes fixed on her now, swivelling towards her.

She found a brick and threw it at the window. The glass cracked a little.

Carrie waited.

The crack spread.

Like a cobweb.

Carrie retreated, afraid she would be crushed by the bodies as they spilled out of the store.

But nothing happened.

She picked up the brick again.

The woman in the store managed to nod her chin a little, encouraging Carrie. The desperate shopper saw hope, now. Hope of breathing freely. Hope of moving more than a milimetre.

Carrie hammered at the glass with the brick.

The alarm wailed and instinctively she stepped back and looked up and down the road.

She returned to the window again and started to smash at it again.

The glass cracked, shards of it showering the pavement.

The knotted bodies began to uncoil. The window exploded. Carrie cried out and stumbled away. She tripped over her feet. The store haemorrhaged bodies. A wall of corpses rolled towards her.

The woman tumbled out on to the pavement. She reached out for Carrie, a smile on her face. But then the smile twisted away and in its place came a look of horror.

Carrie screamed.

The woman disappeared under a sea of bodies as they spooled out of the window.

Screams came from the shop. Shrieks from the freed bodies. Those who were still alive were trying to move, but couldn't. They were broken and mangled, their injuries severe, life-threatening.

The sounds they made were awful, and Carrie covered her ears and retreated.

The human misery she'd unleashed sickened her.

More corpses gushed through the shattered window.

A face glowered at her.

She started to say *sorry*, wanting to apologize for the agony she'd caused.

But then she saw its empty eyes and the mouthful of gore. The blood covering its torso. The kidney in its right hand, half eaten.

Zombie.

Buried in there with the bodies.

Eating its way through the tangle of high street shoppers.

The zombie sprang towards her

Carrie darted for the bike, glancing over her shoulder. More zombies poured out of the store, exhumed from their human crypt.

She screamed and leapt on the bike and pedalled.

The zombies thundered after her.

Eight of them tearing down the road.

She cycled till her legs numbed.

And as she went she saw more people like the ones at WH Smith.

In KFC. In Subway. All along the street. Shoppers and staff crammed inside. Knotted together. Twisted and bent and broken. From floor to ceiling, from back wall to front window. All the shops the same. A street of anguish.

And it was at that moment that she felt herself lose it, her mind slithering away, her sanity splintering.

She imagined zombies buried within those sepulchres of flesh and bone, eating through the dead and the dying.

She screeched, and her voice echoed through the streets, and she realized, then, that she could be the only human left.

Tormented by what she'd seen, Carrie cycled down the road.

A Wetherspoons stood on the corner. Grey brick stained with blood. She turned right down Buller Road, a back street of redbrick buildings.

She looked over her shoulder.

The zombies swept around the corner.

Carrie moaned and quickened her pace.

She swerved left into Redvers Road, passing the rear of the Wetherspoons, into Lordship Road, and then left again, and right into Berners Road.

Head down, she pelted through the empty streets.

No bodies anywhere.

All of them risen, now.

All of them looking for food.

The growl of the pursuing zombies dwindled.

She cleared her mind and focused on one thing.

Mya.

CHAPTER 67.
DOMESTIC.

DREAD leached through Carrie. The house lay ahead. Blood soaked the road. Dismembered limbs were scattered all over the place. Half-eaten corpses baked in the sun. Dogs fought for a human leg. Rats swarmed over a headless body.

By then, she'd started saying Mya's name – a whimper coming from her, a breath, that was all.

The front door stood open.

She felt sick, standing on the front path, looking into the dark hallway.

She skulked inside, and the intense heat became a muggy closeness in the house. Something festered in here. Flies buzzed in the kitchen, and she dreaded what she'd find there.

She was saying Mya's name, gasping it out, over and over.

In the living room, the furniture had been tossed around. Books and DVDs had been thrown off shelves. Blood smeared the panelled wooden floor, and the sight of it made Carrie hold her breath.

She went into the kitchen, her legs shaking. The light spilled through the window. The first thought she had was:

Boyd didn't wash up.

Flies hovered over the dirty plates.

She tried the basement door, and it was locked.

She tried it again.

She crouched down and said through the keyhole, "Mya? Baby? It's Mummy. Are you there?" Her voice quivered, and she wasn't sure if it was loud enough for someone to hear down in the cellar.

Down in the darkness.

She closed her eyes and tried to master the terror coursing through her.

She'd made her daughter go to the place that scared her the most.

The dark.

She tried the door again. She knew it was locked, but felt she had to rattle the handle, hoping it would open.

"Mya," she said, louder this time.

She yanked at the handle, her nerves taut and threatening to snap.

"Mya!"

The force of her voice made her look round, worried she'd alerted someone – or some*thing.*

She leaned against the door and rapped the wood, again saying, "Mya, it's Mummy," but this time more quietly.

The lock clicked. Carrie stepped back, hand on her breast.

The door opened a little.

Carrie nearly fainted. The dark gaped at her.

Tears welled, and she fell to her knees. The door creaked open. Mya stood there, pale in the gloom and wrapped in her pink, rose-patterned blanket.

Carrie unleashed a cry and scooped up her daughter, holding her cold body tight, wailing into her child's hair, smelling her skin.

Something crawled down Carrie's spine.

The coldness of Mya's skin.

She eased the child away and looked into her eyes and thought for a moment they were dead and white.

But their greenness glistened with tears, and when Mya said, "Mummy," Carrie melted.

* * * *

Carrie locked the front door, barricading it with an armchair. In the kitchen, they drank water and ate bread and jam.

Carrie kept her eye on the garden. She feared something could slip through from the alleyway at the rear of the house. The back gate had been hanging off its hinges since Boyd broke through one night when he was drunk. She wanted to ask Mya about him, but let the child eat and drink first.

"Mummy, where have the zombies come from?"

"I – I don't know, darling."

Mya chewed on a piece of bread.

Carrie thought this was the time to ask. "Where – where is Daddy, darling?"

Mya looked up at her mother. "He came back after he went out, and he knocked on the door, Mummy, knocked on this door" – she gestured to the basement – "but he sounded like he was drunk and… and I didn't let him in, like you said. Did I do wrong?"

"No, no darling, you did right. W-where did he go, do you know?"

"He said he was going to lie down."

Carrie stiffened. She couldn't move. Her jaw locked on a piece of bread. Her eyes rolled upwards, to the ceiling, and she pictured him there lying on the bed just above them.

Mya said he sounded drunk. Was he sleeping off a hangover? Or had he been bitten?

"Come here, Mya."

The little girl came and Carrie held her hand.

She thought about what to do. Stay here and wait for... for what? Or go out into the zombie-filled streets.

She didn't know.

She hugged her daughter, because that seemed the only thing she could do. She told her that she loved her, and Mya said that she loved her mummy too.

Carrie tried the DAB radio in the kitchen, but all she got was static. She tried the television, but news channels had messages on screen saying:

THIS CHANNEL IS OFF AIR.
WE APOLOGISE FOR THE INCONVENIENCE.

Really inconvenient, thought Carrie.

She tried the house phone, ringing her friends.

She got no tone. She got nothing.

She told Mya they were leaving and said they should pack up some rucksacks with clothes and food.

Mya wanted to know where they were going, and all Carrie could tell her was: "To a safe place."

"Is there safe places, Mummy?"

Carrie looked her daughter in the eye and said, "There will be."

She got rucksacks from under the stairs, and they packed food first. Carrie wondered if Boyd was in the bedroom. It was like a worm in her belly. She didn't want to think about it, but it squirmed inside her.

A sound came from upstairs, like something being knocked over.

"Mum?" said Mya.

Carrie put a finger to her lips. She whispered, "Go into the kitchen."

"Is that Daddy waking up?"

Carrie felt something cold on the back of her neck, and the hairs there stood on end.

She gestured for Mya to go into the kitchen again.

Carrie looked up stairs. The landing was gloomy. The house felt clammy. She wiped her hands together. They were soaked. She started up stairs.

She was halfway up, and the noise came again. As if someone had stumbled and bumped into something.

She tried to call him, but no sound came from her throat.

She tried again, shaping his name: "Bo – "

The bedroom door flew open.

He stumbled out, onto the landing.

He was in shadow, but she could see him look down at her, see his shape, the shoulders slumped, the head canting to one side.

He stayed there only for a second.

Then he lunged.

Carrie screamed Mya's name and wheeled.

The Boyd-zombie lost its footing and rolled down the stairs.

It pinballed into Carrie, and she yelped, scrabbling at air.

Carrie's dead lover rolled over her, flattening her on the stairs.

The Boyd-zombie grunted and smashed into the armchair blocking the front door and sprawled there.

Carrie slid forward downstairs.

She couldn't stop herself.

She went straight for the creature.

Straight for its gnashing teeth.

The zombie tried to right itself, struggling to find its feet.

She looked into its eyes, and they were dead and white.

It had a wound on the side of its neck, a bite mark. The blood had coagulated now, and strings of flesh flapped around the injury. She thought about the blood on the floor in the living room, about Boyd sounding drunk to Mya.

Carrie bumped down the stairs. She put her hands out in front

378

of her. The Boyd-zombie, on all fours now, scurried to meet her as she slid down.

Her hands clawed at its face and the skin was soft, and her thumbs delved into his eyes, and they popped.

She tumbled into the thing, and it smelled dead.

The creature raked at her, and its jaw snapped, but she held its face away, held its teeth away, her thumbs jammed into the dead eyes.

They struggled to their feet and spun around the living room in a drunken dance.

Carrie clasped the creature's head tightly, thumbs driven into the eye sockets.

The Boyd-zombie's teeth chattered. The creature's fetid breath choked her.

They reeled around the living room. Slammed into the television. Carrie's leg went dead, and she lost her balance. Her hands slipped from the Boyd-zombie's face.

Blinded, it whirled away, flailing, trying to grab at Carrie.

Blood filled its eyes sockets.

"Daddy."

Carrie's scalp prickled, and she screamed:

"No, Mya!"

But it was too late.

The Boyd-zombie stopped careering around the living room and focused on its daughter's voice, turning in her direction.

Carrie hurled herself at the creature, rugby tackling it to the ground. The zombie righted itself. Crawled for Mya. Carrie screamed at her daughter to get back into the kitchen. She grasped the zombie's legs and pulled it back.

The zombie grabbed her arm.

It opened its mouth and bent its head, lips curled back, and Carrie realized she was going to be bitten.

She let go of the thing's leg.

Snapped her arm away.

The zombie's spit sprayed her face, and she recoiled.

She lashed out, scratched the creature's face. Skin came away under her nails. Flaps of flesh hung from its cheek. But the laceration didn't seem to worry the monster.

Carrie scuttled away, towards the stairs again.

The Boyd-zombie lurched towards her.

She threw herself at the creature. Shouldered it in the stomach. The zombie doubled up.

Carrie lunged for the mantelpiece and grabbed the photo of Boyd, Mya, and her on the beach in Morocco, taken the previous summer.

She struck the zombie across the skull with the picture frame.

The scalp split. Blood spurted from the wound.

She struck it again, and its neck snapped back.

The Boyd-zombie wavered. Carrie hit it a third time, slicing its face from chin to forehead. The creature toppled over in a heap.

Carrie straddled the zombie.

Screaming with fury, she hacked at the creature's head with the picture frame. Adrenaline pulsed through her veins, punching her heart. She battered the Boyd-zombie's head till the picture frame buckled and the glass cracked and blood spattered the photo.

She stopped and stared, panting for breath.

The Boyd-zombie's head had been cleaved open. Blood pooled on the wooden floor. Pieces of brain and bone peppered the furniture.

Carrie stumbled away and threw up.

"Mummy."

"Stay in the kitchen, stay in the kitchen!"

Carrie took a moment. She rose, and felt dizzy.

She wavered and thought she'd have to sit. But she found her balance. Staggered towards the kitchen.

The front door flew open, shoving the armchair back against the stairs.

A blood-coated zombie stood in the doorway, glowering at Carrie.

"No," she said, "no," thinking, *I can't do this again.*

CHAPTER 68.
FINDING MUM.

"DAD'S car… it was Dad's car," said Sam.

Craig's heart raced. The fireball mushroomed into the sky. Black smoke billowed. He could smell the fumes.

Sam's squealing made his ears ring:

"Dad's car, Dad's car!"

"Shut your gob," he told her, and she did, gawping at the blaze rising above the service area. The flames had engulfed the zombies.

Craig wheeled the truck and shot down the slip road.

The fire was blinding. Craig felt the heat on his face.

He drove around the blaze, circling the service area.

He glanced towards the garage. The explosion had shattered the windows. No one seemed to be in there.

"That was Dad's – "

"I know, Sam, I know it was our car."

He'd seen it in the forecourt just before the whole place went up.

"They were here," said his sister.

"Maybe. We don't know."

"Should we go out and check?"

He thought about it. Scoped the area. The fire lapped around the forecourt. He stopped the truck.

"There's nothing here," he said.

And then a figure rose up in the garage, hugely tall and black-faced.

Craig's heart nearly burst.

He rammed the truck into gear, ready to flee what he thought was a zombie.

Another figure reared up.

And Sam said, "Mum," her voice a gasp.

It was Mum. Her dark, red hair a mess. Her face blackened.

Craig and Sam leapt out of the truck and raced across the forecourt, crying.

A girl staggered out of the petrol station, hair bloodied, her face black with ash.

Mum stumbled out, and she cried, and her tears ran through the make-up and the soot on her cheeks, and she said their names, and they came to her and embraced her.

CHAPTER 69.
ROGER RETURN'S TO THE CASTLE.

VINCENT said, "If we don't go soon, it'll be dark by the time we're anywhere near getting through to the other end."

"What's different about the dark?" said Teena. She paced the chapel, biting her nails, tears ruining her mascara.

"I don't know," said Vincent. "But at least in daylight we can see those things. And if we get out the other end, we can see them better."

"And the children are more afraid of the dark," said Sandra.

"It'll be dark in those tunnels anyway," said Teena. "My boys, they're not going anywhere till their dad's back."

"Mum?"

She turned to look at her twins. Vincent didn't know which one had spoken. They both looked the same. But the boy spoke again:

"We want to go."

She quaked with fury and said, "What? Your dad's out there trying to save you, and you want to leave him? You ungrateful tykes."

Teena batted at them, and the boys cowered and took off, their mother chasing them out of the chapel, cursing.

Vincent went on:

"We've got to make a decision."

"*Why* do we have to make a decision?" It was Bella. She seemed to have taken over from Oswyn as the advocate of the "stay-where-we-are" contingent. "It's perfectly safe in here. They can't get in."

"But how long can we stay?" said Vincent.

"Till Oswyn and Roger come back," she said.

"And how long do we wait?"

"Someone will come. Oswyn always said someone would come. He knows these things. He knows a lot of things." Her lips tightened, and she folded her arms. "I'm staying put till he comes back – or till someone comes."

Vincent bristled. "Who will come?"

"Let it be, Vincent," said Patty. "You can't change people's minds. I should know – I've tried."

He looked at her. Bert's death had sapped her spirit.

"I've always tried. Tried with Bert, and look where it got him. The old fool. We've been married forty years. It's not the way you expect to lose your husband, no, it's not. But life, at the end, is pain and sadness."

"No Jesus anymore, Patty?" Vincent said.

"God's long gone from here," she said. "From the world and from my heart. Maybe he was never there in the first place."

They were quiet.

And then a scream ripped through the silence.

Teena, outside, screeching Roger's name

* * * *

385

Vincent got to the Gate Next the Sea first, with Gavin close behind. And when they got there, they found Teena screaming and trying to open the door.

Bobby and Jack peered through the murder holes. The boys screamed. They said the word "dad" as they shrieked.

"He's there, Roger's there!" Teena said, yanking at the door. "He's come back for us!"

Vincent lunged at her. "You can't open the door, Teena, no."

He grabbed her, pulled her away. But she'd managed to lift the latch, and as Vincent backed off he saw with horror the door swing open.

Bobby and Jack darted away from the entrance, squealing.

The door gaped open. Silhouettes danced in the sun's glare.

Zombies, thought Vincent. *Dozens of them right there.*

"Move," he said, his throat rasping.

The door creaked, opening on the zombies.

The light flushing the passageway blinded Vincent for a moment as he reared away, trying his best to hold on to Teena. Panic squeezed his heart. His vision adjusted. The zombies poured along the bridge.

Teena screamed, "It's my Roger."

And it was. Roger at the head of the horde. Leading the zombie masses into the castle.

Gavin threw himself at the door, but it was too late.

The zombies jammed the door.

Gavin wheeled and gawped at Vincent. "Go," he said, "go, and I'll do my best to hold them – "

The Roger-zombie dashed through the door, ploughing into Gavin, throwing him to the ground.

Vincent screamed. Teena shrieked. Bobby and Jack yelled for their dad.

Roger, his England shirt stained with blood, his left arm amputated at the elbow, stumbled in and staggered around the gloom of the archway.

386

Teena shrieked again, saying her husband's name.

"It's not Roger," said Vincent, dragging her away.

The Roger-zombie snarled. Spit drooled from its jaws. Its legs were cratered with wounds, bite marks where zombies had fed.

Gavin got to his feet. He stood in the doorway again, wavering.

"Get going, Vincent," he said, his voice spiked with dread.

The zombies flocked through the door.

The Roger-zombie curled back its lips and sprang forward, coming for Vincent, Teena, and the twins.

Gavin hurled himself at the second wave of undead. He screamed and battered at them, fists flying, legs kicking, forcing them back, driving them out of the castle.

He knocked a few off the bridge, into the moat. Others grabbed hold of him, bit into his arms, his neck.

He shouted:

"The door! The door!"

"Jack, the door," said Vincent as the Roger-zombie bolted towards them.

The twin darted towards the door and slammed it shut, his brother joining him to make sure it was properly closed.

Vincent despaired as he heard Gavin shriek. But the attack of the Roger-zombie snapped him out of his grief, and he ran, tugging Teena with him.

"Come on," he said to her.

But Teena wailed, reaching back for the pursuing Roger-zombie.

"It's not Roger," said Vincent as the thing gained on them.

The twins raced from the door, sweeping past their zombie-dad, tears streaming down their cheeks.

The Roger-zombie lashed out at them. Grabbed one boy by the collar and swung him round, throwing him to the ground.

Vincent shouted, "No!"

The zombie-dad pounced on his son. Sank its teeth into the child's cheek. The boy screeched. Blood spurted from his face.

The other twin shouted for his brother and said, "Dad, no – it's our Bobby, Dad, you're eating our Bobby."

Teena tore herself away from Vincent and stumbled back towards her husband and sons.

Vincent's legs nearly gave way. He was exhausted. His chest heaved, and he wheezed with every breath. But he lurched after Teena.

She battered the Roger-zombie around the head as it devoured the twin's face.

The zombie rose and growled, its son's blood pouring over its chin.

The twin panted on the ground, his face and throat shredded. Mutilated by his zombie-father. His brother screamed and backed away.

The Roger-zombie swooped on Teena. She kicked and punched, but he tore out her throat with one bite.

Vincent propelled himself forward and kicked the Roger-zombie in the head. Its neck snapped back and it rolled away from Teena.

Her face had paled. She gasped for breath. Her eyes were wide. She clasped a hand over her throat as blood pulsed from the wound.

The Roger-zombie hunched, setting its sights on Vincent. The scowl was murderous. The teeth were bared, flesh wedged between them, and blood masked its face.

Vincent gawked at the creature.

"Vincent!" came a voice.

He glanced over his shoulder.

It was Holly, staggering towards him with an axe that was nearly half as long as she was.

She dropped it and said, "Oh God, it's Roger."

Vincent tried to heave the axe off the ground. "Take Jack. His mum and brother are dead. Take him."

The zombie charged. Holly scurried away. Vincent cried out with rage and found the strength to raise the axe.

As Holly eased the mourning boy away from his brother's twitching corpse, Vincent swung the axe from right to left.

The blade sliced through the Roger-zombie's legs, hacking them off just under the knees.

The creature cartwheeled. Blood spurted from the stumps. It hit the ground – and began to crawl after Vincent, leaving a trail of blood on the grass.

"Doesn't it fucking hurt, you bastard?" said Vincent.

The zombie kept coming. Vincent lifted the axe. He hacked down and the blade cleaved the creature's skull and wedged in the earth.

The zombie's head dissected. Gore swilled out. The stench from the halved head made Vincent choke, and he rocked backwards. The creature twitched and slumped and stilled.

Vincent stared at the carcass as the flies buzzed in. The insects droned, hovering over the zombie, and their whirr put Vincent in a trance.

"They're dead. Teena and Bobby."

Vincent came to. Bella kneeled over Teena.

"What?" he said.

"They're dead, Vincent."

"Yeah, I know." His blood froze. He held his breath. *Gavin*, he thought.

He bolted for the entrance.

Without thinking, he threw open the door.

A clutch of zombies crouched over a pile of guts and bone.

Vincent yelled out.

The zombies raised their heads. Flesh filled their mouths. Gavin's flesh.

Two of the zombies sprang from the remains and came at Vincent. He slammed the door and then pressed his back against it and on the other side, the zombies raked the wood.

CHAPTER 70.
THERE ARE MILLIONS.

THE zombie stepped in. Blood saturated its body, head to toe. All Carrie could see through the crimson masking its face were its eyes.

Jungle-coloured eyes.

She opened her mouth.

Sawyer said, "There are millions of them. They're everywhere."

He stepped in and kicked the door shut, and she ran to him and became slick with the blood when she embraced him.

While Sawyer showered, Carrie opened cans of fruit and poured them into a bowl. Mya watched her, cowering in the corner.

She told her daughter, "Don't be afraid of him, he helped me, and he'll help us both, now."

"Is he an angel, Mummy?"

"Not quite."

She gave him clothes from Boyd's wardrobe – a Dolce & Gabbana long-sleeved T-shirt that was tight on Sawyer's frame and showed his shape, and a pair of Levis. He washed his walking boots in the bathroom, then put them back on his feet.

They sat at the kitchen table and dipped white bread in the fruit, and ate. Mya looked at him from behind her glass of orange squash, her chin lowered, her eyes wide.

"You've been very brave," he said to her.

Mya blushed. "I don't know. I'm scared."

"We're all scared. It's okay to be scared. But you can still be brave and do the right thing."

"Did Daddy do the right thing?"

Carrie said, "It's not Daddy's fault what happened to him. He got sick, like everyone else has got sick. And when they get sick they… they change and want to do terrible things. It's not their fault."

"Is Daddy dead now, or is he going to wake up again?"

Carrie shuddered. "He's not going to wake up again, Mya."

Not without his head, he won't, she thought.

Earlier, Sawyer had dragged Boyd's body out into the street. Carrie had been shocked, seeing her boyfriend, Mya's dad, lying there – a pile of flesh on the pavement.

But she realized that whatever there had been of Boyd had long gone.

Gone when a zombie bit him.

"Can I go to the bathroom?" said Mya.

Carrie told her yes, and when she'd left, she reached out and took Sawyer's hand. "I thought you were gone"

"*I* thought I was gone," he said.

"What have you seen?"

"I've seen the dead walking. We can't stop them. It's too late. They're everywhere."

"How did you get away?"

His eyes were glassy. He recalled a memory. He ran it in his head:

"I raced back towards Hornsey Park Road. The zombies followed me. Drake and his crew were in a Land Cruiser, trying to get away. I led the zombies to them. They got overwhelmed. I took the van. Drove here. The address you gave me for the TomTom. Remember? I did. I remembered. I saw the dead. Everywhere. *Every*where. The old dead and the new dead. But only the dead. There are millions of them."

She squeezed his hand.

"I wish my baby was yours," she said, and she cried. "You could look after it, be a father. We could be a family in all of this carnage."

He looked her in the eye.

"We're fucked, aren't we," she said. "Oh Christ! My little Mya... my... my... baby... I can't – "

He stood up. "We've got to go, now. It's getting dark. It's not safe here."

She looked straight at him. "Is anywhere safe?"

He said nothing.

CHAPTER 71.
GOING UNDERGROUND.

"THEN why hasn't he changed yet?" said Bella, pointing at Derek, who sat quietly with his head in his hands and a cloth over his throat.

They'd gathered in the inner ward again. The sun glowed strongly, the heat still intense. But shadows now spread across the grass and cooled the ground.

"I think," said Vincent, not really knowing but having a go, "it's because he didn't die. Roger must've died. It's when you die, that's when you... become alive again. But I don't know. I don't."

"We've got to burn their remains," said Patty.

"We've got to leave," said Vincent.

"Don't think you can take charge now you're the only man left," said Bella.

"I'm not doing that. I'm just saying – "

"Say what you like, but Oswyn's not back yet."

Patty said, "He's dead too, dear. Dead and walking, I would imagine. You've got to accept that."

"I'm going," said Vincent. "It's the only way down to the shore without having to fight our way through zombies. The only way.

393

We can't out run them. We can't go out of the door. We've seen what happens. I'm going, and you can come with me if you want. Holly?"

Fear filled her eyes. He held out his hand to her. She stayed where she was. He said her name, but she still didn't move.

"Are you coming with me?"

"Vincent, I – I can't."

"Why not? You said earlier that – "

"I'm – I'm too scared. I can't bear the thought of" – she shuddered – "crawling... crawling through those narrow, dark – I can't bear it, Vincent."

"I'll come," said Derek, his voice a rasp. He tottered over.

Christ, thought Vincent, *that's all I need*, but he knew he couldn't stop him. And he knew he couldn't force Holly either. He glanced around everyone in turn and then spoke:

"Gavin's boat's down there. If we can get to it, we'll be okay. We can sail down the river. We can't stay here, but if we're going to, we need a plan. You can't just wait."

"Why can't we wait?" said Bella.

"Because there's nothing to wait for."

Silence fell. Jack stepped forward. "I'd like to come, please."

"Of course you can," said Vincent.

Bella said, "Your mother wouldn't – "

"My mother's not alive now, is she," said Jack. Bella scowled. Jack fidgeted with the Kodak disposable camera his mother had brought to the castle. Vincent wondered if Jack would ever be able to hold those photos, remember his family's last day together. Perhaps, hundreds of years from now, the images would be exhibited, an artefact of humankind's war against the zombies. But that meant humans had to survive. And deep in Vincent's heart pulsed a doubt that this would never happen.

"I'd like to come," said Patty.

"Good, that's good," Vincent told her.

"But I think I might be too old."

"No you're not," said Vincent. He looked at Holly again. "Holly?" and there was a desperate tone to his voice – he could hear it.

She said nothing.

"I want to go," said Catrin.

Bella told her, "You're in no fit state to go."

Catrin stood. "I'm an adult – that's fit enough."

"Catrin," said Bella, "I'm your line manager now that Oswyn… Oswyn is away, so you have to abide by my rules, and do what I – "

"Oh, shut up," said Catrin. "There are no rules, now. There's no bureaucracy to make you wet, Bella. No Oswyn either." Catrin stomped over to where Vincent stood.

Holly shuffled forward too, joining them.

Vincent said, "Sandra? Penny? You've got to give your kids a chance. And they can make it, too. They can crawl through there like little mice."

"I can't, though," said Sandra. "Look at me." She was plump. That was the one flaw, one of many, in his plan. Another was that he didn't know how wide the channels were, or if they were open at all.

He shut his eyes and sagged under the burden. He might be taking these people into hell, leading Holly to a horrible death. He nearly said, *Forget it, I'll go*. Or even go with Bella's suggestion:

Stay here – and die.

* * * *

"You've got to be joking," said Sandra. Her reaction made the children whine, and Hettie and Maisie had already said they didn't want to go. They wanted to stay with their mum. So the girls had to be hoisted out of the pit.

395

The reek down here made Vincent screw up his face. He thought he'd grown accustomed to the smell the previous time. But the odour clawed its way into his airways and burned away his sense of smell. It brought tears to his eyes.

"I'll go first," said Jack. "I don't mind doing that."

"That's brave of you," said Vincent. "But I think I've got to go first. Then you. And if something happens to me – "

"What'll happen?" said Holly.

"I only said 'if'," he told her. "*If* something happens, Jack can lead. Then after Jack, the kids – okay Bryony, Annalee? – then Penny, Patty, Catrin, and… " He stared at Holly and nodded, and she nodded back. He'd wanted her behind him, but she'd said she couldn't do that: people would accuse them of sticking together, accuse him of favouritism. So she agreed to be at the back, away from him. "… Holly. And Derek, can you take up the rear?"

Derek murmured. Vincent squirmed. He didn't like it that Derek was coming. The man was close to being a zombie. But Vincent hadn't been bold enough to tell him he couldn't come. If the guy was still alive, still human, he probably had a right to save himself.

Vincent tried to forget about it. But thoughts rifled through his mind today. The heat and the stress increased the pressure in his skull. His brain throbbed, and an ache beat through his head.

He looked up. Sandra and Bella gazed down at him. Their faces were pale with fear.

"You want to come?" he called up.

They said nothing. They moved away from the hole, and Vincent found himself staring up at the sky. He shut his eyes and turned away.

"Are we ready?"

They murmured.

He crouched and squinted and stared into the channel. He flicked on the flashlight Catrin had found in a store cupboard in the staff quarters. The beam washed into the tunnel, showing the dirt and the grime.

He said to them, "Stay close to the person in front and talk all the time, okay?"

He took a breath and slid into the channel head-first. The air was muggy, but there was the faint smell of seaweed that had given him hope earlier on. He prayed the odour wasn't imagined.

The channel was narrow. His elbows were tucked under him and, using them, he dragged himself along. He couldn't raise his head very high, and he guessed that by the end of the crawl – if there were an end – he'd be poker stiff.

He wormed his way forward, the sludge squelching under his elbows, his stomach, and his knees.

His lungs burned already. They felt damp, like he had the flu. Thirst had dried out his throat, and the inside of his mouth felt furry. He'd crawled ten yards and fatigue made him limp.

He stopped and said, "Everyone all right – pass it back," and he heard Jack pass it back and then Patty's thin, reedy voice passing it back.

But to whom? There was no one else inside yet. And he heard Derek say, "Get a move on," before he started to crawl again.

He gripped the flashlight in his right hand, spearing the gloom ahead with the beam.

Terror filled his veins with every inch he made through the soil.

At any moment he expected the pipe to taper and seal, blocking him in, the others ploughing forward, him screaming for them to stop.

His heart pounded, panic causing his body to convulse.

Jesus, he thought, the alarm rising in his chest.

I shouldn't have done this.

He quaked and wanted to scream, the walls closing in on him, the channel narrowing, the flashlight showing hands tearing through the earth trying to grab at him.

But he knew they weren't real – his mind careering, that was all.

He moaned, fighting the fear and the grogginess.

He piped himself through the earth, ignoring the queasiness, his quivering guts, his strength-sapped limbs.

The soil brushed against him, and it felt like razors.

On, on, on… he told himself, sweat drenching his body, his lungs heavy.

He stopped and gasped, desperate for fresh air.

Jack nudged his foot and said, "What's the matter?"

"Nothing… just… taking a break," said Vincent.

Then a voice from behind them called out:

"What's the matter?"

Vincent answered with, "Everything's fine… it's okay… I'm just taking a second, that's all – we're all right."

"Are we all right?" said Jack.

Vincent tried to look over his shoulder, but he couldn't twist his neck because the tunnel was too narrow. His bones felt like they were melded together. His muscles seemed to have withered like fruit left out in the sun.

He said, "We're okay, Jack. Honest."

"We – we're not going to get stuck in here, are we?"

"No way. You ready to go?"

"I am, yeah."

Vincent crawled on. He had to constantly fight off the feeling of panic that kept flaring in his breast. His eyes were fixed on the channel ahead, the flashlight showing him the way. It stretched on, and while it remained open, he could still hope.

No need to worry, no need to panic, he told himself.

But he couldn't fend off the fears. They swirled in his head. His belly rolled, and he felt sick and dizzy.

Got to keep moving, got to keep moving.

Water dripped from the roof of the channel, now.

Shit, have we gone too far? he thought. *Are we under the Straits? Is it going to crush us?*

But he knew that was impossible. He knew they couldn't have made it that far. Perhaps they were under the moat. That meant they'd only crawled twenty yards or so. And how long had that taken? It felt like… the word betrayed him. But then he found it: aeons.

A good word to describe the age he felt they'd been under ground:

Aeons.

And how much longer? If it had taken this long to just get to the moat, how long would it take to crawl the two-hundred metres – at least – that lay between the castle and the Straits?

Numbers flashed up in his brain. They flickered like West End lights. They whirled, and he tried to catch them, tried to work out the sum: *how long? how long?*

But the figures swam and swirled and melted and became a carnage of colour in his head, and stars burst before his eyes.

He gagged and puked, retching and twitching in the tunnel.

He kept crawling and throwing up, slithering over his own sick, not caring that the others would have to do the same. He was saving them, for Christ's sake, leading them to salvation. They'd have to put up with his vomit.

Jack groaned behind him, and Vincent said something, but he didn't know what came out of his mouth.

He gasped for breath, the sour taste of sick in his mouth, the smell of puke in his nose.

Is this what going mad feels like?

"What did you say?" said Jack.

"Huh?"

"You said something, Vincent. What did you say?"

"Nothing, I was thinking aloud."

"You said something about being mad?"

"Don't worry about it, I was thinking aloud. Keep going, come on."

"You're not going mad are you?"

"No, I'm not."

"You puked, though."

"Yeah, heavy night." He huffed, his head clearing.

"Vincent?"

"What?"

"Do you think my mum and my brother will come after me?"

Vincent said nothing.

Jack asked again, "Do you?"

"No they won't, Jack. Zombies don't think like that. They're… they're not your mum and your brother any more. Just like that thing wasn't your dad. What was inside is gone, and it's… it's what's inside that makes us… makes us who we are."

"Okay," said Jack.

"We shouldn't talk too much. We should try and save our energy and our oxygen, okay?"

"Okay."

Vincent's chest blazed. He rasped for breath.

We're going to die here, he thought. *We're going to suffocate.*

He thought about Holly, her claustrophobia. The tunnel had narrowed. They were nose to the earth, now. Their heads scraped the roof of the channel and soil showered over them.

What if it falls in on us?

His legs trembled at the thought of being buried alive.

He murmured a prayer and then thought, *Who the fuck am I praying to? There's no one down here. There's no one up there, either.*

His mother came to his mind. She leaned out of the kitchen window, calling him in from the garden, calling him in for his supper, calling him out of the tunnel:

400

"Come on, Vincent, supper's ready, get out of there… look at the state of you, come on… crawl, darling, crawl… supper'll be cold and cold chips'll give you tummy ache… "

"I'm doing my best, Mum, I'm doing my best."

Jack behind him said, "What did you say about Mum?"

Oh shit, thought, Vincent, *I'm going crazy. I'm losing my mind.*

And he could do nothing about it. Keep crawling, that was all. Crawl till madness overcame him. Crawl to hell and let the fires burn him to a crisp. Crawl…

CHAPTER 72.
LEFT BEHIND.

"HOW long have they been gone?" said Sandra.

Bella checked her watch. "Half an hour. They're dead, you know. There's no way they could make it through. There'd be no air, no oxygen."

"Vincent said he could smell seaweed, though."

"No, that's not right. It must've been in his head. Did you see his eyes? They were glazed over, Sandra. The boy was going mad, I think. He's taken Catrin. He's taken those kids to their deaths. He's a murderer, you know."

"I think he was doing his best. If I could, I would've gone with him. And my kids, too. I should've made them go." Her gaze drifted to Hettie and Maisie, curled up asleep on the rug in the corner of the chapel.

"Oswyn will be back, don't you worry."

"He won't though, Bella. Roger came back and… and look what he did – look at Teena and Bobby and… " She trailed off.

"What's the matter?" said Bella.

Sandra said nothing.

"Sandra?"

"Teena and Bobby."

Bella's eyes widened. The bodies lay in the inner ward, roasted by the sun.

Sandra said, "We should check on them."

The women stared at each other. They stayed sitting. Neither of them moving.

Sandra said, "You work here, Bella, so you should… "

Bella rose, dread making her shiver. She crept out of the chapel. Threw one glance back at Sandra, who'd gone to her children and huddled with them on the rug.

Bella sneaked out of the wall passage, out into the heat.

The sun's glare hit her. She blinked, trying to focus on the inner ward.

She remembered where they'd laid Teena and Bobby, and Roger's remains. They'd spoken about burning the bodies. But that had been forgotten in their desperation to escape.

She regretted not going with Vincent and the others. But she knew she couldn't have crawled through those channels – even if they existed. She'd worked here for two years and although aware of them, never thought they were still passable. It was remarkable that Vincent had even found the pit. And really, he shouldn't have gone down there: public property and –

She faltered.

Don't be an ass, Bella, she told herself. *Forget about doing your job, now. There's no job. There's only survival.*

She blinked and gradually began to focus, seeing the inner ward, where the bodies were laid out, and –

She froze.

Only Roger's wrecked corpse remained.

A cold feeling rinsed through her. She stumbled back into the chapel and said to Sandra, "We've got to go, they've got up… Teena and Bobby."

"Go where?" said Sandra.

The children had woken and were crying.

"Shut them up, Sandra," said Bella.

"Where are we going?"

They raced along the passages. Bella's chest tightened with every step. Sweat filmed her body. It got everywhere. Between the rolls of fat on her belly and in her inner thighs, where it chafed. Under her breasts and down her back, where it glued the shirt to her skin. She felt terrible and dreamed of a hot bath.

They came to the latrines and looked down through the hole Vincent had made.

"We're not going are we?" said Sandra.

"We have to, they're here somewhere. Teena and Bobby."

A growl confirmed her fears.

"Oh God!" she said. She lowered herself into the latrine and saw mother and son zombies race across the grass towards them.

Sandra saw them too and screamed. She urged Bella to hurry. And Hettie and Maisie shrieked, leaping about.

The gap was too narrow and Bella's waist was too wide. She wriggled and moaned. Sandra pushed down on her shoulders.

"Pull yourself through, Bella, pull yourself through."

"I'm stuck, I'm stuck, Sandra, I'm – "

The rim of the hole crumbled. The soil fell away. Bella dropped. The air shot out of her lungs. She gasped and plunged into darkness and for a second, she thought she wouldn't stop falling, and a feeling of horror overwhelmed her.

But then she hit the ground and pain shot up her leg, her ankle twisting. She screeched and rolled around in the dirt and the darkness.

Sandra's children, crying and whelping, dropped down into the pit after her.

Sandra said, "Find the tunnel, kids, find it and go."

The children raced past Bella. Up above, Sandra lowered

herself into the hole and momentarily blocked out the light.

Bella heard one of the kids say, "Mum, we've found it."

Sandra dropped down and landed next to Bella.

"Go on then, I'm right behind you," said Sandra.

Bella looked up and saw Teena's and Bobby's dead faces staring down at her.

Sandra grabbed her and said, "Come on," and then hoisted her to her feet, and they stumbled through the darkness, Bella's feet sinking into the soft earth, her ankle on fire. She hobbled, and behind her, the sound of the zombies dropping into the pit made her whine.

Sandra shouted for her children, and they called back, saying they were in the tunnel, and Bella followed the sound of their voices.

"You go first," Sandra told her.

"You're… you're letting me go?" said Bella.

Moments ago, she'd panicked and come down into the pit first, hoping to get away. She'd abandoned Sandra and the children and now wanted to say something, wanted to apologize and thank the woman.

"Please, Bella, they're getting up, they're coming… please go."

Bella crouched and crawled into the pipe in the wall.

She gasped at the sheer blackness, and thought for a moment she'd gone blind. The smell of rot and decay made her cringe. She inched forward, shouting with dread at the prospect of squirming through this narrow space. She heaved herself forward.

And stopped.

She couldn't budge.

The lip of the pipe gripped her waist.

She struggled but couldn't move.

She clawed the earth, fingers gouging the soil.

A cold hand gripped her wrist.

She shrieked.

"Bella, it's me, Hettie," said the little girl. "You've got to move so Mummy can come in."

The child tugged, but Bella wouldn't shift. Her thirteen stone was staying put, jammed into the mouth of the tunnel.

Shrieks burst out from behind her – shrieks and growls and tearing noises.

The zombies had got to Sandra.

Bella said to the child, "You go. Go now, Hettie. Hurry."

The child scurried, her small shape disappearing into the darkness.

Bella sobbed. She tried to heave herself forward again. She thought about Oswyn and how for two years she'd admired him and tried to make him like her. But now he never would, and no man would ever love her. The realization tore out her heart, and she yelled as hope seeped out of her.

The zombies bit into her legs, and she jerked.

They chomped the soft flesh of her thighs, the tendons and ligaments behind her knees, her sturdy calf muscles.

She shrieked and kicked out, but she was stuck.

The pain became unbearable as they ate her legs.

She begged for death, but it didn't come, and her lower half had already been stripped to the bone long before shock finally killed her.

CHAPTER 73.
THE END OF LONDON.

TEMPERATURES soared early into the evening. The sky remained blue, cloudless. They drove north. Carrie didn't know why north. Sawyer couldn't say either. It felt right.

"As right as anything could feel at the end of the world," he'd said.

Carrie had picked up Boyd's BlackBerry before they left the house, and she'd accessed the internet. She typed in the URL of the BBC News site. It took a while to connect, but finally it found the page.

She played a video that was showing on the site.

The reporter was in a helicopter above London. Her voice was high-pitched, laced with panic. The grainy footage shot from the helicopter showed rivers of zombies washing through London.

How long before every inch of the city would be swamped by the undead?

How long before no one living was left?

Carrie felt sick at the thought.

The reporter, looking grey and scared in the helicopter, said things were the same throughout Britain. All the cities crawling with dead. All the living, doomed.

"Welcome to Zombie Britannica," she'd said.

Carrie glanced in the back of the Land Cruiser.

Mya lay wrapped in the blanket. She slept with Dandy in her arms. Carrie thought about the doll. Long and thin, with straggly yellow ponytails and Pippy Longstockings socks.

She remembered clutching the rag to herself when she was scared, when she was sad. She remembered crying into it when her mother left. Embracing it when Boyd walked out for the first time, just before Mya was born.

Carrie wondered if the doll and the blanket would be passed down to Mya's children. But the thought brought anguish. She knew they wouldn't be. Their distribution down the generations would end with Mya. She was the last. No doll. No blanket. No descendants.

Carrie blinked away the tears and scanned the streets. They were on the Great Cambridge Road in Enfield, the A10. Buses lay on their sides, and cars were abandoned. She glimpsed a pack of zombies racing through a housing estate.

"How many do you think have survived?" she said.

Sawyer said he didn't know.

"Do you think we're the last?"

He said nothing.

They scoped their surroundings, taking in the desolation.

She glanced at Sawyer and thought about things, about the two of them, but realized there would be no happy ending.

They were doomed.

He slowed the vehicle.

"What is it?" she said.

"This is the end of London."

"Okay." She stared up at the Great Cambridge Roundabout, where they would follow the A10 towards the M25.

The end of London.

"I'm sorry it's like this," he said.

"I should think so. I've always thought, *Damn that Sawyer, he caused all this.*" She smiled for the first time in hours. Maybe longer than that. She leaned across to kiss him.

She drew away and held his eyes and said, "Had we met before, do you think – "

"You wouldn't want to have met me. I'd've been no good."

She was about to say, "I could've made you good," but realized she'd tried that one before. With Boyd. With others, too. "I can sort him out," was the mantra. "Love will heal him."

She said to Sawyer, "No, I suppose you're right," and sat back in her seat and stared ahead at the road that would lead them from London. Someone had graffitied the letters I LU on one of the bridges, but the next seven letters had been painted out.

Who did you love? wondered Carrie. *And was it worth it?*

Sawyer put the Land Cruiser into gear and rolled it forward.

Mya screamed.

Carrie jerked in her seat.

She whirled so quickly she hurt her neck.

Mya gawped out of the back window.

"Oh, Jesus," said Carrie.

They came swarming through the streets, clogging the A10.

The population of London.

The *undead* population of London.

"Drive," she said.

But Sawyer wasn't moving.

The zombies surged from every street, blocking the road.

A helicopter swooped overhead.

Carrie looked at the BlackBerry. The BBC footage showed a Land Cruiser surrounded by zombies.

The reporter was saying, "And it looks like there are survivors, but they're trapped."

Sawyer gripped the steering wheel. He slammed the accelerator. The tyres screeched. The impact thrust Carrie back into her seat.

The Land Cruiser ploughed forward, scything through the zombies' frontline.

Carrie felt every bump. Mya screamed in the backseat and swayed from side to side as the Land Cruiser swerved. She clutched Dandy to her chest.

Carrie reached over the seat, and grabbed her daughter's arm. The truck sheared through the zombies. They were knocked aside or crushed under the wheels.

Sawyer rocketed up the A10, hitting the roundabout that would take them on to the M25.

The Land Cruiser pitched as it drove over zombies, dragging them under the wheels. Carrie prayed that the vehicle's suspension could take it. It was like driving along a dirt track at high speed. The four-track lurched and rocked. Carrie was tossed about in her seat. She clutched Mya's arm.

Sawyer hammered the Land Cruiser. The engine clanked. Dread froze Carrie's blood as she feared they would stall or break down.

"Keep going," she said, not to Sawyer but to the vehicle.

Sawyer gritted his teeth. Sweat beaded his forehead. His knuckles were white on the wheel. The veins stood out on the back of his hands.

The Land Cruiser powered through the undead. It shaved through the horde, sweeping them aside.

Carrie looked at the BlackBerry and saw their progress on the BBC News site.

She watched as the truck cleaved through the zombies.

"You're nearly there," she said.

The zombies thinned out now, fewer of them here.

Sawyer gave the truck some extra juice, and she felt the surge as the vehicle pulled away.

They sliced through the last of the zombies and the road smoothed and Carrie gave a cry of relief.

She looked behind her, through the rear window. The zombies were following. But the Land Cruiser had hit 70mph, and the dead dwindled in the distance.

CHAPTER 74.
DEREK.

NOW Vincent didn't know what was real or not.

Voices mingled in his head. Images swirled. His stomach rolled. He tried to spit, but had no saliva. He gagged a few times, throwing up. His lungs were shrivelled. His limbs ached.

His elbows gouged into the earth as he heaved himself along. The flashlight's beam reached into the gloom. The channel stretched ahead of him. Narrow enough to crawl through, but only just.

The sense of dread was overwhelming, and it took all his effort to fight it off.

Once or twice, Jack had tugged at his leg from behind and Vincent had stopped, panting.

Jack would say, "Didn't you hear me?" and Vincent wasn't sure if he had.

Someone nearer the back wanted to stop for a moment, Jack would say. Or they wanted to know how far they had to go.

He didn't know how long they'd been going, and wondered if they'd got lost and were crawling down into hell.

He then thought they'd be in this tunnel forever, and would maybe evolve into mole-human hybrids.

Lack of water, exhaustion, and oxygen deprivation had pushed him to the limits of his sanity. Madness lay close by. Far too close. He wouldn't have to crawl much further before he was there, the land of lunacy.

Maybe I should just stop and give up, he'd think. *Curl up here and die. Rot away and let the worms eat me.*

But then he'd have a moment of clarity. He became aware of his responsibility towards those behind him. The burden sickened him, but he couldn't give up.

He stopped now and laid his head on his arms and closed his eyes. His belly grumbled with hunger. His body felt as if it were unravelling.

Jack said, "Are you okay?"

Vincent said, "No, I'm not."

"I'm really tired, Vincent. Them behind me, too."

"Me too, Jack."

"Are we going to get out? I can't really breathe very well."

"I can't either."

"I think Holly's going crazy back there, Vincent."

Holly, thought Vincent, wondering for a second who Jack was referring to. And then remembering.

Jesus, my brain's fucked. I'm forgetting who people are, he thought.

It weakened him further, knowing he'd brought Holly down here into this nightmare.

Claustrophobia couldn't get much worse than this.

He shuddered at the thought of her dread.

He wanted to say, *Turn back*. Wanted to wriggle around and return to the castle.

Bella was right – they should've waited.

If he fell asleep here now, he'd be murdering Holly. He'd be murdering them all. He might have done that anyway, by bringing them down here.

But if he kept moving, they had a glimmer of hope.

Keep moving, he told himself, *keep moving.*

"What did you say?" Jack said.

Christ, thought Vincent, *I'm going crazy.*

There had to be an end to this.

He just hoped it wasn't a dead one.

The scream rifled along the channel.

Vincent jerked, his head thumping the roof of the tunnel, soil raining down on him.

He tried to look over his shoulder, but couldn't swivel his neck.

Jack bumped into his feet and said, "What was that?"

Vincent didn't know – and then he heard the words: "Keep moving, keep moving," filtering down the line.

Patty's voice, Penny's voice, Bryony or Annalee's voice, and now Jack saying, "Keep moving."

The screams kept coming.

It was Holly. He recognized her voice. The sound of her terror.

He wanted to go back, see what was wrong.

Holly was panicking, and it was his fault.

"Keep moving," said Jack again.

"No – no, I have to – "

"Please, Vincent, please. You've… you've got to… we… we'll get stuck here, please… "

And Vincent knew Jack was right.

With a wail, he crawled on, gritting his teeth, tears rolling down his cheeks, Holly's yelps ringing in his ears.

"What's the matter?" he said. "What's going on?"

But no one said anything.

He sobbed, desperate to help Holly.

Had the claustrophobia got to her? Was she having a panic attack? Would she bring the tunnel down on herself, bury herself alive?

And then a word came whispering out of the darkness behind him:

"Derek… "

Vincent's blood chilled.

"Oh fuck," he said.

And then the name again:

"Derek… it's Derek… "

And Vincent knew what had happened and why Holly, second from last, right in front of Derek, was shrieking.

He knew before Jack said, "Derek's dead – and he's coming after us."

CHAPTER 75.
DARKNESS... HOPE.

THEY reached the South Mimms motorway service area on the M25 and found the road blocked by Army vehicles.

But the trucks were unmanned. Some were overturned and others burned out. The soldiers must've been ordered to either stop people leaving London or stop them entering – and they'd faced an unconquerable enemy.

An army of zombies

The sun fell. They sky glowed orange, promising another blistering day tomorrow.

If they had a tomorrow.

Carrie remembered the weather forecast that morning. They said it might approach fifty degrees centigrade. Unprecedented, they'd said. Temperatures never before recorded in the UK.

Perfect weather for a zombie plague, she thought.

Sawyer stopped the truck and got out. Carrie told Mya to stay in the car and then got out herself. They stood in front of the blockade.

"Can we get through?" she said.

"I'll just pile through it." He crouched and picked up a discarded automatic weapon. He rolled it over in his hands, studying the gun.

She said, "What do you think happened?"

"I don't know. The line didn't hold, I guess. They didn't know what they were fighting."

She looked over her shoulder, checking on Mya. "We've got to keep going."

"Do you think I wouldn't?"

"No – no, I'm not saying that. I'm – I'm saying it for myself."

He laid the gun down. "I could do with holding you," he said.

She opened her arms for him, and he stepped into them, and she wrapped them around his back, and he held her too, pressing her to his chest.

Would she have ever done this with Sawyer in the real world?

She opened her eyes and saw seven zombies come from the shadows at a pace, circling the Land Cruiser.

She yelled and pushed Sawyer away. He grabbed her hand and raced for the truck.

"No, no!" she said.

Zombies clustered around the vehicle. They clawed at it, trying to get at Mya, who was screaming inside.

Carrie bolted straight for the zombies.

They saw her coming and turned to face her.

Sawyer shouted for her to stop.

But Mya was locked inside, the undead trying to get at her, and nothing would stop Carrie.

My gospel, my gospel.

The sun fell further, and night approached.

Carrie hurdled up on the bonnet of the four-track.

She kicked out at the zombies. They tried to grab at her. Sawyer ploughed into them, armed with the gun.

He fired, and the zombies jigged as bullets tore into them.

Carrie leapt from the truck. A zombie in a tattered nurse's uniform grabbed her. The nurse-zombie went to bite her face, but she clawed at the creature's eyes and then punched it in the jaw, sent it reeling

She looked for Sawyer.

He tussled with two zombies.

Blood filled their jaws.

He elbowed one in the face, whirled round and shot it.

He shouted, "Get in the truck," and wheeled, firing as he went.

Carrie tried to open the door. Four zombies came at her. She sank to her knees. She looked at Mya.

In the window, she saw a reflection of the sun disappearing behind the horizon.

She waited for death as the light of her last day died.

And nothing came.

She heard groans, but none of the snarls that usually came with a zombie attack.

Gunshots from Sawyer's weapon broke the silence.

She turned, and the zombies lumbered around. They appeared lethargic, dumb. Their limbs were stiff, as if rigor mortis had locked in.

She remembered the cleaner-zombie at The Lexington, teetering in the pub doorway. But when it stepped out into the light, it became lethal. As if life had surged through its dead veins.

"The sun," Sawyer had said at the time, "they're quicker in the sun."

Sawyer, raking the lumbering things with bullets, said, "What happened?"

The zombies continued to attack, but their movements had slowed. Some even fell to their knees and tried to crawl.

"Get in the car," she said.

Carrie drove. They scanned the M25 as they went. Zombies writhed on the road. They loped about in the growing gloom as if drunk. They bumped into each other. It all looked like some old horror film. They weren't the demons she'd seen earlier.

Sawyer asked again, "What happened?"

"The sun. Remember The Lexington? What you said?"

They joined the M1. Zombies, thousands of them, shambled. They keeled over. Piles of them flailed on the motorway, trying to get up, looking for the energy to –

"The sun," she said again.

They drove through an England riddled with the undead.

They stopped at the Watford Gap service area and filled the car with petrol. Sawyer fended off the zombies that shuffled towards them.

Inside the garage, the three of them ransacked the shelves, clearing them of as much food as they could carry – biscuits, bread, water, and cans of beans.

"There's no one living, is there," said Carrie.

Sawyer said nothing. He just watched the undead plod along the motorway. An exodus of zombies going nowhere. They stumbled about, some going south, others north, meandering across the carriageways

When the headlights caught them, they clawed the air and some of the viciousness Carrie had seen before came back into their faces.

Sawyer slept. He looked pale. She glanced at him and felt a glow in her belly. She felt hope now. Hope for Mya and hope for her baby. They would have someone with them.

CHAPTER 76.
THE DRAIN.

THEY were trapped in the tunnel with a zombie.

Vincent dug his elbows into the earth and heaved. He pushed with his knees. Dragged himself along.

He had to speed up to stretch the gap between them – then Jack could quicken his pace, the kids behind him could move faster, Penny and Patty could do the same, and then Catrin... and Holly. Holly could put more distance between herself and Derek.

Keep moving... keep moving...

His flashlight's beam speared down the channel. And showed darkness. More darkness. Lengths and lengths of it.

Vincent cried out. Crawled through the dirt. Pain doused his body. His head thumped, and his heart thundered so hard he thought it would burst.

He was certain that death was close. He wouldn't last much longer. And maybe that would be for the best. Maybe that would end this agony, this torture.

Give it up and die.

But Holly's scream came out of the darkness behind him.

He imagined her being chased by the Derek-zombie. The dead thing tearing through the earth, jaws snapping, eyes fixed on Holly and seeing her as meat.

What would happen if he caught up with her?

A thought came to his mind:

Holly dead, blocking the passage.

And for a second, he thought that would be a good thing.

The zombie couldn't get passed – unless it ate its way through her, and that would take a while.

Enough time for them to gain an advantage on their pursuer.

But then the horror of what he was thinking jolted him, and he screamed, "No!" But what he'd contemplated wouldn't leave his mind, now. It had stained his memory and would remain there, a bruise. The possibilities swirled around his brain, making him cry:

Maybe Derek would leave Holly half-eaten, which meant she'd come alive – and then they'd have two zombies tunnelling after them in this underworld.

And the Derek-zombie and the Holly-zombie would chase and chase and crawl and crawl through these endless tunnels, eating through them one by one, half-eating them, making them into zombies.

Until there'd be only him left.

Him with half a dozen dead things on his arse.

He churned through the soil with his battered limbs, gritting his teeth against the pain.

Adrenaline pulsed through his veins, hammering into his heart. The survival instinct drove him forward.

His smelled something.

His eyes widened.

Holly's screams filled the tunnel.

He clawed forward, elbows gouging the soil.

The others were shouting now – shouting for the one in front of them to hurry, go faster. Patty moaned and prayed. Penny begged her kids to hurry. The children screamed.

Jack said, "It's coming, Vincent, it's coming," his voice shaking with tears.

Vincent quickened again. How much faster could he go? He had no feeling in his legs. His shoulders were on fire. The skin on his arms had been sheared away. Blood came from his nose. His eyes stung with grit and tears.

But then: *the smell.*

He knew what it was.

It had always been there. But it had grown stronger. Stronger with every yard they made.

The sea.

Salt and seaweed.

Vincent gave a shout of hope.

A jolt of energy spurted through him.

In the flashlight's beam, something shimmered.

Light.

Daylight. Twilight. Moonlight. He didn't care which one.

It was light. It was not darkness

How far ahead?

Fifty yards?

He crawled and shouted:

"Almost there! Tell them, Jack. Almost there!"

And he heard Jack shout, "Almost there, keep going, not too far!" and then the children behind Jack saying, "We're nearly there!" and the voices grew quieter and more distant until the furthest one back was swallowed by Holly's shrieks.

Vincent smelled the air and the sea and switched off the flashlight, knowing there'd be zombies out there, not wanting to alert them. He chanced there wouldn't be too many, hoped they would have enough time to crawl out of the pipe and leap into Gavin's boat, any boat, and sail off.

The circle of light grew larger, and he saw that it was dim. Night was coming, the day dying.

Elation flared in his chest.

He'd done it. He'd brought them through. He'd achieved something worthwhile. He'd saved lives.

He couldn't stop crying out, "We're there! We're there!" when he got to the mouth of the tunnel. It was narrow. Weeds draped down like a bead curtain. He burst through them, forcing himself out, and it was like birth.

He shouted with joy as clean air filled his lungs and dim light blinded him.

He snaked out of the tunnel, grabbed for the ground – and gasped with horror.

He clawed at air. Nothing to hold on to. His eyes adjusted to the new light. Beneath him, a shimmering darkness.

He was out of the pipe up to his thighs and had no strength in his legs to prevent himself from falling.

He shouted and spilled out of the tunnel, flapping his arms.

He went head first into the water, the coldness of it biting into his bones.

Beneath the surface, he shrieked, and bubbles shot from his mouth, and he had no breath, and water went up his nose.

He panicked, his lungs about to explode.

And someone grabbed his collar, and he thought, *zombie*, and it dragged him up, and he kicked against the water and reared out into the air, gasping, retching, punching at the zombie.

* * * *

Jack said, "No, Vincent, it's me," and Vincent dropped his arms and settled on the surface of the water. "It's me, we're in a well or something," said Jack. "Or a drain. Look, look up there."

And Vincent looked and saw the darkening sky through a grille some twenty feet above him.

He gave a shout of relief.

Bryony and Annalee tumbled out of the tunnel, dirty and stained by the earth. They splashed, screaming, into the cold water and popped up clean and pale, their eyes wide, their mouths blowing.

Jack said, "We've got to get out of here, there's... there's Derek."

The Derek-zombie. Vincent remembered now. Everything came to him.

He looked around. A ladder scaled the drain's moss-covered wall. The rungs were rusted and festooned with weeds.

"Get everyone out," he told Jack, and climbed the ladder, his arms and legs aching but adrenaline fuelling him now.

He heard another splash as he reached the top of the ladder, Penny spilling out of the tunnel and into the water.

Vincent grabbed the bars of the grille and hoisted. His shoulder pulsed with pain. He had no strength. The grille creaked. He climbed up another rung and put his upper back against the grille. He stabilized himself against the walls of the well.

He saw Patty burst out of the pipe below, disappearing into the water. Jack pulled her up to the surface.

Vincent shut his eyes and gritted his teeth and using his legs, he drove his upper back against the grille. He strained, and the iron lifted, scoring his skin.

He heard creaking, and he didn't know if it was the grille or his bones.

He straightened and the iron slid off his back, and he sucked in fresh air. He threw up on the grass, his head swimming.

Shaking his head, he blinked to adjust his vision. Although the light was dying, to Vincent it felt like staring straight at the sun. His time under the earth in darkness had weakened his eyes, and it would take a while for them to get used to any kind of glare again.

But he didn't have a while.

In the gloom he saw the castle, got his bearings.

They'd come out of the tunnel to the west of the town, a few dozen yards from the water's edge.

He clambered out of the well and collapsed. He breathed sea air, and for a second, everything was all right.

Then he sat up straight, holding his breath.

Holly.

He crawled to the edge of the well. Bryony and Annalee scaled the ladder, Penny behind them.

He looked around, realizing he'd not checked the area for zombies. Towards the castle, he saw a cluster of them – perhaps fifty or sixty. They were pouring in through the entrance, through the Gate Next the Sea.

Christ, they've got in, he thought.

He helped the children and their mum out of the drain and told them to be quiet, keep watch.

Five minutes later Vincent said, "Where's Holly?"

They'd all clambered out of the drain. They huddled together, soaked and covered in slime.

Vincent eyed the zombies. They were still at the castle. But it wouldn't take long for them to sniff out human meat down by the water.

A splash came from below, and Vincent peered down into the drain. A moment later, Holly's head raised out of the water. Vincent gasped with relief. He said, "Come on, baby, come on, there's a ladder – "

And another figure burst out of the water, thrashing around and gnashing its teeth.

The Derek-zombie.

Vincent leapt to his feet, ready to jump into the well.

But Jack said, "Zombies," and Vincent froze.

Three of the undead were headed towards them from the west. Behind the creatures, the sun hung low in the sky.

It would be night soon, and that would make it worse.

Vincent didn't know what to do: leap into the well to save Holly, stay here to protect the others.

He looked down. Holly shuttled up the ladder. The Derek-zombie raked at the rungs below her.

"Help Holly up, Patty," he said and faced the three zombies barrelling along the grass towards them.

Jack had armed himself with a rock. He hurled it at the zombies. Cracked one of the creatures on the skull. The thing's scalp sliced open, blood spurting out. Its legs buckled and it sagged to the ground.

Jack gave a whelp of celebration.

Vincent glanced behind him. Patty helped Holly out of the drain. Then he faced the zombies again, bent down to pick up a rock. Flung it at the creatures. Smashed one in the chest. It reeled, but then regained its balance and staggered on again.

"Come on, kids," said Jack, "let's stone them," and Bryony and Annalee joined Jack, gathering stones and rocks, chucking them at the zombies. The others joined in, stoning the creatures. Pelting them till they were soaked in blood, till they toppled over, and then continued to stone them till they were only piles of gore staining the grass.

"That's enough," said Vincent, and they turned to look at him, and he saw the madness in their eyes – the lust for blood.

He furrowed his brow, fearful of their expressions for a second. And then Holly, behind him, said, "The sun's going down."

"We have to go," he said.

And then Jack lifted a rock and marched towards him.

Vincent stepped in front of Holly and said, "Jack, what the fuck are you – " and he was ready to strike the boy, but the youngster strode past him and Vincent wheeled to see where he was headed.

The Derek-zombie clambered out of the drain.

Jack brought the rock down on its skull. The zombie's head split open. Jack pounded its head again, mashed it till it spread across the grass.

Jack stared at Vincent. Blood covered the boy's chest and face.

His eyes were wide, and he gasped. He said, "I'm a zombie-killer, that's what I am."

"You are, Jack," said Vincent.

And then a small, white arm snaked out of the drain and grabbed Jack's ankle.

CHAPTER 77.
NORTH.

MUM slept in the sleeper cabin, Craig and Sam up front, him at the wheel.

I'm the man around here, he thought. *About time, too.*

Craig glanced in the side-mirrors. The other vehicles followed him. The BMW carrying the tall man and the fat man. The VW camper van driven by the nice American girl, and that muscle-head with her.

That's right, he thought, *they're following me.*

He shuffled in his seat. He felt powerful and in charge. And it was good.

He had responsibility for these people.

He had to lead them to a safe place.

He came to the Broxden Roundabout on the A9 and took the first exit towards Inverness.

North, he thought.

The countryside spread out before them. They saw no humans. Zombies prowled the roads in packs of at least a dozen, sometimes many more.

Cars and lorries lay abandoned along their route. A pram had halted their journey as they joined the A9. It stood on the middle of the highway. Sam had to beg Craig to stop so she could check.

It was him who checked in the end, of course. No way she was going out there.

He'd sneaked up to the pram, shaking with fear.

"There's nothing in it," he'd said to her.

Nothing except for the lower half of a baby.

But Sam didn't need to know that.

They drove on, following the A9. The sky was blue. The sun headed west. The day crept along. Night approached.

And nothing had changed.

Scotland was deserted. It was a zombie nation, now. No human army rumbling across the border from England to save them, their tanks churning over the undead. No government announcement from Holyrood saying everything was okay.

Craig thought, *I've been right all along – no one cares. You've got to look after yourself, and that's the end of it.*

He glanced at Sam and gave her a playful punch on the shoulder. She looked at him and pulled a face.

And look after your own, he thought.

He drove north.

CHAPTER 78.
LAST STAND.

"NO," said Vincent as Jack the zombie-killer raised his rock and prepared to stove in the head of the creature grabbing his ankle, "No, it's Hettie," and he dashed forward.

Vincent hoisted the little girl out of the well, and then leaned down to see Maisie squealing and shinnying up the ladder. He pulled her out and she shrieked in his face, and he said, "You're safe, you're okay," and she threw her arms around him and whispered, "They're coming, the monsters are coming."

Vincent's heart turned to stone.

"Who's coming?" he said to her.

"They're – they're – "

The zombie burst out of the pipe, plopping into the water below.

And when it rose up, breaking the surface, Vincent saw who it was – or who it had been when it was human.

Jack, his voice a hiss, said, "Bobby... "

"No," said Vincent, shoving Maisie towards the others, "it's not your brother anymore, Jack, it's not."

Another zombie spilled out of the pipe, and when it appeared above the water, Jack screamed:

"Mum!"

430

The boy flattened on the earth and reached into the well saying, "Come on, Mum, come on, Bobby, we're safe, we're getting away," and the zombies snarled up at him and clawed their way up the ladder.

Vincent dragged him away saying, "Jack, they're fucking zombies, not your mum and your brother," but Jack fought against him, screeching.

"Holly, Penny, someone… put the fucking grille back on the drain," said Vincent, battling to hold on to Jack.

Holly and Penny dashed forward. They hauled the grille across to the drain.

"Hurry," said Vincent, and then, staring towards the castle he said, "Oh shit."

All the screaming had roused the zombies.

A few were breaking off from the group gathered at the castle and were swarming across The Green.

Holly and Penny shoved the grille into place. The zombies reached through, their hands clawing the air like prisoners reaching through the bars of a cell.

Jack shrieked for his mum and his brother.

"They're gone, Jack – and the others are coming," said Vincent. "We have got to fucking go."

Panic tore through the group. The children were crying. Penny and Catrin wailed.

"Come on," said Vincent, "they're coming, we've got to run."

The zombies pounded down The Green.

They're going to cut us off, thought Vincent, seeing the undead race towards them. He scoped the water. Boats were marooned near the shore. He panicked: *which one was Gavin's?*

In the distance, the sun sank, a shimmering ball of orange on the horizon.

And then he saw the name:

Flower Of The East.

The vessel was a twenty-eight footer. It had a varnished, wooden mast and cabin, the hull painted white. A motor hung off the stern.

"Come on, it's over there," said Vincent, fishing in his pocket for the keys. The group trudged across the grass towards the boat. The zombies barrelled down The Green. Vincent said, "Jump in and swim – it's not far. Just there."

Hettie and Maisie were first into the water, Vincent leaping in after them. He ploughed on, the level coming up to his knees. The children squealed and doggie-paddled. Splashes behind him indicated to Vincent that the others were in the water.

He glanced over his shoulder.

His insides melted with fear.

"Hurry up," he said, his voice a screech.

The zombies stormed towards them. They were murky shapes against the darkening sky.

Vincent clambered into the boat, joining the children. Soaked, he turned and held his breath.

Patty and Holly were still on the shore.

"In the water," he shouted at them, "in the water."

"I can't swim, honey," said Patty.

The boat rocked as the others climbed aboard. Vincent hoped it would hold them all. He shouted again:

"Holly, get in, come on – help Patty, for Christ's sake."

"Don't blaspheme, Vincent," said Patty. "I'll pray for you. You are a good man. Now, Holly, you go – " and she shoved Holly, and Holly stumbled off the sea wall and fell face first into the water.

"Swim," said Vincent and then to Penny, who was nearest to him, he said, "Try to get the boat started, yank that cable… " and he tossed her the key for the padlock that secured the motor.

Holly flapped through the water.

The day dimmed.

Patty kneeled, held her hands in prayer.

Vincent cried out.

The zombies mobbed Patty.

Vincent screamed.

And then:

"Vincent! Vincent! It's not starting!"

He turned, tears blurring his vision. Penny's eyes were wide with terror. She held the cable from the boat's engine in her hand. "Help Holly on board," he said to her, and roughed her out of the way, grabbing the cable.

"They're coming in," said one of the children.

Vincent thought, *No more, no more*, and he looked and saw with horror that the zombies had entered the water.

They paddled towards the boat, splashing and churning up the surface of the river.

Vincent yanked at the cable, his arm weak, his shoulder aching. He had barely enough strength to stand, but he had to do this one last thing.

He pulled again.

Penny hauled Holly into the boat. Vincent glanced at her. She looked pale. She sat on the bench, shivering, her eyes wide and glazed.

The zombies waded deeper into the water, a horde of them inching their way to the boat.

The engine fired.

A gasp of relief went through the passengers.

Vincent yelped with joy.

The vessel headed west, rocking as it went, those on board losing their balance.

"Hold on," said Vincent, and began to steer.

The boat chugged away from the shore.

The zombies kept coming. Vincent had seen them crawl all over a yacht earlier in the day, so he knew they weren't afraid of the water. He had to get as far away from land as possible. He urged the Flower Of The East onwards, the boat rumbling along at a few miles per hour.

The zombies were in the water up to their eyes, now. Their skulls looked like eggs floating on the river.

The sun burned on the horizon. The heat had been brutal all day, but now it was cooler.

The boat drew further away, and Vincent began to relax. He looked down into the water. The engine groaned and churned.

The zombie reared up out of the channel right next to him.

Vincent keeled over. The boat swerved. The passengers screamed. The zombie began to clamber aboard.

Penny, armed with a long pole, lunged forward.

She battered the creature across the skull. It grabbed at the pole and jerked at it, pulling Penny towards the edge of the boat.

The boat pitched. Vincent knew what was going to happen. Penny screeched. She toppled over the side. Splashed into the water. The zombie dived back in after her. Bryony and Annalee squealed for their mother.

Vincent sprang to his feet, stumbled to the stern and shouted Penny's name.

The water churned. The boat circled. He grabbed the rudder and steadied the vessel, shouted for Penny again. Catrin leaned over the side, calling to Penny.

"Oh God, look," said Catrin.

The skulls sliced through the water towards where Penny had plunged in.

She's gone, thought Vincent, *we've got to* –

The water leapt, spraying the boat, everyone tumbling backwards.

Penny reared up, arms flailing.

The zombie shot up behind her, clawing at her.

Vincent grabbed Penny's arm and hauled her in, dragging her up on deck. She fell on him, drenched, and they both screamed and the boat rolled.

The zombie grabbed the edge of the boat, tried to climb on board. Teeth chattering, desperate to bite, slime hanging from its pale, chalky body.

Vincent rolled away from Penny, sprang to his feet. He delivered punch after punch into the zombie's face, mashing the creature's nose. But still the thing held on. It snarled and snapped its teeth at Vincent, and then it grabbed him by the collar. Vincent gasped, feeling himself being pulled over the side.

The sun slid behind the horizon.

The zombie's grip on Vincent slackened. Vincent saw the rage in its face dwindle, the jowls sagging, the eyes drooping. It flailed an arm at Vincent, but he was able to fend it off easily. The zombie's tongue lolled from its mouth. A string of saliva hung from its bottom lip. The creature gave a moan and then slid back into the water.

The eggshell skulls sank beneath the surface, one by one.

A zombie-hand, green and rotten, shot out of the water and grasped the edge of the boat.

Vincent sat down at the rudder and steered. The hand loosened its grip and grabbed at the air before sinking.

The boat chugged down the channel. The Great Orme stood dark in the distance. Vincent remembered visiting the limestone headland when he first moved here with his mum. They'd reached the summit by cabin-lift. He'd gazed out of the gondola on a day that had been as bright as this one. In the distance, he'd seen Beaumaris Castle. He became fixated with the medieval fort. He'd read about it, visited often, and learned as much as he could about life in the late 13th century when the English came to build it.

Now, he never wanted to see the castle again.

He glanced back one more time at Beaumaris.

The sun had gone.

CHAPTER 79.
HUNGER.

HOLLY didn't say anything. She didn't have anything to say. She looked at Vincent but didn't really see him. Saw through him, that's right. As if he were nothing. Nothing but...

She shook her head and shuddered.

Vincent smiled at her now and again, but they were weak smiles. Smiles that asked if she was okay.

But she wasn't.

She'd never be okay. Not now.

She shouldn't have been on the boat.

The water rippled, and she lowered her hand into it. The dark surface held a strange appeal. She pictured herself slipping over the side of the boat and sinking below the surface.

Drink in the river and die, she thought. She wrapped her arms around herself. No, she couldn't do that. Not kill herself like that. It didn't feel right. It wasn't fear, it was... what? What was it? She screwed up her face. She felt weird.

She looked at Vincent again, and when he smiled she looked away. He'd been her knight, after all. More of a knight than she could hope for. Her hero.

He'd led them through hell and got them out.

And this is how she was going to repay him.

A sick feeling rose from her gut. Her head swam, and she started to forget things, like where she'd lived and her mother's face and… and, *What's my name again?* she thought.

But these things didn't worry her at all, for some reason.

She thought again about going over the side but dismissed the idea. Something made her stay put.

An instinct.

A primeval urge.

Her eyes drifted over the passengers in the boat. They huddled together. The children slept. What's-her-name *(Christ, what was the woman's name?)* lullabied the kids.

Holly's belly rumbled, and her jaw began to hurt. Her mouth tingled, and she opened it and then shut it, and opened and shut it again.

What a weird sensation, she thought.

What was it?

The wound on her leg throbbed. Slime and mud coated the injury, so no one had noticed where the zombie had bitten her calf as they'd crawled through the tunnel.

What was the zombie's name, again?

She thought about the incident, and it didn't scare her at all. She didn't even remember if she'd been scared at the time. Actually, thinking about it, she didn't even remember what fear felt like anymore.

What was that sensation in her jaw?

And then she realized:

She wanted to bite something.

It was the last thing she remembered.

CHAPTER 80.
THE POISON IS IN THE
BODY.

CARRIE drove for six hours and came to a village on the outskirts of Berwick-upon-Tweed.

"We have to stop," she said, and he woke up.

His eyes were red-rimmed. They lacked their usual fire, and she felt a chill in her spine.

She said, "We're all tired. We need shelter. It'll be dawn in a couple of hours."

Ivy crawled up the wall of the ancient church. The structure would've fitted into Westminster Abbey's Quire. Carrie thought about that, now. It felt so long ago, another life. But it was only yesterday morning. Not twenty-four hours ago.

The church's graveyard had been ploughed up.

The dead had risen here, too.

Digging themselves out of the earth.

Carrie parked as close to the door as she could.

A few zombies wandered about.

She glanced eastwards. The horizon reddened. Fear coiled in her belly.

"The church for the day, then tonight we get back on the road," she said.

They carried their supplies from the 4x4 into the church.

Sawyer shot any zombie that ventured too close.

Carrie stood in the doorway with Mya. Sawyer eyed the zombies. She said to him, "Come on, we're done."

He stood and looked at the zombies as they crept out of the trees. And then he turned and glowered at her.

"I can't come with you," he said.

She was coming apart and sobbed. "Sawyer, please."

He shook his head and tossed the gun in her direction. It fell at her feet.

"Take it. There's some ammo left."

Her skin crawled with dread. She said, "The dawn's coming. They'll be strong again. We've got to – we – we need you – I need you, Sawyer."

"I can't." He rolled up his sleeve. She knew what he was going to show her. She thought she'd seen it happen at the Army blockade.

He'd been bitten on the forearm. The blood had dried black on his skin.

"The… the poison is in the body," he said.

"No," she said, "no, we can get antibiotics, we can – I can treat it – come on, Sawyer."

"I'm already losing myself, Carrie. My mind is going. There have been moments when I've seen you as nothing but… but flesh and… and my jaw, I can feel it tingle. The need to bite. The need to eat. I can't… come… with you."

Behind him, the zombies clustered. They lurked in the gloom. Swaying figures against the pre-dawn light.

"They're coming, Sawyer. Please, now."

But she knew he wouldn't. She knew he couldn't.

"Go," he said.

"Sawyer – "

"Go," and he turned away from her and faced the zombies, and they shuffled towards him, and she waited to see him taken.

She remembered something and called to him, saying, "What's your real name? Who are you?"

The zombies bunched around him. She waited for them to attack. But they ignored him, and instead shambled towards the church, towards her and Mya.

And then he turned to face her.

His eyes had rolled back in his head, and his mouth hung open.

She cried his name.

But he was gone.

And standing where he'd stood, a zombie.

Carrie retreated into the church, taking Mya with her. She barred the door and slumped to the floor, cradling her daughter.

Outside, the zombies tried to claw their way in.

THE END.

THE END

ACKNOWLEDGMENTS.

The author would like to thank: Emma Barnes and Anna Torborg at Snowbooks for being wonderful publishers. Michelle Farrell, Tracy Law, and Stephen Belsey for reading the manuscript. Tom and Emma Edwards for giving him his name. Marnie Summerfield Smith for her love and support.

ABOUT THE AUTHOR.

Thomas Emson is the author of *Maneater, Skarlet*, and *Prey*. His next novel is *Krimson*, the sequel to *Skarlet*. He is also an award-winning playwright and used to be a singer-songwriter. He is a member of the Horror Writers Association and the Society of Authors. Welsh-born, he now lives in Kent with his wife. Visit his website at thomasemson.net or follow him on Twitter at www.twitter.com/thomasemson